THE SÓLLER SOLUTION

PETE DAVIES

Copyright © 2022 Pete Davies

All rights reserved

The characters and events portrayed in this book are fictitious with the exception of those people who have given their express permission to be included in these books. Any similarity to real persons, living or dead, is coincidental and not
intended by the author.

Every appropriate effort has been made to obtain the necessary permissions with reference to copyright material, both illustrative and quoted. I apologise for any omissions in this respect and will be pleased to make the necessary acknowledgements
in any future editions.

No part of this book may be reproduced, or stored in a retrieval system, or transmitted in any form or by any means, electronic, mechanical, photocopying, recording, or otherwise, without express written permission of the author.

Ebook AISN: B09YMJPPF7
Paperback ISBN: 9798446377190
Hardcover ISBN: 9798446393138

A copy of The Sóller Solution will deposited at the British Library in accordance with the Legal Deposit Libraries Act 2003.

Cover design by: Brian Tarr
(brian-tarr.pixels.com)
All rights reserved

*To all the people who have supported and
encouraged me with my writing.
It's a privilege to share my stories with you.*

THE 3R INTERNATIONAL SERIES

This is the 3rd book in the 3R International series.

Whilst it isn't absolutely necessary to read either The Mallorcan Bookseller, or The Pollensa Connection before this one, I think you'll enjoy it more if you read them in sequence to gain the detail of the back stories to the main 3R characters.

1

"Sam, it's Tony Theakston."

"Tony, good to hear from you, but can I please call you back? This isn't a good time."

Sam Martínez was at the hospital in Inca with Greg Chambers talking to the medical team about Terri, Greg's daughter.

"I just need you for two minutes, I promise. I wouldn't ask if this wasn't urgent."

Sam took a deep breath. Tony was his old boss from the Met Police and he'd been a great friend and mentor and was now Head of Security for an international art gallery.

"Okay, of course. What's up?"

"I've got a ransom situation on the go."

"What's been stolen?"

"Nothing, at least not yet."

"Go on," said Sam.

"Let me start by saying that we don't think it's a hoax. We've been told to pay £10 million by tomorrow, or lose a picture to that value from one of our galleries."

"If you don't think it's a hoax, then that suggests you have some other intel on this Tony?"

"This isn't the first time we've had this. It also happened twelve months ago. We didn't pay up then, or at least, not until a picture was stolen. We then paid the original ransom, plus a fifty percent mark-up, to get it back. We had to, it was on loan from another gallery."

"Why are you ringing me?"

"Our insurers suggested you, 3R International that is. We need this dealt with sensitively, because if galleries start finding out we're losing artwork, then we'll never get anyone to loan us a collection again."

It was the first of three things. All unrelated, or at least that was how it seemed at the time, but all would have major consequences for the 3R team.

*****

"Problem Sam?" said Greg.

"No, it was a work thing from my old boss. I'll fill you in later. What are they saying about Terri?"

Sam tipped his head towards the team of medical staff standing close-by who had been treating Terri, his half-sister and Greg's daughter.

Terri's mother, Josie Anderson, spoke first.

"They're saying it's time. Time to take her out of the induced coma. The head medic says it has achieved what they wanted, that is to stabilise Terri and let her body recover sufficiently to give her a better than fifty-fifty chance to pull through."

Sam saw the strain on Greg's face as Josie said *'fifty-fifty'*.

"What do you think Greg?" asked Sam.

"It's been nearly two months and I, I mean we, we don't want her permanently in this state of just existing."

Simon, one of Greg's 3R team, walked out of Terri's hospital room and nodded at them. Sam had seen the toll it had taken on Greg, but it wasn't just him of course. Simon was a mess too, at least whenever he left her bedside. The tough ex-SAS Welshman would put on a cheerful, brave face when he was sitting with her. But he'd opened up his heart to her, when she lay critically injured, telling her how much he loved her and now he was hurting too at the thought he might lose her.

He had sat for hours with her as she lay in a coma, holding her hand and gently talking to her about everything they would be able to do together when she was better. He had no idea if she would remember anything of what he'd said, especially given the fact that when he told her he loved her, she'd been full of Rohypnol, after Marsden shot her and then injected her with the drug.

Simon, together with Josie, had barely left Terri's bedside since he had brought her into hospital. But when he did, the pain he was feeling for the woman he'd finally opened up to would often erupt and he'd be found huddled on the floor, his back against a wall, knees under his chin and tears flowing uncontrollably down his face.

"She wouldn't want that guys," said Simon quietly.

Sam heard the tone in his voice and knew he was back in his ultra-professional zone, dealing with the life and death issue before them.

"No, you're right," said Greg. "She's a fighter and a damn good one at that."

Greg had made life and death decisions on many occasions since the time he'd been recruited into his former career in the Security Services. But this was by far the hardest thing he had ever had to do. He felt Josie's arm around his waist and he took a deep breath.

She'd flown to Mallorca from her home in Australia after Greg had called her. Sam had found a finca to rent close to the hospital in Inca and she and Simon had been staying there ever since, with the rest of the team using it as a base whenever they were visiting Terri.

Terri was the result of her six month relationship with Greg when she had been in London back in the late 80s, although she hadn't realised she was pregnant until she got back home to Australia.

It was meant to be a holiday romance, but she had been blessed with a beautiful daughter, Theresa Jane Anderson and Greg, whilst living and working on the other side of the world, had been as good a dad as he could, given the distance and time zones.

Dr Jesus Hernandez, the senior consultant, saw the same hesitation he saw in many parents being asked to make a decision on their child's future well-being which may not turn out for the best.

He spoke gently.

"It is the best option, the very best option for Terri. This is the right time, so do I have your authorisation?"

"I think we need to tell them to go ahead Josie. What do you think?" said Greg.

Josie took a deep breath and looked at him.

"Yes."

With tears in his eyes, Greg nodded.

"You're right Doctor, it's time, so yes, please go ahead."

*****

Dr Hernandez said they would know how Terri was responding as things progressed during the next six to twelve hours. They all gave Terri a hug before leaving her to face the toughest personal battle she had ever faced.

Greg saw Simon hesitating, unwilling to leave her side.

"Come on Simon, time to let the medics do their job."

Josie gently eased Simon from Terri's bedside and gave him a hug as she walked him out of her room and into the corridor.

"Come on you big softy. The sooner she's out of it, the sooner you can properly tell her you love her."

Simon looked at her, tears welling up again.

"What if she doesn't remember? About us I mean."

Josie stopped suddenly and grabbed him by his arms and looked into his eyes with a smile.

"Then you'll just have to tell her again then won't you!"

Sam grinned at Greg.

"She's not one to be messed about with is she?"

"She's a typical Aussie is Josie. Heart of gold and with an enormous amount of common sense and good humour. Don't let Lori hear me say this, but I would have married Josie if it hadn't been for the line of work I was in," said Greg.

Whilst Lori Garcia, who was across on mainland Spain didn't hear him, Josie did.

"Well I wouldn't have married you even if you'd asked me you daft Pom. It was bad enough telling my mum and dad my baby was half-Pom without telling them I was going to marry you!"

She started laughing, immediately breaking the tension everyone was feeling.

*****

As they left the hospital they noticed the difference between the cool of the air-conditioned building and the heat of the October midday sun that was reflecting off the car park tarmac.

"Come on you lot, I think you all need some food inside you to get your energy levels back up. Let's go and see Aina at Bar Coral," said Josie.

"Good idea," said Greg. "Sam, I need something to distract me, so whilst we grab some food you can tell me what your phone call was all about."

"Sounds good to me," said Sam getting into the driver's seat of a Kia Sportage.

It was a relatively short drive from Inca to Puerto Pollensa and Greg, Josie and Simon spent the time on their phones to friends and family to keep everyone posted on what was happening with Terri.

Simon rang Lily Green and she was waiting for them as they walked into Bar Coral.

She ran and hugged Simon. "Hello you big Welsh hunk."

Simon smiled and hugged her back. Considering all Lily had been through, she had made a remarkable recovery from the experience she'd had because of Marsden. Maybe it was because she was having to focus on Terri, who had saved her from whatever that bastard was going to do with her? Whatever it was, he'd drawn strength from this young woman who had become a bit like a younger sister to him and she'd spent many hours alongside him and Josie at Terri's bedside.

"She's strong, so she's going to fight hard. So let her do her thing now and she'll be back with you before you know it."

"I hope so Lily, I really hope so."

Aina, one of the fourth generation owners of the restaurant came and greeted them, bringing coffee and pastries.

Aina knew all of Lily's friends by now and Lily had already told her what was happening.

She gave both Josie and Greg a warm hug.

"We are all thinking and praying for Terri."

"Muchas gracias Aina," said Greg.

"Now, I will leave you to sit and talk," said Aina with a warm smile.

"Okay," said Greg. "Now Terri wouldn't want us sitting around here with long faces. She's probably worrying what I've been doing, or rather not doing to keep the business going. So, what was this phone call from your old boss all about Sam?"

2

Sam Martínez put his coffee cup down and wiped away some sugar from around his mouth from the ensaïmada pastry he'd just finished.

"It was a strange one Greg. Tony Theakston was my old Detective Superintendent when I was in the Met and after he retired he joined an art gallery to head up their security team."

"Bit of a come down from being a Super isn't it? Looking after the security on the door?" said Greg.

"I think it's a bit more than that to be fair Greg," Sam laughed. "Have you heard of Adamsons?"

"No, can't say I have."

"They're pretty big in the art world. When Tony joined them he gave me a bit of a guided tour around their galleries in London. They've got a couple. Small, but discreet buildings in the usual sort of places you'd expect to find them at the mid to top end of the market, but they're all over the world too."

"Ah, so when he says he's got a problem, he really has got one," said Greg.

"Yes, I think that's probably very much the case."

"Better tell me all about it then."

"Okay, it seems that Adamsons have been threatened by a person, or persons unknown, that unless they pay a ransom of ten million quid in the next twenty four hours, one of their paintings will go missing."

Greg smiled at Sam's police phraseology.

"How many galleries have they got?" he asked.

"I'd need to check, but I'm sure Tony told me it was eight. They're in New York, London, Milan, Singapore, Beijing, plus there are a few others I can't remember, except I know there's one here on the island."

"Here? Why Mallorca?"

"I'm not sure, but it stuck in my mind as Tony obviously knows I was brought up here."

"Your friend Tony, he's taking it seriously then?"

"Very. They had another threat last year. They thought it was a hoax and of course they didn't pay. Within six hours they'd lost a painting valued at €10 million and had to pay a premium on top of that to recover the painting," said Sam.

"That suggests that whoever did this was already fully prepared to carry out the theft as soon as they got the negative response from Adamsons."

"Looks like it, hence why Tony, not to mention his Board of Directors, is very twitchy at the moment."

"But surely their security must be top notch, especially after they lost a painting last year?"

"The problem is Greg, they thought it was top notch then."

"Point taken."

"What do they expect us to do Sam?"

"Apparently this sort of thing rarely gets anywhere near to the police. The galleries can't risk the publicity, so it's all dealt with through their own investigation teams and their insurers."

"Go on," said Greg.

"Well it seems we've been recommended by one of the insurance investigators as someone who can deal with this particular type of problem."

"You mean we may need to step outside the usual boundaries of law enforcement rules and regs?"

"I think you've hit it on the head."

"Are you okay with that?"

"After what we've been through in the last few months with 3R? I think that's a *'yes'*," grinned Sam.

"Best you set up a meeting with this investigator and Tony then."

*****

"Tony?"

"Sam, thanks for ringing back. I'm sorry if this isn't a good time for you. Anything I can help with?"

Tony Theakston had always been a good boss. Tough, but fair and always had time to listen to a problem, which was why Sam had liked him.

"I'll fill you in later Tony, but for now, can you set up a call as soon as you can with this insurance investigator? My boss, Greg Chambers will also join in as he's in Mallorca with me at the moment."

"You're in Mallorca? Oh God Sam, is it your Mum? Is something up with her?" said Tony.

"No, Mum's fine Tony."

Sam paused for a moment. Trust Tony to remember family details like that. But he wasn't sure if he wanted to bring everything about Terri into this, at least not until they knew how she was responding to coming out of the coma.

"Look, it's a long story Tony and you're under time pressure. So I promise, I'll tell you more later, when we've got through your next twenty hours."

"Okay, as long as you're sure?"

"Positive, now call me back as soon as you get hold of your investigator. By the way, what's their name?"

"Regus, Holly Regus. Know her?"

"No, the name doesn't ring any bells. Right, speak

soon Tony. Doesn't sound like we have a lot of time."

*****

Two hours or so before Tony Theakston first rang Sam Martínez, Doctor Holly Regus had been sat at her desk in her office at Premium Risk International.

It was a non-descript name of the insurance company she had worked at for the last seven years since leaving Durham University with a Masters in Criminology, to which she had recently added a Doctorate from Cambridge.

She had just taken a call from Suzy, the PA to the Head of Risk, Charles Hacker.

"He wants to see you now Holly."

"I was just about to take a call from a claims client."

"He said now."

Before Holly could answer Suzy had rang off.

Hacker was a senior partner at PRI and had a reputation of being brusque, if not downright rude on occasions. However, Holly had soon found that if you returned fire with fire, he would often listen to what she had to say. It didn't mean she necessarily liked him, but she knew she could handle him, but when he said *'Jump'*, it was usually best to ask *'How high?'* and then debate whatever it was concerning later on.

As she walked out her office, she stopped off at one of her investigator's tables.

"I've been summoned Dawn. Please can you take the call from Duttons? You know what's happening. It's a brief catch up, so there shouldn't be any issues you can't cover."

Dawn Thomas was one of her most experienced investigators. Holly had hand-picked her to be on the team and knew she could more than handle any issues from the MD of Duttons.

"No problem Holly. Good luck with Mr Hacker," smiled Dawn.

Holly smiled back and as she went up the three floors in the lift to the Executive Suite she thought about her time at PRI. She had started as a junior investigator, but had quickly been identified as a 'flyer' within a world that rarely received the publicity or plaudits it perhaps deserved.

She knew Hacker liked her style - professional, tough and although he didn't often tell her, she was damn good at her job. But then again, whilst he didn't often say it with words, he had chosen her, from a short list of other highly skilled investigators in the industry, to head up a new team called Specialist Risk Investigation.

It was a new department set up as a response to a number of high value cases affecting not just the art world, but all areas of the PRI business where they faced significant claims and that meant anything over three million pounds.

However, by the very nature of their work, insurance investigators in this specialist field were usually managing much more than just the financial element of an insurance claim. They were often dealing with the reputational damage limitation of PRI's most trusted clients, something which was worth considerably more than any high value insurance pay out.

As she approached Hacker's office she saw Suzy, his PA, grimacing.

"Go straight in Holly. He's a bit tense."

Holly knew what Suzy's understated comments to describe Hacker meant, so she pulled a face back at her and knocked firmly on the door before entering the office.

"Good morning Charles."

"Don't you usually wait to be invited into a senior partner's office," Hacker said tersely.

"Not when Suzy has said you wanted to see me immediately."

She thought she saw a faint smile.

'Another mini-test. If he just got on with being a boss, he could be a bloody good one instead of all these mind games.'

"Well, yes, fair point. Good morning to you Holly, but it's not actually a very bloody good morning."

She could see he was agitated and she looked at the file that was on his desk. It had 'ADAMSONS' printed across it. They were one of PRI's most important global clients and as such, all of their business portfolio was managed through the London Office.

It was one of their key claim cases last year that had been the catalyst for Hacker to set up the SRI, the Specialist Risk Investigation team. But before she could say anything, he barked at her once again.

"3R International. Ever heard of them?"

"Risk Reduction something or other isn't it?" said Holly.

"Yes, Risk Reduction and Resolution. So what do you know about them?"

"Run by a guy who used to be a field agent with MI6 I think, Gary Chambers?"

"Greg Chambers," corrected Hacker.

"Yes, that's him. Why do you ask?"

"We engaged them on a job about eighteen months ago. It was an engineering company that was losing equipment out the back door at one of their sites in Africa. Our in-country GM out there had heard that Trent MacDonald were using them."

Holly nodded, she knew they were a huge global engineering company.

"Well, they had used this guy Chambers because he had the ear of Trent MacDonald's Chairman, Sir John MacDonald. It seems that this Chambers guy has a knack of resolving those difficult issues that can challenge your typical law enforcement agency operating methods."

"You mean he doesn't stick to the rule of law?" said Holly.

"Let's just say this he works within the overall guidelines of righting wrongs."

"That seems conveniently vague Charles and who is he to decide what's right and wrong? Unless of course he's God."

"No he isn't, but in our world, the client is. Anyway, how he does things might be a bit vague in terms of the law, but he's bloody effective."

"So how much of the stuff did he get back in Africa?"

"Ninety five percent of property recovered."

Hacker left the words hanging.

"Impressive," murmured Holly.

"And no police involvement and more importantly the engineering outfit's client had no inkling of what had been going on, so there was no…"

"Loss of organisational reputation." She finished his words.

"Quite."

"Is there another problem with Adamsons then?"

Hacker looked quickly down at the file.

"Yes, it looks like the bastard who hit them last year is at it again."

Holly knew about the case. A ransom before the theft and Adamsons had to pay out a hefty on-top 'fee' after they took it as a hoax and they didn't advise PRI until the subsequent theft of a £10 million painting two days later.

She knew things had got very sticky because whist the lack of notification of the threat gave PRI their opportunity to step back from any liability, they did make a £2 million contribution as an act of good faith, although it was effectively to help retain the Adamsons' business.

"What do you suggest this 3R can do for us Charles?"

"I don't know, but that's for you to find out. Speak to Bill Warner on the Africa Desk. He dealt with Chambers and when I just spoke to him he said 3R have recently been expanding and taking on more staff. We need to know precisely whether or not they can do something for us, without it ending up on the front page of every major newspaper."

With that Hacker sat down at his desk shouting, "Suzy, more coffee." Before adding, "Please."

Holly knew this meant the meeting was over, but as she went to leave he said, "Oh and Holly, as good as I know you are, this needs a damn good outcome for both our sakes."

She half turned to look back, but she knew exactly what he meant and had no doubt as to whose head the axe would fall on if she failed to deliver.

3

The security guard saw something flash across the CCTV screen from the camera on the roof of the building. He checked the next camera. Someone was on the roof. It was difficult to tell if it was a man or woman, but by their size Mark Flowers guessed it was a man.

He checked the daily log. There was nothing to indicate they were having any maintenance work up on the roof. He flicked the switch on the microphone on his radio.

"Mark to Jim, you receiving, over?"

Silence.

He tried again as he saw the man on the roof take what looked like a flying leap up the side of one of the maintenance blocks before spinning in the air and landing serenely back on his two feet in an almost theatrical display.

"Jim, come in, over."

Still nothing.

Flowers knew he should do something. He called to Tina, one of the reception team that he was going to check a man he'd seen running about on the roof and that if he wasn't back in five minutes she should call the police.

"Okay Mark, you be careful up there," said Tina.

'Was she smiling at him?' thought Mark, or was he just imagining it. *'Did she think he was joking?'*

"No I mean it Tina. There's a man up there and I need to check it out."

"Okay, yes, you go and see Mark and I'll be sure to call the police if you don't come back."

Reassured that she'd got the message, Flowers got in the lift and inserted his security key into the override to allow him to access the roof level. A few seconds later he felt the lift come to a halt and he waited a moment after the lift door had opened.

He took hold of his 4 battery cell torch like a weapon, holding it above his head. *'Better to be safe than sorry.'*

He moved quickly, getting out of the lift and making his way towards the maintenance block where he'd seen the man almost run up the side of. He saw a shadow, it was him!

"Jim, Jim, come in!" He whispered urgently.

Still silence from his radio.

He took a deep breath and stood up straight.

"Stop! Stop now!" he shouted. "What the hell are you doing up here?"

The man was dressed head to foot in black lycra clothing. He slowly stopped and turned to face the security man.

"You're new here aren't you?"

The man spoke quietly and seemed to be smiling at him.

"Never mind that. Who are you and what are you doing up here?" said Flowers.

"Jim didn't answer your radio call did he?" said the man.

"No," said Flowers, regretting immediately that he'd answered the man's question. He straightened up again, holding the torch like a club in is hand. "Look, I'm going to have to call the police if you don't tell me who you are and what you're doing up here. You're trespassing for a start."

"Well I don't think I am," said the man, "because that would mean the owner of the building would object to me being here."

'He's bloody confident, I'll give him that,' thought Flowers.

"Look. You shouldn't be here mate, so just give me your name and I'm sure we can sort this out."

"I'm sure we can. So to answer your question, I'm Jake Sutton," taking off the balaclava he had on.

Flowers thought he recognised the face from somewhere. Then the name hit him like a train. Jake Sutton was the owner and President of SIS, the company Flowers worked for.

"Mr Sutton, I'm so sorry, I didn't know."

Sutton smiled.

"Don't worry about it. Try calling Jim now and I expect he will miraculously answer."

"Mark to Jim?" said Flowers tentatively.

He heard the crackle of the radio as Jim responded immediately.

"Met the Boss have you?"

Flowers looked to the floor. He'd been had and presumably Tina was in on it as well. He looked sheepishly at his boss.

"It's Mark isn't it?" asked Sutton.

Flowers nodded to him.

"Yes Sir."

"No need for sirs around here Mark. Look, it's a bit of fun Jim sometimes has with new members of his team. Look upon it that you've just passed the bravery test. I mean fair play to you, coming up here to confront someone armed only with your 4 cell Maglite. Good to have you as part of the team. Now perhaps we should both get back to work?"

"Yes, yes, of course Boss and thank you."

As Flowers stepped out of the lift back on the ground floor there was a reception committee for him. Everyone was lined up applauding him and waving the business journals that had Jake Sutton's face on the front cover. That's where he'd recognised the face from. Jim had given him a copy just that morning when he started work but he'd been so nervous on his first day that he hadn't had time to read it.

He grinned with embarrassment and then joined in their laughter. He saw Tina, who winked at him and then ran up and gave him a hug.

"You did so well!" she whispered. "Sometimes they don't even go to look, but they're the ones who don't seem to last here very long."

After the clapping had finally stopped, Jim grabbed him around his shoulders.

"Welcome to SIS, Mark. You've officially passed the response test and you've met the big boss all at the same time!"

"Thanks, I think," grinned Mark. "But what was Mr Sutton doing up there anyway?"

"He'd have been doing his morning exercise. I think they call it free-running or parkour, or something like that anyway."

"Isn't that the stuff where they go running across rooftops?"

"Yep, dangerous shit if you ask me," said Jim, "but he loves it."

*****

Jake Sutton was still smiling at Jim's bit of a fun with the new member of his team as he ran down the staircase from the roof and into his office suite, on the top floor of a smart business centre in the Docklands area of London.

Twenty nine and a multi-millionaire after Sutton Innovation Security Ltd, his start-up electronics business, had taken off with the revolutionary alarm system that had swept through the corporate security market.

After he showered and changed, he grabbed a coffee from the machine and walked into his work area and picked up a file. Sales had increased again over the previous quarter and SIS had opened two new international offices in Singapore and Milan to go with those in New York, Paris, Frankfurt and Sydney.

He didn't have a desk as such, but more of a set of comfortable chairs and low coffee tables which had on them an assortment of business journals, papers and athletics magazines.

He saw his face looking back at him from one of the journals. It was from a recent interview he had been asked to do about new entrepreneurs.

"Jeannie," he called out.

Jean Marshall stuck her head in through the door.

"At your service," she said with a grin.

He smiled back at her. She was around thirty years older than he was and had originally helped him set up SIS as his principal investor.

Seven years ago she had been looking for something to keep her mind busy after deciding to step back from her role as a senior VP at an investment bank and get out of the rat race.

A colleague, Graham Sykes, had heard about a brilliant young electronics graduate through a friend, Geoff Hoskins, a tutor on Jake's Masters' programme who had been impressed by the complexity of the designs he had seen from the young man.

Hoskins had tested and questioned Jake about his designs, finally challenging him to produce a full system working model for his final assignment.

She remembered her friend's words well.

"Jeannie, Geoff says this young lad Sutton just needs some investment. I know we say this all the time, but I can really see this taking off," said Sykes, "so this may be something you might want to get on board with."

This had started a working relationship with Jake that saw her go from an advisor and investor to becoming CEO for the fledgling company, leaving Jake free to focus on the design and manufacture of his products.

Her thoughts were brought back to the present as Jake asked, "What's happening with the negotiations with Adamsons?"

"Same as last year Jake. They're still playing hardball at the moment saying they're getting all they want from their current system. Surprising really, seeing as last year someone broke into one of their galleries in the US and walked off with a painting."

"Serves them right," said Jake with a half-smile.

"Do you want me to have another go with them Jake?"

He thought for a moment. Adamsons were a high brand international art dealers with galleries all over the world. He'd like the business, but he wasn't going to let them try to dictate a contract that only benefitted them.

"No, it's their choice. If they think their current set-up is fine for their needs then we'll leave them to see how they get on. So who else have you got in your sights Jeannie?"

He asked the question but wasn't really listening to her as she went through a number of high profile prospective clients. He was thinking about the email he'd sent Adamsons with the ultimatum to pay £10 million by tomorrow, or lose another picture.

*****

Sam was still sat with Greg and the others at Bar Coral when he saw the Zoom invite ping through on his phone from Tony Theakston half an hour later.

"We should get back to the finca to take this call Greg."

"Okay, we'll see you guys later," said Greg with a wave to Simon, Josie and Lily.

As they drove the short distance back to the finca they'd been using as a base when visiting Terri, Greg wanted to know more about Tony Theakston.

"He's one of the good guys Greg. He was always very thorough in his approach to what he was doing, so I'd imagine he's been through a complete review of the previous ransom incident, so it will be useful to find out what they learned from that."

"This Dr Regus sounds interesting too," said Greg. "I wonder if she is more an academic researcher than an investigator?"

"I don't know, but I'm hoping she can bring something useful to the table, as I don't particularly think art theft is in either of our skill sets is it?"

Greg laughed.

"No, it's a new one to me, that's for sure."

He paused.

"Quick question. Do we want this one Sam? I mean, with what we've got going on with Terri?"

Sam knew Greg had stepped away from much of the business side of things with Terri being hospitalised for so long, but he was feeling a pull of loyalty to his former boss and mentor.

"Look, let's just listen to what they have to say. It may be I can take care of this on my own, or bring in Tommy if need be."

"And we shouldn't forget Anna. How's she getting on with that job in London?"

Anna Martínez was Sam's mother and he'd grown up with no inclination that before he was born, she had been an MI6 field agent and had in fact recruited and trained Greg in covert operations.

Stranger still, he'd only discovered from his mother in this last year that Greg was in fact his biological father, the result of a brief affair in the week after he'd completed his training with her.

Sam sometimes pondered how it all seemed very complicated, working with his mother, biological father and his half-sister, Terri. But strangely enough it wasn't. He liked Greg, but he didn't look upon him as his father, because that had been and always would be Luis, who had adopted him after he'd married Anna. Luis had always treated him like his own son and maybe it was because of Terri, but Sam was only just beginning to realise how much he missed his father since he'd died from cancer almost ten months ago.

He remembered Greg had asked him about his mother.

"I spoke to her earlier to let her know what was happening with Terri. She says she's almost done. It was a review of some case Martin wanted her to look over, so she should be set to come home sometime this week."

"Good," said Greg. "That'll give us some more capacity if we decide to take the job."

Sam drew the car to a halt at the front of the finca and they made their way inside out of the early afternoon sun that was still very warm for October.

"You get the laptop set up Sam and I'll put the kettle on," said Greg.

Sam grinned. He knew that Greg was a lot more technically savvy than he gave himself credit for, but he'd take every opportunity to do something else other than get involved with setting up video calls and suchlike.

No sooner had Greg brought in the mugs of tea when Sam saw the incoming Zoom call.

"Good to see you Tony," said Sam. "This is Greg Chambers. Dr Regus, good to meet you too."

"Holly's fine please. Good to meet you Sam, you too Greg."

"Okay, how do you want this to work Holly?"

She immediately liked Sam's business-like approach. Tony had given her a quick rundown on his background, which was a lot more than what she'd been able to find out about Chambers.

"Tony's given you an overview?"

"Yes, it seems you have a repeat of a ransom demand from last year. Copycat or the same person?" said Sam.

"We can't be a hundred percent sure, but it's the same communication method. Untraceable email, same formatting of the words, so it looks like the same person. Cards on the table," she paused, "we don't connect with the police over matters like this, at least not unless we absolutely have to. The potential loss of organisational reputation is critical, so we just can't let this get out into the public domain."

"We get that," said Greg. "So how can we help?"

"You guys can operate beyond the usual parameters of the police. Bill Warner told us what you were able to do for him in Africa and I need the same sort of approach to this problem."

"We still operate within the spirit of the law Holly. I just want to point that out," said Sam.

"Yes, of course, but you're not hindered by some of the legislation that might slow things up when it comes to surveillance and recovering property."

"If you mean things like the Police and Criminal Evidence Act and the requirements for search warrants, then yes, as a private company we can work around those pieces of legislation."

Greg smiled at Sam's use of the words *'work around,'* thinking back that it was only a few months ago when Sam was questioning the legitimacy of 3R's tactics when they'd first met.

"Okay Holly, maybe we can help, but I'm still not clear what we can do if you have nothing for us to go on," said Greg.

"Thefts of fine art are rare. They're usually very well protected and contrary to what you might think, most incidents come from opportunists rather than, let's call them criminal masterminds."

"I didn't know that," said Greg.

"And I certainly never investigated a high value art theft," said Sam.

"Like I said Sam, we don't usually involve the police on this type of thing. We prefer to resolve it ourselves, which often means paying some sort of ransom. However, when it's an opportunist thief, it's generally a fraction of the value of the art."

"What's the usual M.O?" said Sam.

For Sam, the Modus Operandi, or the way things occur, was vital to determine any trends in this type of crime and it was always one of the first things an investigator would want to know.

"A thief will sometimes just walk into a gallery, takes the frame off the wall and walks out unchallenged. Because who would think that would happen?" said Holly.

"Okay, so that's where they take the whole frame. But what about where they cut the painting out of the frame?" said Sam.

"The purists hate that. They'd rather the thief took the whole picture, because by cutting it out, no matter how carefully they think they may be doing it, they're damaging a piece of art and worse still they then roll it up which usually causes irreparable damage to the surface."

"So you'd rather they just walk out with it?" said Greg.

"Yes, in effect. Art has been stolen for hundreds of years and yet the pictures eventually turn up and come back into the public domain, even when stolen from private collections. So it's much better if they remain intact as far as the art world is concerned."

"What about the insurance companies?" asked Sam.

"We don't mind either. Most of these pieces aren't actually insured. They're too valuable and anyway they're irreplaceable."

She saw confusion cross Greg's face.

"We provide security advice and effectively insure the buildings that contain the artwork, as well as some cover for the ransom pay outs, although we don't obviously call them that in the policy cover."

"So how are they described?" asked Sam.

"Oh, it's something like administrative charges arising from x, y and z….if you get my gist?"

Sam nodded with a grin.

"Okay, so Tony will now give you what've we actually got," said Holly.

4

The second of the seemingly unrelated events was when Francis Alan Walker stepped out of the gates of HMP Belmarsh, one of the UK's highest security prisons.

He saw the black BMW 7 series waiting with the driver holding the back door open for him.

"Boss," said the driver. "Welcome back to the outside."

Known as Frankie to his closest associates, but to everyone else he was the 'Boss.'

"Thanks Bob. Now take me to the pub, a strip club and then home to see the missus, in that order."

"The brief's in the car too Boss," said Bob quietly.

"Let's see if he wants to come with us then shall we," said Frankie with a smirk.

As Walker got in the car he saw his solicitor.

"Ah, Mr Rogers of Rogers, Rogers and who's the other one?"

Philip Rogers didn't like Walker, not one iota, but he paid well, so he took his usual deep breath.

"It's Smithers, Frankie. You know that and yet you always ask me the same question."

"Because I'm paying you so bloody well Philip, so I can ask you anything I bleeding well like."

Philip Rogers softened. Walker had been inside for almost a year, part remand and part sentence and so he wasn't likely to be in the mood for any light hearted banter.

"Of course Frankie. Now I heard you're off to the pub. I'd love to join you, but I have to get to Court."

"Philip, I haven't seen you for a year, so you will stop and have a drink with me."

Rogers heard the tone in Walker's voice.

"Of course, let me make a quick call."

"Good and then you can come to the strip club too, but don't go thinking you can then come home and have a bit of my missus. She'd like you with your posh accent, but don't go getting any ideas, you hear me?"

"No, no, of course not Frankie, I never, I mean she's a lovely a girl, but she's…"

"Way out of your league? Is that what you were going to say Philip?"

Rogers nodded. It was going to be a long afternoon with Walker, but his thoughts were interrupted when Walker asked him, "So how did you get me off Phil?"

He hated Walker calling him Phil, but like many other things in their relationship, Rogers put up with it, because to do otherwise meant he might lose the very hefty retainer Frankie Walker gave him, which with two divorces and three children at private school was something he could ill-afford.

Worse still, he had seen what Walker did to people who fell out of favour with him and he shuddered at the thought of the sight Walker had made him look at after he finished one of his punishment beatings.

"It was a technicality dear boy. The Old Bill hadn't declared that part of the information about the robbery you were accused of had come from a paid informant. But we did some digging around and called them out on it in the Appeal process."

"So you got me off even though they had me bang to rights? Especially after I shot that copper!"

"We pushed the agent provocateur angle, meaning you would never have committed the crime without being coerced into it," said Rogers.

"I know what it bloody well means," snarled Walker, before continuing in his usual more upbeat voice, "Well fair play to you mate. There'll be a bonus in this month's retainer Phil."

Rogers smiled.

"Thank you Frankie, that's most…."

"Do we know who the snout was?" asked Frankie quietly, ignoring Rogers's response.

"Er, no, not for certain. They wouldn't divulge that and so we can't be sure, so it would be wrong for me to…."

"Who do you think it is Philip?" Again the quiet voice, but this time Walker's voice had taken on a more menacing, even frightening tone.

"Frankie, I'm not sure this will help. I mean if he should suddenly disappear the police will know it's you and you can't afford to be in their spotlight so soon."

"But I can afford you Philip and you seem to be able to let me get away with almost knocking off a copper, so let me do the thinking around what I will or won't do to the piece of scum who set me up. Now who was it?"

It wasn't a request, it was a demand, so Philip Rogers wasn't about to try to defend the man who had sold any sense of loyalty to Walker down the road.

"We think it was Paul Robbins, or Robbo as I think you call him."

Walker showed no emotion, which surprised Rogers. He simply nodded, but Rogers knew he had just in effect signed a death warrant for a man he barely knew.

*****

As Walker got out of the car to walk into the pub, he turned to his driver.

"Bob, find out where Robbo is and get him taken to the lock up down by the river." He looked at his watch. It was just after 11am. "Get him loosened up for me and I'll be there around three."

Rogers winced as he heard Walker giving his instructions.

"Come on Philip, what are you looking so down about? Let's go for a pint."

It was actually three pints later when Walker decided to leave and to Rogers' relief he released him from the torture of spending even more time with him.

"Now don't go billing me for this time Philip. Remember I bought the drinks."

Was this the violent psychopath's pathetic attempt at a joke?' thought Rogers. *'Something else I have to pretend to laugh at.'* He forced out some sort of noise that he hoped Walker took for a laugh, whilst once again regretting the day twenty plus years ago when he'd first seen the young juvenile in the cells at Fulham Police Station when he'd been on the Duty Solicitor Scheme.

"Right Bob, next stop, the strip club and some fun. I need something to get me in the mood for later."

Bob nodded, although he wasn't too sure if his boss wanted to get in the mood to then see his wife, or to see the unfortunate Robbo.

*****

Paul Robbins was sat at his kitchen table drinking coffee when there was a knock at the door.

"Someone at the door love," he heard his wife yell down the stairs.

"I've got it."

That was the last Mrs Jill Robbins heard of her husband until two weeks later she was asked to identify his body at the mortuary with a police detective by her side.

Robbins looked through the spyhole and saw it was two of his team.

'Strange, they're looking a bit shifty,' he thought. 'Didn't think it was that cold out there.'

He took his hand away from the baseball bat he kept by the side of the door, as he undid the twin security locks and opened the door.

He immediately regretted he hadn't thought about why they might be there, as the first man lunged at him with crowbar and caught him across the side of the head, knocking him to the floor.

"Are you alright down there love?"

The two men ignored the call from Robbins's wife as they wrapped plasti-cuffs around his wrists and ankles and roughly stuffed a gag in his mouth. They then got him back on his feet and then dragged him backwards out to the van that was waiting engine running and the driver ready to go.

This wasn't an area where anyone would report a strange incident to the police and Robbins wasn't liked anyway, so as far as his neighbours were concerned it was a case of good riddance.

He lay still in the back of the van, trying to take in what had just happened. He raise a shoulder, but felt the plasti-cuffs tightly bound on his wrists and when he moved his leg, they bit in on his ankles. That's how he would have done it too, no, that's how he had done it many times before, when he'd been sent to get someone for the boss.

He tried talking through the gag in his mouth.

"Guys, what's going on?"

But he was asking a question that he already knew the answer to. He'd been happy to take the money from the Old Bill over the years, only giving up odd snippets of information, but there was nothing too serious until a few years ago when they gave him a new handler. He really started turning the screw on him, threatening to tell Frankie about him if he didn't give up more and more information.

'But how the hell had Frankie found out?'

"Shit!"

One of the men pulled out the gag.

"What's that Robbo? You talking to me?" said the man, giving him a sharp kick in the ribs.

"No, no."

"What no, you weren't talking to me, or you don't want another kick?"

The man kicked him again, but this time harder. Robbo could tell the man was enjoying this. Robbo was a bully, even within his own team and as far as the man sent to get him was concerned, he was going to enjoy loosening him up ready for the boss.

"I wasn't talking to you," said Robbo.

"Good, so have another of these then."

Another kick.

Robbo was thinking, so didn't even feel the pain. He wasn't afraid of these guys, but he tensed as he thought about the boss. A shiver ran through his body.

"Won't be long Robbo. The Boss has just gone to say hello to Mrs Walker. Shouldn't take too long after a year inside, hey?" the man sniggered.

The other man joined in the laughter.

"Did you hear? He said the Boss shouldn't take too long."

Robbo waited and got the expected kick in his chest.

"Okay, thanks," he forced out a reply as another rib cracked.

5

Sam and Greg took notes as they listened to Theakston's fifteen minute overview, noting the areas they wanted to explore with him in more depth.

"So that's what we've got and before you say anything, I know it's not a lot," said Tony.

"So basically, you've got no one and nothing of evidential use to go on?" said Sam who wasn't trying too hard to disguise his frustration.

Even through the video screen they both saw Theakston squirming in his seat.

"Well, yes, if you put it like that."

"I appreciate your confidence in us," said Greg. "However, I think the point Sam is making is that it's a little thin," he added diplomatically.

"The point as you say Greg, is taken on board, but that's precisely why we're taking this out of house and asking you guys for help," said Holly, her voice calm, but firm.

'Not a woman to be messed with,' thought Sam.

He could tell he'd annoyed her. It had been unprofessional to let his frustration show through. After all she was the client and he didn't want to let Greg down in front of her. He looked at Greg and he gave a hint of a nod.

"I'm sorry if I came across a little unenthusiastic Holly. We've got a family matter on the go and I think it perhaps distracted me for a moment."

"No need to apologise Sam. I just want to know if you guys are willing to help us."

She had softened in a moment.

"Yes, we like a challenge don't we Greg?"

He didn't wait for an answer before continuing, "What's your plan to deal with the ransom demand?"

"I can take this Holly," said Theakston. "Last time we had this situation we realised the thief was very precise with the painting valuation. He said he'd take a £10 million painting and that's precisely what he took a couple of days later. It was by an Italian artist and had been recently valued as part of a catalogue review."

"So the thief is well-versed in how the art world works then?" said Greg.

"Yes," said Theakston, relieved that Sam and Greg were back on board. "We undertook a post-case review of our entire portfolio across the globe and we only had six pieces of art that had been valued at £10 million in the last twelve months."

Sam saw where Tony was taking this. He was narrowing down the potential locations of where the thief might strike next.

"If I'm reading you right Tony, you're about to tell us how many £10 million pictures you've currently got?"

"You're spot on there Sam. As of now, we've got eight. One in each of our galleries as that spreads the risk. Now if it was simply a matter of putting a dozen guards around them, then we'd do that," said Tony Theakston.

"But that would set alarm bells ringing with the art world that would massively impact your reputation as a safe haven to store and auction fine art," said Greg.

Dr Holly Regus was impressed. She'd heard this 3R outfit was good, but she was hearing them ask the right questions and coming up with some sound conclusions.

"So it's too many for you to effectively cover without giving the game away, what's your gut feeling on say your top three from the eight possibles?" asked Sam.

"My turn for this one Tony," said Holly. "My analysis suggests we're looking at one in London, one in Singapore and one where you currently are, in Mallorca."

She saw the surprise on Sam's face.

"Yes, it's slightly odd Sam, given that you guys are out there at the moment. Whilst there's a lot of very good art often on display on the island, it's not necessarily the usual spot for high value art exhibitions."

"Where is it being shown then Holly? Palma?"

"You'd think that would be the obvious place, given the number of galleries in the city such as Es Baluard Museu, but it's actually in Sóller."

Greg looked at Sam for some clarification.

"It's on the west coast, the place you get to by the train through the mountains Greg."

"Yes, got it now and then you go by tram down to the Port."

Sam nodded.

"So why Sóller Holly? What's the attraction?"

"Part of my role with PRI is to research the areas our clients are placing their artwork for sale and advising them on not just the risk elements, but also the market potential. Sóller is continuing to attract wealthy new residents from countries such as the UK and Germany, but the real wealth is coming in from Russia and China."

"Okay, so that explains Sóller. And I'm assuming

you've got London and Singapore in there as they're such high profile fine art centres?" said Greg.

"Yes, correct. I'm not going to waste your time explaining why I don't think it's the other five places, because I'm pretty certain it's these three."

Sam saw the confidence in her. It would be a waste of time as she said, as what did he know about the art world anyway when she was the expert?

She saw Greg and Sam nodding at her.

"What's your immediate thoughts guys?"

Sam spoke first.

"The thief has too much of a head start for us to think we're going to make much headway as to who he is. And I'm only calling him 'he' for convenience sake, that is until we have some clearer indication as to whether we're dealing with a male or female."

"Go on Sam," said Holly.

"How much of a stomach do you think Adamsons have to play this out?"

"What are you thinking Sam? That we let the thief take the painting?" Holly asked the second part of the question slowly.

"I think we need to be realistic given the timescales of this latest ransom. If he's going to do anything, it's going to happen before we've really had time to sort something out."

"Okay, so what are you suggesting?"

"We get ready for the next event, not the one we're currently dealing with. We accept a painting is likely to be stolen if we don't pay the current ransom. Then the ransomer is going to demand the fifty percent mark-up to return it, which I don't think they should pay."

"I'm not sure I like this, but carry on for now," said Holly.

"We call his bluff! Let's see what happens and find out more about how they go about stealing the picture.

Then we build more of our profile of the thief, based on the first time they did it and we get more from this second time. The more data we have, the better the opportunity to identify who it is."

"Hmm, not sure how my boss is going to like telling Adamsons they need to accept another £10 million loss."

"Agreed, but as I said, I'm being realistic. I don't think we can stop the theft of this next picture, do you?" said Sam.

"I suppose not, especially given the fact that there is little or nothing to go on in terms of the M.O. on the previous thefts. We don't really know how the thief got in, nor how they got the painting out," said Theakston.

Holly thought for a moment.

"I think the bigger problem is how do we put it to my boss?"

"Think you're right there Holly, so how will you do that?"

"I think you mean *'How will we do that?'* Sam," said Holly.

"Point taken. Set up the call."

As they came off the Zoom call with Holly and Tony, Greg grinned at Sam.

"Welcome to the 3R international management team."

*****

"You're seriously suggesting we just let this thief go ahead and steal another £10 million painting, so you can build your profile on how they're doing it?" asked Charles Hacker incredulously.

It had seemed to Sam that the conference call would go better when he'd been planning it, but it had quickly backfired.

"I know it sounds somewhat risky," started Sam.

"Somewhat! How exactly do you expect me to get

this past the senior managing partner?"

"Let's turn this on its head shall we?" said Sam, trying to wrestle some positivity back into the discussion. "If you advise Adamsons to pay the ransom now, then you'll just be back to square one, waiting till it happens again and you, or rather Adamsons, will have to keep paying it again and again."

"But Sam, you can't guarantee catching the guy can you?" asked Hacker.

"No, I can't, but you stand little or no chance of catching him anyway if you do nothing and just keep paying up, do you?"

He realised that Sam had a point. It sounded a foolhardy approach until you brought in the alternatives. Then it almost seemed a sensible option.

"I'll need to package this in a way that he sees what I've just seen, but much earlier."

"I can help Charles. I'll come and talk it through with you if it helps?"

"That would help, but please chose your words carefully. PRI's managing partner is liable to go off the deep end if he doesn't see this working and he's already told me that I'll be looking for a new job if this goes wrong."

"Got it," said Sam. "When do you need me to meet them?"

"Like yesterday," said Hacker.

"Right, well I'm booked on the late afternoon flight into Heathrow, so I can be in your office first thing tomorrow morning, along with my mother. I can meet your managing partner and then we'll set up a Gold Suite in your offices and manage the on-going activity from there."

"Gold Suite Sam? Your mother? Can you explain?"

"It's a Command system we used in the police Charles. It helps determine roles and responsibilities and keeps everyone in the loop. The Gold Commander has overall responsibility, sets the strategy that type of thing. But he, or she, delegates roles and specific tasks to a Silver Commander who in turn does the same with their Bronze Commanders and their teams. I'm only thinking of using the concept as a loose fit for our needs here, but with Adamsons and you, representing Premium Risk International it will help keep everyone up to speed with what's happening."

"Okay, now forgive me for asking what seems like a daft question, but why are you bringing your mother?" said Hacker.

"I should have explained. She's in London at the moment in her professional capacity, she's ex-MI6, like Greg and still does some work for them."

"Hello Charles, you still there?"

"Yes sorry, I was just taking that last piece of information on board and I look forward to meeting her. So, I like the Gold Suite idea," said Charles. "I know the Adamsons' Board are getting very anxious about what is going to happen, so maybe some structure will help settle their nerves a bit."

"Hopefully yes, but of course it won't stop the inevitable happening. This guy, if it is a guy, is way too far ahead of us at the moment. But I think we can manoeuvre things to our benefit if Adamsons will just hold their nerve."

"That's a big 'if' Sam, but I think you're right. Okay, Holly, let's run with Sam's idea."

6

The Adamsons file was still on Jake Sutton's coffee table. They'd declined his offer to help them with their security again. This time with a very firm rebuttal, which he'd taken as a personal affront.

They had done the same the previous year and he'd made them pay. So he'd do it again this time, especially as he didn't think they'd cough up the £10 million he'd demanded in his latest email.

'They'll pay, one way or the other.'

He checked his personal mobile again for his non-personalised email account. Nothing. Adamsons hadn't responded, but he'd expected that. They were probably desperately searching in the dark for anything to identify where the emails were coming from. But the only thing they'd find would be a false trail he'd laid suggesting the emailer may be in Thailand.

He knew that security guy with Adamsons, Theakston, had people sniffing around their sites across the world, but no one would ever catch him again, not after the year he'd spent in Feltham Young Offenders Institution. It had been tough, but he'd learnt a lot and realised how careless he'd been to get caught in the first place.

He smiled to himself. Even back then, as a fifteen year old kid, he'd only given up what he wanted the police to know and he knew they couldn't prove half of the roof top burglaries he'd done, other than by him telling them.

But it was like he was seeking their approval. He wanted them to know just how good he was, but then again, he didn't want them to know why he was so good.

It was the same now. It didn't matter to him whether he took a £10 million painting, or the family photograph of the Olympic coach who had sacked him from the athletics programme when he was fourteen.

He typed another short email.

'You've had six hours. Stop wasting your time looking for me. You have another eighteen to go, after which you'll lose another of your precious pieces of art.'

He pushed SEND.

*****

The Suttons had lived in North London. His dad was a bus driver and his mum was a business administrator for a small building company.

Jake was their only child and came as a blessing after they had tried without success for a number of years to have a baby. As often happens, it was soon after they stopped 'trying', that his mum fell pregnant.

As young Jake was growing up his parents realised he was blessed with a number of special gifts. He was clever, really clever and well ahead of most of the other children, especially with his reading, as even in his last year in pre-school, he was tackling books of the age groups two to three years ahead of him.

As his mother waited to pick him up from infant school one day, one of the teachers approached her.

"It's Mrs Sutton isn't it? I'm Tim Horton, I take Jake's

year group for sports."

"He's not in any trouble is he?"

"No, not at all. In fact I wanted to ask you if I could put Jake's name forward to the county athletics people?"

"Why? What? I mean, I know he can run but I didn't know he liked athletics."

He could see she was confused. Jake was only six and to be picked out as having potential at such an early age was unusual, but Horton had been a sports coach for long enough to know when he could see potential in a child.

And so it started.

It was all very informal to start with, with the county coaches telling his parents they would just be keeping a watching eye on young Jake, checking his progress and waiting to see which of the events he particularly liked and which ones he was especially good at.

His mum and dad soon came to understand the demands Jake's talent would place on them, running him to training and then competitions, not to mention the financial burden that came with it.

"At least he's not into swimming," Bill Sutton grinned to his wife one day after hearing about the 6am training sessions some of the parents were having to transport their kids to.

"This is bad enough Bill," she replied, "but we've got to give him every chance haven't we?"

"Yes, of course," said Bill.

But he was worried. Worried about the increasing cost of taking Jake to competitions that seemed to be further and further away from home now he was competing in the Under 17s events, even though he was still only fourteen.

As well as the petrol and the wear and tear on Bill's

old Ford Mondeo, his son seemed to need more and more specialist kit, especially for his feet because the coaches kept telling them that these were Jake's golden ticket to success and they needed to protect them by getting him the best kit they could afford.

Sheila Sutton's initial experience of buying running shoes had been down at the local supermarket. So when they bought Jake his first pair that cost over £100, she had to wind in the housekeeping budget for the next month just to make ends meet.

He was good at all of the athletic sports, but when Horton saw Jake exercising on the gymnastic apparatus one day he was taken by the ease of movement and agility of the young boy.

He had seen many talented youngsters in his time, but Jake Sutton was head and shoulders above them all and by the time he was fourteen Jake was regularly competing for England in international events, specialising in the parallel and uneven bars, the still rings and the pommel horse.

The BOC, the British Olympic Committee, were also now involved in Jake's development and he was being watched with interest as a potential Olympian of the future. Everything was going well in Jake Sutton's young world, including his academic work at school, Jake's other gift that his parents had discovered when they realised his reading ability was far ahead of that of his friends and classmates.

Even with all of the training sessions he was attending for his gymnastics, Jake never fell behind with his school work. In fact he was excelling at school and his science teachers were already earmarking him as a star performer.

But then Bill Sutton was made redundant after he failed a routine medical for his Public Service Vehicle licence to drive a bus.

"They say I've got something degenerative with my eyesight, so it's not going to get any better and basically I'll never drive a bus again," he told Sheila after he got home from work with the news.

Sheila was shaken, but tried not to show it.

"We'll manage. We always have and anyway, it's time you did something different," although the reality was she was really worried how they'd manage, not to mention how they'd be able to keep taking Jake to his competitions and kitted out properly.

*****

Jake wasn't initially sure what his dad's redundancy meant to the family. Whilst they weren't rich, far from it in fact. His mum and dad had always scrimped and saved to make sure he had the best trainers, the best rucksacks and kit and now he was part of the England set-up he did get quite a lot of the extra kit given to him, so he never felt overshadowed by the richer kids at his school.

For a while everything was okay and Bill and Sheila Sutton struggled on as best they could, but this was 2008 and the banks had just imploded and most companies had either stopped recruiting, or were laying people off themselves, so Bill struggled to get another full time role.

This was now making money tight for the family. They had intended to use the small amount of Bill's redundancy money as a nest egg, but they'd already had to start dipping into this, just to keep them afloat.

Jake had no real idea of how bad things had got until the day when his Mum told him quietly that they couldn't afford to buy him the latest Nike trainers like his friends had.

"Mum, it's fine," he said. "I don't really need them. I was just having a look."

She knew by the look on his face that he was

disappointed, but also worried and she gave him a hug.

"Thank you," she whispered, tears welling up in her eyes.

It wasn't fair that Bill had lost his job and it wasn't fair that she couldn't afford the things her son needed for his blossoming gymnastics career.

Jake knew it wasn't their fault, far from it, but the harsh world of the 'haves and have-nots' would have a significant impact on his life and he was damn sure he and his family would never be part of the 'have-nots' ever again.

*****

"Holly, we've had another email, telling us we've had six hours. I've sent it through to you," said Theakston.

She pushed a button on her laptop and the message appeared.

"He's playing with us Tony, telling us to stop looking for him. What else does he expect us to do? Have you spoken to Sam or Greg yet?"

"No, just about to though." He paused. "You are happy that we're bringing them in aren't you?"

"Yes, I like him, I mean them. They aren't afraid to challenge, so I don't see them just taking the fee and going through the motions."

"That is something I am a hundred percent sure of," said Theakston.

"Why did he leave the Met?"

"It was a mix of things I think, but it started when he was on a firearms operation to prevent an armed robbery. One of his team, Sam's best friend in fact, was shot by one of the robbers. They were staked out waiting for the gang to do the job and Sam blamed himself for taking his eye off the main offender as a little girl came into his line of fire. The robber realised it was a set up and started firing, catching Sam's mate

Jimmy and putting him in a wheelchair."

"But surely Sam shouldn't be blaming himself should he? Isn't that what you guys call an *'operational incident'*?"

"Exactly, but knowing the theory and living the practice are two different things. Seeing Jimmy in the wheelchair every day at work just seemed to make it harder for Sam. He hid it well, I mean the PTSD as I certainly didn't see it in him, but then I retired and Sam and my DCI got bumped up a rank, I mean Sam was promoted to DCI, Detective Chief Inspector."

"Yes, got it Tony."

"He apparently managed okay for about a year or fifteen months, but then he lost it big time and nearly laid out his new boss. That was when the bosses realised what he was really going through."

"So he left the police because of that?"

"Like I said, I don't think it was specifically that. He took some enforced leave. He was damned lucky his boss at the time was a really good close friend who wasn't going to support any sort of assault charge against Sam, but he made sure Sam took extended leave to help him sort things out."

"So he lives in Mallorca?" said Holly.

Theakston had been a detective long enough to know when he was being pumped for information. He smiled. He liked Holly Regus, so why not let her find out some more about Sam.

"Yes, his mum is English and his adopted father was from Mallorca. That's another thing, his father died earlier this year, from cancer."

"Thanks Tony, that's useful background. So, I take it you haven't responded to this latest email?"

"No, I've stuck with the tactics we agreed on, to wait until we were twelve hours in before sending anything, but do you think this changes anything?"

"Well he's not done this before, has he? He's always just sent the one message and then a follow-up after he's stolen the painting and yes, I'm still calling him a 'he'. I'd advise that you send a holding response that the matter is still being considered at Board level, but maybe run it by 3R first to get their view?"

"Okay, good idea. I'll get back to you as soon as we have anything," said Theakston.

*****

"Sam, it's Tony, can I run something by you?"

Theakston briefed Sam on the conversation he had just had with Holly Regus. Both were experienced in ransom and kidnap investigation from their time together in the Met Police, so the exchange was like a quick-fire Q&A session.

"Interesting that he has said *'you will lose another painting'*," said Sam.

"Yes, good point. We'd missed that to be honest Sam, but it's definitely positive re-enforcement that it's probably the same guy."

"Yes, good use of the word *'probably'* to keep our options open. Now this email you want to send? What do you hope to gain Tony?" asked Sam.

'Always a classic question,' thought Tony. Actions have consequences and often unintended consequences.

"Nothing beyond a holding position."

"Do you think the ransomer cares?"

"No, I don't suppose he does. I think he may even think he holds all the cards at the moment and maybe considers us to be powerless to stop anything he may choose to do."

"Yes, I agree," said Sam. "So let's keep him thinking just that by sending the holding message."

*****

Sutton's private mobile buzzed with the incoming

email. He was sat with Jean Marshall going through a presentation he was to deliver to a Security Expo where he was the keynote speaker.

He quickly glanced at the email and smiled. It was from Adamsons. A holding email telling him the Board was considering the ransom demand.

"Anything I need to know about before you swan off to Singapore for this conference?" said Jean.

"No, it's just a message from a friend," quickly replacing his phone into his pocket. "And I'm not swanning off to Singapore as you put it," he said with a grin. "It's an important conference and we need to be seen there. Why aren't you coming with me again?"

"Because it's you they want to see, not some old woman who just does all the backroom work," she grinned.

"Jeannie, we both know you do a damn sight more than that. SIS wouldn't be where we are without everything you've done. So come on, why not come out and enjoy a few days of sunshine with me?"

He could see she was tempted. It was already particularly grey and damp in the UK for October and Singapore would be really nice at this time of year. It would be nice to have her out there with him, not only because she was good company, but because she was a skilled networker who could share the focus with him. He also knew that having Jeannie out there would provide a useful smokescreen for the other activities he had in mind to do whilst he was out there.

She looked at him. Singapore sounded fun. She'd originally said 'No', because she had some key client meetings coming up, but one had cancelled and so she did have time, even if it was just for a few days.

"All right then, why not?"

"Great, it'll be fun. I'll get the tickets and hotel sorted. Bring a couple of dresses, one cocktail and one for the evening as we've got a black tie for the final night. I'm so pleased you're coming."

She smiled. He seemed genuinely pleased when for most of the time he was happy to travel the world on his own to these types of events.

7

Greg and Josie were back at Terri's side when she came round. They'd had a call from the medical team to say she was responding well having been given the release medication to bring her out of her coma.

"Your daughter is a fighter Señor," said one of the nursing team.

He smiled at her. She had been there all of the time looking after Terri and he could see she was as anxious as they were to see how she came through. He held her hand and smiled.

"Muchas gracias."

"Greg!" said Josie. "She's coming round."

Dr Hernandez checked the data readings on the mass of dials on the equipment around the bed and looked across reassuringly to Greg and Josie.

"You can talk to her now Josie."

With tears streaming down her face, Josie started talking quietly to her daughter.

"Terri, Terri, can you hear me my love? I'm here with your dad and everyone else is waiting to see how you are."

They watched on hoping to see something. Terri was breathing easily and unaided, but hadn't yet fully woken up.

"It may take a little while, but she's doing very well," said Dr Hernandez.

"We can't wait for you to wake up my darling girl. You've got a lot of catching up to do and your dad will be so relieved to get back holding the reigns at 3R."

"That's right sweetie. We've been just about managing to keep things afloat, but the sooner you're back the better," said Greg, choking slightly, his words coming out in a stilted fashion as he fought back tears. "Sam's outside, so is Lily and of course we've got Si…"

He didn't finish what he was saying as Terri's eyes flickered open.

"Simon, is he okay?"

Greg waved Simon in through the door and he came in hesitantly, not wishing to steal the moment from Terri's parents.

"Get in there Simon and tell her you still love her for God's sake," whispered Josie.

"Do you?" said Terri softly, a tear falling on to her cheek.

Simon gently brushed his hand across her face taking the tear with it.

"Always have and always will."

She heard his words in his soft Welsh accent.

Greg patted him on the back. He could think of worse son-in-laws to have in the family than a guy who had saved his bacon on more than one occasion.

"She still needs to rest guys," said Dr Hernandez, "so we should leave her to sleep now, but it will be a natural sleep and you can still sit here quietly with her."

The doctor was looking at Simon, who smiled back at her.

"Doc, can Lily and Sam come in, just quickly?"

"Si, pronto, pronto," she grinned.

Lily Green came in to the room with Sam and she

knelt down by Terri's bed.

When they had first met just a few months ago, Terri had had to spin Lily a story as to who she was so as not to arouse her suspicions over how she was trying to help her. Then there had been the incident when Terri's bike had been tampered with on the ride back from the Formentor lighthouse, not to mention them being kidnapped and both of them almost killed by Marsden.

"I'll see you soon hun. We've got so much to catch up on when you can tell me all about the real you," she said with a smile. "You take good care of her in the meantime," she hugged Simon around the back and gave him a kiss on the top of his head.

"So pleased to see you awake Sis," said Sam gently kissing her on the cheek.

As Greg and Josie went out they both embraced Doctor Hernandez.

"Thank you so much and your team for all you've done," said Josie.

"Do you think she's going to be okay Doctor?" asked Greg.

"It's been our pleasure. Now I've got nothing to suggest anything otherwise than she's going to be fine. Yes, it's early days, but she clearly knows who you are and she has retained her mid-term memory of whatever went on with Simon," she said with a smile. "The physical injuries are healing very well, but we need to see how she deals with any psychological issues from the incident, but I think you guys have your own experience of PTSD, yes?"

"Sadly Doctor, they do, and in bucket loads," said Josie.

*****

Jake Sutton and Jean Marshall got out of the taxi at Terminal 5 London Heathrow. It was reasonably quiet at the Business check-in and they were soon through the Fast Track Security and waiting for their flight in the BA Lounge.

"Have you been to Singapore before Jeannie?"

"Yes, a number of times when I was working for the bank," she replied. "But I haven't been for a few years, so I'm looking forward to this."

"Good," said Jake. "So am I."

Although for him the trip was less about the Security Conference keynote speech he was going to give and much more about the enjoyment he was going to have, making Adamsons sweat after he'd taken the painting from their gallery in Orchard Road, the city's primary high street shopping area.

8

Anna Martínez was at Heathrow airport to meet her son on the flight in from Palma de Mallorca.

She held him tightly in her arms.

"Hello Sam, how are you?"

He'd felt the intensity of her holding him. It was nearly a year now since Luis had passed and she must be missing him so much and it must have all come flooding back with them nearly losing Terri.

"I'm good Mum and so relieved about Terri."

She knew it had been a pretty tumultuous time for him over the past year or so. He'd had the firearms incident at work to deal with where Jimmy had been shot. Then the breakup with his long term girlfriend and then she knew herself that she'd probably piled on the pressure, when she told him Greg was his biological father and that Terri was his half-sister who he'd then nearly lost after she was shot.

"Yes, I wish I'd been there when she woke up, so thank you for keeping me posted on what's been going on. Now tell me, what's happening with this new job with Adamsons?"

'Typical mum,' he thought. *'Absolutely caring about people, but then when she knew that everything was okay,*

she was straight back down to business.'

"What are you smiling about now?" asked Anna.

"Nothing," he grinned. "Right, this is what we've got."

And he took her through the call from Theakston and the subsequent follow up conversations with Holly Regus.

"What do you need me to be doing tomorrow Sam?" she asked.

"This will be fast moving I reckon Mum, so I'm thinking two heads are better than one, especially as we could be having questions fired in from both Adamsons and PRI."

"Understood. So you're not thinking of even adding security to the three priority locations Dr Regus has identified?"

"I don't see how we can without potentially alerting the art world that something fishy's going on, which is apparently the last thing Adamsons want. I think in truth that they'd rather lose another painting than risk their reputation, although that sounds a bit odd in itself doesn't it?" said Sam.

"Yes, I suppose it does," said Anna. "Losing a painting risks their reputation, but if no one knows about it, then no one is the wiser. Telling the art world they've actually lost a painting is tantamount to putting their own reputation on the chopping block and waiting for the axe to fall."

"You've got it in one Mum. Now, what about some dinner? I guess you aren't staying at The Savoy this time?"

She laughed.

"No, Martin's budget wouldn't stretch to that this time around. By the way he sends his regards."

Martin Carruthers was his mother's MI6 contact and had helped them resolve the IT scam issue that had first got Sam involved with Greg and 3R.

"Well not to worry. I'm sure we can enjoy a nice evening meal somewhere and charge it to PRI, Holly's outfit."

"Ah, Holly now is it?" said his mother.

"Stop match-making Mum!"

She smiled at him, but underneath her smile she really was concerned that he didn't seem able to hold down any sort of long term relationship and wondered how much of an effect the PTSD from Jimmy's shooting was having on him.

*****

At 9am the following morning, the two of them walked the short distance from their hotel to the PRI offices.

Charles Hacker, Holly Regus and Tony Theakston were waiting for them, together with a Director from Adamsons, Christine Harrison.

"Good morning everyone," said Sam after the introductions were over. "Thanks for coming Chris and thanks to you too Charles for hosting this meeting."

"PRI are here to help Adamsons in any way we can Sam. So how will this Gold Suite of yours work?"

Sam motioned to everyone to sit in the chairs around the Board Room style table where their individual nameplates were positioned.

"Holly has set up the room with direct line phones that immediately connect to key contacts who we may need to speak to in the remaining twenty four hours of this cat and mouse game the ransomer seems to want to play."

Chris picked up the phone in front of her and a voice immediately answered.

"Mrs Harrison, it's Kathy."

Chris Harrison immediately recognised the voice of the Chairman's PA.

"How can I help you?"

"Just testing Kathy, thank you." She rang off.

"I'm impressed Holly."

Sam continued outlining the set-up of the room. Three of the phones connected to the three galleries identified as priority locations, whilst another was a general number that any of the other galleries could call on if they needed to reach the Gold Suite.

"What are the other ones for Sam?" asked Hacker.

"They are for the 3R teams who are out and about at the three priority locations. We've got a couple of people here in London, Greg is in Mallorca, plus we have a team from India who should now be just about in position in Singapore."

"But you said you didn't think you could stop the thief stealing the painting?" said Chris Harrison.

"I still think that Chris, however, I wanted our people on the ground to respond to what happens if, or rather when we expect a painting to be stolen."

"What are you specifically looking for from me Sam?" asked Harrison.

He liked her. Friendly and easy to connect with, but already he could sense she was assessing each of them in the room.

"You're a decision maker for Adamsons Chris. Although you'll be able to call your Chairman, I understand he's empowered you in the event of me needing a fast time decision?"

"Yes, that's right."

"That's great. These Gold Command suites work much better when you have people in the room who can actually make a decision on behalf of their organisations," said Sam. "So what I need from you and you too Charles, is first of all your buy-in to what we're doing here and second, this may end up being a fast moving scenario where I might need your immediate go-ahead on a particular course of action. Now, the plan today is to establish which location the thief hits and then ensure we grab that Golden Hour to capture as much information as we can at the scene."

"Golden Hour?"

"Sorry, more police-speak Chris. It's as it says on the front of the tin, it's that first hour after an incident occurs when key evidence can be seized or lost. No disrespect to your teams Tony, but I want my people out there to get to the scene as soon as possible to give us the very best chance."

"Surely there's a logical process you investigators go through at a scene, so how can evidence be lost in this Golden Hour?" said Chris.

"Good question and if we lived in a logical world then yes, there wouldn't be a problem. But we're dealing with people here and in the heat of the moment things can and do get missed, often because tensions are running high, not to mention the chaos that can surround an event where people may have been hurt, property damaged or stolen. Let's not forget the person doing this knows we will be looking for them. So we should expect distraction tactics."

"Can we do anything to prepare ourselves against these distractions?" asked Holly.

"That's a tough one Holly. Even by briefing your teams to be mindful of any unexpected incidents, you know, like the fire alarm maybe going off, we can sometimes prime them to focus so much on those possibilities that they inadvertently become blind to other things happening, such as the thief perhaps taking a picture that's worth significantly more, or even less, than the £10 million one he's threatening to take."

"True, but I'm still not sure we shouldn't warn at least the team leaders Sam," said Tony Theakston.

"Again, that's a good point and I'm open to discussion around that Tony. You know your teams better than I do. I'm not averse to telling the team leaders at these sites if that would reassure you?"

Theakston looked across at Christine Harrison.

"I'm happy to go with what you guys think. But the option to at least tell the heads of security at the individual sites seems a good idea."

"Done," agreed Sam. "Tony, can you make that happen? I'll work though a short briefing note with you. We'll also tell them about our 3R guys being nearby and that they should allow them free access should anything happen. Is that okay with everyone?"

Harrison and Hacker both nodded and murmured their agreement.

"Now what do we do?" said Holly.

"We wait," said Sam walking across to the refreshments that had been placed in the corner of the room. "Coffee or tea?"

"Before we do that Sam, this seems a good time for us to brief my managing partner."

Sam nodded and followed Hacker as he walked towards the door.

*****

Five minutes later they were in an office on the top floor, the Executive Suite according to the lift button signage.

Hacker introduced Sam to Keith Smalling, senior managing partner at Premium Risk international and then started explaining Sam's plan.

"But wouldn't Adamsons have wanted to have this Gold Suite at their offices?"

"No, Sam's thinking is that they won't want to attract any unwanted attention to themselves. Having it here just makes it look like any other meeting," said Hacker.

"Sam, the plan to allow the ransomer to steal another painting and possibly another one on top of that seems a very high risk strategy?"

"Yes it is Keith. However, if you keep advising Adamsons to pay the ransom then you will never get out of this cycle. I think that's the definition of insanity isn't it? Doing the same thing over and over and expecting a different result?"

Sam thought he saw a thin smile appear on Smalling's face.

"That's why we need a different type of intervention Keith. You could go to the police, but that risks the issue getting out into the public domain, or you can…"

"Allow your 3R organisation to use your own particular skills," said Smalling.

Hacker knew his boss had made his decision and was backing Sam's plan.

"Charles, it's high risk and I'll hold you responsible for the outcome, so let's hope for your sake that it works out as Sam here thinks it will."

As Sam followed Charles out of the room, he said, "He's not leaving you in any doubt there is he Charles?"

"Name of the game in corporate life my friend, it's the name of the game." As they stepped into the lift to go back down to the Gold Suite he added, "And I liked the definition of insanity bit Sam. Nice touch that certainly wasn't lost on Keith."

*****

Anna had already set to work checking on the positions of the 3R teams who were either at or making their way to the three priority locations.

"Hello Anna," said Greg. "I've got Simon with me down in Sóller. We've been in to see the painting Holly indicated might be the target. It's a Miró."

"Ah, yes, Luis loved his work. So you're okay? Nothing to report in?"

"No, it's pretty quiet down here. You wouldn't really know this was a high end art gallery unless you know the art world. Don't get me wrong, it's in a very nice building just off the main square, but it's low key and the people coming in here just aren't walk-ins. There's money here Anna and a lot of it."

"Okay, great. Any more news on Terri?"

"She's doing well. Josie and Lily are with her today. I think it's doing Simon, and me for that matter, a lot of good to get out and about on a job again."

"That's so good to hear. Let's catch up later."

Anna then moved onto the London team. Tommy, who had been with Greg almost from the start of 3R was with Sharon, one of the UK based team leaders.

"Good morning Tommy, how are you my dear?"

"Lovely to hear from you Anna. We're all good thanks. We've been in for a walk around and can confirm the picture is still there. It's pretty quiet and the Adamsons security team looks to be on the ball. Sharon has a couple of her team keeping a watching brief close by in case we need back-up."

As Hacker and Sam came back into the room Anna looked up.

"Things seem pretty quiet in both London and Mallorca. It's really interesting looking at how the thief actually got into the gallery the previous time. I've read the papers and Tony has walked me through it and there's nothing, nothing at all to identify how they got in. We've got the time when the picture was originally stolen, but all the CCTV suddenly went off and there was nothing from the facial recognition cameras to identify anyone of interest before that happened."

"What about Singapore?" said Sam.

"You've got people out there?" asked Holly. "We only spoke to you yesterday, so I can't believe you've got that covered as well!"

"We've got a team based out in Mumbai, so it's actually less than five hours flight time," said Sam. "Any contact from Eschaan?"

"Not yet, just about to call him."

Anna made the call.

"Anna?"

"I think it must be good afternoon by now Eschaan?"

"Yes, Anna. We're in position around the gallery, although it's been difficult to get inside. Do you still want us to hold off and not make contact with the security teams?"

Sam, nodded. He was taking the role of Gold and so Anna would refer any key decisions to him.

"That's an affirmative Eschaan. No contact unless absolutely necessary. I've just texted everyone to let you know we're telling the heads of security on site, so you'll be given immediate access should anything happen, but their teams won't be briefed by them. We want to keep this as quiet for as long as we can and see how it plays out."

"Yes, yes," replied Eschaan in the traditional double confirmation of surveillance teams.

"Which of the team have you got with you?"

"Hello Anna, it's Ruha."

Anna heard her South London accent. Ruha was one of Terri's three new recruits in the Mumbai office. She was a former Met police officer who had decided to relocate to Mumbai where her parents' grew up.

"Hi Ruha, how are you finding Singapore?"

"It's great. Never been here before, but Eschaan has, so he knows his way about."

The niceties over and Ruha was straight back into her professional reporting mode.

"We've got good cover over here. We're dressed up fancy and made a point of visiting some of the high value shops in Orchard Row before we approached the Adamsons. We reckon they'd already clocked us because they buzzed us through the security doors straight away."

"I hope that's why they did," muttered Tony, concerned that his team may have been too lax.

"Did we know there's a Security Expo on here at the moment?" asked Eschaan coming back in on the conversation.

"No, we didn't," said Sam. "That's helpful guys. Can you check it out?"

"Already got tickets sorted. It's by 'Invitation Only,' so we've booked it using the 3R International name to get us a corporate ticket. There's some interesting stuff there on personal and building security."

"Okay, check it out when you get an opportunity. Speak later," said Anna.

"Sam, I'm impressed you've got feet on the ground already, especially Singapore," said Hacker.

Holly looked across at Sam and smiled.

'This guy's good at this stuff. Maybe, just maybe, we might have some luck in identifying this thief.'

9

After they checked into the Shangri-La, a short walk from Orchard Road, Jake suggested a drink in the executive lounge which they had access to because of the rooms they had in the Valley Wing.

He'd quickly changed and was now in chinos and t-shirt, but he had to look twice when Jean Marshall walked into the lounge. He was so used to seeing her over the past eight or nine years they'd worked together as the very smartly dressed, highly professional, businesswoman at work, that he realised he'd rarely seen her away from the workplace in any sort of social situation.

"Wow, Jeannie, if I may say so, you look stunning!"

She smiled. It was like a son telling his mum she looked beautiful. She never looked upon him as a son because first and foremost, they were business partners, but the age gap wasn't lost on her as she could quite easily be his mother.

"That's very nice of you to say Jake. Thank you."

She was touched, as he rarely made personal comments about her appearance. Jake was also the only person at SIS who she allowed to call her *'Jeannie'*. He was a brilliant young entrepreneur, but if she had a worry about him, it was because he was almost entirely fixated on his business and seemed to spend very little time on his personal life, other than with his exercise regimes.

They each ordered a gin and tonic and sat back listening to the woman quietly playing background music on a harp.

"Has your package arrived at the conference centre?" asked Jean.

"Yes," said Jake. "It should add a little something to the presentation." Although he was also thinking it played nicely into his plans for a visit to a certain art gallery on Orchard Road.

*****

Maggie Walker lay in the bed next to her husband. She was surprised that the sex had been so gentle and loving. Not that it usually wasn't, but she'd expected it might be a bit more rushed, *'maybe a rougher ride,'* she smiled to herself, especially given the fact Frankie had been inside for over a year now.

Then again, he hadn't exactly rushed home. He would have got out around 11am and he hadn't got home till around two. She could smell the beer on him, so guessed he'd stopped off at the pub. She knew her husband well, so he'd probably been to a strip club too. She didn't like it, of course she didn't, but she'd accepted it as long as he didn't parade it in front of her. Anyway, it was all part of the 'show' he put on for the outside world she told herself.

They'd been married for over ten years and she knew what he was when she married him. He was a criminal. He'd been one since he was a teenager. In and out of trouble, in and out of borstals and the only thing she'd hated then was that he was small fry. He wasn't even a big fish in a small pond.

She'd been the one who had pushed him to do bigger

and more daring jobs. He'd been against it at first, because it meant he had to work harder at what he was doing. Plus the fact he wasn't sure he liked his wife telling him what to do. That wasn't the sort of thing that happened where he came from.

Walker lay next to Maggie. He'd enjoyed the love-making with his wife. He loved her. Always had and always would. Like his Dad had been with Mum. He had a lot to thank Maggie for. If it had been down to him they'd still be in the council house they'd first moved into when they got married. But she'd changed his life and now they lived in a five bedroom house, with two kids at a private prep-school and he was the boss of a very lucrative business.

'Hell, it's a bloody mansion with a bleedin' Bentley parked outside!'

It was Maggie who called it a business. She was definitely the brains and he was the brawn, but she'd taught him and taught him well and now they made a bloody good partnership.

The only thing he'd asked, when she'd told him to get off his arse and let her help him become a *'proper robber,'* was for him to still be the one his people thought was the actual boss.

Maggie knew this was a bit of male vanity. Part of her wanted to be the one who people knew was running the organisation, but she also truly loved her husband, so if that made him happy, then she could go with that and she knew he loved her all the more for it.

"Rogers has told me Robbo is the snitch Maggs."

She sat bolt upright in bed and looked at him. Frankie looked down at her breasts and smiled. Almost self-consciously she pulled the sheet up to cover herself.

"Concentrate lover-boy" her voice hardening. "Now tell me again. What do you mean Robbo is the snitch?"

She had thought someone had given Frankie up for the robbery where he'd shot the copper, but Frankie wasn't so sure and thought it was just bad luck.

"Well it was an almighty bit of bad luck, if that's what it was Frankie," she'd told him at the time.

It had all been a bit too convenient that the police happened to get some information that a robbery was going to take place. She had been the one to tell their slimy brief, Philip Rogers, to start digging amongst the undisclosed police evidence to the CPS. It had to be a far better way of finding out, if someone had given Frankie up, than fishing around the team creating suspicion and unrest that certainly wouldn't help maintain performance whilst he was inside.

Only one member of the team had created any sort of fuss when she walked into the meeting after Frankie had been arrested and put on remand in prison.

Frankie had enough support from a couple of very loyal guys and at her word, they soon stepped on the one decrier, Hughie Morris, who looked after the stripclubs. She had sat down at the head of the table, in Frankie's chair and stared straight at him.

"Hughie, this isn't a discussion about me taking over whilst Frankie's inside. You toe the line, or you start looking for alternative employment with two broken legs."

Hughie and the rest of the team heard the menace in her voice and she waited for her words to sink in.

'She sounded just like Frankie did when he went off on one,' one of them said later.

Hughie had chosen 'toe the line' and to be fair there had been others who had been less vocal in their support for her. However, in the year she'd been heading up the organisation they'd seen she was tough, but fair and she certainly wasn't a shrinking violet when it came to managing the dirtier side of things. Far from it in fact. If people performed, she rewarded them well, but anyone thought to be holding back on what they could deliver were soon reminded of what would happen if things didn't improve. Even Hughie hadn't been any trouble since and actually, he'd been doing a pretty good job of running the strip clubs and had been very respectful to her.

Frankie looked at her, hearing her voice change tone. She'd been brilliant since he'd gone inside. It was the first time he'd been in prison since he was a teenager. That was down to her. She'd made sure his planning was well thought through and he'd covered all the angles. Yes, he'd been nicked a few times, but the Old Bill had never had enough to pin anything on him and he'd always been released without charge by the end of the day.

"Rogers got it from the undisclosed stuff just as you said he would but he didn't want to give up the name to me."

"I thought there was something he wasn't telling me. Remind me to cut his retainer. Pissing me about like that," said Maggs. "Where's Robbo now?"

"Down at one of the lock-ups. I'm going down at three to see what he has to say for himself. Do you want to come along?"

"No, I've got the kids to pick up, so I'll leave that to you."

Maggs looked across at the digital clock on the bedside table. 14.45. She looked at Frankie and pouted her lips.

"Come on then big boy, show me what you got," as she let the silk sheet slide down her body. "You've got two minutes, what are you waiting for!"

*****

Frankie looked down at the blood on his hands. He was disappointed it had gone on his shirt too, but he knew he'd be getting rid of it anyway.

It had been Maggs's idea to have the sound proofing and the portable shower put in at the lock up. The team and even the plumber who installed it weren't sure why the shower was being fitted. But Frankie knew. This was the punishment centre and Maggs had long ago identified the need to erase any chance of any blood, DNA or anything else of evidential use being found. This meant anyone carrying out a punishment beating immediately showered afterwards and their clothing was incinerated.

When the beating resulted in the permanent demise of the victim, she also made them strip the victim and put them through the shower for the same reasons. Frankie knew this was one of the primary reasons the police had never been able to pin anything on him. Maggs was way too savvy for anything like that to happen to him.

"So Robbo, tell me again, who was it you told about the job in Hackney?"

Walker added another violent uppercut to Robbo's chin and thought he almost heard the noise of some of the man's teeth rattling loose.

Robbo spat another mouthful of blood out. He'd taken the decision that the best policy was to tell everything and just hope Frankie made it quick, whatever he was going to do with him.

"I said it was Tony Theakston. It started when he was a DI. He'd just been promoted to some Major Crime Unit and wanted to make an impression. I swear Boss, until then, I'd only done a few bits of rubbish and it was just because I was trying to get into them myself. You know, to turn one of them and make them ours."

It was a tactic Frankie knew others had tried sometimes with cops. Give them a little bit and then draw them into what you wanted from them.

Sometimes with money, or maybe access to some high class girls or boys. It did work sometimes, but he wasn't convinced Robbo had enough about him to pull anything like that off.

"Good try Robbo, but you're just not smart enough for anything like that my old mate."

For good measure Frankie threw in a left hook that caught the side of Robbo's head, almost knocking him off the seat he was tied to.

"Do you still speak to this guy Theakston? I thought he'd retired not long after the Hackney job?"

"No Boss. He stayed on for a bit, but only because you'd er, you'd shot that copper."

"Ah yes, the gun bloke. I caught his mate looking at the little kid as she stepped across in front of me."

Frankie's voice was almost jovial, but Robbo had heard him like this before, when he'd been the one standing behind the chair watching some poor bastard get a beating off the boss.

'It won't be long,' he thought to himself. *'At least I hope so. It'll be over one way or the other.'*

"But I'm not going to bloody beg."

"What was that you said Robbo?" Again the menace in Frankie's voice.

'Shit! Did I say that out aloud?' Panic started to set in with Robbo.

"Did you say you're not going to beg?" asked Frankie quietly.

Frankie's face was pressed so close to Robbo's that he could feel Frankie's breath against his cheek. He smelled of beer and a woman's perfume.

"No, no, I didn't mean it."

Robbo could hear the fear in his voice and knew Frankie must have heard it to.

"Please Frankie."

"I thought you said you weren't going to beg? But

I reckon that after you got me put inside for the last twelve months Robbo for a few measly quid, I think we'll just see how much you will beg you miserable piece of shit."

Whether Frankie Walker heard anything Robbo said after that was debateable and even when the chair Robbo was sat on tipped over, as Frankie smashed punch after punch into him, the two men standing behind it just picked it up and Frankie carried on and only stopped hitting Robbo when he fell to the floor with exhaustion.

Bob looked on showing no emotion, but even he hadn't seen Frankie being quite as vicious with anyone before.

"I reckon he's gone Boss."

"I don't like grasses Bob," said Frankie regaining his composure.

"None of us do Boss. Good riddance to him. Now there's a change of clothes by the shower. I'll see that Robbo is cleaned up before we dump him."

"Thanks and Bob? Find out what you can on what this guy Theakston is up to now."

10

Jake Sutton stood at the podium in the Shangri-La Hotel Conference Room and looked out at the audience. The organisers had planned for a thousand delegates and as he looked out across the rows of people seated before him he felt a slight twitch in his stomach.

'Nerves. Good,' he thought. As a young competitor in the world of gymnastics he'd long ago realised the power of harnessing his nervous energy and using it as a positive release to deliver his best performance.

He looked across at Jeannie Marshall and smiled. He'd seen her perform on stages like this and she set the bar very high with her professionalism and skill in working the audience. He turned back to face the audience and breathed in slowly.

"Hello everybody! I'm Jake Sutton."

There were a few murmurs, but not much of a response. He tried again.

"I said hello everybody!" This time he yelled it and jumped down into the auditorium and started running around shaking people's hands. He could sense the growing noise in the crowd.

"Come on everyone. Say hello to the person next to you."

He could hear their voices. He looked at Jeannie, who smiled back at him, nodding her head. She knew he'd got them.

"Okay, so have you introduced yourself to the people next to you and behind you?"

This time, there were shouts back to him from people in the audience. He checked to see where they were coming from. He'd positioned some of his Singapore SIS team in the audience just in case he got no response, as they were primed to call out if need be, but he was pleased to see the shout-outs were coming from other areas. He relaxed, he really had got them now.

"So how do you know they aren't going to now go and steal your identity?"

He pushed a button and an image flashed up on the screens situated behind him and around the room.

Identity Theft
How to do it and how to stop it

The audience went into a hushed silence as many of them started to realise what he'd done and just how easy it could be for an identity thief to get into their lives.

Jake spent the next forty minutes of his presentation keeping them on their toes. He fired out questions at them and kept the energy levels high as he focused in on how these thieves went about their business, before going into how they could protect themselves and their businesses.

"You see the best way to protect yourself is to know how they do it. Once you know, you can use the ideas I've given you to combat their tactics and keep your identity secure."

He could tell it was going well and their engagement and applause he was getting seemed to confirm that.

"Now, I've got one final thing for you. If you'd all like to look under your chairs you'll find a small gift from me to you as a thank you for you taking the time to listen to me."

He watched as the audience fumbled around under their seats with their hands and then saw as they started to bring up the bags containing the gift.

"By the way, all the bags are from recycled paper, so please either deposit them in the bins we've provided for you on the way out, or take them home and recycle them yourself."

He saw the first few people put the glasses on. Some were sunglasses and some had clear lenses. Others were looking at them a little puzzled, whilst there were a few in the audience who realised what Jake had given them.

"Okay, so who's guessed what these are then?"

Some hands went up in the audience and there were a few shouts.

"Say that again," said Jake to a woman in the third row.

"Are they anti-facial recognition glasses?"

"Yes, you're absolutely right."

He flicked the slide switch again and two images appeared on the screen.

"So the first is a picture of me with a pair of ordinary sun glasses on and you can see a facial recognition CCTV camera has picked up my image. Now, not all current systems can pick up facial recognition through sunglasses, but all the latest gear can. Okay, so I'm seeing by the look on some of your faces that you hadn't realised that."

Again, there were murmurs in the audience as he'd struck a chord with them.

"So, as well as those of you who may wish to protect your own privacy from CCTV surveillance across the towns and cities where we live, there's another reason I highlight these types of glasses. With your permission," he said holding up a handheld video camera, "I'm going to turn this camera towards you and your face will come up on the screen. Now if you don't want your face shown up on screen, or if you're just interested to see what happens, then put your glasses on now."

He saw lots of glasses being put on in the audience.

'They're either all hyper sensitive of their privacy, or they want to see what happens,' he smiled to himself.

"Okay, let's start with Jeannie over here," Jake pointed his handheld camera at her. "Some of you may know her already, but if not, this is Jean Marshall, CEO of SIS and my long time mentor. Say hi Jeannie."

Jean waved at the audience, who waved back or called out to her. She wasn't wearing the glasses and she saw her face flash across the main screen. Then as the facial recognition software started to work, capturing the geometry of her face, a second image appeared next to the live image of her – as the software matched her image to a previously uploaded picture from her conference name badge and a CONFIRMED ID message appeared on the screen.

"Looks like it got you Jean. Now what about the rest of you? Now is there someone who doesn't want to be identified as being here today?"

He picked a guy at random in the audience in the front five rows. He ran down the stage steps and focused in on the young man with his camera.

"What's your name my friend?"

"Bill," said the man in an Australian accent.

"Just to confirm to everyone here Bill, do we know each other, or have you ever had any contact with me?"

"No mate, on both counts."

"Let's see if I can find you with this software then

Bill."

Jake turned the software switch on with the camera still pointing towards Bill's face. Jake was looking up at the screen too and heard the noise from the audience before he saw their reaction for himself.

They'd seen a white blob appear around Bill's face on the screen.

"Well thank goodness for that," said Jake laughing. "It works."

The audience laughed too, but they had seen and understood the impact of the anti-recognition glasses.

"How do they work?" Someone shouted out from the back.

"Great question. There's different types and designs of these glasses, but these particular ones have two things that can stop the facial recognition software working effectively. First of all there's a reflective layer within the lenses. This bounces light back at the camera, so this works best when the light is very good, or when there's a flashlight involved. The second thing which you will have to look very hard to see is the frames have tiny LED lights embedded in them."

He saw lots of people taking the glasses off and turning the frames around in their hands trying to see the LEDs.

"If they're there, then they look like they're part of the frame," a dark haired woman called out from the rows at the side.

"Oh they're definitely there," said Jake. "Look, I'll put the camera on my pair and focus right in on the frame. There can you see those dots? They're the lights, but they're actually pretty much invisible to the human eye, but they appear like big blobs of light to any CCTV cameras looking at them."

He turned the camera off and looked out across the audience.

"Look guys, I hope you've enjoyed this presentation and go on to enjoy the rest of the conference, but please, what I need you to remember is that some in the criminal fraternity know about this technology as much as the security industry does. We suspect, no let me correct that, we know that some are already using it when they carry out a recce of a property or location they are intending to attack. Now this isn't your local shoplifters after a bottle of wine or a few clothes. This is the organised crime gangs who are sending out teams of shoplifters to flood a town or city for a day, or it may be those criminals who commit high value robberies or burglaries. What's for sure is that no alarm system is completely fail-proof and ladies and gentlemen, I include my own SIS products in this and I should know because I designed them."

The audience started talking amongst themselves, taking on board what one of the leading lights in the electronic alarm industry had just said.

"Now this isn't a sales pitch for SIS, far from it. All I ask is that whoever's system you currently use, please make sure you regularly check with them for the technological advances they should be making and if they aren't?" He gave a laugh and threw his hands up in the air. "Then you know how to find me. Thank you."

He left the platform to more applause and found Jeannie who smiled at him.

"You know, you're getting rather good at all that stuff Jake. You had them in the palm of your hand."

"Thanks Jeannie, I learned from one of the best," he winked at her. "Come on, let's go and get some fresh air."

As they walked out of the hotel, one of the doormen offered them both Shangri-La umbrellas. Jake looked up at the sky. It looked pretty clear.

"Take it Jake. It's almost four o'clock. The rain will be

here shortly. It's regular as clockwork."

He took the umbrella a little reluctantly, but Jeannie had been right. They had only just got as far as Orchard Road when the heavens opened and with umbrellas going up all around them, they made their way into a coffee shop.

They took a table looking out onto the road and Jake smiled as he saw a number of passers-by wearing the glasses he'd given them.

"Do I want to know how much a thousand pairs of those glasses cost?"

"Probably not, but I'm sure you can write it off to marketing or something," said Jake, although the real reason he'd got them was much more about what he intended to do in a little while in the nearby Adamsons gallery.

11

Anna had continued to make regular checks into the teams and none of them had anything to report other than the estimated numbers of people visiting the galleries.

Tony Theakston had confirmed with the individual heads of security at each location that the alarm systems were all in good working order and there had been no unexpected staff absences that might suggest any sort of collusion by anyone with the thief.

Sam had suggested to Charles Hacker and Christine Harrison that they might as well continue with any of their other work and whilst Hacker went back to his office, Chris Harrison grabbed the office adjacent to the Gold Suite.

"I've read and reread your reports on the painting you lost last year Tony and from the moment the alarm went off until it was noticed that the painting was missing, no one seems able to bring anything to light to say how the thief got it out of the building?" said Sam.

"That's right. It's like a black hole. It doesn't sit well with me Sam. There's always got to be an explanation, but I've not found it yet, nor has anyone else."

"The painting that was stolen was pretty big wasn't it? About four foot by three?"

"Yes, so you'd think someone would have seen it if the thief just walked out with it," said Theakston.

"And as the frame wasn't found discarded there's no suggestion that it was cut out before being removed from the gallery?" asked Anna.

"No, but we thought it might have been because the GPS located in the frame indicated the painting, or at least the frame was still on site," said Holly.

"That wasn't in the report. I didn't know about any GPS," said Sam.

"Oh hell, I'm sorry about that," said Tony. "I think I sent you the abbreviated file. We keep things like the GPS under wraps. It's a pretty well-known secret, but the industry as a whole tries not to publicise the fact that GPS chips are fitted on all frames containing high value art. They're tamper proof too, so we'd know if a thief was trying to take the chips off the frame."

"What happened when the alarm went off?" asked Anna.

"A back-up should have cut in, but it didn't. The alarm company weren't sure what had happened, but the alarm showed a problem with another part of the building some distance from where the actual painting was stolen."

"So when the alarm went off in one area, the whole system went down? Is that usual?" said Sam.

"No, far from it. They think it was perhaps some sort of blocking or diversion device. Certainly there was nothing untoward in the location where the alarm activated, so it looks to have been a distraction."

"Your heads of security know that Tony?"

"Yes, we ran some training sessions post-event to get the message across, so in theory, they shouldn't all go running to where the alarm indicates."

"You don't sound too convinced by your own theory Tony?" said Sam.

"It's the human element to it all Sam. I think we've all seen enough of what can happen if someone sees or hears an alarm of some sort. It takes discipline and a lot of training to not go running to the place where the alarm tells you there's a problem."

"Plus, if you're an entry level security guard, the fact that if you don't at least cover the location the alarm is telling you, then you risk being called out for not covering the basics by the likes of me and Tony," said Holly.

"Fair point Holly," said Sam. "Okay, for now, we only have the one incident from last year to go on. It's likely that with your twenty four hours about to lapse very shortly, we're going to have to learn some very quick lessons when the thief strikes again."

*****

The thief they were talking about was now back in his hotel room after his walk and a coffee with Jean Marshall. He had told her that he was going for a quick nap and would see her around seven for drinks before dinner, but he was soon back out of the hotel and walking towards Orchard Road.

Even with the torrential afternoon downpour the pavement was already drying out as he strolled towards the Adamsons gallery. He knew there was a good chance the gallery would have people out looking for a potential thief. He'd plotted this out for some time and had cross-checked all of the scenarios he could think of and countered each one with a different strategy.

To start with he'd created the opportunity for a distraction. He'd ensured there was a mass of free tickets to the Adamsons gallery made available for the conference delegates. They were already spread around the hotel as it was a marketing ploy often used by galleries and high-end shops to attract new clients staying in the city.

Jake reckoned that out of the thousand delegates there was a good probability that maybe five percent might take up the invite and that would be fifty people. More than enough for what he had in mind.

He doubted Adamsons had brought in the police after he'd emailed them the ransom threat. They couldn't afford the chance that it might get leaked to the press by some loose lipped copper. That meant they were dealing with this in-house or more likely, they'd brought in some outside team. Now that did concern him a little. It all depended on the team. He knew from his industry experience that many private security companies were good at guarding things, but not much else. However, he did know others and he'd need to be mindful of the different and much more effective way they went about their business.

Finally and it seemed simple to him, he'd threatened to steal another £10 million picture. Well clearly they'd all be looking at the pictures recently valued at ten mill and put extra security around them. He wasn't stupid but maybe they were. He wasn't going to steal a ten million picture, but one that was worth around seven or eight million, depending on which valuation you took into account.

He had left the hotel wearing his own clear lensed anti-facial recognition glasses. He knew he'd have no difficulty getting in there if he just walked up to the front door and said who he was because he'd been in a few months ago when he was researching the Adamsons' security business. However, that meant his photo would be somewhere on their database, or at least it should be if their system was even half as good as his SIS products. That's why he needed the anti-facial recognition glasses.

One of the gallery assistants would be looking at

him as he approached the front door. It was their job to use their experience to determine whether they let him in or not. This was a critical time as he was taking a gamble as to whether or not the assistant would have access to the camera facing the front door.

He knew the cameras were only viewed by the back-room security team as when he last tried to poach their alarm business he had checked and confirmed the gallery assistants at the front of the building didn't have any access to the CCTV screens. This meant they were effectively blind and reliant on the back-room staff, a key point Jake highlighted in his report to Theakston and the rest of the Adamsons' Board, only to still be rejected because of some apparent unwarranted loyalty to their current supplier.

Jake waited patiently for a moment at the gallery's front door, before he heard a click. It was very quiet, because potential buyers didn't necessarily want to feel like they were in a prison, but then again, it was also to contribute to the whole experience of going into a top-end gallery.

As he walked in he saw a number of other people mingling. He guessed they must have been delegates at the conference because they were wearing the same type of glasses he was. He felt the inside of his chino's pocket and clasped the black box in his hand. He'd estimated he had about two minutes. After that it was highly likely one of the backroom security staff would notice the faces of a fair number of the visitors to the gallery were all showing as white blobs on the CCTV screen.

*****

The phone by Anna rang.

"Anna, it's Ruha. This may be nothing, but we've got a whole bunch of people, maybe ten, fifteen of them who have all walked in wearing the same type of glasses."

"Sam!" called Anna. "Okay we're on speaker phone. Where are you now Ruha?"

"We've just stepped inside the gallery and they've let us in. Anna, I was doing some work around privacy glasses, the sort you wear to avoid facial recognition cameras and it's a bit of a long shot but I'm thinking these might be the same thing."

"Could it be a coincidence Ruha?" said Sam.

"I don't know Sam, copper's gut feel, or rather ex-copper's gut feel that something's not right."

Holly and Tony looked at Sam.

"Ruha was in the Met before she decided to move to India."

"Ruha, it's Tony Theakston from Adamsons. How many of them are there wearing these things?"

"Hi Mr Theakston. Wait one please."

Eschaan had been listening in.

"I think we've got about fifteen or so. They're in small groups of between two and four."

"Did you get that Mr Theakston?"

"Ruha, it's Tony and yes we did."

She knew he'd been a Detective Super when he'd retired and even though she'd also left the service, old habits died hard when it came to talking to rank.

"You're the ones on the ground Ruha, what's your plan?" asked Sam.

"We're going to…."

She went quiet.

"Hang on. The security guys keep flicking their radios. This could be it. Now the alarm's gone off. Something's definitely happening."

"Ruha, can you hear me?"

"Yes, yes. So I think whatever has hit the electronics is only affecting the shortwave radio and maybe the internet."

"Okay, we think last time the alarm was a distraction and took the security guys away from the main picture, so you guys need to get to the picture we sent you. You know where it is?"

"Yes, yes, it's in the room in the back right area. We're heading there now."

They didn't notice a young man in a t-shirt and chinos wearing a set of clear lensed glasses walk calmly past them in the opposite direction.

12

As soon as Jake had flicked the switch on his blocking device the alarm at the gallery had gone off. He'd programmed the fault to show as a fire in one of the back rooms. Diversion One.

He waited thirty seconds and watched a number of men and women, some in a uniform and some not, but all were clearly Adamsons' security staff, start to move towards the back of the gallery. He was standing just to the side of the room where the £10 million picture was and quickly glanced in. There was one guard still there.

Time for Diversion Two. Another flick of the switch and judging by the confused looks on the faces of the security team as they tried their radios, he'd successfully jammed their radio comms and with it the CCTV cameras.

He was looking around for anyone who didn't look like security, but who might be police or insurance investigators. He saw a number of people including an Indian man and woman. They looked like they might be together, just by the way she was talking to him. Probably worried about the alarm.

He walked quickly to another room that was just across the corridor from where the alarm was indicating there was a fire. He knew the fire service should be there soon and they would create their own added confusion. Even if the gallery rang through to say there wasn't a fire, the fire service would still attend to carry out their own checks, especially in a building of this size.

As Jake walked in to the room he smiled as he saw it was empty. *"Like taking candy from a baby,"* he sang softly to himself, before going straight to the painting on the wall behind the door. Even if someone walked past and looked in they wouldn't see him, not unless they actually poked their head behind the door.

He looked at the painting. It wasn't that he particularly liked it, it was one of the lesser known works by Claude Monet, but it was still worth around eight million, so would do just fine to make his point to Adamsons.

'I can take anything I want, at any time I choose because of your pathetic alarm system,' he thought.

*****

"Ruha, what's happening?"

"It's chaos here Anna. We've found the Head of Security, a guy called TC Hao, but he's focused on the alarm that's saying it's a fire. I think he knows it's a false alarm set off by the thief, but he's adamant he wants everyone out of the building to RV at the fire points. He says if he doesn't he'll get slaughtered by the local Fire Chief."

"Tony, did you get all that? I think your guy is more worried by the fire chief than losing a £10 million painting."

"I'm on it Anna, I'm calling him direct."

"Ruha? Tony Theakston is ringing the guy direct, so you should get some cooperation shortly," said Anna calmly.

Ruha saw the Head of Security take the phone call from his boss back in London. He looked sheepishly across at Ruha and nodded.

"I'm sorry, but the fire regs are so prescriptive over here."

"Don't worry about it TC, but what we need to make sure is that no one gets out of here without us knowing exactly who they are because someone in here is the thief!"

Eschaan was impressed by Ruha's handling of the situation. He thought she was good when he and Terri hired her, but he was seeing first hand that she was some way better than good.

"I think he's played us Ruha," said Eschaan. "We've been focusing on the ten mill picture Adamsons told us about when I think he's banked on us just concentrating on that and he's gone for another picture. We need to check the other rooms."

Anna was still on the phone to Ruha and had heard what Eschaan had just said. She turned to Sam and the others in the room.

"Eschaan thinks the thief might have played us. He thinks he's gone after another picture."

Sam thought for a moment. *'That would be a bloody effective tactic.'*

"We need to stick with the original plan, even if the thief has side stepped us. The objective remains the same – we need to get more data on how he does this, but without him realising what we're doing, so tell Eschaan to go carefully."

"Okay Sam," said Anna. "Eschaan, from Sam, go carefully when checking the other artwork. The thief will be watching for anyone outside of the Adamsons team, so don't let him know you're there."

*****

Jake Sutton was too busy taking the Monet down from the wall and so hadn't seen the discussion Ruha was having with TC Hao.

He knew that pretty much every gallery took the same approach in how they affixed their framed artworks to the wall with plates attached to the frame and secured to the wall by either one, two or three screws depending on the size of the frame. On the back of the frame there should be a security chain linking it to an alarm sensor on the wall.

Ordinarily gallery specialist cleaning teams would work in pairs to carry out minor cleaning around the frames, removing the wall screws and then with one holding the frame, the other would clean the area at the back of the frame, all without having to compromise security by not having to disconnect the picture from the main security system.

Jake could see the Monet had four plates held to the wall by just single screws. Holding the frame just away from the wall he took a pair of wire cutters from his pocket and snapped the security chain. With the alarm blocked he knew the sensor wouldn't activate but when he'd planned his attack on Adamsons last year he knew that taking a picture out of a gallery in broad daylight was unlikely to succeed, especially if it was still in the frame.

He'd spent a lot of time in different Adamsons galleries across their portfolio when he'd been preparing his bid for their contract. They were very brand conscious and every gallery looked the same. Minimalist decoration with plain walls, soft lighting and flat seating positioned in the centre of the room and this had all been part of his considerations when making his mind up as to how he'd get the pictures out of the galleries.

'Hide it in almost plain sight.'

The flat couch-like bench seats were oblong in shape, about five by four metres, designed to allow people to sit facing out around the room, so it could take about twelve comfortably positioned around the seat.

The seat base, supported by four sturdy metal legs, was fifteen centimetres in depth. He'd measured it, and there was a gap of twenty eight centimetres between the base and the floor, again he'd measured it.

There was a reason he was choosing the pictures he was stealing and it had less to do with the actual value and more to do with the size of the frame, which had to fit under one of these bench seats.

Once he had the Monet off the wall, he checked the doorway to the room. He'd heard the fire engine sirens and could now see some fire officers down the corridor. He'd need to work quickly now and secure the frame to the underneath of the bench seat.

He flipped the seat up on its side and it took nothing more a few well positioned strips of gaffer-tape he'd had wrapped around his belt, to hold the frame firmly in place in the centre of the seat. He had just flipped the seat back over and repositioned it in the middle of the room when one of the fire officers came in.

"You shouldn't be in here!"

"I'm sorry. I got lost in all the rush. Which way to the fire RV point my friend?" said Sutton in the best mid-Atlantic drawl he could come up with.

The fire officer didn't see this guy as his friend.

'Why the hell don't people get out of a building when they hear a bloody fire alarm!'

"Straight down the corridor and turn left and please be quick. We don't know if this is a false alarm or not, so you need to treat it as real until you're told otherwise."

"Of course. I'm going now," said Jake knowing only too well that it was a false alarm.

"Please go now sir!" yelled the fire officer.

"I'm gone," said Jake with a grin, who once out in the

fresh air made no attempt to stop at the Fire RV point. He put a pair of wireless earphones on and started heading slowly back towards the Shangri-La hotel.

After a hundred metres or so he took the jamming device from his pocket and flicked the off switch. He smiled again as he heard the fire alarm at the gallery go silent, before moments later the sensor then activated on the wall where he'd taken the Monet and the alarm bell started to sound again.

13

"I hope this plan of yours has worked Sam," said Hacker. "I can't help thinking we've just stood by and watched a £10 million painting go out of the door."

Sam was working hard to control his own nerves, let alone those of the rest of the group. It had been a bold plan, but it still made sense to him that unless they got more information on the thief, they wouldn't be able to change the situation they were in where the thief could pick off Adamsons anytime he, or she wanted, but then he got an unlikely ally in the form of Christine Harrison.

"It's a tough one Charles, but I think we've got to stick it out. Things aren't going to change until Sam's team finds out more about this thief and although I can't say I'm enjoying the prospect of explaining the loss of another painting to the Board, I do think we need to hold our nerve."

They both looked at Sam.

"You're right of course Chris. This is a question of holding our nerve. Let's see what we've got at the scene back in Singapore. Mum, can you get hold of Eschaan or Ruha again?"

Anna was already dialling Eschaan's mobile.

"You're on speakerphone Eschaan."

"Hello Anna, I was just about to ring you. We've got a missing picture, but it's not the one you thought it would be. TC's identified it as a Monet. It was in another room. Value is about £8 million. The security chain has been cut and by the way, the alarm is back up and working. Looks like the thief has turned the jammer off."

"I can hear it now Eschaan," said Anna.

Sam saw Hacker holding a hand over his face. He seemed to be the one who was more anxious about the picture, whereas Chris was looking calm, albeit serious. Sam looked across to Holly, who nodded slowly back at him. He knew that she thought this was worth the gamble, because to do nothing wasn't an option.

"Eschaan, it's Sam. I appreciate it's no doubt pretty chaotic there, but what's your sense that the thief is still in the building?"

Eschaan looked around the gallery. Fire officers were moving from room to room ushering everyone who was still there to quickly leave. He'd had to already tell three of them that neither he nor Ruha were going anywhere.

"I'd say they're long gone Sam, otherwise why would they reactivate the alarm? The fire alarm hasn't helped either, as it's definitely thrown a spanner in the works with regards to us keeping any sort of lid on the crime scene with the fire crew trooping through here, but at least there wasn't an automatic sprinkler system."

Sam knew exactly what Eschaan was talking about. He'd seen it happen enough times when he'd turned up as the SIO, the senior investigating officer, to find a scene completely doused in water with the resulting impact on the chances of recovering anything of evidential value. But he knew the fire officers had a job to do and it was all about priorities and theirs of course, was to negate any possibility of a fire in a city centre building surrounded by some of the most expensive real estate in Singapore.

"Not your problem Eschaan. But use Ruha's skillset to see what she can figure out."

"She's already on it Sam," said Eschaan.

"What size is the Monet, Eschaan?" called out Holly.

Eschaan was in the room where the Monet had been and could see the slight difference in colour where the frame had been against the wall.

"It looks like it's maybe three and a half, possibly four feet by three. Now we didn't see anyone going out of the building carrying anything of that size. Just a minute, I'm going to clear this room."

"Are you thinking what I'm thinking Eschaan?" asked Ruha as she helped to move all but TC, the Head of Security out of the room.

"Maybe. TC, can you get one of your guys outside the door and make sure they stop anyone coming in whilst we check the room out?"

TC nodded and spoke quickly in Mandarin Chinese to one of his team who immediately acknowledged him and took up his position, closing the door as he did so.

"Ruha, there's a hell of an elephant staring us in the face in here," said Eschaan turning his head to the bench seat that was in the middle of the room.

"It couldn't be that simple could it?" said TC starting to walk towards the seat.

"Whoa, hold on just a moment," said Ruha. She spoke so suddenly and firmly that it made TC jump. "It's not likely, but let's check it for prints."

She took the backpack off her shoulder and opened it up, taking out a small box.

"Sam, you still there?" said Eschaan into the phone.

"Yep, still here and we're picking up where you're

going with this."

Ruha was now down on the floor looking underneath the seat. She didn't want to get ahead of herself by simply turning it upside down. If this guy, the thief, was as clever as they seemed to be, she needed to be mindful of possible booby traps, even explosives.

She flashed a mini torch underneath.

"Bingo," she whispered.

"You got something Ruha?" said Sam.

"Yes, yes." Again the police-speak came naturally to her. "We have the painting. Confirm. The painting and the frame."

"Thank God," said Charles Hacker and even Christine Harrison breathed a sigh of relief.

"What are you thinking Ruha?" said Eschaan.

"This looks too simple."

Sam smiled. She was good. It was too simple. What was this guy playing at? Did he think we'd miss this?

"He's playing with us, isn't he?" said Sam.

"Looks that way Boss," said Ruha. More police-speak as that's what she would have called anyone who was an Inspector or above in the Met, whether they were male or female, such was the hierarchical culture within much of the force.

"I can't see anything like a sensor. If it's here then he might have it pinned under the seat legs, or somewhere underneath the seat. But I'm guessing he or she is some sort of electronics wiz if they can jam alarm systems at will, so presumably they could have put anything in here if they'd wanted to and we might not spot it."

A few hundred metres away, Jake Sutton was listening to what was going on. He'd not only left a sensor to tell him if the seat was moved, but also a listening device.

"You're better than I thought you'd be lady," he said quietly to himself.

Back at the Gold Suite it was Tony Theakston who had been furiously scribbling down *'He might be listening to all of this!'* onto a piece of paper which he hurriedly passed across the table to Sam.

Sam read it and showed his mother and mouthed the word 'text.'

A moment later Eschaan's phone pinged with a text. He read it and realising the noise could have been heard by the thief he calmly said, "My reminder to feed the cats."

Ruha turned and looked at him. She hadn't known Eschaan very long but one thing she did know was that he didn't like cats. She saw the look on his face and then read the message on the mobile screen.

"You and your cats! What are you like?" said Ruha with a laugh.

Eschaan then slowly eased TC away from the seat to the corner of the room and putting his finger up to his lips he then showed him the message too.

TC's eyes flashed and he started looking around the room, before Eschaan gently took hold of his arm and walked him to the door and out of the room.

"We'll just go and get some coffee Ruha. Back in a moment."

Eschaan closed the door after them and took TC away to one side out of earshot from the rest of his team.

"You think the thief could be listening to us?" said TC.

"We need to be aware that they might be. Anna, Sam, are you getting all of this?" Eschaan still had his mobile on speaker phone.

"Yes, loud and clear. If the thief is listening then they know we've found the painting, but like you guys say, this is all too easy, so we're checking with the other sites to double check nothing has gone from there."

"What do you think he's playing at Sam?" asked Eschaan.

It was Holly who spoke first.

"I think you summed it up well Eschaan. He's playing with us. He's seeing it as a game. That suggests it was never his intention to steal from Adamsons for profit. I think this changes a lot Sam."

Sam was already thinking past the possibility Holly had come up with. Motive was always a key issue in any investigation. The 'why' somebody would do some sort of act was always a significant factor in determining the 'who.'

"Eschaan, let's go through this as though we hadn't thought there might be any listening device in there. Get back inside to Ruha and let her know and then go through the whole room with a fine tooth-comb and then again with the rest of the gallery. You'll need some specialist kit to check for devices, but hey you're in Singapore, so what better place to source that type of stuff. Chris, Tony, we should be able to get the whole gallery done overnight, so you can open up as usual tomorrow morning and no one will be the wiser."

"That'll work Sam, and we can say the Monet has been removed for cleaning," said Tony.

"Yes, I like that plan," said Chris Harrison.

"Okay, I'll sign off for now guys and after I've briefed Ruha, I'll go and source some kit with TC and then we'll make a start going through the room."

*****

Jake was pleased with the reception he was getting through his earphones. He'd heard the man they'd called Eschaan. He'd been the one with the phone and had gone out saying he was going for coffee. Since then he'd heard the woman's voice as she'd whistled softly to herself. He'd have liked to have put a camera in there, but the listening bug was much easier to fit in a hurry and besides he didn't need to worry about angles of vision and so on.

'So you think you've done very well finding your precious picture don't you? Now let's see if you take your eye off the ball whilst you focus on the Monet?'

14

Sam sat down in one of the chairs in the Gold Suite. Things had actually turned out a lot better than he could have hoped for. They'd recovered the painting and discovered a lot more about the thief's MO and perhaps even more importantly, their motive.

"So I think the critical thing here is the motive you came up with Holly."

"Yes," said Holly slowly. She'd been running through scenarios in her head since she'd first suggested the thief wasn't necessarily stealing for personal gain. "I'd been looking at this from the perspective of the money and have been a bit blocked to the possibility of them having some other reason."

"Easily done Holly, so don't beat yourself up. After all the thief did keep the £15 million Adamsons had to pay last year, so it's not as though he or she is some sort of Robin Hood, or at least not as far as we know," said Charles Hacker.

"No, but I'm annoyed I didn't at least consider the option Charles."

"Okay, but let's take this as a win for us," said Christine Harrison. "We're much further down the road than we were even just a few hours ago. It was a bold strategy Sam, so well done. It's paid off, but what now?"

"Good question Chris. We're likely to be getting an email sometime soon, so we need to be ready for what our response will be. But you're right, it is a win, but it won't be worth a lot if the thief just targets another of your galleries. Thinking of which, how would you guys go about finding out if there were any other galleries being targeted by the thief. It would be good to confirm if it is just Adamsons that's being targeted."

"You're right Sam and we did ask a few contacts some carefully worded questions when it happened the first time, but it's tricky. This industry is a bit 'dog eat dog,' so we couldn't give the game away that we'd lost a painting otherwise they'd be like hyenas closing in on an injured animal," said Holly.

"I don't think we've got any option but to ask the question again, but at least this time we can talk with some more authority about a thief we've been able to prevent from stealing a painting, so perhaps best that we don't mention the previous incident," said Hacker.

"I think that's sound thinking Charles," said Sam. "There's no need to tell the whole story, so stick with the positives and put it out there like an industry warning and see what comes back."

"Sam, just to let you know, I've stood the teams down in London and Mallorca as there's been no movement at either location," said Anna.

"Good, when you get a moment, can you get hold of Greg? I'd like to get his perspective on this too. Can I suggest a short break whilst we all brief our respective people? Holly, can you start to draw up a possible profile of the thief on what we know. I appreciate there will be some key blanks in there, but it might help us focus on the areas that we need to explore."

Holly nodded and immediately started to work on her laptop.

"Sam, I can't thank you enough," said Tony Theakston. "We were getting nowhere on this and now we've at least got something we can be working on."

"Still a way to go yet Tony, but yes, it's definitely progress."

"Mum, what else do we need to do that we haven't yet covered?"

She was a master planner, something he hadn't known when he was growing up as she was just, well, just his 'Mum.' Since finding out she was ex-MI6, he'd realised that it wasn't by chance that the Martínez household used to run like clockwork.

"I'll keep an eye on how Eschaan and Ruha are getting on. I can't see us getting anywhere fast with the sensors and listening device that might be under the seat. The thief has shown they aren't stupid, so there's not likely to be any leads from those. I'm wondering if we hadn't spotted the picture whether the thief would have come back into the building at some later stage and if so, how or rather where might they have tried to get in?"

"Do you think one of us needs to get out there?" asked Sam.

"I don't think so Sam. Eschaan and Ruha definitely seem to know what they're doing, so let's leave it to them. I do think we could get Anju to see if she can do any more with the technical side of things?"

Sam nodded. Anju was the second of Terri's three new recruits in India and she'd already shown her worth with the last job they had taken on, when she'd created a smokescreen website for a fake banking corporation.

"Agreed. I think we've only just scratched the surface with her skillset so far."

"I'll get Eschaan to brief her," said Anna.

*****

"So Anju, it looks like the thief is very good at hiding their trail, both with their emails, but also with the £15 million Adamsons had to pay out last year. It went into some sort of black hole and they lost all trace of where the money went."

"Okay Eschaan. I can't promise anything, but I'll make a start straight away. The difficult thing is that it's quite easy for people to hide their identities using VPN's, sorry for the techy terms. They're virtual private networks, then there's proxy servers and Tor custom browsers that can make it very challenging to find out who they actually are. Basically they route everything through multiple countries – it's a bit like them taking on a new disguise, you know a false beard, a change of clothes and hairstyle every time they re-route their connection."

"Woah!" said Eschaan, "you lost me on proxy servers Anju. So how do we catch these people?"

"It's usually when they make a mistake, or sometimes we can drop some malware into their system which can give us an in."

"Again, you've lost me, but it's good to know that you know what you're doing," he said with a grin.

"I do, so don't worry. It may take a while, but I'll check it all out and we'll see just how clever he or she is at covering their back," said Anju.

*****

"Greg, it's Anna. Yes, we've had some movement in Singapore. A picture was taken and secreted under a bench seat still within the gallery. Ruha found it, so we're currently sourcing kit to be able to sweep the seat and then the whole gallery for sensors. Plus we think the thief maybe listening in to what we're saying."

"That's interesting, but first off that's some great work by Ruha. What's the next move?"

"Sam wants to talk that through with you," said

Anna.

"Okay, no problem. We'll get back to the car and tell him I'll call him on the way back to the hospital."

"Have you had any more updates on Terri?" asked Anna.

"Just a few texts from Josie. She's doing well and the doctors are happy and they'll be starting some light physio later this afternoon."

"Wow, they don't hang about do they?" said Anna.

"You're right and when they told Terri that's what they wanted to do she was really up for it."

"That's so good to hear. She's tough Greg, that's for sure."

"Yes, I suppose we may just need to keep an eye on her to make sure she doesn't overdo it. But that said, I don't fancy my chances telling her not to do something when she's set her mind on it."

"I think this is where Simon will need to play his part as she'll probably listen to him more than her mum and dad."

"Yes, good point Anna. Okay, we'll be about five minutes and then I'll call Sam."

15

The rooms in the Valley Wing of the Shangri-La were big and roomy and were a long way from the ones he stayed in when he was on the British Olympics training programme. But Jake Sutton was completely oblivious to the beautiful hotel room he was currently in.

Had he underestimated the Adamsons security team, or had they brought someone else in? He worked things through in his head again and decided that whichever it was, he'd made a mistake, something he didn't like doing.

"Sod it!"

He'd been careless in his approach, but now he'd need to recover the situation to try not to give them, be it Adamsons or whoever they had engaged, any indication that he was fallible.

He opened his laptop and started composing another email. The proxy server he was using would route it though over twenty five servers, which he knew was almost as many as the Chinese hackers were reputed to have used in the Equifax breach in 2017 when the personal information of 145 million people was hacked, so whoever might be looking for him shouldn't stand a cat in hell's chance of finding him.

One thing was for sure though. Dr Holly Regus had been right when she'd recognised that Jake Sutton wasn't doing this for the money. He was doing it because he could and because he got a kick out of it.

The £15 million he'd extracted from Adamsons the previous year had been used on a number of climate change projects that Jake had an interest in. He'd had to be careful because Jeannie had casually asked one day where he was getting the money from to invest in the projects. Jeannie was never casual when it came to money, so he knew she must be getting a bit concerned that he may be over stretching himself. He managed to fob her off saying it had come from a small group of generous benefactors who wished to remain anonymous, but he wasn't entirely sure if she had accepted his explanation.

He needed to make sure he took more care and made no more mistakes. He looked down at the email he'd prepared and read it through again, then pushed SEND.

*****

"Looks like it went pretty well this morning Sam," said Greg.

"Yes, we've got more than we had before Greg, which was the primary objective. But now it's a question of what next, so I just wanted your thoughts. Just so you know, you're on speaker phone, but it's just me and Mum in the room at the moment."

"Okay understood. Now, the first thing that occurs to me is that we're probably still in a reactive mode at the moment. Anna's told me about a possible listening device and that you'll be going through the Singapore gallery with a fine tooth-comb, but essentially we're waiting for the thief to make their next move aren't we?"

"Yes, but I can't help thinking there's another tack we could take on this, to try to get ahead of what may be coming next," said Sam.

"I know where Sam's going with this Greg," said Anna, "but like him, I'm a bit stuck on what that might be."

"Well I like where you're going with Dr Regus working on the thief's profile. Before we had nothing to go on, or rather we assumed this was driven for financial gain, when it looks as though they may have another motive. That could be the move we're looking for. See what the good doctor comes up with and start the data research on the names who might fit such a profile, whether or not they've ever come to the attention of any sort of law enforcement agency before now."

Anna could see Sam smiling. She could see he liked the idea.

"Like it Greg. Give Terri a big hug from me."

With that Sam was out of the room and on his way to find Holly.

*****

"Everything okay Greg?" said Simon.

"Yes, seems to be. Sam was just checking in. Interesting though, it looks like the thief may not be doing this for the money. Not sure if that may make it easier, or harder to track them down."

"Follow the money is always the plan isn't Greg? So maybe it might be harder. But what about the £15 million from last year? If he isn't doing it for money, what's he done with that? Can't see the thief just leaving it sitting around can you?"

"Hmm. It's worth a look at any sort of community ventures that have had a sudden influx of backing."

He speed-dialled Anna's mobile.

"Simon's just suggested we take a look for any community events last year where there was perhaps an anonymous donor or donors. Bit needle in a haystack, but fifteen mill is still a fairly significant bit of dosh."

"He's not just a pretty face is he?" said Anna.

"No, I'm not Anna," laughed Simon, leaving Anna realising Greg had his mobile on speakerphone.

*****

Simon and Greg walked back into Terri's hospital bedroom expecting to see her, but just saw her empty bed. As they walked back into the corridor they saw her coming around the corner holding onto a zimmer frame with a nurse and a physio either side of her, just in case she lost her balance.

"Hello Dad!" yelled Terri.

"Hello my girl. Good to see you up and about."

"It feels so good and before you say anything, I'm not going to overdo it. Small steps, small gains, before I look to start stretching things."

She then looked at Simon.

"Well? Don't just stand there! Aren't you supposed to kiss me or something?"

Simon looked suitably embarrassed by Terri's public announcement.

"Would you like us to all turn away for a moment?" said Josie.

Simon was about to answer when he realised she was joking. He took a deep breath and took hold of Terri and kissed her tenderly on the lips.

"I feel like Cinderella!"

"I think you might mean Sleeping Beauty," said Lily who was just behind the physio. "So how does it feel to be in love you big Welsh dragon?"

Josie saw Simon's face getting flushed and decided he'd had enough teasing for the moment.

"Come on Terri, let's get you back into your room and off your feet shall we?"

The physio nodded. This was going to be hard work,

keeping this one down. She really was a live wire.

"Si senora, Terri, you've done mucho bueno today. Rest now and we'll be back tomorrow, okay?"

"Gracias Maria. See you tomorrow." She waved to the physio and the nurse as they left and then turned and looked at her father.

"So Dad, are we still in business?"

He wasn't sure if she was asking a serious question, or whether it was his turn to be teased before he saw her smile.

"Oh good one daughter. Yes, whilst you've been lying around having a sleep, we've just about managed to keep 3R afloat."

"Don't you mean 3R International?" she teased him back.

"Nothing wrong with your memory then?" her father said.

She grinned at him.

"Now Mum's told me you've just been to Sóller. Where's Sam and what's this latest job all about?"

He could tell she was tired. Her eyes were like saucers, just like they used to be when she was four or five and was trying desperately to stay awake to see her Dad who had travelled half way across the world to see her.

"I'll go and get some coffees," said Lily.

Greg started to tell Terri about Adamsons and the ransom demand from the thief, but by the time Lily came back with the coffees Terri had fallen asleep.

"Just like when you were four," he said quietly and he felt Josie squeeze his hand.

As they filed out of the hospital room Greg felt his mobile buzz and as he saw the text he said, "We've had another contact."

16

Tony Theakston had read and re-read the new text a number of times now and had already forwarded the message to Christine Harrison, Holly and Sam.

'Well done for finding the Monet, although I would have been worried if you'd have missed it given that it was the only likely hiding place for you to search. Now the thing is…. What to do next to test your ability to prevent me taking another one, but this time I'll be removing it from the building?'

"What do you think Sam? Have they really just been playing with us all along?"

"You know what Tony, I think they intended to come back and get the painting, maybe later tonight. So whilst I think you're partly right that he or she's playing with us, I reckon we've also just pissed them off just a little bit. I've a hunch that they didn't expect us to find the painting, possibly because they didn't think Adamsons or you would have taken on some additional help."

Holly came into the conversation.

"I've finished my first draft of a profile of our thief and that's the first thing. I think it's a man and that's based on his propensity for arrogance." She turned and looked at the men in the room. "No offence guys, but you tend to just be better at that arrogant bullshit than us girls."

"None taken Holly," said Sam with a laugh, although he didn't see Charles Hacker laughing much who'd just come into the Gold Suite.

"What about the second sentence?" said Holly. "You could read it that he's teasing us, but maybe he's not actually too sure himself what to do because he now knows we're ready and on high alert for him."

"I can go with that idea to an extent Holly," said Anna, "but I think he can run with a bit of a waiting game, which we can't necessarily afford to do. Teams on maximum alert can only be sustained for a relatively short period of time, otherwise experience shows a new concentration norm is formalised, with a diluted level of alertness."

"Before we go on, tell us more about your profile?" said Sam.

"Okay, we can pitch his age group as somewhere from late twenties to late thirties. That's based on likely need for agility to cope with the potential access points of the first gallery he hit, even though we don't actually know how he got in. So as a follow on from that, his build is likely to be athletic."

Both Hacker and Harrison were getting ever more engrossed in the detail of Holly's profile.

"Is this all just guesswork Holly? Because I'm thinking in any moment you're going to show us a picture of the thief," said Christine Harrison.

"I wish I could Chris. I'd rather say they're assumptions balanced with analysis of studies of criminality, but yes," she smiled, "there's still an element of calculated guesswork in there if that's what we want to call it."

"But they're often very near to the mark in my

experience," said Sam.

"Where does the motive, or rather lack of motive take us Holly?" asked Anna.

"I hesitate to say this, but I think in some ways it helps."

She waited for the reaction, which wasn't slow in coming from her boss, Charles Hacker.

"How can it possibly help Holly? Surely you're just firing darts in the dark?"

"It felt like that at first Charles, but then I realised that we weren't looking for what I'd best describe as the stereotypical criminal here, by which I mean one driven by money. No, we're looking at the other motivations we see in criminals, like those of passion and vengeance."

"If you put it like that Holly, then looking at those three motives, then I'd be happy to put some money on vengeance," said Hacker.

Sam looked around the room. Whilst they still didn't have a name for the thief, Holly's work had brought the Gold Suite to life and there was now a buzz going around, suggesting they'd taken something of a leap forward towards identifying a list of possible suspects.

"I think we should look at what vengeance might mean to the thief and do some board-blasting around that?" said Holly.

Anna was already pulling off a couple of sheets of flipchart paper and grabbing some marker pens.

They then spent the next ten minutes calling out possible reasons for vengeance. After a couple of them tried to dive in to start exploring some of ideas in more detail, Anna pulled everyone into line.

"Just the ideas everyone. Once we've got those down, then we'll dig deeper into them."

Sam smiled at his mother as she managed the group

and kept them focused.

When the calling out dried up, Holly took the lead again.

"Good. Now let's see which ones we put together into mini-groups."

It didn't take long to pitch the ideas into groupings.

"This is interesting," said Holly. "It looks like we've highlighted three distinct sets of people who could bear a grudge against Adamsons. We've got disgruntled customers, disgruntled employees and disgruntled competitors or suppliers."

"Guys, we've moved this issue a bloody long way since we all walked in here at nine o'clock this morning," said Sam. "Now tell me your gut feeling as to whether you think we're barking up the wrong tree with any of this?"

Holly appreciated that Sam had said 'are we barking up the wrong tree?' as this was very much all based around her profile, but there were immediate comments supporting the thinking they had all contributed to.

"I can think of some names belonging to all of those mini-groups Sam," said Christine Harrison. "Tony? I think you can put a few in there as well can't you?"

Theakston nodded and smiled. He'd told himself on a number of occasions that he wasn't missing 'the job' as retired coppers called their work, but the buzz of the room had brought back many of the feelings he'd felt during much of his career when like Sam, he'd been leading a room of talented and committed people in solving problems and detecting crime.

Sam whispered to his old boss, "I take it you enjoyed that?"

"Was it that obvious Sam?" laughed Theakston. "Don't get me wrong, I love what I do now and the getting home at a reasonable hour of the day and not always being on call for the latest serious crime. But this got my juices going, especially because you and Anna have brought new energy to all of this."

"Okay everyone, the next bit is something neither Anna nor I can help you with. So we're going to order some more refreshments in and put you guys to work."

He waited until he saw them go to pick up their pens to start writing before he injected his final instruction.

"Now it's really important you don't overthink this. You're compiling a list of possible names that could fit one of these three descriptors. These are not, I repeat not, suspects, so do not go eliminating names based on just your gut feel. Leave that for later when we've all had a chance to consider them. Only then will we look to turn information into actionable intelligence."

He saw them all nodding at him.

"Come on Mum, let's go and get some fresh air."

*****

Jake Sutton was sat in a restaurant with Jeannie Marshall but he wasn't enjoying his meal and she knew something wasn't right with him as he was usually such good company when they were out.

"What's up Jake? You don't seem yourself?"

"Oh it's nothing. I was thinking over the presentation again and I think it could have gone better."

He wished he'd thought of a better response because she immediately knew something was wrong. The presentation had gone really well. She knew it and he knew it too.

"I'm not going to nag, so just tell me what's up, or tell me to shut up and I'll stop." She said it in a jokey way, so was taken aback at his response.

"Well shut up then."

He realised his mistake immediately. He'd never ever said anything like that to Jeannie before.

"Oh God, I'm so sorry Jeannie. I didn't mean it."

She was tough, but he'd never spoken to her in that tone before and it had surprised, but also hurt her.

"I'm not your mother Jake, but when I ask if you're alright, I do so out of consideration as a colleague, as a principal investor and I thought as a friend. Do not ever speak to me like that again. Do you understand?"

She rarely cried, but she was definitely holding back the tears and he could see that.

"I can only apologise Jean. I must have more on my mind than I thought and I have hit out at you. I promise I will never speak to you like that again."

He had shocked himself. He couldn't bear to think he'd hurt the woman who had been such a rock for him in supporting his fledging business and helping him turn it into a global success. He cursed himself.

'What a complete dickhead! Taking all this out on Jeannie when it's your own mess you've created with Adamsons.'

She could see he was deep in thought and she dearly hoped this was a one-off, as she certainly wouldn't tolerate another outburst from him. But it was also so unlike him. That meant he was definitely troubled by something, but for some reason he wouldn't talk to her.

His mind was all over the place. He'd clearly upset Jeannie, but he was drawn back to what he was doing with Adamsons.

'Why haven't they replied to my text? What are they playing at?'

Even the sounds Jake was getting from the listening device at the gallery had died off. He could hear some sort of noises and suspected they may be sweeping the area for bugs. If they hadn't already they'd soon discover there was just the one sensor and one listening device. Did that mean the tables had turned?

17

Frankie Walker drove himself home and left Bob to dispose of the remains of Robbo. He felt no particular emotion from having just ended the life of a man he had known since they had started getting into fights and petty thieving as teenagers.

As he parked the BMW on his driveway he saw the curtains twitch in the lounge. It had to be Olivia. She was the oldest and her mum would have told her that daddy was coming home. As far as the kids were concerned daddy worked abroad sometimes and couldn't come home for long periods of time.

He grinned to himself.

'They must think there's no bloody airplanes where I work!'

The front door flew open as he approached the house and his two children, both girls ran towards him and threw themselves at him.

"Hello my beautiful girls! I've missed you so much."

"Have we got presents Daddy?"

"Oh my, how could I ever forget."

He hoped Bob had done the usual and bought something at Harrods and put it in the back of the Beemer.

"Let's go and see shall we?" he looked across at his

wife and held up his hand with his fingers crossed. She just nodded back. She'd told Bob what to get.

"Hello darling," said Maggie. "How did you get on this afternoon?"

She saw he was in different clothes. He'd used the shower and Bob would have got rid of his clothes in the incinerator.

'No evidence, no chance of conviction.'

"All good hun. That lock up set-up is bloody excellent."

Maggie glowered at him.

"Sorry sweetheart, I meant it's excellent. Sorry kids, Daddy used a bad word."

"Not as bad as what Mummy sometimes said whilst you were away Daddy," said Olivia, with the innocence only a child can have when they say such things.

Maggie looked at Frank and both tried unsuccessfully not to laugh, before the children joined in with their giggling too.

"Out of the mouths of babes," grinned Maggie.

*****

Later with their children in bed, they sat down to dinner.

"We need to meet with the Costa guys Frankie. They're playing hardball and we need to get this sorted."

He knew Maggie wasn't referring to the local coffee shop as she had kept him up to speed with how the business was going when she visited him at Belmarsh.

"I know you said you'd been having some difficulties, but I thought you felt you'd straightened things out with them?"

"I thought I had, but the last shipment was a kilo light. Admin he called it."

"Admin! Jesus Maggs, that's a hell of a lot of bloody admin," said Frankie. "What was that then? £25K?"

The kilo they were referring to was high quality cocaine that they'd brokered a deal with a Spanish crime gang based on the Costa Del Sol.

"And the rest Frankie."

"I thought Alejandro was a decent bloke!"

"Me too hun, but I wonder if he's having to manage his own internal politics. I think it might be his father who is the one making things difficult, or it could be a test? Old Man Sanchez is getting on and he's not yet chosen his successor."

"But Alejandro is the oldest son isn't he? Wouldn't he just choose him?"

"You'd have thought so, but Alejandro is apparently more like his Mum. Tough, but a thinker."

"Like you my love," said Frankie.

She smiled at him, "Whereas the second boy, Diego is more like his Dad, very tough, no make that vicious, but not so much of a thinker, so he could be winding his dad up with stories that they aren't getting enough from this collaboration."

"Do we need to have words then?"

"No, this needs dialogue. They're way too strong for us to try strong-arming them into anything. Remember hun, they're on their territory out there, so we're best off not starting anything we might not be able to finish."

He'd loved her since he'd first seen her across the school yard when they'd started secondary school and nothing had changed since then. She was definitely the brains of the partnership, but he loved the fact she had helped develop his way of thinking as to how they ran their outfit.

"Should we meet on neutral ground then?" he asked.

She was so proud of him. He'd have never considered such an idea when he was younger, but he'd taken on board almost everything she had told him about how they could run their 'business' and she could pin it down to when he came out of Feltham at nineteen and he'd dramatically improved his reading and writing.

"I like that idea. Why don't we take the kids away? Half-term starts this weekend, so let's grab a holiday too. You could probably do with one couldn't you?"

"Too right I could, and it would kill two birds. I'm thinking Majorca love," he said, sounding the word with a hard 'J'.

"It's Mallorca hun. Say it with a 'Yuh'," said Maggie.

"Mayorker."

He said it grinning with an almost perfect New Jersey American accent.

"Sounds much posher Maggs. Always said I was boxing well above my weight when I managed to hook you."

"Well I won't argue with you there my big hunk. So what's it to be? Do you fancy a bit of dessert, or a bit of me?"

She knew his answer as he got up from the table and came and picked her up in his arms.

*****

Alejandro Sanchez was pouring a glass of wine as his father came in to the room.

"Alejandro, have you sorted out that English woman about the new arrangement?"

"I have Papa, but she isn't happy and she wants to meet to discuss it. She's suggesting we have lunch in Mallorca in a few days' time."

"Why doesn't she want to come here? Isn't our villa good enough for her."

Alejandro could tell his father was annoyed, so he trod gently as he tried to explain.

"No, of course not Papa. They're going on holiday with their kids and thought it would be nice to meet up whilst they're close by and just resolve the issue of your additional admin charge."

"It's our admin charge my boy. Just make sure you're singing off the same page as me when we're meeting these people. Now what news on the police? They're sniffing around far too near to some of the distribution points. Can't we throw some money at this and shut them up?"

"No, it won't work with the GEO Papa." He knew the Grupo Especial de Operaciones were pretty water tight when it came to corruption. "We're best off not overreacting. Give them a couple of small wins and make them think they're getting the upper hand whilst we transfer most of our efforts to our other routes."

He knew as soon as he'd said it that he shouldn't have used the word 'overreact.'

Alejandro was taller than his father by some six inches or so, but just a look from his father could still be very intimidating.

"Do you think I'm overreacting then Alejandro?" Sanchez said quietly.

As his son went to say something his mother came into the room and he immediately saw the look on his father's face change to the one that he always used to see when he was a little boy. Caring, smiling, happy and loving. His mother never saw the other side of her husband and the way he could be with people who had 'disappointed' him as he would say.

Maybe if he hadn't have been persuaded to go into the family business Alejandro would have, like his mother, continued to only see the best side of his father. However his father had been very persuasive, saying he needed both his sons with him as they were the only people he could truly trust. But it had come at a price for both boys as they soon saw a different side to Papa.

"What were you two talking about? Not work again?" said Adelina Sanchez.

"We won't say another word my dear," said Sanchez giving his wife a warm embrace. "We'll speak later Alejandro, but yes, fix up your meeting with your friends in Mallorca."

"Mallorca? If you're going there, then I'm coming too," said his wife. "It's about time we got back out there as we haven't been to the villa for a while Alberto."

"Why not indeed, we can make it a long weekend, eh Alejandro?"

"I'll get it all sorted Papa."

18

When Sam and Anna Martínez walked back into the Gold Suite with coffee and pastries, they could see a table of names projected on to the wall from Holly's laptop.

"This looks like good work guys," said Sam.

He glanced down the names without any of them standing out at him. There were six names each in the Customer and Competitor/Supplier lists and four names in the Employee list.

"We started throwing the Employee names around as we were waiting for you and think we can dispense with two of them as not having the wherewithal to put something like this together," said Theakston.

"Good, I won't bother asking your criteria as you've obviously worked it through. Now what about the two other lists?"

They spent the next half an hour talking around the twelve names on the remaining lists finally managing to whittle them down to six, all of whom were thought to have not only the resources, but the mental aptitude to potentially be the thief.

"So now we have eight in total," said Sam. "Holly, we're going to need profiles of each of these. Can you pull this together and do you need any help? We've got

Anju over in India who can do this type of thing as well."

"It would be a massive help if Anju could start trawling the social media sites for our eight people and I'll focus on what we know of each of them from an Adamsons and PRI perspective."

"I've just sent her an email and copied you in on it Holly and here's her mobile too."

"It's hard to not run before we can walk with these eight names Sam," said Chris. "There's a couple there who I think could be possibles, but I know this is a better way. We need to use the data to inform our decision-making."

"Yes, although if we don't find anything meaningful in the data then it might just have to come down to that thing we all know as a gut feeling," said Sam.

"I've got Eschaan on line one with an update too Sam, if you're ready?" said Anna.

"Yes, let's see how they've got on."

"Hi everyone," said Eschaan. "I'll let Ruha lead on this as she's managed the search."

"Thanks Eschaan. Well I'll start with the overview. We've recovered a balance sensor and a listening device, both from under the seat. The sensor would have activated if we'd have turned the seat over. We tried to get some sort of reading from it, to see if Anju could track it back Sam but we couldn't get any sort of fix on it, but anyway, we turned the seat over to let the thief know we'd found it as we knew he'd pretty much guessed that from the email he sent you."

"Have you negated the listening device too?" asked Holly.

"Yes, again for the same reasons. He knew we were being careful, so I've taken the battery out."

"Hi Ruha, it's Tony Theakston. Nothing else in the rest of the gallery either found or out of place?"

"Hi Boss, I mean Tony. No, we've swept the rest of the gallery with the kit TC managed to source with Eschaan. It's good quality stuff, so I'm happy I haven't missed anything. As regards anything being out of place, we've had TC go around each room to confirm nothing is untoward and that includes the outside and roof too."

Theakston gave Sam a nod of approval.

"Good job guys and thank you. We really appreciate your professionalism here working alongside TC."

Sam smiled. It was a nice touch from Tony and he knew it would have been appreciated by Ruha and Eschaan.

"Just finally Ruha, how did the thief attach the painting to the underside of the seat?"

"It was gaffer tape Sam. Four strips about eight inches by two. This is strong stuff, but not so strong that you'd expect it to hold for any great length of time."

"So you're thinking if the thief was planning to come back for it, then it wouldn't have been that long a time before they'd have done so?" asked Sam.

"Exactly. We've taken a good look around the building and if I was to take a punt at the most likely POE, sorry I mean point of entry, I'd say it had to be the roof."

"But that's really well covered by the alarm, as are all the stairs and levels down to the ground floor," said Theakston.

"True, although the thief has already shown they can jam the alarm as and when they want," said Anna.

"Good update Ruha. Thanks again. Eschaan, time I think for you guys to move out when you're done," said Sam.

"Will do Sam," said Eschaan. "Just one more thing that may, or may not be connected."

"Yes, go on."

"When we got the CCTV back up and running we played it back to see if we could spot anything prior to it being jammed. There was a fair number of people in the gallery wearing anti-privacy glasses, you know the ones that blur your face on infra-red CCTV cameras, which is basically pretty much every CCTV system except some very specialist military hardware."

Sam looked across at Tony Theakston.

"Yes, ours is infra-red, although we've got facial recognition as well."

"What about the facial recognition software Eschaan?"

"Actually makes it worse Sam. The person's head just becomes a white blob of light then."

"How many people were wearing these glasses?" asked Anna.

"Maybe ten to twelve."

"Are people so security conscious in Singapore then?" asked Sam.

"We did a bit of digging and there's a Security Expo on at the moment. We'll go and take a look when it opens up again tomorrow."

"Okay, good plan, thanks Eschaan," said Sam.

Anna looked at him.

"Just a coincidence do you think?"

"If it isn't then it might give us another clue to our thief."

*****

He wasn't looking forward to the flight home, but they were only an hour in when Jake started working on something he could go back to Adamsons with.

"Okay, if you're into games, we'll play one and then let's see if you can solve this little riddle."

"What's that Jake? Did you say something?"

"Nothing Jeannie, just musing out aloud." He'd been

talking out aloud and hadn't realised!

Things seemed to have settled down a little between him and Jeannie, but he knew he still had some way to go to regain her trust. Although that said, it was a good job that she had no idea what he was up to with Adamsons, as she'd never condone anything like it.

It was about an hour later that he settled on the wording, but only after he'd researched crossword writing and then been through a number of ways to try to solve the riddle.

Using the plane's on-board wi-fi he accessed the proxy server again and then pushed SEND.

*****

"Chris, Sam he's sent one," said Theakston seeing the message ping on the Adamsons' info email account.

'A car that detours to a place may help to show you something small.'

"Anybody any good at cryptic crosswords?" asked Sam.

No one said anything.

"Well I'll take the deafening silence as a no then," said Sam. "Okay then, before we do anything let's get it across to Anju. She might be good at them, or she might even have a programme that does them."

"Any ideas at all anyone?" said Hacker. "I confess these leave me cold. My wife is great at them though, so I could ring her if I wasn't persona non-grata with her."

He saw the confusion on their faces.

"Mucky divorce."

"Right, so do we have anyone else we could call on?" asked Sam.

"Tommy," said Anna.

Sam looked at her.

"I wouldn't normally associate ex-paras with cryptic crosswords Mum."

"No, possibly not, but I remember it was something

he mentioned to me a while ago. He said it helped him de-stress in the waiting time before an engagement."

"Can't do any harm, Give him a call."

Tommy hadn't long left the gallery and was sitting in a coffee shop just off Threadneedle Street with Sharon and her team.

"I'll be with you in about twenty minutes Anna."

"Thanks Tommy see you then."

"Anything we can help you with?" asked Sharon.

"Not unless you or any of the guys are any good at cryptic crosswords?"

Her look was enough as a response.

"Thought not," he grinned. "Catch you soon guys."

*****

Frank Walker was in his car on his way to one of his clubs when his mobile buzzed. Traffic was only moving at a snail's pace, so he chanced a glance at the screen. He saw it said 'Maggs.' He flicked the screen.

'Flights and hotel booked. We're off to Mallorca!'

He smiled. He knew she was looking forward to a break. She'd hidden things well, but he had seen how stressful the last year had been on her. Bringing up the kids and running the business. He smiled again. He wasn't sure which one would have been the harder for her to manage!

She'd been the one who had encouraged him to take up with the Spanish. He'd seen the figures she'd calculated for him and knew it made sense financially, but it was hard enough making collaborations with other gangs working in London, without having to work with guys with whom he literally couldn't talk their language.

Maggs had realised from the start that they needed to do something to make the collaboration work and she'd enrolled in Spanish evening classes. He'd laughed so much, when she told him on one visit about the first class she went to, that the prison officer had told him to quieten down.

The tutor had asked everyone to introduce themselves and to tell the class why they wanted to learn Spanish. Maggs had told him that by the time it got to her, she'd heard so many people say it was to be able to talk a bit of Spanish whilst on holiday, that she couldn't resist saying with a deadpan look, *'So I can better engage with the crime gang we plan to work with on the costas.'*

Then she'd watched the reaction from the tutor and the rest of the group to see if she meant it, before she laughed it off as just a joke.

Anyway, Maggs got the chance to try out what she had learned when they'd first flown out to Alicante to meet the Sanchez family. Old Man Sanchez had been particularly impressed and Alejandro had given Maggs and Frankie a wink indicating they'd definitely scored some good points with his father.

It had all gone well to start with and it was bringing in a lot of money to the business. And it was a lot of money, with a kilo of cocaine at one stage going for over forty grand on the street and they were bringing in over fifty kilos a trip. He wasn't too sure why things had changed, maybe because the prices were coming down, but Maggs had said they were now being squeezed by the Spanish. She suspected it might be the younger son, Diego, who was stirring things up, but hopefully this 'clear the air' meeting would work and even if they had to pay a bit more, Maggs had said they still had a really good margin to make it worth their while.

19

Tommy took one look at the clue Sam showed him the thief had sent and realised it wasn't going to be a simple solution.

"But you think you can have a good crack at it Tommy?"

"Let's put it this way Sam, I'm usually pretty good at this sort of thing, so I'll give it my best shot."

"Good enough for me chum. I'll leave you to it. You can use this breakout room and just shout if you need anything."

Holly Regus was waiting for Sam as he walked back into the Gold Suite.

"Okay here's what we've got on the eight possibles. There's two customers who seem to have taken exception to the fees they were charged, despite having previously agreed to an industry recognised sliding scale. Both are from the Middle East and have significant resources and I mean significant."

"So both are showing good potential then?" said Sam.

"Yes, I've asked Anju to start checking their movements around the time of the incident last year and for this latest one. I hope that was okay?" asked Holly.

"Yes, of course. Who else have you got?"

"I think we need to look deeper into one of the ex-employees, but the other I think we can discount. I've asked Charles to find out more from the Department Head who sacked the guy I'm interested in. That leaves us with four in the Competitor/Supplier list. I'm struggling to get this number down."

"What's the split Holly?" asked Anna.

"Two competitors, two suppliers. I'm siding more with a supplier being the more likely, but like we've said before, this is a tough industry, so could I put it past another competitor making trouble for Adamsons? I just don't know to be honest."

"They sound like a tough bunch then Holly and I thought the spy world was difficult."

"I've allocated each of the four remaining Competitor/Suppliers to a specified lead, as I can't see anything jumping out at me to make me choose two, let alone one to put all our focus on. I've taken Johnsons, one of the galleries, with Chris taking the other one, Mastersons. That leaves us with the two suppliers. One is SIS, a security company who keep pushing Adamsons to give them their business and I've got Tony doing some work on them and finally there's a facilities outfit, Facultex. They lost their contract to Adamsons last year around the time of the first painting being stolen. Sam, can you take a look at them as we're now a bit stretched?"

"Of course, no problem Holly. Okay, I think we've reached a point where we can shut this room down for the time being. We can start it back up again if and when something concrete comes in, but for the time being we're better off keeping things fluid and just touching base when we need to. Agreed?" asked Sam.

There were nods and murmurs of agreement from the group with Christine Harrison adding, "Sam, Holly, thank you. I probably don't need to tell you how concerned Adamsons have been with all of this, as it's just felt like we've been sitting ducks. But now we have something we can work with and before you say anything, I know there's no guarantee that any of the now seven possibilities may be responsible, but at least we're doing something."

"Thanks Chris, glad to help. Now," he paused, "let's get to it!"

*****

"Tommy, we're closing the Gold Suite down, but you can stay here as long as you want. Any early thoughts?"

"Cheers Sam and maybe. I tried the obvious thing, as in it might be an anagram, but there's nothing in the clue to suggest the descriptive word that the anagram might be. I'm pretty sure it's just a cryptic clue, so it's just a question of time of working my head around how this guy's brain works."

"Okay, good luck with it. I'm not anticipating any issues with the follow up stuff we're doing now, but keep your phone on just in case we need the cavalry."

"Will do Sam," and he got back to his crossword clue.

*****

Tony Theakston had met the boss from SIS, Sutton Innovative Securities about a year ago. It had been when he'd made a pitch to Adamsons for their business. Jake Sutton had delivered an impressive presentation and Tony had been happy to vote for a change, particularly because SIS were promising to bring new technology, something their current supplier couldn't match.

Theakston had been a little disappointed that his Board hadn't followed his recommendation, especially because he had been fairly new in post and it felt like a dig at his professionalism.

However, since then he'd come to realise some of the Board members were very traditional in their outlook and having been with the current supplier for many years, they weren't minded to change.

The fact that it was a year ago that SIS were rejected was definitely a factor, but it seemed a massive leap to make this a motive. As a business SIS were clearly flying in the security world and he'd seen Jake Sutton's picture on the front of one of the financial magazines recently, so it seemed unlikely that either Sutton himself, or maybe an ambitious employee with them, would take such drastic action against the gallery.

Theakston had worked his way up through the Met Police in various ranks of detective, intelligence and surveillance before he'd started moving up the promotion ladder. Therefore, whilst he'd been a bit of a desk detective, heading up a major crime team for the last few years, he still knew enough of the basics as to how to take a closer look at Jake Sutton and SIS.

The first thing he did was buy the financial magazine that had Sutton's face all over the front cover and read the interview.

"So he's clever, very clever," he said out aloud. But Sutton was now clearly a very wealthy young man, so it definitely didn't look like he'd be doing it for the money, which fitted the profile Holly had come up.

"Would not getting the contract be enough of a snub to him to take him down a road of criminality?" he mused.

He didn't like asking for favours from his old colleagues, because he knew it put them in a difficult position to say 'no.' But when he did, he always asked in a way that would allow them to answer in such a way so as not to necessarily compromise themselves in terms of data protection. Well, that was what he told himself anyway, because whichever way you looked at it, they were going out on a limb for him.

He put the call in.

"Jimmy, it's Tony Theakston."

"Hello Boss, how are you?"

Again the reference to him being the boss. *'Was it just a Met thing?'* he wondered, but answered himself quickly, with a grin. *'Probably not.'*

"Jimmy, I need a favour."

"How can I help?" asked Jimmy Mellor, a Met Intel Officer.

"Can we play our usual game of yes and no?"

"Yes."

He heard Jimmy laughing on the other end of the phone. It was like an unspoken rule between them of 'don't ask too much' and 'understand if I can't answer the question'.

"Ever heard of a guy called Jake Sutton?"

Theakston could hear the keys on Jimmy's desktop tapping.

"Yes."

"Recent?"

"No and before you ask, it was about ten years or so."

Theakston had read that Sutton was twenty nine, so that probably meant that anything he had in terms of a police record was from when he was a juvenile, a young offender under the age of eighteen.

"Did he have to go and stay away on some sort of extended holiday?"

"Yes, almost twelve months, but he wasn't far away and by the way, he's a nice quiet lad."

"Thanks Jimmy, I won't trouble you anymore."

Jimmy's coded words suggested Sutton wasn't violent. Therefore it must have been something like burglary that got him twelve months in a Young Offenders Institution, and that must have been Feltham as Jimmy had said it was nearby.

"Oh and Boss, one other thing I thought you might want to know. Frankie Walker is out. He got out of Belmarsh yesterday."

"What!"

"He got out on a technicality. Remember his dodgy brief, Rogers? Well he's been digging about for any undisclosed stuff. We've literally been bombarded with loads of Freedom of Information requests and he must have found something that gave him enough leverage to suggest a snout set the whole job up, said they'd been an agent provocateur."

"But he wasn't and he didn't!" shouted Theakston. "Sorry Jimmy, I didn't mean to shout. It's not your fault. Is the snout still in touch?"

They both knew the snout was Paul Robbins, 'Robbo.'

"No, it's gone very quiet. His handler's getting a tad concerned."

"Does Sam know? About Walker I mean"

"I haven't told him Boss, I wasn't sure I should. He's still not over the whole bloody incident, even though I keep telling him I'd have done the same thing when it came to the little girl."

"I can tell him if you like Jimmy? I'm working with him on something at the moment, but I'll hold off for a while. No need to go telling him just for a minute though, as I can't see it helping him."

"Agreed Boss, that's why I hadn't told him."

"Thanks again Jimmy and I'll let you know if and when I tell Sam about Frankie Walker."

20

Jake Sutton already knew which Adamsons gallery he was going to strike at next, but he hadn't yet chosen the painting he was going to take. But by the time his BA flight from Singapore had landed at London Heathrow he'd made up his mind as to his next move.

"Jeannie, if it's okay by you I'm going to take Friday off and have a long weekend away somewhere."

"Good idea."

She had got over her reaction to his outburst and thought she may have overreacted a little, but either way, things seemed to be back on an even keel as they'd chatted like they usually did on the flight coming home.

"Sounds like a great idea. I'm going to do the same and see some old friends down in Dorset. Where are you thinking of going?"

"Oh I don't know, maybe here, or I might grab a flight to somewhere sunny," said Sam, although he'd already booked his flight from London City to Palma de Mallorca for the following day.

*****

Terri was continuing to make good progress, although both the doctor and her physio, her Mum

Josie and Simon had to keep telling her to rest and take things easy from time to time.

"She's actually doing far better than I would have expected, even given the fact that she was a very fit and healthy young woman before she was shot," Doctor Hernandez was telling Josie and Simon, "but you're doing exactly the right thing in making her slow down sometimes."

"When do you think she could leave here Doctor?" asked Josie.

"I know she's desperate to get out and get home Josie, so as long as she commits to coming back a couple of times a week to start with so we can check up on her, then I'm happy to let her go in a day or so."

"Can we tell her?" beamed Josie.

Terri had been sleeping after a good workout in the gym with the physio, but she woke as the door to her room opened.

"Hello guys, sorry I think I nodded off."

"It's good for you to get your rest. You seemed to have had quite a workout my girl," said Josie.

"But it felt good Mom, so good to be back feeling my body react to the endorphins kicking in."

She held her arms out to Simon who hugged and kissed her warmly.

"Won't be long and I'll be giving you a run for your money," she said, before kissing him again. "It was almost worth getting shot to get you to finally tell me what you thought about me."

Simon shook his head.

"Look, I just didn't know if you felt the same. You never said anything."

"I'm going to leave you two love birds alone whilst I go and ring your dad. Tell her what the Doc said Simon."

Terri's eyes widened.

"What did she say? When can I go home?"

The last thing Josie heard as she left the room was Terri yelling "Yes!"

*****

"So she can come home then?" said Greg.

"Yes, in a day or so. I know it's only been a couple of days Greg, but boy has she made progress. I think it's more a case of keeping her just a little bit in check as she builds up muscle strength, but the Doc is really happy the wound is sound."

"That's great to hear. Now, I've just been doing a few calls, but how about lunch? We can pick up Lily on the way and bring her up to speed."

"Yes, it would be good to give Terri and Simon a bit of space. You are okay with them being, you know?"

"An item?" laughed Greg.

"I can't see either of us getting very far if we tried to tell that daughter of ours anything about who she should, or shouldn't be with, do you? Besides, Simon really is a great bloke. A trained killer yes, but as gentle as a lamb and I honestly do think he really loves her."

"So do I, although I'd rather you'd left the trained killer bit out of your description of him."

Greg laughed again.

"But that's only when he needs to be and if anybody else ever got between him and Terri? Then I think they'd go the same way as…"

"Okay, I get the message, can we move on?"

Maybe it was something in his genes that had led their daughter to the life she had chosen in the Australian Army? Josie had never really known about Greg's background, at least not until he'd left MI6, or whoever he had been with. To her, he'd been a handsome young civil servant when she'd met him when she was in London on a gap break before she went back home to Uni.

But Terri had certainly grown up to be a headstrong young woman. That must be my genes, Josie smiled to herself, but the stuff Terri had done in the Army? A lot of that had to have come from Greg.

"Now then, where shall we go for lunch? Lily's favourite? Bar Coral?" asked Josie.

"Sounds great to me. Pick you up in about twenty minutes," said Greg.

*****

"I was going to ask Mum, what are your thoughts on staying here in London, or getting back home?" asked Sam.

"I'd really like to get back and then I can get to see Terri too. Greg says she's doing really well, but I do need to tidy a few things up here, so why don't you get a flight sorted now and I'll join you in a few days?"

"Sounds like a plan. The people Holly wants me to look at are actually US based, so if anywhere, I should be there, but until I get something concrete coming in from the work Anju is doing for me, then I'm not going over to the States just on a wild goose chase. So that effectively means I can work from anywhere, so I might as well get back home for the time being. I'll check with Holly and make sure she's okay with it, but I'm sure it'll be fine."

He called Holly a few minutes later.

"Yes, I've got no issues with that Sam. We've got so much to be going on with and anyway and you're only a couple of hours away at most, so by all means get back to Mallorca," said Holly.

*****

If there had been any space on the early flight out of London City the following day, Sam could well have found himself sitting alongside Frankie Walker and his family in the Club Europe seats up at the front of the plane.

Instead he was booked on the afternoon flight after them, whilst they were on the 7.00 am, the first one out of London City, with a pair of very sleepy children.

Once they were aboard and settled in their seats, they had the second and third Club rows left of the aisle, each sitting with one of the children, Walker looked back at his wife and smiled.

"I'm looking forward to this."

"Bet you are my love. Was it tough in there?"

She hadn't asked him about Belmarsh for the whole time he was in there. It was like an unwritten thing between them that they'd agreed a long time before.

"It was okay Maggs. If people leave me alone and don't bother me, then I won't bother them."

This wasn't entirely true as Frankie had decided early on that he needed to stamp his authority on the inmates around him. It was always likely that someone inside might decide they could take on this so-called tough London gang boss, so he didn't hang around to find out who it might be.

There were a number of inmates in there who he knew and it didn't take long to get around them and ask a few questions as to who they thought might have the balls to go up against him.

He'd acted as soon as he found out about a young Turkish Cypriot lad, Akbas, who apparently had ambitions to be the big 'I am' in his wing at Belmarsh.

There was a good enough supply of weapons in Belmarsh, both home-made and those smuggled in, for Walker to easily get hold of a blade. It had started life as one of the short plastic toothbrushes issued in prison, but it had been ground down and sharpened into a something that now more resembled a cut throat razor than a toothbrush.

Frankie had spoken with a couple of guys, who for the price of some fags and a cash drop when they got out, were more than willing to manufacture a small disturbance that took the attention of the screws, the prison warders. It was over in a flash and Walker had rearranged the facial features of the young Turkish Cypriot.

He didn't need to kill him to get his message home, besides, that would have brought too much attention from the subsequent investigation. It would be put down to a bit of internal squabbling, which the prison officials were more likely to leave well alone if it didn't spiral into any sort of tit for tat retaliation, something which Walker had no intention of allowing to happen.

"I'm glad," said Maggs and it pulled Frankie back from the moment he had the young lad in a headlock as he'd told him a few home-truths about not getting above his station.

"So, we're due to meet the Sanchez lot tomorrow, which means we have today for a bit of sunbathing, chilling and playing with the kids."

"I'll be sunbathing and chilling Frankie, you'll be playing with the kids!"

He grinned and kissed her.

"Yes, of course, my love."

21

Jake Sutton was also on the same morning flight. He'd been surprised by how busy it was. *'Must be half-term judging by the number of families with school age children.'*

He couldn't remember if half-terms started on a Friday, but maybe they were taking their kids out a day early to benefit from the cheaper holiday costs. He knew they'd have to face the potential wrath of the education system, but he doubted any fine would put those parents off who either wanted to, or because of their work had to, go a day or two earlier than the school holidays officially started.

He'd seen one family at the gate and thought he recognised the man from somewhere, even though he was wearing sunglasses, which Jake thought was a bit odd given it was only seven o'clock.

They were now sat in the two rows immediately behind him. He wasn't listening in deliberately, but there was something about the guy's voice.

An hour into the flight he noticed the guy get up from his seat behind and walk the few steps to the front before going into one of the toilet cubicles. Jake wasn't intentionally waiting to see him as he left the toilet, but as is often the case he found his eye-line drawn towards the movement at the front and he saw the man, but this time without sunglasses.

Frankie also locked eyes with the man in the row ahead of his. For an instant he wondered why he was being stared at and was about to tell him where to go, when he heard him speak.

"Frankie?" Jake spoke hesitantly.

Frankie looked at him. The guy was nearly ten years older than when he last saw him, but he was the same build and same short, wavy hair.

"Jake, mate, is that you?"

Maggs heard her husband talking and sat up and looked through the gap between the seats to try to get a better look at the man he was talking to.

Jake had got up by now and moved towards the galley where he could stand up properly.

"You're looking good Jake!"

"You too Frankie." Jake turned and saw Maggs and smiled. "Is this your family?"

"Yes, yes, this is Maggs, my better half and my kids. The kids you can have Jake," he grinned, "but not Maggs. She's a keeper."

Jake looked at him, puzzled for a moment.

"What's mine is yours…" said Jake slowly.

"And what's yours is mine too. Not that you ever took anything off me. But you could have done Jake. Anytime you wanted, you did know that didn't you?" He heard the earnestness in Frankie's voice.

"Yes, I did Frankie, but I was just so bloody grateful you put your arm around me."

It was Maggs's time now to look a little confused.

"Does Maggs know?" Jake looked at Frankie for confirmation that he wasn't letting any past secrets out of the bag.

"God, yes, I've told her all about you. Maggs, this is Jake Sutton. You know, the one who taught me to read and write properly."

He realised he was talking quite loudly and other people where now listening in. He turned and glared at them.

"What? What you lot listening too. Just mind your business unless you want some of this." A clenched fist appeared in his hand and the people who had been wondering what was going on immediately lowered their heads and started to concentrate on something, anything, that was in front of them.

"Frankie, calm please."

"Yes, of course, sorry folks. Early flight, what was I thinking. Miss, you can bring some of your complimentary champagne the people in the posh seats get and dish it out all down the plane? I'll settle up in a minute."

This time he turned with a smile to the rest of the passengers and those who had ventured a look at him smiled back.

"Jake, it's great to see you. Hey, we've done alright haven't we? Up here in the posh seats?"

"Yes, it's pretty cool Frankie. So what do you do now?"

"Oh, this and that."

Jake realised straight away that maybe Frankie Walker hadn't moved away from the life of criminality that had led them both to be in Feltham Young Offenders Institution. Jake had been in for the burglaries he'd committed to help provide money for his folks, whilst he knew Frankie was inside for violent assault.

"Never mind me. What about you?" said Frankie, before he saw Maggs holding up a magazine. "What's that you got there hun? Christ Jake, that's you on the front page of that bloody mag!"

Jake could feel his face starting to flush as the

passengers near the front could all hear Frankie, as he wasn't exactly speaking quietly. Then he saw some people were picking up the financial magazine they'd got as they boarded. He saw the recognition in their faces as they could now see it was the smaller built guy at the front who was on the front cover.

"So Jake, you're SIS!" said Maggs. "I'm impressed, they're pretty big in the security industry. Good for you,"

Jake quickly realised Maggs, although clearly very pretty, was far from some sort of trophy wife. Although he didn't immediately switch on as to why she should know about SIS and their position in the industry.

'Maybe she has just read the magazine article?'

Maggs Walker had read the article, but she was already aware of SIS, just as she was of the other major security companies. She ensured Frankie had a full research report on the strengths and weaknesses of the security system of each of the buildings the Walker crime gang targeted.

These weren't house burglaries, as she had made her husband move away from that level of crime a long time ago. Now their usual targets were warehouses and security lock-ups, each containing hundreds of thousands, if not millions of pounds of high value stock that could be easily disposed of on the black market.

"Yes, I've had a lot of luck and a lot of help, but things have gone very well," said Jake. "So I'm assuming you guys are off on holiday?"

"Yes, I've been away for a while," he gave Jake a wink, "so we've been looking forward to getting away, although we've got some business to take care of over in Mallorca too."

Maggs shot Frankie a glance. She didn't want him broadcasting what they were primarily going over there for.

"Oh Maggs, Jake's sound. It's just a business meeting that's all."

At the back of the plane, Tony Theakston couldn't believe his eyes when he saw Frankie Walker talking to the man he'd followed onto the plane.

'What the hell's the connection between you two?'

*****

Theakston had thought he was dreaming when he heard his phone ringing, that was until his wife angrily shook him awake and told him to answer it, or turn it off.

He looked at his bedside clock. It was 5am. He swiped his phone to take the call.

"Looks like the airport Tony," said Jon Hall.

"London City Jonny?"

"I think so mate, I'll confirm in five."

Hall had been sitting on Sutton's flat in Canary Wharf since the previous evening, watching for any movement. He was parked up in his van, which he'd kitted out with some very hi-tech equipment when he'd turned himself into a surveillance consultant for hire after he retired from the Met.

With the help of some magnetic signage and different colours of vinyl film, he could quickly and easily change the look of the van by wrapping the film around all or just some of the panels, all within a matter of ten to fifteen minutes.

It currently looked like it was some sort of roadside maintenance vehicle, especially as he'd also put out a row of traffic cones to mark it off in the road, all of which added to the illusion that it was 'officially' parked.

He'd done this sort of thing for literally years and had long ago learned that patience and focus was the key to good surveillance. After he'd watched the lights go out in the flat at 11pm, he'd made sure he regularly stretched his arms and legs to keep the circulation flowing, whilst taking sips of water to stay hydrated. Once he'd seen 2.00am appear on his watch the area became very quiet, with very little foot or vehicle traffic.

It stayed like that until he saw a light come in Sutton's flat at exactly 4.45am. It might be a toilet visit he thought, but anything that happened dead on a particular time always suggested a planned action and when the light didn't go out after five minutes Hall started watching for a car to either turn up, or leave from the underground car park.

'Bingo!'

At 5.00am, the light went off in the flat just as a car arrived outside. Hall had his phone primed on speed dial for Theakston and pushed the button as soon as he saw Sutton walking with a flight bag and getting into the back of the car, which he guessed must be an Uber or private hire taxi.

By the time Hall had phoned him the second time, Theakston had changed, grabbed his pre-packed overnight bag and was already heading down to his car in the car park.

"Jonny, what you got?"

"Definitely London City. I'll keep a loose follow and if I can, I'll see what flight he checks in on."

"Great work Jonny. I'm on my way."

Theakston once again felt the buzz he'd been missing, not just for the last year since he'd retired, but for the past ten years or so, or was it even more since he'd been a desk jockey?

He knew Jon Hall would be careful. He'd been running surveillance training for the Met for donkeys' years before he'd retired and was one of the best. He'd been lucky to get him at short notice, as Jon's work was now in real demand, but he'd asked him as a favour and Jon had been more than happy to help an old friend.

By the time Tony had parked up at the airport Jon had lined everything up for him

"It's Palma de Mallorca. I saw him check in on the machine. He's in Club, but I couldn't get the seat number. I checked with the BA desk and there's a few seats left and I've reserved you one, so get yourself booked in because I think they're about to board any moment now. I'll go and keep an eye on him as he goes through security."

Theakston managed to get his ticket and get through security just as he heard the Last Call announcement. As he boarded the plane he made sure he kept looking straight down the back of the plane avoiding contact with anyone in the Club Europe seats at the front.

That was why he'd missed recognising Frankie Walker, but it was probably just as well as he was pretty sure Walker would remember him from his trial.

He'd need to tell Sam Martínez as soon as he could. There was no point in worrying about how he might take it. Sam would no doubt be damn annoyed at Walker's release, but figuring what if any connection with this guy Sutton was now much more important.

When the plane landed Theakston kept at the back of the plane until he saw Sutton and Walker disembark. He saw Maggs Walker was there too and their two kids.

'Is this just a holiday they're on and so it really is just a coincidence?'

If was just a coincidence it was a bloody big one, that was for sure. As soon as he got off the plane he made the call.

"Sam, I'm in Mallorca."

"What the hell are you doing there Tony?"

"I followed Jake Sutton here this morning. I had one

of my guys sitting on his place and he called me when the cab turned up to take him to London City."

Sam was thinking on his feet.

"Are you thinking Jake could be going to look at the Adamsons gallery in Sóller?"

"Well, yes, but there's more. He met up with Frankie Walker on the plane."

"Walker! What the hell's he doing out of prison?"

"I don't know, some sort of technical cock-up I think, but he's here with his missus and the two kids. Look, I've got to go and see where they go. I'll call in later."

"Tony! Wait, slow down. Look, I'm not telling you to back off, but mate, you've been out of the game for a while and Walker's shit-hot on surveillance techniques. I'm catching the afternoon flight over, so just hang fire will you? Just till I get there?"

Theakston couldn't hide the disappointment in his voice.

"I might be old, but I'm not stupid."

He rang off. He'd see where they went and then he'd call it in later.

Sam realised Tony had hung up.

"Shit! I hope you're bloody careful Tony."

He pushed a speed dial on his mobile.

"Sam, good morning. All still set to see you and Anna later this afternoon?"

"Hi Greg, that's a 'yes,' but in the meantime we might have a problem with a retired Detective Chief Superintendent who thinks he's still got his street surveillance skills."

"What sort of problem Sam?"

"He's just landed at Palma."

"What's he doing here?" exclaimed Greg.

"He's followed Jake Sutton who caught the early flight from London City."

"What's he going to do Sam? Nothing stupid I hope?"

"Not intentionally Greg. He's not stupid, but I am afraid that he's rusty. There's something else too."

"I get the impression I might not like this extra bit?" said Greg.

"Well I certainly don't. Sutton met up with Frankie Walker on the plane."

"Walker? The guy who shot your mate Jimmy? I thought he was locked up?"

"I thought so too. I'm about to put a call into Jimmy, but I know what he's going to say. He didn't want me getting wound up. Which is fair enough, that is until you factor in the possible connection he seems to have one of our seven possible suspects with Adamsons."

"What do you want me to do?" asked Greg.

"It might be a needle in the haystack, but can you get down to Palma and try ringing him on the way. I think I upset him and he rang off."

"Upset him? How? Oh, hang on, you didn't go down the road of you've been out of this business for a while did you?"

"Sadly yes. Problem is Greg, he has and not just for a year or so. He was a long way removed from the field for his last ten or more years. He's a bloody amazing strategist and decision maker, but it's been a long time since he was on a live surveillance job."

"Not a great recipe Sam. I'll get straight down there. There's not time to pick up Simon as he's still at the hospital, so I'll have to go on my own," he paused, "and before you dig yourself another hole, don't tell me to be careful either," but Sam heard the humour in his voice this time.

"No Boss, of course not," he laughed. "Speak soon."

22

Frankie Walker walked with Sutton as he went to collect their cases from the baggage hall. He could see Maggs waiting at the exit doors with the kids.

"Where are you staying Jake?"

"I'm booked in at the Portixol, so I'm going to grab a cab and then pick up a hire car tomorrow. Listen we should meet up, but probably better when we're back home. I've got a few things on and you look like you're pretty busy with Maggs and the kids."

"That sounds great Jake. Look forward to it. Let me ping you my number."

Frankie took his phone out and dropped the contact to Jake via airdrop. "Honestly mate, you don't know how much I need to thank you for helping me. You know, to read and write properly."

"You made it easy Frankie, because you wanted to learn. And if anybody needs to thank someone it's me who should be thanking you. I was way out of my depth in Feltham mate and they were starting to make mincemeat out of me before you stepped in."

"Couldn't have them messing up my personal tutor could I?"

A cold shiver ran across Jake's back as he thought

back to the first few weeks he was in Feltham. He was fifteen coming up sixteen, so he was in the younger group of 15 to 18 year olds who were kept separate from the older lads, the 18 to 21 year olds. But it was no kindergarten and he'd never come across the levels of violence he was seeing.

He'd tried to keep himself to himself, spending as much time in the education centre as he could. The tutors soon recognised he was bright, some even realising young Sutton could walk rings around them academically. Jake saw this as a possible way to stay out of trouble and away from the violence, at least during the day by volunteering to help teach some of the lads who showed an interest in trying to get an education whilst they were in there.

It wasn't that he wouldn't, or couldn't stand up for himself. He was strong from years of gymnastic training and his fists were rock hard from the work on the rings and parallel bars, so he could fight, but he wasn't used to the extreme violence or the use of handmade weapons and worse still, the gang attacks on individuals.

He'd taken a couple of bad beatings himself, from a group of South London boys who seemed to take exception to him being smarter than they were.

"What's up swot, can't fight? You'd better learn quickly before you become my bitch. Is that what you want big boy?"

Jake went to retaliate, but there were three of them and he saw one of them had a blade.

'How the hell had he got that in here?'

"Oh, he nearly bit. See that boys, the swot nearly hit back. Come on what's stopping you?"

He'd had enough and was about to lash out and take the inevitable beating when he heard a voice he'd recognised from a lesson he had been helping to run earlier in the day.

Frankie Walker didn't usually intervene in squabbles. He was above that and he'd made sure that no one now came and bothered him after dishing out a few beatings soon after he'd been put on remand in Feltham for GBH.

A Section 18 was what the Old Bill called it. He had no idea it was a Section 18 assault occasioning grievous bodily harm contrary to the Offences Against the Person Act 1861, because he couldn't read the charge sheet he was given.

He was going to be there for at least twelve months the brief had reckoned, because he'd left the boy in a pretty bad way. Maggs had told him he needed to come out better than he went in, but he knew she didn't necessarily mean better as in he wouldn't commit crime. He was from a family with a long criminal history, so he wasn't likely to become a reformed character anytime soon. No, she meant 'better' in that he'd be smarter and wouldn't get caught so easily next time.

Frankie had always struggled with the tutors at Feltham, they talked too quickly and he couldn't follow what they were saying. But this afternoon he'd seen this young guy, one of the inmates who he'd heard being called swot and he'd seen how he was when he was working with the other lads.

Frankie actually left the lesson that day being able to read a couple of paragraphs in a book. It made him feel good. So when he saw the swot being attacked he made a decision that wasn't some sort of righteous act to prevent him being beaten, far from it in fact. This was for purely selfish reasons, as at last he'd found someone who could help him learn and that was exactly what Maggs had wanted him to do.

"Now lads. Give the swot a chance. He's new alright,

so leave him alone and run along."

The leader of the South London boys, Charlie, stopped and looked at Walker. This was a clear challenge to his authority, but he was wary of Walker, although he reckoned with two of his boys there they could take him.

"Who do you think you are Walker? Coming in here interfering with something that's none of your business?"

"But Charlie, you see it is my business. I like young Jake here because he's helping me, so I'm going to help him. Now back off and we'll have no issues. Otherwise…"

"Otherwise what?" said Charlie.

"Wrong answer."

Frankie didn't think Charlie would back down and he certainly wasn't going to give him a chance to get a punch in first. He hit him with a lunging right hook that put Charlie straight on his back and Frankie wasn't one not to kick a man when he was down.

He started kicking him and didn't stop. Jake Sutton looked on, unable to take his eyes off what was happening, as Walker kicked him again and again.

"You two can stay and get the same, or wait outside and then carry your mate to the hospital wing and tell them he fell down a stairwell. What's it to be?"

Charlie was trying to get up when Walker growled at him, "Stay down, or you'll get really hurt. Now boys I asked you a question?"

"Could we take him now Frankie, if you're done?" said one.

"What do you think Jake? Is he done or do you want a kick for good measure?"

"No, I'm good thanks Frankie," said Jake, trying to keep from throwing up.

"That's alright then. Now remember boys, he fell

down a stairwell. Got that Charlie?"

Charlie grunted through the blood in his mouth.

"I didn't hear you."

"Yes, Frankie, sorry Frankie."

"Just remember what's mine is yours anytime you need anything Jake, okay? I mean it, I'll always have your back."

"And what's mine is yours too mate, although I haven't got much, but yes, I'll always have your back too," said Jake.

And that had been how things had been for Jake's year in Feltham. He'd seen Frankie Walker every day during the week in the education centre and then at weekends they'd spent time in the library where he'd show Frankie a whole range of different types of books.

Jake sometimes found it difficult to separate the quite softly spoken young lad, who initially struggled to read and write even the simplest of words, with the guy he saw outside the classroom.

There Frankie showed a jungle instinct for survival, the same as when he'd saved him from another beating from Charlie. Jake had seen it again when Frankie had viciously slashed a young Greek Cypriot lad across his face, apparently just to show who was boss on the wing.

It was a strange friendship brought together because of circumstance, but it had worked and they had both got something significant from it. Jake had stayed safe and by the time he was due for release Frankie Walker could read and write to a very good standard.

"You could take exams if you wanted to you now Frankie, you're bright enough."

"Thanks Jake, but I don't think my career path is destined to take me down a route where I'll need exams or qualifications, but honestly mate, you've set me up for life."

Now as he watched Frankie pull his cases off the baggage carousel in Palma airport, Jake thought about how they had talked about staying in touch. They'd been pulled together in unusual circumstances and had become close friends whilst it lasted, but then they'd gone on to live and move in very different circles after they left Feltham.

Jake continued with his education, going to University before going on to set up SIS, whilst Frankie, together with Maggs, started creating their own fledging crime gang, which in time grew to have the same level of success as Jake's more legitimate pathway.

"Jake? You look like you're a million miles away mate? Give me a hand with these will you?"

Jake smiled and grabbed a couple of the bags and lugged them on to the trolley before they moved across to Maggs and the children and stepped through the sliding exit doors and out into Arrivals.

Tony Theakston was watching from behind one of the pillars. He'd seen Sutton talking to Walker, but couldn't hear what they were saying, although it worried him that they looked like two old friends talking, rather than two blokes who'd just met on the flight.

He wished he hadn't over reacted with Sam. It would have been handy to get him to ring Jimmy to try to find out some more about a possible connection.

He watched as Walker and his family turned to their right and then he saw them immediately start talking to another man who seemed to be waiting for them.

'*Maybe a driver?*' thought Theakston.

But he wasn't just the driver, it was Alejandro Sanchez.

*****

"Welcome Señor and Señora Walker. Bienvenidos a

Mallorca amigos."

"Muchas gracias Alejandro. Es bueno verte," said Maggs. "It's good to see you."

"Señora Walker, your Spanish is very good," said Alejandro in perfect English.

"Hello mate," said Frankie Walker.

"Frankie, good to see you looking so well. I hope your time away from home wasn't too difficult."

"Er, no, thanks, it was fine."

Walker nodded at Alejandro Sanchez, appreciating how he'd taken his kids into consideration in describing his time away in HMP Belmarsh.

"Alejandro, this is a friend, Jake. We met by chance on the flight out. Haven't seen him in ages."

Jake saw the Spaniard looking at him suspiciously.

"Buenas dias amigo, I'm Jake Sutton."

"Relax Alejandro, he's sound mate, honestly. Can we give him a lift to his hotel on the way? He's at the one in Portixol."

Alejandro tried to show he had relaxed, when he was actually nowhere near to relaxing. It was supposed to be a private meeting and this idiot had brought some other guy into the frame.

"Of course, that's no problem at all. Come in with me Jake."

"Look, if it's going out of your way, I'll just grab a cab."

"No, Señor, it's fine," said Alejandro, but Jake heard a firmness in his tone that indicated otherwise.

"That's very kind of you then. Gracias."

Maggs could see the tension developing in the situation and tried to bring things around.

"Kids, this is Alejandro, say hello," said Maggs.

"Hola Alejandro!" both of the children yelled on cue.

"Ah, I see you have both been learning Spanish too. Well done amigos. That must deserve el helado, yes?"

Maggs heard Alejandro's voice returning to its usual friendly and calm intonation.

"Si, si, si!" they yelled again, recognising the word for ice cream.

"We have a car waiting to take you to your hotel. I'll follow in my car to make sure you get there okay and then I'll leave you to enjoy the rest of the day."

"That will be perfect Alejandro and thank you," said Maggs.

There were two Mercedes GLCs waiting outside in the coach waiting area, the two drivers were outside the vehicles, ignoring the gesticulations from some of the coach drivers, who soon stopped when one of them pulled back his suit jacket revealing the butt of a hand gun.

The two drivers put the luggage into one of the SUVs which the Walkers got in to and Sutton got in the other one with Sanchez.

"We'll meet tomorrow at eleven o'clock. I'll come and collect you and take you back to our villa to see my parents. Is that okay for you guys?"

"Yes thank you Alejandro, that will be great," said Maggs, although she was a little concerned that he'd said *'their villa,'* as that put a different perspective on the neutrality of meeting in Mallorca.

Tony Theakston watched from the taxi rank, quietly urging the taxi master to get the people in front of him away. The next cab immediately pulled up and he quickly got in.

"¿Hablas inglés por favor."

"Si, a little my friend. How can I help?"

"Can you please follow my friends in those two black Mercedes SUVs?"

"Yes of course," said the cab driver. "So there was no room for you in the cars Señor?"

"No," he laughed.

The cab driver pulled in behind the second GLC and could see there looked to be a space in the back seat of the Merc.

'Odd,' he thought. *'Maybe they had a lot of luggage?'*

Then he flicked the switch on his meter and slipped into the traffic behind the two cars.

"Which hotel Señor?"

"Ah, that's the thing, I'm not sure. It was all a bit of rush, so can you just follow them?"

"Si," said the driver thinking this was the sort of thing you usually saw in films. *'Follow that car,'* and all that stuff. *'Ha! I'm imagining things now.'*

The two car convoy, with the cab following, turned on to the motorway towards Palma and it wasn't long before they turned off at the Ciutat Jardi exit and headed towards Portixol.

In the Merc ahead of them Sanchez spoke to Sutton.

"So you met by chance then Jake, what a coincidence?"

"Yes, it was a surprise seeing Frankie again after all these years. We were sixteen or so when we met," said Jake.

He didn't know who this guy Alejandro was, but given the interaction he'd had with him, plus the look of the drivers, he knew he wasn't part of a holiday pick-up service.

"So what brings you here to this beautiful island then amigo?"

"Part business, part pleasure."

"What sort of business is that then Jake?"

"I run a security business and we have some clients over here."

It wasn't an interrogation as such, but the next few questions from Alejandro were very clearly intended to ensure he knew all he could about this stranger who had 'by coincidence' met up with the London gang boss his father was due to meet tomorrow.

"Well I don't suppose we'll see each other again, will we Jake?"

Again, it was more of a statement, than a question.

"No, I don't suppose we will, although Frankie suggested maybe having a drink together, but that might need to wait till we get home."

"I think that might be best Jake. We have a very busy schedule with the Walkers, so I don't think they will have time for you whilst you're here."

A friendly sounding voice, but a very definite message which Jake heard loud and clear.

"I think perhaps you're right. Ah, I think we're here now. Thank you so much for the lift and give Frankie my regards."

As Jake got out of the car he saw Frankie waving at him from the other GLC.

'I hope you know who you're involved with Frankie?'

Theakston saw the two Mercedes slowing down as they drove through the Portixol marina and turned first right towards the port and then right again.

"Looks like they're going to the Portixol Señor," said the cab driver.

"Actually I think this will be fine amigo. It looks a bit busy up there, so can you please drop me off here."

"No, it's fine Señor, I can get in close."

"No," said Theakston firmly. "Stop now, please."

"Okay, okay, okay," said the cab driver. There was something definitely going on here, but now he could see the look of the guys in the two black Mercs, he didn't want to get involved. He knew that look and it was trouble.

Theakston leant forward towards the driver and quietly said, "Muchas gracias amigo," as he pushed a hefty tip into his hand.

"I don't know what you're doing my friend, but I

think you should take care, a lot of care," said the driver.

Theakston nodded and then as he got out of the cab he saw Sutton get out of the Mercedes GLC and walk into the Portixol Hotel.

"Got you!" Theakston said quietly.

23

Alejandro Sanchez watched as Sutton walked into the reception of the Hotel Portixol. He didn't like coincidences, so who was this guy?

"Boss, I didn't like to mention it in front of the guy we just dropped off, but I've got a feeling we were just followed from the airport."

Pablo, the driver, had been with the Sanchez family for over ten years and so Alejandro knew that if Pablo had a concern then there was good reason to listen to him.

"What car and where is it now amigo?"

"It was a Skoda, it stopped just the other side of the marina and an old guy got out with a cabin trolley."

"Get someone down here Pablo and find them and whilst they're at it, they can keep an eye on this guy Sutton too, okay?"

"Got it Boss."

"Good work Pablo. I don't know what's going on here, but there's something that doesn't feel right."

*****

Theakston still hadn't picked up any of the messages he'd left him. Sam rang Holly again.

"I know I'm asking a stupid question as I know you'd have told me, but have you heard anything from Tony?"

"No, what the hell's he playing at Sam? Going off on his own like that. I mean for God's sake he's not as young as he used to be and more to the point, he's been out of the game for too many years to be running around out there on his own."

He could hear the concern in her voice. He could tell straight away that she was more worried than angry at Theakston.

"I've got Greg heading down to Palma, but of course we don't even know where to start looking. I don't suppose you had the tracker App put on his phone did you?"

"Wish I had, but I didn't think he'd be going AWOL in Mallorca did I? What time is your flight Sam?"

"I'm at the airport now, so we should be boarding shortly and if we're on time we should be landing around 6.30pm."

Just then he felt his mobile buzz with an incoming call.

"Holly, it's him. I'll ring you back."

Sam pushed the cancel call/accept call indicator on his phone.

"Sam, look I'm sorry."

"Never mind that. Are you okay? We've all been worried to death about you?"

Theakston felt the hairs on the back of his head bristle again.

"Sam, I'm not a damn child! I used to do this stuff for a bloody living, remember?"

Sam realised he'd said the wrong thing.

"Tony, look I'm sorry." He softened his voice. "It was just a bit of a shock and then with you being in the air, we obviously couldn't get hold of you."

Theakston took a deep breath. He'd seen the dozen or so missed calls and a bunch of text messages from both Sam and Holly, so he could understand where Sam was coming from.

"Okay, I get you. I'm sorry but it was too good a chance to miss."

"Understood, so tell me, what have you got? Last thing you said Tony, was that Sutton had met Frankie Walker of all people. I've tried getting hold of Jimmy but he's not picking up. What's Walker doing out and what the hell's he doing in Mallorca? Have you spoken to Jimmy?"

"Sam, slow down. Jimmy does know, but we decided not to tell you in case it upset you."

"Upset me? Of course it was going to bloody upset me Tony. The guy nearly killed my best mate and now he's out? What sort of cock-up was it?"

"Something to do with undisclosed material and his brief saying it was a case of agent provocateur, so the conviction was quashed."

"I don't believe this. Who was responsible for that crock? No, don't tell me, it won't help will it. So it was just quashed with no retrial?"

"Yes, I think it was politics between the Judiciary and the CPS, to teach them a bit of a lesson as there's been a number of these high profile cases that have folded in the past couple of years."

"Trust it to be Frankie Walker who gets off an Attempted Murder of a police officer scot-free."

Sam was lost in his own thoughts for a moment before Theakston brought him back.

"Sam, Sutton has booked in at a hotel in Portixol, but I don't know where the Walkers are."

"Walkers? God yes, you said he's out there with his missus and two girls?"

"Yes, so maybe it's just a holiday Sam and them meeting really was just a coincidence?"

"That's a big 'maybe' Tony."

Sam went to speak again but Tony interrupted him.

"The strange thing is, they were picked up by three guys in two black Mercedes SUVs. Two were drivers and one was very much the boss."

"Spanish? British?"

"They all looked more Spanish Sam, but of course they could be ex-pats out here, but I don't think so and I didn't get that sense. Don't know why, just a feeling."

"Nothing wrong with a bit of gut feeling Tony. Look, I'll be out there with you soon. Greg is coming down to Palma to tie up with you. Give him a call and go and grab a coffee or something and I'll see you at the airport later on this afternoon."

"Great, look forward to it Sam. Feels like old times."

"Yes," said Sam, smiling and it did. It was a good feeling too.

*****

Greg saw the text from Sam. It was about Tony Theakston and was quickly followed by a call from Tony himself.

"Looks like I've been worrying the youngsters," said Tony.

"Yes, but it's nice they worry," said Greg. "Where are you Tony? I'll come and find you and you can fill me in on what's happening, then we can sort you out a place to stay."

"I'm in a bar looking directly across at the Portixol Hotel."

Twenty minutes later Greg found Theakston sitting at an outside table of one of the bars surrounding the marina.

"Coffee Greg?"

"Please."

"I think I've pissed off Holly and Sam."

"Think you're right there Tony. But they were just worrying about you. They forget the fact that we were doing this stuff whilst they were still in nappies."

"I know, but I shouldn't have just gone AWOL. It was just for the first time in a quite a while I felt…..well, like what I was doing was worthwhile."

Greg smiled.

"Tony, I've got a couple of years on you, so I know all about what you're thinking. Don't worry, they'll get over it and hey, it was a good lead and worth following, although Sam was apoplectic when he heard Walker was out."

"Yes, I've no idea what could happened there. The SIO was a good bloke, so I can't see how anything like that could have happened. Maybe it was someone at the CPS who held it back? I don't know. But whatever it was, it's meant Walker is out and about and not even up for a retrial."

"Well, we need to park it for the time being and figure out what, if any, connection we've got here between Sutton and a London gang boss. What's your feeling from what you saw?"

"I couldn't hear anything Greg, but to be honest, it looked like they were both surprised to see each other."

"What did you make of the guy who met them at the airport?"

"If you didn't know otherwise, you'd think he was a businessman meeting a client. He was smartly dressed, suit trousers and jacket, white shirt, no tie and it looked expensive gear."

"But?"

"Unless I've really lost my touch, he had crime gang written all over him Greg."

*****

Greg wasn't the only one to have seen Theakston. Sat in a different bar, one with a view of both the Portixol Hotel and the bar Theakston was in, was Andres Da Costa, called in by Pablo to find the man who had followed Alejandro's convoy.

It had been much easier than he'd thought. It was the cabin trolley that had given the man's position away, plus he didn't look like a tourist. If it had been mid-summer Andres knew it might have been like looking for a needle in a haystack, but this was October and whilst still reasonably busy, there was a distinct separation of what the tourists and the locals were wearing clothes-wise. With the temperatures now down to late teens or early twenties, only the tourists were still dressing like it was a warm summer's day, whilst many of the locals were already in sweaters and some were even in coats.

The man looked to be in his late fifties, quite stocky, but seemed to be carrying a bit more weight now than maybe he did when he was younger. He was on his second coffee when Andres saw another man turn up and sit at the table.

'Now who are you?'

He texted Pablo and saw the immediate response.

'I'm sending some more guys down to you. See where these people go.'

Pablo had said the boss wasn't happy about Sutton and had been even more concerned about the guy in the taxi, so this third person turning up was another proverbial spanner in the works.

He acknowledged his boss's text and sat back to wait for the reinforcements.

24

Alejandro Sanchez was feeling very uncomfortable standing before his father. He was trying to explain the apparent coincidence of not one, but now three people, who may know about the meeting between their family and the Walkers.

"Alejandro," said Alberto Sanchez quietly. "This was your idea to bring us all across for a private meeting with your friends, the Walkers."

Alejandro didn't miss his father's emphasis on the word *'your'*.

"Papa, I think it may just be a series of strange coincidences…"

"Yes, you've said that Alejandro, but I'm not convinced and neither is Diego, are you son?"

"No Papa, one maybe, but then two more people arrive on the scene. Come on Alejo, I know you want this to succeed, but even you must see this doesn't look good."

Only his brother called him 'Alejo.' He smiled at Diego, but there was little love lost between them. They were like chalk and cheese. Diego was usually the rash one, whilst he would generally take the more cautious option. He much preferred working on the lowest risk margin, but still with a good return, ensuring the business stayed safe and out of the watching eyes of the police, especially the GEO, who seemed to have made the Sanchez family one of the primary targets in the last year or so.

Now Alejandro realised that he was the only one who wasn't seeing a possible threat by thinking this was just a set of unconnected coincidences.

"Okay Papa, what do you want to do? Shall I call it all off?"

His father thought for a moment. He wasn't getting any younger and he needed both his boys to step up to take responsibility for running the business.

"You make the decision Alejandro. I'll go with whichever way you decide."

"Thank you Papa. I'll do some more digging around who these people are, but for the moment, I think we should still meet with the Walkers."

"Good, that's settled then," said Old Man Sanchez.

"Hope you're doing the right thing," whispered Diego, as he walked past his brother on the way out of the room.

*****

As he followed his brother Alejandro stopped him and took him to one side.

"Diego, don't mess this up for me."

His brother feigned a hurt look.

"You're doing that on your own Alejo. You didn't need any help from me. But if you want some help, you know you can just ask."

The sarcasm came through as thick as treacle. Help from Diego was the last thing Alejandro was likely to ask for. He remembered when things were different, when they had been close when they were growing up, but whilst he'd gone to university, Diego, despite being just as bright and intelligent, had dropped out of school as soon as he could.

Seeing less of each other over the four years he was away doing a Masters had just seen them grow more apart, but what hurt Alejandro more than anything was how Diego somehow seemed to delight in undermining him at every opportunity he could. He didn't know if it was jealousy of his university education, or because he was the older brother and it seemed likely that his father would make him head of the business when he decided to pass it on.

There had been a time when he thought he would do something completely different and not join his father, but those ideas had been quashed very early on by his father. He'd reminded him in no uncertain way, by taking him out and forcing him to watch a punishment session of a dealer who had tried to double cross his father, that his education had come from crime and that a lot of blood had been spilt to make the money that had paid for his expensive university education. Like it or not, he was part of a crime family and his father had made it very clear that he had a family duty to continue to provide for the people who relied on his father for a living.

That had been then, when he was fresh out of university. But there was nothing soft about Alejandro. He was as tough and ruthless as his father, but perhaps in a more considered way, whereas Diego was often hot-headed and Alejandro had lost count of the times his father asked him to clear up a problem his brother had caused.

To convince his father that he was the one who should take control of the business meant that Alejandro needed this to go right. The Walkers had got a good hold on their territory in South London and that meant there was a lot of potential to increase the amount of cocaine they were shipping into the UK for them.

His father had given him responsibility for the cocaine business three years ago, when he had told his sons that he wanted to start winding down his participation in the business.

This was another reason Diego was upset, because he had been his father's Number Two with the drugs side of things and he expected his father to give it to him. However, Alejandro knew that part of the reason his father had wanted him to go to university was to ensure he came back with the ideas of how to elevate the business to something more than what it was.

He'd done that too, with new collaborations with the producers in South America and improved efficiency from the traffickers in the transit countries of North and West Africa. Profits had rocketed, whilst he had still made sure the family maintained a low profile with the GEO, the Spanish police unit tasked with tackling major drugs crime.

He checked his watch, Pablo should have his extra men by now. He called him.

"Pablo, qué tal amigo? How's everything my friend?"

"Everything's good Boss. No movement, but I've got enough guys here to respond if we need to. We've been into the Portixol, but there's no sign of Sutton. My guy didn't even try getting anything from the reception team, as he didn't want to draw attention to himself."

"Good call Pablo. Now if you get pulled in too many ways, then here's my priorities for you. One: Are the two men in the coffee shop definitely following Sutton? Two: Where are they staying? Three: Who are they? Whatever course of action you choose has to be to meet one of those objectives, is that clear?"

"As crystal, Boss."

"Okay, I'll leave you to it amigo. You know what

you're doing, but call me if you need anything."

Pablo liked it when he worked for Alejandro because he was so clear and specific in everything he did. Diego was fun, but a complete bloody nightmare, as he was forever changing his mind and making things up on the hoof.

'Okay, come on guys, time for one of you to make a move.'

Across at the coffee shop Greg and Tony had finished another coffee.

"Look Greg, why don't we split up? If you can get rid of this bag it'll free me up to be able to better respond if Sutton does go walkabout."

"Yes, good thinking Tony. It's not going to help for sure, you banging your cabin bag along behind you. Here, give it to me and I'll take it across to my daughter's place. You can stay there tonight, it's just across the road."

Tony looked across at a smart looking block of apartments and nodded.

"Thanks that's great. I'll keep you posted on any movement."

Theakston knew he'd have to move fairly soon as well. He'd been there a while and although he'd brought a book with him to pretend to read as cover for him just sitting there, it was pretty obvious that he'd need to do something soon to avoid arousing suspicion, even if it was to go for a walk and then come back for some lunch.

Greg had told him that he'd walked around the hotel a couple of times before when out for walks with his daughter. As far as he could recall he didn't think there was an actual exit at the back. But there was only a low wire fence, so it wouldn't be any sort of barrier to Sutton if he chose to go out that way, rather than use the main entrance.

It was probably a mix of Pablo's team being well-disciplined and trained and Theakston being more than a bit out of practice with surveillance. In any event, Theakston didn't see any of the Sanchez team as he walked, despite passing within metres of two of them as he strolled around the marina towards the Portixol Hotel.

"Hold there guys, no need to move in. Let's just keep watching him," radioed Pablo.

"Okay Pablo, understood," came the response via the covert radios they were all wearing.

Theakston was monitored all the way as he walked slowly around the marina road into the one way system, stopping occasionally as though looking in the shops.

What neither Theakston, nor Pablo realised was that they were also both being watched.

25

She had been tempted to go with Pérez and the team when the intel came in that the entire Sanchez family were on their way to Mallorca.

It was so difficult to get any surveillance anywhere close to them when they were in their huge, and it had to be said, impressive hacienda on the Spanish coastline just south of Alicante.

But Lori Garcia knew it wouldn't have been professional. Her team knew about her relationship with Greg Chambers, whose daughter lived on the island, so she didn't want them feeling she was taking advantage of the situation. She knew they probably wouldn't, but that wasn't the point, so albeit a little reluctantly, she just sent Pérez with the Alpha team. Besides, there had been no intel linking the Sanchez family with any activity with the Balearics, so perhaps it was just a holiday?

However that idea was soon dismissed when her other Sergeant, Nino Castilla, shouted through the open door to her office.

"Boss, I think you need to come and listen to this."

"You're on speaker phone Fernando, I've got the boss here," said Nino, as she walked towards him.

"Hi Boss, things are getting interesting here."

By the time he got to the part when he'd seen Greg Chambers, from 3R International, turn up at the coffee shop and sit down with the guy who'd followed the Sanchez convoy in a cab from the airport, Detective Inspectora Garcia couldn't contain herself.

"What the hell is he getting involved in now? He's supposed to be looking after his sick daughter!"

She'd been thinking it and hadn't realised she'd said it out loud.

"I don't know Boss and we still have no idea what the connection is with the guy in the Portixol and the Sanchez outfit, nor do we know who the family are," said Nino, who had been running the checks.

"No hits on the guy or the woman then?" asked Garcia.

"No, they couldn't get close enough for good enough pictures, so we're running up a number of possibilities. We're down to about twenty, but we're just checking with Interpol and the Met police in London to see if they recognise any of them."

"Maybe try Sam Martínez's friend Jimmy? Sam says he's one of their best intel guys. I'm sure Sam wouldn't mind a bit of name dropping."

"Okay Boss, do we know which team this Jimmy is in?"

"Ah, good point. They're a pretty big outfit." She walked quickly into her office and came back with a business card. "Here, this is one of Sam's old cards with a direct dial office number. Try that."

Nino nodded and went to another desk and picked up a phone.

"Fernando, how's your cover?" asked Lori.

"Cover is good Boss, I'm on a boat. The rest of our team are holed up in various places. Sanchez's guy Pablo has a got a team of five. Have to say, they're pretty well organised. He's got them laid up on a bike and two cars, so it's pretty busy down here," he laughed.

"What do you mean, you're on a boat?"

Pérez had a reputation of somehow getting into all manner of places when he needed to quickly find an OP, an observation post, so she wondered how on earth he'd managed to get access to a boat.

"Ah, well," he paused as if telling a story. "We were by the marina when the Sanchez convoy started slowing. I was running as footman in the last car, so I jumped out and this looked as good a place as any to get eyeball on everyone. It's plenty big enough, it's about fifteen or twenty metres. Luckily enough I found a very helpful a member of the crew, she's the boat captain actually. She's literally just arrived an hour or so ago after she brought it across from France with another crewmate. It's brand new."

"You never fail to amaze me how you do it, but make sure you do the necessary forms when you're done."

"Yes Boss," he grinned. Unlike on the cop shows on TV, where you never seemed to see anyone filling in any forms, anything connected with a police surveillance operation always required a ream of paperwork.

Garcia had also heard him say, *'she's the boat captain.'* She rolled her eyes because Pérez was known to be a bit of a ladies' man, so if anyone could charm his way onto a brand new, multi-million euro luxury cabin cruiser, then he undoubtedly could.

"And Sergeant?"

"Yes Boss?" said Pérez.

"Keep your mind on your job!"

"Always," he said, smiling as the attractive boat captain looked across at him with a smile and a bottle of water in her hand, motioning if he wanted a drink.

*****

"What are you going to do Boss?" asked Nino.

"Good question Nino. I need to ring Greg and

see what he's up to walking into the middle of our operation. Give me a minute, but I think we need to get some more reinforcements over there too."

"I'll get the Bravo team called in and get them on the overnight ferry. I'm assuming we'll go as well?"

"Yes, but we need to get there tonight. Try and get us on the next available flight Nino."

He was picking the phone up as he nodded to her, but she was already on her way back to her office making her next call.

Greg saw 'Lori' appear on the mobile screen and he smiled.

"Hello my love, what a nice surprise."

"Can you talk?"

He frowned. He recognised the tone in her voice. It was her professional, no messing voice.

"Yes, what's up?"

"Where are you Greg?"

"Portixol. Why?"

"I know that. But where specifically are you?"

"How do you know I'm in Portixol?"

"Just answer me Greg, please."

Again, she spoke with some urgency.

"I'm walking back to Terri's apartment. And before you ask, if I've wandered into something then I'm sorry, I had no idea you were operating here. But if you are, why didn't you tell me?"

She heard his voice and realised he maybe didn't know what he had stumbled into."

"Look, this is a fast moving Op. Do you remember Pérez?"

"Yes, of course. Is he here?"

Greg didn't start looking blindly around as an inexperienced surveillance operative may have been tempted to do, but instead he kept walking slowly as before, talking into his phone.

"Yes, he's there with his team. He's seen you and another guy, a white male, mid to late fifties, sitting at a bar drinking coffee looking very interested in the Hotel Portixol. Greg? Now, tell me, what are you doing there?" she asked quietly.

"It's that job I told you briefly about? The one for an insurance company and the art gallery?"

"I remember."

Like her, he would tell her just enough about his work to let her know he was okay and where he was. But neither of them went into any of the detail so as not to compromise his client, or in Lori's case, any police operational confidentiality.

"Can you tell me who you are looking at?" asked Lori.

"Is it important? No, don't answer that. You wouldn't be asking. Okay, it's Jake Sutton and Lori? I know I probably don't need to say this, but this is extremely sensitive, He's a very high profile entrepreneur, so this can't get out."

"Understood and it won't. Is it just him?"

Nino came in at that moment and passed her a piece of paper. From Jimmy at the Met. She nodded to him and mouthed *'Gracias,'* to him.

"Well it was, until the chap I'm with, Tony Theakston, he works for the gallery, just told me Sutton met a London gang boss called….."

"Frankie Walker," said Garcia.

Greg paused.

"Lori, I swear I didn't know anything about this. But you know Walker is the one who shot Jimmy?"

"Yes, we've just spoken with Jimmy. Listen, Sam isn't anywhere near you is he?"

"Not at the moment, but he's on his way from London. He lands later this afternoon and before you say anything, I'll look after him and make sure he doesn't do anything stupid."

"Make damn sure you do Greg. This is a two year Op we've got on the go and he can't go messing this up if he has a PTSD attack."

"I know, I know. Now you might choose not to answer this, but in the spirit of sharing, are you looking at the same two? Or is there someone else in the mix?"

"We didn't know anything about Sutton, so I can't say if he is involved in this at all. Jimmy is doing more checks on him and Walker at the moment. But Walker? Again, we didn't know for sure if it was him who our target was meeting until we just got the partial photos identified by Jimmy."

"That hasn't exactly answered my question Lori?"

"I know."

He smiled. He took the silence as her answer. She wasn't going to tell him, or at least not yet. Well, to an extent he was in the same position with not being able to tell her anymore about the theft of the paintings from Adamsons, again because of the strict confidentiality they had required from him.

"You don't need to tell me anymore, but this is presumably an OCG?"

"Yes, they're una pandilla del crimen organizado, but yes, in English, an organised crime group and they're from the mainland."

"Okay, so do you need me to move Tony out?"

She thought for a moment. Pérez had told Nino that he felt the Sanchez outfit already knew about this other guy with Greg, Tony Theakston. Therefore, it might be better to wait for the Sanchez team to make a move that Pérez could respond to.

"Let's leave him there for the time being Greg. But I'm only telling you this because I don't want you blundering into this any further. The people we are looking at are watching both you and Sutton, okay?"

"Presumably they aren't nice people either?"

"Far from nice, so watch yourself and definitely watch your friend Theakston."

"Other than that then, are you all okay sweetheart?" he asked, trying to lighten things up a little.

"Don't joke with me on this one Greg. These are not people to be underestimated, do you hear me?"

He could hear the concern in her voice.

"Yes, of course, I was just…"

"I know what you were doing and that's lovely. Now, the good news is that I'll be across later this evening. So book a table for a late meal. Make it somewhere nice in the city as I need to stay close to what's going on."

"Do you need picking up at the airport?"

"No, I'm good. I'll have Nino with me and we'll have people there to collect us."

He smiled. Even having seen her husband murdered in front of her and her children when they were young, had not deterred Lori from working in what was one of the highest risk areas of policing within the GEO.

"Okay my love, I'll see you later."

26

Greg carried on walking towards Terri's apartment. He decided against ringing Tony as he wasn't sure he might not start looking around for either the GEO team or the Spanish OCG guys, but he did need to tell Holly Regus about what they'd stumbled into.

He was about to ring her when he got a call from Tommy.

"Hi Tommy, what's up?"

"I've solved it Greg!"

"Solved what?"

"Sutton's riddle."

Greg thought for a moment.

"I don't want to steal your thunder Tommy, but it would be bloody good if your solution to his riddle is Sóller."

"How did you know?" asked Tommy, feeling as though his little bubble of success had just burst.

"Sutton has just arrived in Palma de Mallorca, so to be honest, it was just a guess, but it's great that we've now got confirmation that one, it's pretty much certain that it's Sutton we should be looking at and two, it looks like he's planning to steal the next painting from a gallery in Sóller."

"Oh good, I'm happy now that it was worth me doing," said Tommy, his voice immediately cheering back up to his usual happy, rolling Bajan lilt.

"Definitely mate, that's brilliant, how did you crack it?"

"Sheer brilliance Boss, but basically it's trial and error, looking at all the words and possible alternatives. I was floating around other words for car and came up with streetcars, which I looked up and found was what trams were first called. Trams obviously run in many cities across the world, but cross referenced with Adamsons galleries and it was just San Francisco and Sóller."

"And the riddle says it will *'show you something small'*," said Greg. "Meaning Sóller, rather than SanFran."

"Exactly."

"Well done again Tommy, we're another step forward because of this. Now it changes things a lot as well. I'll probably need you out here at some stage, so be ready for the call, but in the meantime can you just keep an eye on things on the everyday business over there."

"No problem Boss, catch up soon."

Greg grinned as he rang off, smiling at how Tommy always seemed to call him Boss regardless of the number of times he'd told him he didn't need to.

He rang Holly to bring her up to speed.

"Holly, I've got an update and yes, Tony's fine."

"Good, I'm so relieved to hear that. Now what have you got for me?"

She listened as he briefed her on what Theakston had seen and then his conversation with DI Lori Garcia, ending with Tommy's breaking of Sutton's riddle.

"The Sóller Solution, that's fantastic Greg," she paused. "I don't mean to pry, but is Lori your girlfriend?" she asked slowly, "because if so, haven't we got a conflict of interest here?"

"That's the last thing we've got here Holly. She doesn't know who I'm contracted to and I don't know who the Spanish OCG is that she's looking at. Look, that's just the way we are Holly. Call it years of experience of having to hide secrets if you like, but I promise you, there isn't an issue of any sort."

She heard the sincerity in his voice and knew he wasn't trying to bluff her.

"That's fine then, but where does this leave us and more importantly, are you happy leaving Tony out there in the middle of what seems to be a policing Op and some sort of Spanish OCG stake-out?"

"No, I'm not happy and now the more I think about it, I think we should pull him out of there. We know, because of what Tony's followed up on, that Sutton is on the island and where he's staying. I just need to think of another way to make sure we find out when Sutton makes a move."

"Any ideas how?" she asked.

"Not at the moment," he admitted, "but Sam's about to get on a flight out here, so leave it with me and we'll come up with something."

"Now, do you need anything else from me?"

He thought for a moment.

"I may need to break the confidentiality clause at some stage by telling Lori what we're doing. It will only be if I absolutely need to, but can I do that?"

"That's a big ask Greg, but given the people we've found ourselves dealing with, then I think it's a fair question and I'll take it to Charles and Chris and come back with a decision. Is that okay for the time being?"

"Perfect and let's do a catch up call with them tomorrow morning at 9.00am your time."

"That's good for me and Greg? Take care of Tony will

you? Don't let him go wandering off again."

He heard the concern in her voice. This was a long way out of her usual remit of risk and loss analysis and she'd clearly been worried by Theakston going off on his own.

"Of course Holly. He's a good bloke who can look after himself, but I'll make sure we keep a good eye on him."

He dropped Tony's cabin trolley off at Terri's apartment and thought for a moment about the secret storage Tommy had installed for his daughter that housed all manner of firearms and weaponry.

But with the GEO looking at them, he couldn't afford for any of his 3R International team to be stopped and found in possession of what would be an illegally held firearm.

That said, there was a chance Sutton might hire a car and he knew Terri had got in some more tracking devices. He flicked the hidden switch and as the sliding doors opened, he walked into the storeroom.

He was still amazed the hidden storeroom Tommy had built for her, not to mention how his daughter had managed to get so much equipment transported covertly on to the island. There were semi-automatic guns, hand pistols, body armour, night sights, plus the sniper's rifle she'd taken to Armenia and India.

He stopped at a rack when he saw what he was looking for.

"Let's have a couple of you shall we? Just in case," as he picked up two tracking devices and slipped them into a backpack.

*****

It didn't take very long for DC Jimmy Mellor to find the connection between Walker and Sutton. It was Feltham. They'd both been there as young offenders, although there was nothing in the intel files to suggest they'd had any contact since then.

Finding out Frankie Walker was in Mallorca meeting the Sanchez crime group was news he needed to tell his boss about.

"What are they up to Jimmy?" said DI Sandra Chisholm.

"I don't know Boss, but it doesn't look like Frankie and Maggs are just out there on holiday."

"And the GEO are all over this?"

"Yes, a DI Lori Garcia is OIC. I've spoken to her before, about Sam Martínez."

"Sam, he's your mate isn't he Jimmy? But hasn't he left the job now?"

Chisholm was new to the Intel team and hadn't met Sam before.

"Yes, best mate actually. He's back living over in Mallorca now, but he's doing consultancy stuff with an outfit called 3R International."

"Haven't heard of them, but Sam has a strong reputation hasn't he? A good cop."

"He was very good Boss, but the whole thing with Walker and this," he looked down to his wheelchair. "Well, it got to him a bit. Thinks it was his fault the daft sod."

"Was it?"

He was taken aback by her question. No one had ever asked it in such a direct way before.

He smiled back at her.

"No Boss, far from it, at least not in my book and I reckon I'm the numero uno here in relation to whom it matters most. Well, me and the little girl."

Chisholm smiled back at him. Jimmy also had an outstanding reputation, not only as a very good cop himself, but also as a really good bloke. So she wasn't surprised as he turned the conversation away from himself and back to the little girl who, because of Sam's actions, had avoided being injured.

"You're a good friend to him Jimmy Mellor," she smiled. "Okay, let's give DI Garcia as much help as she needs. We need to know what the Walkers are up to down there."

*****

"Nino? Jimmy Mellor from the Met. I've got the connection between the Walkers and Sutton."

"Si amigo, please go on."

"They were in juvenile prison together when they were around sixteen, or seventeen, for around nine months. They were in Feltham, what we call a Young Offenders Institution."

"Si, si, we have the same type of thing over here. Sadly sometimes it just creates better, more skilled criminals."

"Aye, you're right there Nino. Now we've got nothing telling us that they've had any contact since."

"So this may be a coincidence?"

"Possibly," said Jimmy. "Now can I ask, do you have anything else you can tell us at the moment?"

Jimmy heard the pause.

"Don't worry Nino, I gather there's more, but you can't share at the moment."

"Si Jimmy, gracias amigo." Another pause. "Have you spoken to Sam recently?"

"No," said Jimmy slowly. "Should I?"

"It may be good to catch up with him. Maybe sometime soon, but as a friend, not as a cop. You understand?"

"I read you Nino."

*****

Sam saw the text come in from Jimmy's mobile.
'Where are you?'
Sam rang him straight away.
"Jimmy, I'm at London City chum, waiting to board

a flight back home. What's up?"

"You've heard about Walker haven't you?"

Sam heard the hesitation in his friend's voice.

"Yes and don't worry, I get why you didn't tell me. And hey, I'm cool with it. If he's got away with it then so be it," as Sam said the words he saw his hand starting to shake.

"Sam, that sounds remarkably unlike you."

Sam forced a laugh.

"Didn't think that would work Jimmy. So, no, I'm not bloody okay with it, especially now he's walked into something we're looking at."

"Ah, so that's it."

"What? Did you know? Or rather, what do you know?" asked Sam.

"Well I think I've got two halves of a story, but they weren't joining up. There's Tony's part and now I've just had a call from Lori's DS, Nino, something to do with Walker meeting a Spanish OCG, the Sanchez family. He couldn't tell me anything, but suggested I give you a call, you know? As a mate."

"He's a sound bloke is that Nino. So who are they?"

"A major crime group on the Costas. In to everything. Run by the Old Man, Alberto and his two sons, Alejandro and Diego."

"I'm loving your Spanish accent Jimmy."

"I learn it from a book," laughed Jimmy in pidgin Spanish. "Anyway, this is a pretty significant team Sam."

"And the GEO are looking at them?"

"That seems to be the case. I think that's why Nino dropped a less than subtle hint for me to ring you."

"Okay, I'd better ring Greg. I've been off air for a bit getting through airport security. You alright otherwise mate? How's your new DI?"

Jimmy had told him a while ago that there were a

few changes going on and he was getting a new boss who had no previous intel experience.

"She's good Sam. She might not have been in this intel world before, but she's got a shed load of experience as a DS on a drugs squad, so she knows what she's doing."

"Better than some bosses you've had then?"

"Oh yes, she's so much better than you obviously."

He heard Jimmy laugh again and could only marvel at the way his friend had reacted to the shooting that had left him wheelchair bound.

*****

They still hadn't called his flight, so Sam rang Greg.

"So the plot thickens then?"

"Yes Sam, it certainly does. I take it you know about Walker? Are you okay with it? Let me rephrase that. I know you won't be okay with it, but can you manage it?"

"I'm glad you rephrased it. Can I manage it? With him not standing here right in front of me, then yes. Ask me again if I happen to come across him and it may be a different story."

"Well I appreciate your honesty Sam. No point just saying you'll be fine if you think there's a chance you might react differently. So let's see how it goes. Anyway, we don't know for sure what, if anything, this connection is between him and Sutton. Tony seemed to think the meeting was a surprise to both of them."

"Yes, but the Sanchez thing? The OCG connection with Sutton, or again is that coincidence?"

"I didn't know the OCG name, Lori didn't tell me."

"I think that's why Nino got Jimmy to ring me, you know, as a mate. Looks like Lori was just ensuring a bit of professional distance with you."

"Yes, I get that," said Greg. "Difficult situation, but more than one way to skin the proverbial cat. So I gather the Sanchez clan are not to be underestimated?"

"No, so where's Tony and does he know?"

"He's still sat up in the coffee bar, but I haven't filled him in on the new info. I didn't want him to start wandering about until I can get back and we can walk out of there together, but I'm on my way there now to take him away from there."

"Does Holly know?" asked Sam.

"Yes and before I forget, remember the riddle on the email? Well, Tommy's sussed it and it's Sóller."

"Bloody hell! How did he do that?"

"Easy when you know how apparently and no doubt Tommy will regale you with the full ins and outs at some stage, but it makes things fall nicely into place doesn't it?"

"The proverbial plot really does thicken then."

"Yes, very much so. By the way, I've asked Holly to give us some leeway on the confidentiality clause, because I reckon we may need to tell Lori and possibly Jimmy about our connection with Adamsons sooner or later. She's going to confirm it with Hacker and Christine."

"Good. What's our next step Greg?"

"I was about to ask you the same thing."

"I suppose it's back off completely for the moment and let the GEO do their thing. That way we remove the risk of us getting pulled into something with the Walkers and Sanchez family that may be entirely unconnected with Sutton."

"My thoughts exactly Sam," said Greg. "Just wanted to see what you were thinking. Okay, I'm close by to Tony, so we'll be moving out shortly and leaving the GEO to it."

27

Terri was on the cross trainer pushing herself hard. She'd been buoyed by the news that she could go home in a day or so and was determined to make it the next day if she could.

"Don't push too hard Terri. Slow and easy and then we'll pick up the speed as you get stronger."

"You talking about the cross trainer, or something else Simon?"

She saw him flush and grinned at him.

"What! You getting embarrassed? We're going to have to do something about it at some stage!"

"I know, but…."

She slowed the cross trainer back down to a fast walk and then to a stop before she turned and let him take her in his arms as she stepped off the machine.

She kissed him gently.

"You know it was you who kept me fighting don't you?"

She saw the tears in his eyes and realised, perhaps for the first time, just how close she'd been to losing that fight.

"You must have been so worried," she said with tenderness.

"I thought we, I mean I…" She saw his Adam's apple

wobble as he swallowed. "I thought I'd lost you."

She kissed him again, this time on his cheeks, wiping away the tears that had fallen.

"But you didn't and now you're stuck with me forever," her voice growing stronger and louder as she hugged him and held him tight.

Josie had been watching from across the other side of the gym and she saw how happy her daughter was in the arms of this man. It was getting near the time when she knew she should be thinking about going home, back to Australia. It was a thought tinged with sadness, as she'd be separated once again from her now not so little girl, but at least she could leave her knowing she was in safe hands with both Greg and now Simon there to make sure she was okay.

"Hey you two, come on now. Stop all this soppy stuff and get back on that treadmill."

She saw them both laugh and Terri beamed across at her.

"I'm on it Mum."

Josie too had thought she'd lost her, but she could now see the sparkle back in her daughter's eyes. She was getting fitter by the day and it was pretty clear too that she was deeply in love with the man before her.

She spoke quietly to Simon as her daughter ramped up the speed on the cross trainer.

"You make sure you look after my girl now, do you hear me?"

Simon heard the emotion in Josie's voice and turned to face her.

"I will, I promise, with my life."

"You just make sure you do. Because I never want to have to come here again and see her like this and if you think her father is tough, then you've got to know that an Aussie mum is on another level."

She patted him on his chest and gave him a hug.

"Understood Josie," he whispered to her.

*****

Anna was reviewing where they all were with the actions that had come out of the Gold Suite, including Tommy's news on solving the riddle. She checked her watch, Sam's flight might not yet have taken off.

He picked up her call straight away.

"Sam, have you heard about Tommy solving the riddle?"

"Yes, I spoke with Greg just a minute or so ago. It's making it look like he's our man for sure."

"Especially as I've got an update on those sunglasses, the anti-face recognition ones, that people were wearing in the gallery in Singapore?"

"Go on Mum."

"Jake Sutton's SIS company ordered a thousand of them for the conference where he was the guest speaker."

"A thousand pairs of glasses? That's a lot of money Mum. It's got be £50K or more hasn't it?"

"At least Sam, so it's a pretty significant outlay for a presentation."

"But not when you lay it up against a £10 million painting."

"No, but I keep coming back to why is he doing this? I mean, he's made millions through his company. What do you think it is? What's he looking for? Is it for the adrenalin kick, the challenge, or something else?"

"I don't know. What do you think Mum?"

"I think he's an adrenalin junkie, that's for sure. I was reading something in one of the business articles on him and he's into that Parkour training regime, plus he was an elite athlete, albeit only at a junior level, so maybe it's as simple as that."

"Parkour is a tough sport, bloody tough in fact. But do we know if SIS is any sort of financial trouble?"

asked Sam.

"They don't seem to be as they appear to have some strong backers, although some of them seem to stay under the radar, as though they're hiding away from the limelight, which isn't entirely unknown. Anyway, from the work Anju has done with some in-depth financial background checks on him, there's nothing at all coming back to suggest they are doing anything but smashing the security market with their products. SIS is the proverbial goldmine for their investors."

Sam thought for a moment.

"Sam, you still there?"

"Yes Mum. I was just thinking if there's any merit in just approaching this guy Sutton and just fronting him out. After all, our remit isn't to catch him, but to stop him."

"I like that idea. Who are you thinking should do the approach? You?"

"I was actually thinking this may come better with a softer touch, at least from his perspective, but believe me, I know you're far from any sort of soft touch after the way you handled Sergei Grigoryan in Armenia."

Anna smiled. Her son hadn't known anything of her previous life before he was born, when she'd been an undercover field agent for MI6, so she'd been more than comfortable in confronting the crime boss at the café in his home city of Yerevan.

"I'm happy to do that and what do you think about me taking Holly with me? After all, she's got all the details about the previous theft."

"Do you think she's up for it? I mean, she seems to be a really good analyst, but this is a different ball game, fronting Sutton up."

"I think she is and besides she'll be with me."

"Point taken Mum. Will you speak to her?"

"Yes and you tell Greg. This is your show, so he'll be

happy to go along with this."

"Especially because you came up with it," he smiled.

"Not at all Sam. He trusts you absolutely. This is not nepotism of any kind. He's got you and Terri on board with 3R International because you are bloody good at what you do."

"Thanks Mum and I think the same can be said of you too."

It was her turn to smile now. Things had changed dramatically since Greg Chambers had walked back into her life just a few months ago. But the best thing, she thought, was that it was a change that had come at a time when she needed something to fill the void of losing her husband Luis.

"Well that's as maybe. Anyway, let's get back to this should we?"

There she was again, thought Sam. The consummate professional in what she did. There was time to chat and a time for action.

"Okay, they're finally calling my flight. I'll probably see you later on in Palma then?"

"Yes, I'll speak to Holly now and make the arrangements."

*****

"Anna, I'm not sure. Do you think…?"

"Before you go on Holly, I do think you can do this, as does Sam, otherwise I wouldn't be asking you. We'll have someone nearby to us all the time, but you've seen the research on Sutton and know there's no suggestion of him being violent in anyway."

Anna waited for Holly to speak. She didn't want to force her into this, but Anna really did think Holly could take this on and work with her in challenging Sutton.

"I think I should speak to Charles first."

"He thinks it's a good idea."

"You've spoken to him already?" stammered Holly.

"Yes. Now listen, there's no pressure on you at all. I will lead the discussion with Sutton. I just thought it would be a good idea to have you there with me for the detail."

She saw Holly suddenly push her shoulders back as though she'd reached a decision.

"I'll do it. When do we leave?"

"In three hours. The flight's booked and we fly from London Heathrow T5 and should get into Palma around nine."

"You've booked the flights already?"

"I had a feeling you'd rise to the challenge and say yes."

"So have you actually spoken to Charles?" Holly slowly asked.

"No," grinned Anna. "We can do that now."

28

An hour later they were on their way to London Heathrow. Charles Hacker had shown some initial reluctance to the idea of Holly going with Anna to confront Jake Sutton directly, something Holly had actually found quite touching and definitely surprising that he should be concerned for her safety and well-being.

However, he'd agreed after Anna had explained about the back-up that would be on hand from the rest of the 3R team.

"What if he denies everything Anna? What do we do then?"

"I think we're on a win-win here Holly. Whether he admits it or not, our goal here is to stop him doing what he's doing. Adamsons have made it quite clear they don't want any publicity and so that means no arrest, no trial and therefore no press. They know that this might come at a cost, meaning that whilst they'd obviously like some, or all, of the £15 million back that Sutton extorted from them the first time, that might have to be the price of keeping all of this under wraps."

Holly thought for a moment.

"Can I ask what exactly you did in the intelligence services Anna?"

"Yes of course my dear," smiled Anna, who then said nothing.

"Point taken."

*****

Greg and Tony Theakston were at Palma de Mallorca airport to meet Sam as he walked through the Arrivals gate.

"Guys, thanks for the welcome. Anything new to report?"

"No," said Greg. "I got the call from Anna about her and Holly coming out and we'll pick them up later. They should be in around nine this evening."

"You're happy with the thinking around approaching Sutton Greg?"

"Yes, absolutely, especially as we seem to have inadvertently run into one of Lori's operations. Probably best we keep out of her way."

"I'm sorry I asked Jimmy to keep the news about Walker from you Sam. I thought it was best at the time, plus I didn't think it was relevant to what we were doing with Sutton," said Theakston.

"Tony, it's fine mate, honestly. I was saying to Jimmy, I'm obviously not thrilled with it, but we've both been in the job long enough to know that justice isn't always seen to be done."

"So you won't…?" Theakston started to ask a question.

"What? Go all vigilante and sort Walker out myself? Er, no. I might have left the Met Tony, but I'm not such a lone wolf to go out after Walker. I'm still into justice, rather than any sort of vengeance."

Sam saw just a small, almost imperceptible nod from Greg. He hadn't realised there had perhaps been as much concern that he might go rogue on them and go after Walker.

'Is that what they think? I'm a loose cannon?'

He put the thought to the back of his mind, at least for the time being.

"Okay, what's the plan? And if we haven't got anything specific on, I'd like to go and see Terri."

"Thought you'd like to do that Sam, she's expecting you. She's back home in the apartment, so you can go there now. I'm having dinner later with Lori after she gets in."

He saw the look on Sam's face.

"Yes, things must be stepping up as she's on her way over now, so whatever is going on between Walker and the Sanchez family, it seems to be pretty big."

"Okay, let's catch up later. By the way, do you still think we're being watched?"

"Not by Pérez's team, but I think we may still have eyes on from the Sanchez lot. There's a car outside. They're not exactly subtle, it's a black Merc SUV with dark tinted windows. I'm pretty sure they haven't sent anyone in after us, so they won't know we've met you. But we need to shift them somehow without bringing more attention on us, so can you pick Anna and Holly up later?"

"Good idea," said Sam.

He left Greg and Theakston to walk out on their own and stayed back inside the terminal and looked out. As Greg had said. It wasn't the best surveillance vehicle to blend in and he saw it waiting across from the coach parking area.

*****

Alejandro Sanchez had gone to the airport after Pablo had reported the two men in Portixol had gone first to an apartment block and then on to the airport. He'd then left his driver and was now sat in Pablo's Mercedes.

"Do you want me to send someone inside the terminal Boss?"

"No, we'll wait here and see who they come out with. I don't like this Pablo. Who are they and what's their connection to the Walkers and this other guy Sutton?"

Pablo knew it was a rhetorical question. Sanchez often spoke out aloud and he knew better than to offer advice unless specifically asked. That wasn't how Alejandro, or in fact any of the Sanchez family operated.

He saw Alejandro shift in his passenger seat.

"Okay Pablo, this thing with the Walkers is too important to wait to see what these other guys are doing here. Get your team to move in and we'll pick one of them up, both if we can get them. Focus on the first one you saw, the one who followed Walker and Sutton from the airport. Give me five minutes to get clear."

Sanchez didn't wait for an answer. He was out of the car and walking back towards the multi-storey car park where his driver was waiting. There was no need for him to be anywhere close to the pick-up.

Sam Martínez saw the man leave the black SUV and after putting on a pair of sunglasses, the man had started walking towards the car park.

"What are you up to?" he said out aloud.

"¿Disculpe señor? Pardon me sir?"

Sam hadn't realised there was someone standing so close to him who must have heard him talking out loud. He quickly apologised in Mallorquin and said there was nothing to worry about and the man walked on by.

The Mercedes was still parked with just the driver in the vehicle. It looked like he was on the phone. It was probably nothing but he thought he should let Greg know what was going on, so he took his phone out to ring him. No service.

He could still see Greg and Tony and they were

almost in the car park, where Greg would have parked. He tried again. Three bars showing on his phone, so he pushed dial.

There was a ring tone, but Greg wasn't picking up and by now Sam couldn't see either of them.

'Maybe in the lift by now,' he thought.

Public parking started on the second floor, so they could be anywhere. Sam had that feeling in his stomach. The one he got when he just had a sense something bad was about to happen.

He tried ringing again and then he started to run towards the car park. He glanced across towards the Merc and that had gone too.

"Shit! Greg! Answer your bloody phone!"

Pablo already had two men waiting near to Greg's hire car that was parked on the fourth floor and he had four more on the way up the ramps in another Merc.

"Pablo, we're almost in position. You want both picked up?"

"If possible amigo, but go for the first guy we saw, okay?"

"Si, amigo, we're there now."

As the lift stopped at the fourth floor, Theakston stepped out first, to make room for a young couple with a pushchair. Greg held the lift door button on open as the man manoeuvred the pushchair through the lift doors and waited until the couple were clear of the lift before he got out.

"Gracias señor."

"¡De nade!" said Greg.

All of this didn't take long, but it was enough to distract Greg and he momentarily lost sight of Theakston who was already through the car park doors heading towards their car.

*****

Theakston thought Greg was just making room for

the young couple to get clear of the lift and that he was still behind him as he went out of the car park doors.

As he heard the doors close behind him, he turned to look back for Greg and so missed the black Merc as it pulled up alongside him.

"Señor?"

He heard the voice and looked back and saw a man in an SUV with the passenger window open.

"Si," said Theakston.

The man in the car lifted up a piece of paper and half showed it to Theakston, as though he needed some help. It was another distraction, enough to take any focus Theakston may have had about the situation and he missed the man who came up behind him until he felt something hard pushed into his back.

"In the car, now!"

He'd been around firearms enough in his police career to sense it was a handgun being pressed into him.

"Okay, okay."

Greg was only just coming through the car park door as he saw the Merc accelerate hard, tyres screeching as they bit for traction.

"Tony? Tony!"

His phone rang.

"Greg, where are you?"

Sam. No pleasantries and he was breathing hard too.

'Was he running?'

"Fourth floor."

"Be careful, the Merc has moved."

"I know, I think they've got Tony."

"Shit!"

Sam lost contact again. He hadn't bothered with the lift but had run up to the second floor, the first floor for public parking, but he was now back in the stairwell and running hard up the stairs.

Greg started towards his car that was parked close to the car park doors. He was now on edge, his senses picking up on his surroundings. If they'd taken Tony they'd know about him too. A quick glance around showed no other cars approaching. He got to the car, a blue Ford Kuga and clicked the door switch, opening the central locking.

"Señor, we'd like you to come with us and join your friend."

Greg calmly turned and saw a man standing about ten feet away. He was tall, well-built and was wearing a jacket with pockets. He had his hand in the right pocket.

'Gun, knife?'

Greg thought there must be another one near-by and then he saw the shadow. A second man, about fifteen foot to his left, partially hidden by a pillar.

"We just want to talk Señor, that's all, so please come with us?" said the first man.

"Or what?" said Greg.

He hoped Sam was getting close because he couldn't take on these two alone. Besides, if it was a gun, he wouldn't get anywhere near to him, although the fact they hadn't shot him straight away suggested they wanted information.

"Or I will shoot you Señor," said the first man, taking out a hand pistol from his pocket."

"What? Here? They'll have CCTV amigo and your car would have been recorded coming in here. Maybe you haven't got your tactics right today?"

Greg saw the hesitation from the man. It wasn't much, but just enough for someone with his experience to recognise he had got the guy thinking. He'd presumably thought this would be an easy lift and hadn't planned for contingencies.

'Sloppy.'

Another shadow. Greg caught just a slight movement, but the second man missed it.

'*Sloppy again.*'

29

As Sam got to the fourth floor stairwell, he paused for just a moment, he needed to get his breath back. No use going out there puffing and panting into whatever he might find.

A quick, but careful glance out of one of the car park doors and he saw a young couple with a pushchair loading up their car. He went to the other side of the lobby area and looked through that door. He could see Greg in the middle of the driveway. He was standing still, but the way he was standing suggested there was a problem.

He seemed to be talking to someone, although it looked like the person was somewhere just ahead of him. If he was in trouble, then Sam reckoned there would be at least two of them. He made a calculated guess. The other one had to be to Greg's left. He doubled back and went out through the other doors and worked his way around the lift block and slowly back towards where he'd seen Greg.

He saw the second man almost immediately. He wasn't trying to hide as such, but he was beside a pillar. Maybe a good ploy to not show out to Greg, but it put the man at an immediate disadvantage as he wouldn't be able to see Sam approaching him.

Breathing slowly now, Sam eased his way between the row of cars. There was still a fair amount of noise both from other cars on the floor, as well as the wind that was blowing in through the open walled car park.

This wasn't a time to ask questions. Sam got within a yard before the man sensed him and went to half turn, but he wasn't quick enough to react to Sam's headlock.

"Hey amigo! How about we call this a draw and you back away and I release your friend here?" Sam spoken in Spanish.

The man with the gun looked confused for a moment.

"Stay out of this. This has nothing to do with you amigo. You don't know who you're dealing with?"

The gunman replied in Spanish and seeing more people coming out of the car park doors he put his gun back in his pocket, but it was still clearly pointing at Greg.

"Oh, but you see, I do," said Sam. "Now, yes, you have a gun, but I have your partner here and we're getting a bit of an audience aren't we? So how do you think your boss, Señor Sanchez, would react to you being seen to commit a murder and losing this guy with me?"

More hesitation from the gunman, but the man who Sam had in a hold seemed calm and almost unfazed.

"Pa..‚ the gunman started to say, but the second man cut him off.

"Phone the boss. He'll know what to do."

Again the gunman hesitated. Greg saw it instantly and quickly ran to his right, away from the gunman's line of fire, to safety behind a pillar.

Sam started shouting at the people by the car park doors to get back inside the lift block and wait there. He saw uncertainty and confusion, before shouting again, in Mallorquin this time.

"Señor, we have a stand-off. Do as your friend here says. Tell your boss he can have his man back if we get Tony Theakston back to us unhurt within the hour."

"You said you'd release my partner."

"Yes, but that was when you had a gun on my friend amigo and now you clearly don't."

The man Sam had in the headlock had been passive until then, but he made his move to try to wrench himself free. But with a firm twist of his forearm, Sam applied more pressure on the man's neck that quickly forced him to start patting Sam's arm in submission.

Sam knew this was a critical and dangerous point as he could see the gunman was now well and truly unsettled. Clearly, this wasn't how the man had expected things to go. He was now faced with backing down and then having to explain things to his boss, who wasn't likely to be happy with the outcome.

"Ring your boss amigo and I suggest you do it quickly, because one of those people out there could have called the police by now."

*****

"Boss, it's Pepe, I have a situation in the car park."

"What do you mean a situation? You were just supposed to pick up the second man," said Alejandro Sanchez.

"I did Boss, I did, but someone else arrived and they've got..," Pepe went to say one thing and then changed his mind, "one of our guys."

"Who is it Pepe?"

"It's Pablo Boss," the first name that came into Pepe's head.

"Pablo? He's with me."

"No, Boss, I mean the other Pablo."

Alejandro went to question Pepe again before he realised what was going on. *'Shit!'* Diego must have got involved and now they'd somehow taken him!

"Ah, that Pablo. Okay Pepe, I understand."

'Damn.'

It had been a mistake not to send someone in as Pablo had suggested.

Alejandro swore again.

"Boss?"

"Shut up Pepe."

"Si, Señor."

"Is there an audience Pepe?"

"Si, Señor. People are coming back to their cars."

"Presumably they want their friend back?"

"Yes, Boss," he paused. "Unharmed, within the hour."

Alejandro couldn't help but laugh. They'd hardly want him back dead.

Pablo heard his boss laugh.

"I'm sorry Boss."

"Yes, yes, we'll deal with all that later. Ask your new friends to move to somewhere a little less conspicuous and they will have their friend back in an hour in exchange for our 'Pablo'."

Pepe nodded and turned to Sam.

"Señor, my boss says we should move to somewhere less conspicuous for the exchange. He'll bring your friend back in an hour, unharmed."

Greg had been trying to follow what was being said between Sam and the gunman.

"Sam?"

"His Boss has asked us to move somewhere without an audience and they'll do the exchange within the hour."

Greg thought for a moment.

"Okay, tell them we'll meet them on the front at Ciutat Jardi. No cars. On foot right by the seafront, where you took us for coffee the other day and Sam, tell them a maximum two people."

Sam knew Greg must have done many of these types of exchanges over the years, as it sounded like he was reciting a well-rehearsed plan.

"I understand what you just said Señor," said Pepe and re-stated the conditions into his phone to Alejandro.

"Tell them I agree Pepe. Now is Pablo okay?"

"Si, Boss. Although he looks mad."

"I bet he is Pepe. Tell him not to kick off and now get the hell out of there and quickly."

"Si, Boss."

He took his hand out of his pocket and started walking away.

"My boss agrees to your conditions. Pablo, go with them and the Boss says don't kick up. We'll get you back in an hour. Okay?"

The man Sam had in the arm lock seemed to snarl, more than acknowledge Pablo, but Sam felt the man stop any sort of resistance and after a moment to check he wasn't likely to try to jump him, Sam released Pablo from the head lock before taking firm hold of his arm.

"If you try anything Pablo, I will break your arm, do you understand?" Sam tweaked the man's arm just sufficiently to make it quite clear what would happen.

"No problemo Señor. I have my orders. There will be no trouble."

The man seemed to spit the word *'orders'* out.

"Bueno. Okay Greg, let's go."

*****

Alejandro stood for a moment. This hadn't gone well and having to now hand the guy back was definitely not part of the plan. One small piece of luck was that the man didn't know they were about to hand him back.

He looked down at the man sitting on a chair before him. He was in his fifties and looked like he had been sat behind a desk for too long and had lost any sort of athletic build he might have had as a younger man.

"Okay Señor, now you have already caused me a certain amount of inconvenience. I simply have just a few questions to ask you to which I'd appreciate answers. And one thing Señor, please do not try to be brave and hold anything back."

Tony Theakston looked back at the man in front of him. He wondered if he was one of the Sanchez family. Not the father, as he wasn't old enough, but he could be one of the sons Greg had told him about, Alejandro or Diego. If he was, that might not be a good thing as once the questions finished, they might not have any need to keep him alive.

He was in some sort of garage lock-up. The man asking him questions had turned up not long after they'd got there. He seemed to be the one with the authority, whereas there was a guy standing almost behind him who seemed to have muscles coming out of every inch of his body.

It had been a long time since he'd been an operational police officer, but he'd not lost any of the courage he'd had as a young recruit when he'd first been called on to act to protect others.

Alejandro sensed the man before him wasn't afraid. Maybe he could have made him if he'd had more time, but he didn't.

"Señor, this needn't be combative. We saw you leave the airport and follow our little convoy into Portixol. Yes?"

Theakston had been thinking as the man had been talking. He was wresting with whether to cooperate, or try to hold out. But hold out for what and for why? This wasn't a situation where he needed to protect informants and he couldn't see there were any life and death issues linked to this, except perhaps his own.

"Yes, that's right."

"Why did you follow our convoy Señor….?"

The man waited for Tony to provide his name.

"It's Theakston, Tony Theakston."

"Gracias Tony. And the convoy? What's your interest in us?"

"I have no interest in you Señor and nor in Frankie Walker."

"So you know who Frankie Walker is?"

"I should do, I've tried to lock him up often enough," Theakston almost laughed.

"So you're a policeman?"

Sanchez was trying to maintain his calm, but if this guy was a British police officer then it would bring a whole lot more problems.

"Retired Señor Sanchez. It is Sanchez isn't it?"

Tony was feeling emboldened, but soon regretted his decision to go beyond simply answering Sanchez's questions."

"You might think you're clever Theakston, but do not, I repeat, do not try to be clever with me. Answer my questions and I will ensure you are not harmed whilst you are here."

He felt like he'd been told off and by a younger man. He remembered the first time his boss was younger than he was. She was a Commander and in the Met, this was equivalent to an Assistant Chief Constable in a non-metropolitan force. It wasn't the fact his boss was a woman, far from it in fact as he'd always supported and encouraged the women in his teams. And anyway, she was good, bloody good. No, it was because she was younger than he was and not just by a bit, but by almost twenty years.

It also didn't matter whether his boss was right or wrong. But the age thing just seemed to be so out of kilter to him. He'd been used to a society where your teachers were always older than you, but this was a time of rapid promotion within policing and he'd had to accept it or move on.

He'd accepted it, but now he wondered why this particular memory had come back now? When an OCG boss was quizzing him on what he was doing on Mallorca. He smiled.

"Why are you smiling Señor?" asked Alejandro. "Do you find this funny?"

The Englishman was beginning to annoy Sanchez. Maybe he'd forget the exchange and just have this idiot dumped in the flood channels running down from the hills into Palma.

Sanchez's change of tone snapped Theakston's attention back into play.

"No, I'm sorry. I just realised you are quite young to be at the head of an organisation. It reminded me of my old organisation."

Sanchez's voice softened.

"Was that the Met Tony? But you say you're retired now?"

"Yes, to both of those Señor."

Whilst Theakston had decided there seemed to be little point in holding back that he had no interest in Sanchez or Walker, he wasn't sure about what to say about Sutton.

"Señor, I find myself in a difficult position. I have told you I have no interest in anything you or Frankie Walker may be involved in, however, the reason for looking at Jake Sutton is confidential, but I can assure you that it has nothing to do with you or Walker."

Sanchez looked at the man. He'd seen the look on other men's faces after he had broken them. It was something in the eyes, when honesty came to the forefront of a man, or woman's thinking.

"Hmm, Señor, I think I believe you about my family

and Walker, but I wish there was something else you could tell me to persuade me about your interest in Sutton."

He didn't wait for Theakston to answer, but nodded at the man standing next to Theakston. Without hesitation, the man punched Tony hard in the kidneys, taking the wind right out of him.

"What happened to the bit where I wouldn't get hurt," said Theakston forcing the words out through gritted teeth as he tried to recover.

"Oh, that isn't getting hurt Tony, that's just a little, what do you say, a little tickle."

With that, the man hit Theakston again.

"So, why are looking at Sutton Señor? Please just answer my question."

Decision time. He'd had two warning shots across his bow and they'd bloody hurt, so he knew he wasn't going to stand up to any sort of beating. He also didn't think Adamsons would expect him to hold out against an OCG thug.

"Okay, okay, we think he might be involved in some sort of art theft."

"But he's a multi-millionaire businessman isn't he?"

"Well, so are you of a sorts, but it doesn't stop you getting involved in the dirty end of your business Señor."

Alejandro Sanchez smiled. The Englishman had a sense of humour.

"Okay, you see? That was all fairly simple. Now we can get you back to your friends."

Tony went to flinch in case that was some sort of code for another punch, but nothing happened. Instead the man who'd hit him grabbed him by the shoulders and shoved him up out of the seat and pushed him towards the lock up garage door. Another man there opened the door and he was pushed into the back of the Merc.

Sanchez got in and as he pulled his seat belt across he said, "Buckle up now Tony, we don't want you getting hurt on the way back do we?"

30

They drove in silence towards Ciutat Jardi, coming off the motorway at the hypermarket junction. Pablo was sat in the back with Sam whilst Greg drove.

"So Señor, you live on the island then?"

Sam recognised the man spoke with a Spanish, rather than a Mallorquin accent. Presumably he'd come across with the Sanchez outfit for whatever business they were doing with Frankie and Maggs Walker.

He wanted to ask Greg if he thought they should have spoken to Lori before arranging the exchange, but he wasn't sure how much English Pablo understood.

"I do, yes," answered Sam, but he decided against elaborating any further on his response.

"This should do here," said Greg," pointing a finger towards a parking space on the one way street on the sea front.

"Okay Señor, just sit where you are," said Sam.

"Of course," Pablo answered in English.

'Good decision,' thought Sam, 'not to start talking about Lori in front of this guy.'

Greg had got out and opened the rear passenger door to let Pablo out, when Sam tugged his arm back.

"No tricks Señor."

"I won't run away Señor, I promise."

He was laughing at them. He knew he was being exchanged, but Sam was getting a nagging feeling that something wasn't right.

'Why were they so quick to agree to getting this guy back?'

Just then Pablo's phone rang. Sam took it out of his pocket. The screen display said ALEJO.

"My boss, Señor," said Pablo. "Would you like to talk to him?"

Sam took the phone.

"Si."

"I can see you're on time Señor. This won't take a minute," said Alejandro, again in English. "We're walking towards you now. Just me and one other plus your friend Tony, just as you requested."

Sam had seen them. Tony had two men walking with him, one at each side. He went to give the phone back, but Pablo told him to keep it.

"In case you want to speak to my boss again."

Sam went to say something, but then saw the taller man next to Tony say something to him. Theakston nodded and then started walking towards Sam and Greg.

"Okay, go on, you can go too," said Sam.

"Muchas gracias Señor."

Pablo set off, but then turned and said, "I sense we may meet again amigo."

It wrong-footed Sam for a moment. Why would this guy think he'd see him again? He took out his phone and called out, "Hasta la vista amigo."

As Pablo turned, Sam took a picture.

"Bit of research?" said Greg.

"Something doesn't feel right, so I want to find out more about this Pablo."

Theakston had reached them and he breathed out a big sigh of relief.

"Greg, Sam, thank you and before you ask, I'm fine."

"No injuries?" said Greg.

"A couple of bruises, but nothing that won't mend quickly."

They turned and started walking back towards their car, when they suddenly heard a screech of tyres. Sam saw it first. It was one of the black Mercs. Whoever was driving must have done a quick lap of the one way street and come back down towards the seafront and was now heading at speed straight at them.

"Look out!" yelled Sam, pushing Greg to one side.

He heard a sickening thud and then saw Tony flung into the air as the driver deliberately drove in to Theakston.

"Tony!"

Sam ran to Theakston. He was still breathing, but his injuries looked serious.

"What the hell!"

Sam saw the Merc had stopped about thirty yards from them and the driver got out. Sam saw it was Pablo, the man they'd just exchanged, who had taken out a phone. Sam felt and then heard the phone in his pocket ring, the one Pablo had told him to keep just moments before.

"Just a little message Señor."

Sam recognised the voice.

"You bastard. The agreement was that he'd be brought back unharmed."

"And he was Señor, but that agreement ended the moment we did the exchange. Now stay out of business that doesn't concern you. Understand?"

Sam went to say something, but the phone had gone dead.

"Whoever that was Greg, he was no ordinary foot

soldier. I should have guessed."

"No, we should both have guessed. Why else would they agree to the exchange so quickly? Forget it Sam, we were turned over. Now we need to get Tony to hospital."

Sam was already dialling 061, the Spanish emergency number for an ambulance.

"Stay with us Tony mate, the ambulance is on its way," said Greg.

He'd not known Theakston long, but Greg felt a responsibility for him, particularly after what he'd said to Holly Regus.

"Come on, let's get you comfortable."

Theakston was just about conscious and they made him as comfortable as they could, without risking moving him too much in case he had any neck injuries.

The ambulance was with them within ten minutes and the paramedic sedated Tony, to give him some relief from the pain. After checking which hospital they were taking him to, Sam rang Simon.

"Sam, what's up?"

"We've had a problem with the Sanchez's mate and they may know where Terri lives, so …."

"Okay. Understood," interrupted Simon. "Where are you now and what do you need?"

"Ciutat Jardi. They've done a hit and run on Tony. He's breathing, but it was a hell of an impact. We'll be back with you shortly, but a quick check of the outside of the apartment would be helpful."

"I'm on it. Shall I tell Terri?"

"You tell me as I think you're best placed to make that call."

Simon looked down at Terri, who was sitting on the sofa with her Mum. She was looking at him and he knew that look.

"I'll tell her."

"Tell me what?"

Sam heard Terri ask question.

"I'll leave you to it. See you soon."

*****

"Something's happened to Tony Theakston. He's been in some sort of hit and run," said Simon.

She'd been making really good progress on her fitness, but she'd not got involved in any 3R business so far, so Simon wasn't sure how switched on she'd be.

She looked at him. "Perimeter check?"

He smiled.

"Why are you smiling?" asked Terri.

"Nothing."

"You were wondering how sharp I'd be Simon Barnes! Go on, admit it."

"Maybe."

He kissed her on her forehead.

"Perimeter check it is then Boss. I'll be back in a few minutes. Greg and Sam are on their way from Ciutat Jardi. Tony's breathing, but it was a big hit."

In just a few sentences he'd briefed her and she was up and heading for her bedroom.

Josie was still sat on the sofa, trying to take in the conversation she'd just heard. She knew Greg and Terri operated in a high risk business, but she was rarely exposed to this level of detail.

Terri came back into the lounge. She'd changed into a pair of casual trousers and a top from the gym kit she'd been wearing. She saw the look on her mother's face and sat down beside her.

"It's okay Mum. This is just what we do."

"But that poor man, Tony?"

"Dad and Sam will have made sure he's okay and he'll be on the way to hospital now."

"Where's Simon gone?"

"He's just going to check the outside of the

apartment. To make sure we don't have any unwanted attention."

Terri tried to talk in as calm a voice as she could, but she was also conscious of how she was feeling. She felt excited. For the first time since, she'd woken up from the medically induced coma, she felt like her old self.

"You're smiling?" said Josie.

"I know Mum and I don't really know why. Maybe it's another corner I've just turned. But now I need to go to work. I'll still be here, but I need to put some calls in, is that okay with you?"

Josie saw her daughter's face. It was bright and alive with colour. She smiled back at Terri.

"Get to work then girl."

*****

Greg saw his daughter's name appear on his mobile screen.

"Hello, how are you?"

"Good, honestly I'm good. Simon's briefed me. Where are you now?"

"Approaching Portixol. Anything from Simon?"

"No, he's just gone out and about. He'll call you if he has anything to tell you."

He could hear it in her voice. She was great in these situations. Calm, professional and decisive. He could almost sense her strength surging back through her body as the adrenalin kicked in.

"Good to have you back my girl."

"Glad to be back Dad, but not at Tony's expense. How did he look?"

"Not great to be honest Terri. It was a hell of a hit. It was the guy we were exchanging. He was driving. He's clearly no foot soldier and we missed that."

She heard the concern in his voice.

"Dad, let it go for the minute and focus on the here and now."

He smiled as he heard her coaching him. It reminded him of the things Anna used to say to him when he was going through his undercover training.

"Yes, you're right."

"Dad, just a thought. Do we need to think about giving Tony some protection? I'm just thinking, might they go back if they want him silenced completely?"

"Good point. I must admit I think Sam and I thought it was just a message and it wasn't a deliberate attempt to kill him. I think they'd have just shot him otherwise."

"Fair point. What about Lori?"

"You ask the most difficult questions daughter of mine."

"She'll find out as I guess there were people around weren't there?"

"Yes, a few, but whether anyone will want to get involved I don't know, but you're right, I shouldn't bank on the fact that she won't find out and better I tell her before someone else does."

31

Jake Sutton finished his call with Jeannie and sat back on the bed in his hotel room. She said it had just been a catch up, but he knew she was checking up on him. His outburst towards her had been so out of character it would have stood out a mile. He cursed himself for letting his emotions run away with him.

One set back. That's all it was. Adamsons had got lucky in Singapore, but he wouldn't make the same mistake again. He'd scope the layout at the gallery in Sóller the following day.

He was thinking some more about his next attack on Adamsons when he saw the text from Frankie Walker.

'Fancy some dinner? Just me and you?'

He didn't have any other plans, although he didn't fancy a long night out, so he texted back.

'Yes, 8pm my hotel?'

Walker immediately responded and just after eight he walked into the bar at the Hotel Portixol. Sutton stood up and greeted him with a warm handshake that Walker quickly changed to a bear hug.

Jake had wondered if there was anything more to the dinner than merely two people with a connection from the past meeting up. It wasn't. Frankie explained that Maggs had wanted the kids to have an early night and she was happy with some supper in their hotel room.

Frankie had been genuinely pleased to see Jake after so many years and wanted a catch up, although there wasn't perhaps a lot of detail he could go into about his own line of business, but he was really interested to hear about Jake's success.

It was still warm enough even in October to sit outside on the Portixol terrace and Jake had the view of La Seu, Palma's beautiful Gothic cathedral that lit up the city's skyline.

"So Jake, how did you go from a sometime teenager burglar to multi-millionaire security industry giant my friend?"

Jake thought about Frankie's choice of word. 'Friend.' Had they ever actually been friends? He'd thought of their relationship as more of a service agreement, or was that just his business-speak that he'd become accustomed to?

He'd taught Frankie to read and write whilst they were in Feltham and in exchange Frankie had kept Jake safe from bullying and worse still from some of the more predatory inmates. He'd be forever grateful for that, but once he'd left Feltham Jake soon lost contact with his protector, because that was more the term he would have used.

"Jake, are you listening mate? I asked you how you became the big 'I am' in the security world?"

"Sorry Frankie, I was thinking back to, well you know when, when we met. You made it bearable for me Frankie. I'm not sure I could have survived, at least not unscathed, without your help."

"Unscathed, well we are posh now aren't we? More like you weren't buggered senseless!"

"Quite," Jake smiled awkwardly.

"Anyway, nothing to thank me for Jake. You gave me a gift I'd chosen to ignore as I was growing up. By the time I came out of Feltham you had me reading bloody Shakespeare!"

He heard Frankie's belly laugh and grinned back at him.

"Yes, you were! But to answer your question, I've been fortunate and also very lucky. Right place, right time for the ideas I had around a new type of security system and it took off. Add in some amazing supporters and the business has gone from strength to strength. What about you Frankie? Still in the same line?"

Another belly laugh.

"Yes, you could say that, although we've now expanded into the import side of things as well."

Walker gave him a wink and it didn't take much thinking by Jake to realise Frankie was talking about the drug trade.

"High risk, but presumably high reward Frankie?"

Walker responded with just a small smile, but it was enough to give Jake the answer to his question. The conversation moved into more general topics and continued easily throughout the meal. When they'd finished Jake sat back, a little surprised that he'd enjoyed Frankie's company quite as much as he had.

"What's up Jake?"

"I was just thinking how much I've enjoyed seeing you again."

"Surprised that you could still relate to a gangster are we?" said Frankie with a wink, as he looked at Jake over the top of his brandy glass.

"That's not what I meant," said Jake, a little flustered.

"Sure?"

"Well, maybe, just a bit. But it's been a while Frankie

and to be honest, I'm not sure I knew what to expect."

"Well I don't go around putting people in concrete coffins all the time you know."

"I know, I know…"

"Just some of the time," interrupted Frankie.

Jake wasn't sure if he was joking or not, but even with Frankie grinning at him across the table he thought there was still probably a modicum of truth in Frankie's last comment.

"So what about these Sanchez people? Sure you can trust them?"

"Bloody good question my friend and to be honest, I don't know. Maggs thinks we can and she spent a lot of time setting up the deal whilst I was, well otherwise engaged."

Jake had got the message that Frankie had been inside for the past year, but he hadn't said why and neither had Jake asked him. He knew he could Google it if he wanted to know, but why did he need to know? Would it make it any better or worse knowing what Frankie had been getting up to recently? Probably not.

"So you're really over here on a working holiday then? That's why you brought the kids with you?"

"Yep, mind you, we had thought Mallorca was going to be neutral ground until we discovered the Sanchezes have already got a place over here."

Jake noted how Frankie said Mallorca, pronouncing it 'Ma-your-ca.' He smiled. Tough, violent criminal this man may be, but he'd come some way from the young thug he'd first met in Feltham who could barely string two words together before he'd hit someone.

32

Lori Garcia stood on the escalator as it took her and Sergeant Nino Ruiz down the slope towards the baggage collection area.

Rather than turning left at the bottom of the slope to go towards the baggage collection area, they walked straight on towards a side door where a uniformed police officer was standing. Garcia showed her badge.

"Inspectora, welcome back to the island."

"Gracias."

She smiled and walked through the Personal Autorizado door and out into the evening air. Although it was now well into October, it was still reasonably warm given it was just gone eight o'clock.

Outside the door that the police used to exit the Palma de Mallorca terminal Detective Constable Juan Moriarty was waiting by a car, an unmarked blue BMW M4,

"Buenas noches Inspectora," said Moriarty.

"Hola Cecil," said Garcia. "Glad you brought the car tonight."

Juan 'Cecil' Moriarty grinned. He was the surveillance team's motorcyclist and was usually seen astride an assortment of high powered bikes that when called upon, would see him flying through the traffic to create spaces for the following surveillance cars, sometimes almost throwing his bike down onto the tarmac to bring the oncoming traffic to a stop.

Surveillance driving was a risky business at the best of the times and it was widely acknowledged, across all of the policing agencies, that the surveillance motorcyclists were all just a little bit mad to do what they did.

Known by his nickname from the time he joined the unit five years ago, 'Cecil' Moriarty's name came from a former Chief Constable of Birmingham, Cecil Moriarty, who wrote many of the police training books during the 1950's, rather than from what some thought, which was perhaps the more well-known fictional character from Sir Arthur Conan Doyle's Sherlock Holmes stories.

"Is Pérez still on his boat Cecil?" asked Nino.

"Think so Sarge, but he might have moved as he asked me to get the boss to ring him as soon as she could."

"Things been happening then?" asked DI Garcia.

"Si, there's been movement with the 3R guys, but we couldn't cover them and watch Walker and Sutton."

"Okay," she went to call Greg when her phone buzzed.

"Talk of the devil," she said, as she answered her phone. "Hello, I was just hearing something about you?"

"Hello my darling," said Greg.

"Do I want to hear what you're about to tell me?"

Greg paused. Perhaps she hadn't heard the detail yet, so at least he could get his excuses in early for once.

"I'll let you be the judge of that, but let me just say, we didn't start this."

"Start what? And please don't tell me Greg that you've got involved with the Sanchez family."

Silence.

"You'd better tell me what's happened."

"Okay, but like I said, we didn't start this. They took one of our guys, Tony Theakston."

"I'm listening."

"We'd gone to meet Sam at the airport and they were waiting for us in the car park, the multi-storey. They tried to get me as well, but Sam managed to get in behind them and we got one of their guys."

"Hang on, what do you mean, you got one of theirs? Have you still got him?"

"Like I said, we grabbed one of theirs and then they rang to do an exchange."

By now she was shaking her head.

"Greg, I specifically told you not to get involved with this outfit."

"I know and we weren't engaging with them, honestly. They came for us, although I don't know why. Anyway Theakston is now in hospital, unconscious."

"What do you mean he's unconscious? What the hell happened? I thought you said you were going to do an exchange?"

"And we did, down at Ciutat Jardi, out in the open. But then the guy we exchanged jumped in one their cars and swung around the block and came back and drove straight at us. Sam pushed me out the way, but the car hit Tony and threw him up over the bonnet."

Nino could tell something had happened. He motioned to Cecil to head off and mouthed 'Headquarters' to him.

"How is he?"

He heard her voice soften. Whatever she thought he may, or may not have done to get in the way of the Sanchez investigation, she had immediately switched her concern to Theakston.

"He's badly hurt. It's his right leg and pelvis. They're

operating at the moment, so we'll know more later. Look we got a picture of the guy we exchanged. We thought he was a foot soldier. His mate called him Pablo. I'm sending it now."

He heard the ping as it arrived on her phone.

"We think he may be something more than just a foot soldier, otherwise why would they be so quick to exchange him?"

Lori took one look at the picture on her phone.

"He's not called Pablo, Greg. This is Diego Sanchez, youngest son of Alberto Sanchez."

"Oh shit!"

"Yes, you can say that again. All of them are vicious thugs Greg, but Diego has a mad streak in him. You're damn lucky he didn't get you and Sam too!"

"No bloody wonder they did the exchange so quickly. I was so keen to get Tony back I missed the fact he was more than just a foot soldier."

Greg turned to Sam.

"Did you get that? Pablo was Diego Sanchez!"

"It wasn't Pablo then. The other one was going to call him Patrón, that's another Spanish word for Boss! I didn't think of it at the time as I'd normally use el jefe," said Sam.

"Lori, I'm sorry, if we'd have known it was Diego I'd have told you immediately."

"It's done, don't worry about it."

But Greg could tell from her tone that she was disappointed. Or was it just frustration? Having Diego as a principal offender in a kidnapping would have given Lori a lot of leverage with the Sanchez family.

"Where are you now Greg?" asked Lori.

"On our way to Terri's place."

"Okay, I'll ring you back after I've checked in with Pérez."

He heard her pause.

"And Greg?" she said slowly.

"Yes?"

"Please take care. These guys will not hesitate to use extreme violence if they need to."

He got the message loud and clear. Perhaps he'd underestimated them, something he wouldn't do again.

"I get that. Probably best I cancel dinner?"

"Yes, too much going on I think."

She was in her full-on professional mode. He knew there must be a lot riding on this investigation and he, or rather Tony Theakston had somehow managed to become entangled in whatever was going on between Frankie Walker and the Sanchez family.

"Greg?" she said.

"Yes?"

"I'll call you later."

He smiled. She'd lost the police speak voice.

"I look forward to that."

33

Simon Barnes slipped out of one of the back doors of Terri's apartment block in Portixol. From the outside it was difficult to tell that it was a door and Terri had told him that she'd only found it by chance when she was having a good look around the maintenance corridors within the block after she'd bought her apartment.

He doubled around the front of the building that looked out on to the Portixol marina. He saw him straight away. It had to be one of Sanchez's men. Standing by a lamppost, it was as though he was making no effort to hide his presence. Maybe it was because after the exchange to get Theakston back there was no need for any pretence.

Keeping to the shadows, Simon moved further around the block looking for anyone else who may have eyes on Terri's flat. Greg had told him that Lori had one of her surveillance teams in the area looking primarily at Jake Sutton, but after ten minutes of circling the area he'd still only identified the one Sanchez guy.

He was in two minds as to whether to tackle him, when he heard a voice nearby.

"Señor, do you have a light?"

The voice had come from just behind him. Simon

didn't think anybody could see him, but whoever it was would also be out of sight of the Sanchez man.

"Don't worry amigo. I'm a friend, but I'd appreciate it, as would my boss, DI Garcia, if you didn't do anything to interfere with the Sanchez lookout over there."

"Do you have a name friend?" asked Simon.

"Pérez, Fernando Pérez."

Simon had heard a lot about this guy. Tommy really rated him, as did Sam. He'd been the one who had taken the shot on one of the Armenians who'd kidnapped Anna.

"Pleasure to meet you. What would you like me to do amigo?"

"Just ease back into the building and can you call Señor Chambers and let him know not to take any action too?"

"Of course."

Simon had missed Pérez coming up behind him. Maybe he was slowing down? He'd been out of the Regiment for a good few years now and working in the private security industry was nothing like living on the edge, as it had been during his time in the SAS.

It was still no excuse that he'd missed Pérez and it was a bloody good job he was a *'friendly.'* Two minutes later he'd made his way down into the underground car park before accessing the residents' lift back up to the third floor to Terri's apartment.

"Everything okay down there?" said Terri, seeing a strange look on his face.

"Yes and no. I saw the Sanchez guy who's watching us, but I missed one of Lori's men, Pérez."

She saw the look on his face. Disappointment, or was it maybe concern?

"He's good hun, so don't take it to heart."

"I know he's good, but I should've been better. How

can I….?"

"If you're about to say 'protect me', then don't, alright?" she snapped.

He looked across at her. She wasn't happy and he knew why. He'd promised himself he wouldn't get like this, all protective of her.

"I'm sorry. It's just…."

"Look, I get it and in a way I love you for it, but don't you dare go smothering me."

She laughed and hugged him and he knew she'd already forgiven him.

"I won't."

She looked at him again, with eyebrows raised.

"I promise," he said.

She laughed again and he smiled back at her.

"Look, I should ring Greg. Last thing we want is for him or Sam to take a poke at the Sanchez guy after I've just been warned off."

*****

"Fernando, what's happening?"

"Welcome back to Mallorca Boss. I've just intercepted one of the 3R people, Simon, the ex-SAS guy."

She could feel the tension rising in her hands.

"What was he doing, or about to do?"

"Well to be fair, maybe nothing. But he'd clocked the Sanchez lookout, although in fairness, the guy was making no effort to hide the fact he was keeping a lookout on Señor Chambers's daughter's place."

"So you had no problem with him, Simon, I mean?"

"No, no, none at all. He's gone back inside and said he'd ring Greg to let him know about the lookout."

"Good. Now what about Walker and Sutton?"

"Both still in the hotel, presumably enjoying their dinner. I'll get a couple of the team to watch Walker, to make sure he goes back to his hotel and I'll keep an eye on Sutton in case he decides to go out and about."

"Good work Fernando."

"Gracias Inspectora," he grinned.

*****

"Greg, are you still on your way in?"

"Yes Simon. Any problems?"

"We've got a Sanchez guy on lookout duty. He's not trying to hide the fact he's watching us, so you should spot him straight away. He's across the road at about three o'clock to the front of the apartment."

"Okay, we'll keep an eye out."

"Greg, I got tagged by Pérez. He spotted me when I was out looking at the Sanchez guy."

"He warned you off?"

"Oh yes, very much so. Told me to ring you."

"Fair enough. We don't know what we've wandered into, but Lori's over here now too, so whatever it is she doesn't want us anywhere near it."

"But what about Theakston? Are you going to leave that with Lori too?"

"I'm not sure it's high on her priorities. Don't get me wrong, if she gets a chance she'll use it as leverage against Diego Sanchez, that's for sure, but she has bigger things on her agenda than poor old Tony getting run down by that maniac."

"What are you thinking then Greg? No harm in parking it for the moment. We can always go back to it when Lori has finished."

Greg thought for a moment. Simon had a point. They didn't need to go rushing in for some sort of retribution against Sanchez for what he'd done to Theakston. And anyway, what exactly was he going to do with Sanchez? The police were investigating the family and this was a police matter, so yes, he'd leave it with Lori and then go back to it if and when he needed to.

"That's a sound idea Simon. We'll park it as you suggest and leave it with Lori. That way she's happy and we can focus on Sutton and making sure Adamsons don't lose another ten million quid."

Greg had just turned off the main road and onto the Portixol marina road. He saw a man standing on the right side of the road, as Simon had described and looked across at Sam, who nodded to him that he'd seen him too. A minute later he was parking up in the underground car park of Terri's apartment block.

*****

"Okay, I should get back to Maggs amigo," said Frankie Walker. "And mate, I really enjoyed tonight."

"Me too," said Jake Sutton.

He still wasn't sure why he was surprised. Perhaps it was because he hadn't necessarily expected to enjoy spending time with Frankie. Maybe he was afraid it would rekindle memories of Feltham that he'd long ago hidden away.

As he walked Frankie out to his taxi that was waiting at the hotel entrance, Walker looked up and saw a plane in the sky over the Bay of Palma making its way in towards the airport.

"More touristicos coming in on the late flight Jake. All coming for a bit of this island paradise."

Jake smiled back at him.

"You're a bit of a romantic at heart aren't you Frankie?"

"I am mate, but if you tell anyone, I might just have to kill you," grinned Walker.

He'd said it with a smile, but Jake couldn't help but feel a slight chill across the back of his neck. As much as Walker had been good company during the evening, he was still someone who lived in a very different world to his, one that was dominated by crime and drugs and where violence and even death was never far away.

"Give my best to Maggs."

"Will do Jake. Now if we don't catch up again on the island, let's do something back in London? And quiet-like. I know you have a reputation now, as a big shot entrepreneur, so you won't want the pictures of us two partying spread across the tabloids."

Again Frankie was grinning, but Jake took it as a genuine effort for them to see each other again, without perhaps causing him any organisational damage if he was seen to be connected to be a major London criminal.

"I'd like that Frankie."

He waved him off and looked across the marina at the boats, some with their evening lights on. It was a still night and there weren't many people about. He was drawn to someone who was standing under a street light just across the marina. They were about a couple of hundred yards away, on the opposite side of the road to an apartment block. He was just standing there.

"Funny place to stand," he said out aloud, before walking back inside and making his way to his room.

34

The Airbus A320-200 touched gently down onto the tarmac at Aeroport de Son Sant Joan, Palma de Mallorca. Anna changed her watch, adding on the hour for the Central European Time zone. It was just past 9pm.

She checked her phone. There was a message from Greg.

'Tony's been injured. Need to see you so I can tell Holly. Ring asap.'

"Problem?" said Holly.

Anna hadn't realised her face had given something away to Holly.

"Greg wants me to call that's all."

As soon as she got through border control, she rang him. He picked up almost as soon as the dialling tone started.

"You get in all okay?" he asked.

"Yes, the flight was pretty quiet and so we got through the border control checks quite quickly."

Anna turned her head away from Holly and lowered her voice.

"What's happened?"

"The Sanchez family tried to pick me and Tony up after we'd come to collect Sam. They got Tony, but they missed the fact Sam was about and we ended up getting one of theirs, who we then exchanged."

"But you said there was more?"

"Yes, the one we'd exchanged Tony for turned out to be Diego Sanchez and it seems he has a particularly vindictive side to him. As soon as we did the exchange, he jumped in a car and came around the block like a bat out of hell and mowed Tony down. He's in hospital and he's stable, but he's taken a hard hit to his lower body, especially his right leg."

"I see," said Anna calmly, "so do you want to come now to explain things, or shall I take care of it?"

Greg thought for a moment. Anna could easily cope with telling Holly, but he'd wanted to do it personally. That said, he didn't want this left hanging in the air.

"Maybe it's best you tell her now, sooner rather than delaying it just for me to get down there. I'll head for the airport and see you in about ten when I can fill in any of the blanks for you both."

"Greg, with all this interest the Sanchez lot are showing in you, do you think it might not be a bad idea if I keep a low profile, just for now?"

He didn't need to think for too long before he replied.

"Good job one of us is still on the ball Anna. That's a bloody good idea. Tell Holly I'll come and pick her up. She'll probably want to go to the hospital anyway, won't she?"

"Yes, I think you're right. I'll get a cab home and we can talk later."

Anna turned to Holly who was now standing in front of her as they went down the travel escalator. She waited until they'd both stepped off the escalator, before she gently touched Holly's arm.

"Holly, Greg's coming to meet us. But he's got some bad news. Tony's been injured in a hit and run.

He's been taken to hospital and they've stabilised his condition."

She saw Holly taking in the information and trying to digest it.

"But Greg said he'd take care of him. To make sure he didn't get into any more trouble."

"I know, but it seems that the Sanchez family had other ideas. They grabbed Tony at the airport and tried to get Greg too, but they seem to have missed the fact that Sam was there and he somehow managed to stop them grabbing Greg as well."

"Is he okay? Tony I mean?" Holly's voice faltered.

"Greg said he's stable, although Tony's right leg was badly injured in the collision."

She could see Holly's shoulders had dropped, as though the stuffing had been knocked out of her.

"I know it's a shock Holly, but Greg will take you straight to the hospital. Now, I'm going to just wait back here for a moment. Don't worry, we're just taking extra precautions by not showing all our cards at once. You go with Greg and I'll make my own way home."

"You think they may be watching us?"

"Maybe, but probably not, but there's no need to take unnecessary chances if we don't need to. Now off you go and see how Tony is doing. And Holly?"

Holly turned to look at her.

"Tony's a tough old cop, so he'll be fighting hard to get through this."

"I know."

Holly forced a smile that quickly turned to a frown.

"But they can't get away with this, can they? This Sanchez gang?"

"One way or another, we'll make sure that whoever was responsible for this won't get away with it Holly. Now come on, let's get you through the Arrivals door and see if Greg is there yet."

It was just a few minutes' walk from the bottom of the escalator to the Arrivals exit at Gate C.

Anna watched as Holly walked tentatively through the doors. The young woman she had first met in the PRI offices had taken quite a knock to her confidence, which Anna knew she'd need to quickly get back if she was going to front up Jake Sutton in the next day or so.

Greg saw Anna was watching him, just from inside of the Arrivals doors and he gave her the briefest of nods, before he waved at Holly. Anna saw him open up his arms and Holly walked straight into them. She could see Greg reach into his pocket and then give Holly a tissue. Greg was now talking gently to her, so it seemed the shock about Tony had now hit her.

"Holly, I'm so sorry. I know I said I'd look after him, but…"

"It's okay Greg, I know you couldn't keep him wrapped up in cotton wool."

"Let's get to the hospital and we can see how he's doing? Sam's outside waiting in the car for us."

Holly suddenly stopped.

"Will Anna be okay?"

"Yes Holly," he said with a smile. "She's probably the very best of us in regard to looking after herself."

Holly looked back at him.

"What exactly did she do in the intelligence services Greg?"

"Ah, I gather she didn't give you the detail on that, so forgive me if I don't either. Suffice it to say Holly, she really knows what she's doing."

"Okay, I'll stop asking questions that I'm not going to get an answer to."

A small grin had appeared on her face and he could see the tears had stopped.

"Right, let's go. If we're quick we should just make it before visiting time finishes."

"One last question Greg, why would they run Tony down?"

"Good question Holly and right now, I don't think I've got an answer for you."

*****

Frankie Walker paid the taxi and as he walked towards the front door of the smart five star boutique hotel he saw a black Mercedes GLC waiting close by with two men inside.

"Señor Walker, you're alright! We were worried about you," said the receptionist as he walked through the door.

Frankie looked at her with a puzzled expression.

"Anyway, I'm glad you're okay and I have a message for you. The gentleman who left the note said he was a friend."

He took the note from the young woman.

'Why would she think something was wrong with him?'

The note was in a small sealed envelope. He flipped open the flap and took out a single sheet of paper.

> *Frankie,*
> *We need to talk.*
> *We're very concerned about your sudden reconnection with your friend Jake Sutton.*
> *Please come to the villa immediately, we have a car waiting for you outside.*
> *Do not be alarmed, but we have arranged for your wife and children to come as well.*
> *I look forward to seeing you very soon.*
> *My best wishes*
> *Alejandro*

Frankie Walker went cold as he read the note.

"Is everything alright Señor Walker?"

"Er, yes, yes, gracias. Did you see my wife go out this evening?"

"Si Señor," said the receptionist smiling. "Although she seemed a little upset, but the man she was with said it was because you were in hospital?"

'So that was it!'

They must have told her he'd been in some sort of accident and were taking her to see him.

"Señor? So are you alright?"

Walker ignored her and turned instead to see one of the men he'd seen in the Merc was now standing at the hotel entrance. He didn't need to say anything. Frankie knew what was happening. They'd taken Maggs and his kids.

'But why?'

There was no point asking these guys. They were just foot soldiers obeying orders. He had no one to call on and no back up to take to wherever the Sanchez villa was to get Maggs back. He might as well go with them. If Sanchez was going to kill him he'd have done it by now, a drive-by shooting would have done the trick, so there must be some room for negotiation here.

'They want something,' he thought. *'But what?'*

*****

Maggie Walker had been surprised when she'd heard the knock on her hotel room door, but it soon turned to shock when the man said that Frankie had been involved in a car accident.

"Is he okay Señor?"

"I don't know Señora. Señor Sanchez just told me to come and get you and your children and take you to the hospital."

"How did it happen? And which Señor Sanchez? Was it Alejandro?"

"I don't know Señora. But yes, it was Señor Alejandro."

"Wait a moment, let me call him."

She rang his number.

"I don't think he can answer Señora, I think he may be at the hospital."

"Was he there? Frankie was supposed to be with Jake this evening."

"I think Señor Sanchez found out and went to the hospital to check your husband was alright. He didn't want to call you until he knew how he was, but he now thinks you should come quickly."

"Oh my God. Give me two minutes."

She went quickly into the children's bedroom and gently woke them up.

"Come on kids, we need to go for a little ride. Just get some clothes on over your PJs and quickly please."

The children saw the look on their mother's face and didn't ask questions. The eldest, Olivia, squeezed her mother's hand.

"Is Daddy alright Mummy?"

"I think so sweetheart. We just need to go and check on him that's all."

"Okay, come on Sis, let's get ready," said Olivia, aged seven, taking charge as she usually did with her younger sister, Charlotte.

By the time they were dressed and downstairs and sitting in the back of the Mercedes, Maggs Walker had started to have second thoughts. She didn't know why. It was just a feeling, something she couldn't explain, but it was certainly one she didn't like.

"Which hospital are we going to?"

"It's a local one, not far from here."

"But which one? I need to know to be able sort out any medical insurance."

"There is no need to worry about that Señora. It will all be taken care of by the Sanchez family."

"But I want to know. Please stop the car and let me get out!"

"I can't do that Señora. I'm sorry but I have my

orders to take you to...."

"The hospital, so you said," finished Maggs.

She sat in silence and this time she squeezed Olivia's hand as she looked up at her with worry in her eyes.

*****

"Ah, Señora Walker. I'm glad you could make it here. Welcome."

"Alejandro! I don't know what bloody game you are playing, but it's not funny. Is Frankie okay? Your man here said he'd been in an accident and we were going to the hospital."

"Oh no, I'm sorry, that's some sort of misunderstanding. It must have been lost in translation. Frankie will be joining us soon. We just thought it would be better if we were all here, under one roof."

The same feeling she'd had in the car came flooding back over her.

'What's happening here? Frankie, where the hell are you?' she thought.

"I can see you're confused and I'm sorry Maggs. This isn't how I wanted things to be, but we've had certain events happen and it's best we have a discussion about them."

"But it's the middle of the night Alejandro. My kids were asleep in bed."

"But the night is still young in Spain Maggs. Some Spanish families are only just going out for their evening meal now! So relax. The children will be fine, we can put them straight to bed if you like?"

She thought for a moment. The feelings hadn't gone away, but perhaps they'd subsided a little. She knew that the Spanish often didn't start dinner until late on into the night and that their children would still be up and about well past the usual bedtimes of British kids.

"Well okay, that would be a good idea."

Just as she spoke, Maggs saw an older woman come striding into the room.

"Alejandro! Why didn't you tell me our guests had arrived?"

"Margarita, welcome. My son has told me all about you and these are your two beautiful daughters. Come now children. Let's get some milk and biscuits and then go and find your bedroom."

The children looked at Adelina Sanchez. She looked like someone from a fairy story, like a nice kind old grandmother.

"Yes please, gracias," said Olivia.

"Your Spanish is perfecto young lady. Come, let's go."

As they walked out of the room, Maggs half-turned to the woman.

"Gracias Señora, but may I ask, do you know why we're here?"

Adelina Sanchez stopped and faced Maggie Walker, the kind face of the fairy-tale grandmother had gone.

"Oh I think you know all too well why you're here, but for the sake of the children shall we keep this little charade going?"

Maggie Walker felt a chill go down her back.

*****

As the car approached the villa gates Frankie Walker had the realisation that there had been a major flaw in Maggie's thinking. Mallorca was not neutral ground. Far from it. The Sanchez family clearly had a permanent base here and this was it. That meant it would be heavily protected and away from the watchful eyes of the police, so there was no hope he could get the Spanish Old Bill onside, even if he'd wanted to.

As the car pulled up to the front door Frankie saw Alejandro was waiting for him.

"You'd better have a bloody good reason for this Sanchez. And if you've harmed a hair on either my wife or my kids…."

"Stop there Frankie. They're all fine. But a good reason? Let's try Tony Theakston shall we?"

Sanchez saw Theakston's name stop Walker in his tracks.

"What? He's here? On the island?"

"Yes and he's been looking at your friend Jake Sutton and because of that he knows you're here too."

"Oh shit! Alejandro, I had no idea, honestly. Look listen, I didn't know Theakston was looking at Jake and why would he? The bloke's a multi-millionaire, not a crook. Anyway, I haven't seen Jake in years, almost ten years."

"But the problem is Frankie that too many people now seem to know about you being on this beautiful island and that includes a retired London cop."

"But I told you, I don't know why he's here. Now where's Maggs?"

"I'm here Frankie," said his wife as she came out of the front door. "I'm fine and the kids are in bed. Señora Sanchez here has given them some milk and biscuits."

Frankie saw Adelina Sanchez appear smiling behind his wife. From the look on his wife's face he realised that whilst the Sanchez woman had given his kids some milk, his wife had clearly gained a very different view of this woman from the happy smiling one he saw before him.

"Shall we cut the crap then Alejandro? What do you want from us?"

It was Maggs Walker who was asking the question.

"So you aren't just the trophy wife then Margarita?" said Adelina Sanchez, with a wry smile.

"Does it look like I am Señora? Now come on, I'm sure we can sort out whatever your concerns are."

They'd walked back inside the villa and were now standing in the main living area.

"I'm sure we can, but it will cost you ten million euros."

A new voice. Maggs and Frankie turned to see a man they hadn't met before, but they both guessed by his demeanour who he was.

"May I present my father to you, Señor Alberto Sanchez."

They both knew he was the head of the Sanchez Crime Syndicate and whilst all their discussions had so far been with his eldest son, Alejandro, any business they had undertaken either in the past, or the future, would ultimately be sanctioned by Alberto.

Maggs took the lead.

"Señor Sanchez, what a pleasure to meet you, isn't it Frankie?"

Frankie Walker had been well-schooled by his wife over the years in his development as a London crime boss and he knew what was expected now, despite the undisguised threat this family had shown his wife and children.

"Yes Señor. It's a pleasure, although…."

He hadn't been able to help himself from making at least some sort of response, but Maggs quickly cut him off.

"Although we're sorry it's taken a little while to actually get to meet you Señor."

No one was under any sort of misapprehension of what had just been said, however, there had been no offence spoken out aloud.

Alberto looked at the Walkers.

"You appear to have brought some unwanted attention to my family. Therefore there will need to be some compensation for this inconvenience. I think I mentioned ten million euros?"

Maggs and Frankie both looked at him open-mouthed. This time it was Frankie who spoke.

"Señor Sanchez, I have explained to Alejandro here that I haven't seen Jake Sutton for over ten years and so I have no idea why Theakston may have been watching him. Tell me where Theakston is now and I will personally go and speak to him and find out what is going on."

"You won't be able to do that Señor, my son tells me Theakston met with an unfortunate accident and is now in hospital."

Maggs was taking a moment to try to think. She had nothing to barter with and worse still, they had her kids here too.

"Ten million euros is a lot of inconvenience Señor," she said. "What sort of accident did Theakston have, because if this was a result of some action by your family, then I'd politely suggest the inconvenience should become a matter for negotiation, because we will now be the ones subject to severe inconvenience when we return to London. He was a senior Met copper for God's sake, the one who locked Frankie up!"

She saw the reaction to what she'd just said.

"Ah, so you didn't know that Señor? So which of your idiot foot soldiers decided to put Theakston in hospital?"

There was an awkward silence before another man stepped forward.

"Señora Walker, I'm Diego Sanchez."

Maggs realised there was little opportunity to retreat from the statement she'd just made, although it was now pretty clear that it hadn't been a foot soldier who'd put Theakston in hospital.

"Encantado Diego. Perhaps you feel that you had good reason to harm Theakston?"

Diego Sanchez wasn't bothered to play the games he

had been witnessing.

"I didn't need a good reason and I certainly don't need to explain to you, or your gofer husband here, why I did it. You've messed up what was a perfectly acceptable arrangement between our two organisations and now if you want to continue to do business with us, it will cost you an additional ten million euros."

Maggie Walker was watching Alejandro as Diego was making his outburst. She could see he was unsettled. There was obviously something else going on here. Sibling rivalry, or a power struggle of some sort? Whatever it was, it wasn't helping as she didn't know who she was supposed to be negotiating with.

"Look, perhaps I was a little hasty. I can go with it if you had good reason to take Theakston out, but ten million euros! We can't lay our hands on that sort of money quickly. You'd have to give us time."

"Señora Walker, I'm not sure you completely understood what I was saying," said Alberto Sanchez.

He was smiling at her, his voice soft and almost charming, but she saw his eyes were cold and there was an edge to his voice that didn't match the words.

"No, I don't think I do understand Señor."

As he spoke two men, who had appeared at one of the side doors to the room, suddenly moved forward and grabbed Frankie Walker from behind and one of them kicked his legs away from under him, taking him to his knees.

Frankie looked up to see a pistol aimed at his forehead.

"Let's be sensible here, shall we?" he growled.

"I don't think you have any grounds to be leading this discussion Frankie," said Alejandro. "Now you heard my father say he wants some compensation. Why don't you go and see your multi-millionaire friend Jake? I'm sure he could lend you the money? In the meantime, your delightful wife Maggs can stay here with us, together with your darling children."

"Wait, just wait!" said Maggs. "What if he hasn't got ten million either?"

This time it was Adelina who spoke.

"Well let's just hope he does, especially for your children's sake my dear."

35

Frankie Walker was dropped off by Sanchez's men at his hotel and immediately got a taxi straight to the Hotel Portixol. He phoned Jake on the way, who had quickly got dressed after he heard what his friend said.

Frankie went straight to the second floor, to Jake's room, where they could talk in private.

"Ten million euros Frankie!"

"I know, I know. It's a stupid amount of money and I wouldn't ask, but they've got Maggs and the kids Jake."

"Look Frankie, I don't know what the hell you've got yourself into with these guys, but isn't this something you should be thinking about talking to the police about? I mean, they're threatening your family mate."

"Jake, be serious! I'm in bloody Mallorca for Christ's sake. The Old Bill in London wouldn't lift a finger to help me, so why would they out here? This is something I've got to do myself, besides, I don't want to lose this deal. In fact I can't lose it Jake, I've got too much already invested and promised to other people back home."

Jake looked at Walker for a moment, then took a deep breath.

"Look, I would if I could, I owe you a lot from

Feltham, I know I do, but honestly mate, I don't have ten million lying around and even if I did, I'd have too many questions to answer from the people who manage my business for it not to go unnoticed."

Frankie was pacing up and down the hotel bedroom. Jake poured him a drink from the minibar to try to help calm him, then he poured himself one.

A year ago, he'd actually had fifteen million euros in a private Swiss bank account, the money he'd received from Adamsons for the safe return of the picture he had stolen. But although SIS, his company, was doing well on paper, the reality was that the huge research and development costs meant it was swallowing money far faster than they could make it.

He'd transferred nearly all of the Adamsons' ransom into different off-shore bank accounts before putting some into some climate projects and then reinvesting the rest back into SIS through a smokescreen of a small number of 'new' investor identities he'd created.

"Look, I could probably get one to two million fairly quickly Frankie, but I'm sorry mate, I don't have anywhere near ten million euros locked away just sitting there, let alone spare that I could just hand out to you."

"But I thought your business was doing so well?"

"Smoke and mirrors Frankie, smoke and mirrors, although to be fair, it is doing bloody well, but the on-costs, to keep me ahead of the competition, well, they're just frightening mate. So we're only just keeping our heads above water."

He saw the impact of what he'd just said on Frankie's face. Whilst he was, at least on paper, a multi-millionaire and was far better off than his mum and dad had ever been, the Adamsons money, which had started off as nothing more than a way of getting one over on a client who wouldn't do business with him, had turned into a very necessary lifeline for SIS.

"Maybe you could offer something up as a first stage payment and negotiate around the rest?"

"Negotiate Jake! With what? Shall I tell Sanchez to just kill one of my family whilst I get the rest of the money!" snarled Frankie.

"I was just trying to help," said Jake quietly.

Frankie Walker saw the look on Jake's face.

"I'm sorry mate, I know you are. I'm just so wound up. I can sort out my own battles usually, but this is different. Nobody and I mean nobody has ever dared threaten my family. If they so much as touch a hair on any of them…"

"Frankie, focus on the problem we've got, not what might happen in the future."

Walker looked at Jake.

"You said the problem we've got? Look Jake, this is my problem. You can't afford to go getting involved in this. I mean it could wreck your business if anyone found out."

Jake was taken aback by the concern Frankie Walker, one of the most dangerous criminals in London, if not the UK, was having for his well-being, when his own wife and kids were being held captive by a Spanish OCG boss.

"I meant it Frankie. It's our problem. Without what you did for me back in Feltham I don't think I'd have survived in there, so there wouldn't be any SIS."

Frankie managed a smile.

"You were a bit out of your depth, weren't you mate?"

"Just a bit," grinned Jake. "Now look," he said slowly, "I might have a way to get their ten mill, but it wouldn't be cash, so we'd have to negotiate. I need some time to see if it's feasible, so I'll get back to you tomorrow."

"What are you thinking Jake," said Walker, with at

last some hope in his voice.

"Look, I don't want to raise your hopes Frankie. It's a long shot, so I'll tell you more tomorrow."

"Okay and Jake, thank you mate."

The little hope Walker had started to feel had quickly deflated, but he knew he needed to be patient with his friend.

****

Holly stood at the side of Tony Theakston's hospital bed with Greg and Sam. Greg had warned her that he might be asleep as they'd given him a pretty hefty dose of sedatives, but she was shocked to see the extent of the bruising across his face, arms and legs.

Greg saw the concern on Holly's face.

"You shouldn't go thinking you're responsible for any of this Holly. Tony was an experienced police officer and would have faced danger in his line of work on many an occasion. If anything, this is down to me for not anticipating some sort of response from the Sanchez family."

"It's just that…, well he could have been killed Greg. And for what? Some stupid painting that half the world thinks is amazing and the other half has either never heard of it, or thinks a two year old could have done a better job."

"Ah, but art has and always will be in the eye of the beholder Holly, so whichever way we look at this, the paintings that Adamsons deal in all have a value and in most cases, it's an extremely high value which it's your job, and Tony's, to protect."

"The doctors did say they thought he'd be okay though?"

"Yes, but he was lucky. The break to his leg dug deep into one of his veins and he was losing a lot of blood. Another half inch or so and he'd have probably lost so much he'd have been in real trouble, so let's take the positives. He's okay now and he's stable." He paused a moment, judging if this was the right time. "This might sound a bit callous Holly, but now you've seen Tony, I really need you to focus on what you came out here to do. We need to front up this Jake Sutton and bring this whole thing to a halt before it gets out of hand. Okay?"

Holly was still looking at Tony lying so still on the bed, but hearing what Greg said, she lifted her head and nodded.

"I hear you Greg and Tony's an old pro isn't he? He'd be telling me to stop worrying and get on with the job in hand."

"Couldn't have put it better myself. Come on, let's go and get you sorted for the night and we'll make a clean start in the morning."

As he turned to leave the room, he took a final glance back at Theakston and thought, *'You'd better make sure you pull through this now old boy, as she won't forgive herself if you don't.'*

36

The following morning Greg was sat at Terri's breakfast table with Terri, Sam, Simon and Holly, whilst Anna was on speaker phone on her mobile listening in from her villa, just a short distance away near Illetes.

Josie had made coffee for everyone.

"Okay," said Greg. "I'll do a quick update for everyone. Tony is stable and doing as well as can be expected. Anna, I think it was a good call for you to stay away from the rest of us, just in case we need a new face who neither Walker, Sutton nor the Sanchez outfit have seen."

There were nods and murmurs of agreement from around the table.

"Now Holly, I need to drop this on you. By keeping Anna under wraps, you'll have to front up Jake Sutton."

He immediately saw Holly start to say something. He also saw her hand tremble, so he quickly carried on.

"You won't be doing this alone. I've asked Terri to go with you, okay?"

He saw the tension in her relax almost immediately, but this time it was Simon who started to say something.

"If you're about to say, *'Are you ready?'*" barked Terri.

"Actually," said Simon in his quiet Welsh accent. "I was about to say what a good idea it was and that I'd be happy to give you both some cover from outside the Portixol hotel, if that's where you intended to see Sutton?"

"Oh," said Terri. Then she mouthed *'sorry'* across the table at him.

"So Holly, are you up for this? And by the way, just so you know, I wouldn't ask you if I didn't think you could do it. That's not my way," said Greg.

Again, there were more nods from around the table.

"Not by a long way. It's good, we've got this Holly," said Terri, looking directly at her, "haven't we?"

She'd only met Terri that morning after Sam picked her up from her hotel and they'd gone to Terri's apartment. On the way, Sam had mentioned that she was his half-sister and that she was still recovering from an injury, although he didn't say what it was.

She'd been struck by the positivity of the woman. She was so full of energy and had just come back from a run with Simon, who seemed to be her boyfriend, or partner.

This was new territory for Holly, that was sure, but she was certain she wasn't going to let Sutton get away with this, especially not now Tony was lying in a hospital bed.

"Yes, Terri's right, we have got this," she said, with a firmness in her voice that made the others sit up. "So shall we move on it today?"

"That's great Holly," said Greg, "and yes, let's do this before lunch."

He wasn't completely confident that Terri was a hundred percent operationally fit, but she'd assured him that she was good enough for what should be a non-combative interaction with Sutton and having Simon nearby, to give them some protective cover, was a good mitigating factor.

"Greg?" said Anna. "Did you get anything else on the Sanchez group from Lori last night?"

"No, but she told me very politely, but equally very firmly, to stay away from them because they are not nice people, so if anyone sees anybody who looks remotely like they are from the Sanchez team, then we back away."

"Not like you to pull away from a threat Greg," said Simon. "Is Lori that worried about us?"

"Concerned more than worried I suspect Simon. She knows we can look after ourselves, but I think it's more to do with us not putting her two year operation at risk."

"Okay, I get you. Terri, I'll sort out comms and then can you take Holly through the set up?"

Terri nodded and looked across at Holly. "It's just an earpiece and microphone, so the team can hear what's going on."

"Sam?" said Greg. "Anything to add?"

"Just keep a lookout for Frankie Walker as well. We don't know what he's doing hanging around Sutton, but he's another one to be mindful of, because he can be very violent."

Greg checked his watch. "Okay, let's get in place. Simon, Sam, I'll leave you guys to do a recce of the hotel and then call Holly and Terri in."

"Roger that," said Simon.

*****

Frankie Walker was in his hotel room making arrangements with his bank, or at least he was trying to. It was Saturday morning and he knew they'd be closing soon at midday UK time. He'd called his branch manager's direct line to tell him he'd be ringing in a day or so to transfer money to a Spanish bank account.

"I'm sorry Mr Walker, but Mr Tanner isn't available

at the moment. We can do as you ask, however we'd need a bit more notice and there's a couple of forms you'd need to complete sir, but you can do it on-line," said the Assistant Manager, trying to be helpful.

"Listen chum. I'm not filling in any bloody forms. Just take this call as my authorisation when you get my next call, alright?"

"But Mr Walker, I'm sorry, we just can't do that. I mean, how do I know it's really you?"

"Oh, you'll know it's me sunshine next time you see me if you don't do as I bloody well tell you."

"Mr Walker, please understand I am trying to help, but I need to protect both you and the bank from fraud."

"Listen mate, just get me your bloody boss will you? I know you said he's in a meeting, but tell him Frankie says, 'Hello and how are you getting on with the gee-gees at the moment?' I'm sure he'll find time to come to the phone then."

Frankie had tried calling Tanner, the branch manager, on his mobile, but he kept getting an ansaphone message, so he'd phoned Tanner's direct landline which had been redirected to the man he was now talking to.

"I'll try Mr Walker, please hold."

The Assistant Manager stepped out of his office and knocked tentatively on the office door of the branch manager, James Tanner before opening the door and walking in.

Tanner looked up from his desk in surprise, as did the customer who was sat across the desk from him.

"What is it Mark?" he demanded. "I asked not to be disturbed."

"I'm sorry Mr Tanner, however, I have an urgent message for you. 'Frankie says hello and how are you getting on with the gee…'"

The Assistant Manager didn't finish what he was saying as Tanner stood up, his face going pale.

"Yes, yes, Mark, that's fine. I'm so sorry Mrs Ball, however, I must just take this call. Mark, get Mrs Ball another coffee and I promise I'll be back in a couple of minutes."

Tanner was pushing his assistant out of the office.

"What's going on Mark?"

"Mr Walker wants us to transfer money across to an account in Spain sometime in the next day or so, but he won't do any of the online forms I told him he needed to complete."

"Is he here?"

The Assistant Manager could see his boss was sweating.

"No, he's on the phone."

Tanner checked his own mobile and saw the missed calls from Frankie Walker.

"Shit!"

"What's up Mr Tanner?"

Mark couldn't understand his manager's response. Walker's account was significant to the branch, but nowhere near as important as that of Mrs Ball, the customer his boss had been meeting with.

"Never mind, never mind, please get Mrs Ball another coffee and keep her sweet. We were talking about moving some of her investments around, so just keep her talking as to what she wants. I'll be back in a minute."

Tanner waited until Mark left him alone in the assistant's office, then took a deep breath and picked up the phone.

"Frankie, what a pleasure. I'm so sorry I missed your calls I was just…"

"I don't care what the hell you were doing Tanner. The deal was I sort your fifty grand gee-gee bill with the bookies and you be on the end of the phone whenever I need you. I've never asked you to do anything dodgy, just to be there on the end of your phone should I ever need you quickly. So you've spectacularly failed on that one thing I asked from you in exchange for me getting you out of the shit!" he snarled.

"I'm sorry Frankie, I'm sorry. I was …"

"I said I don't care what you were doing. Mess me about again and your bosses at headquarters will get a little call about your betting problem. Got it!"

Tanner felt himself go cold and saw his hands shaking.

"Yes Frankie, I completely understand, now how can I help? Mark says it's about you needing to transfer some money to Spain maybe in the next day or so?"

"Yes, I'll need to do it quickly and can't be messing around with any forms. I just need you to do it when I call."

"That won't be a problem. Just call me the moment you need it. How much are you looking at?"

Tanner was back in control now, talking about a simple transaction where he could action all of the necessary authorities later.

"One, maybe one and a half mill. Whatever's in our joint savings account. You can do that can't you?" Walker said sarcastically.

Tanner didn't bother mentioning that the movement of such an amount would fall into the realms of a check down the line by his bank under the financial regulations governing money laundering investigations. He'd deal with that as and when the time came. Right now, he just needed to get Walker off his back and make the problem go away.

"Is everything alright Frankie?"

"None of your damn business. Just tell me, can you do it on a phone call?"

"Yes Frankie, that's no problem at all, leave it with me and just call when you need the transfer."

"Just make sure you answer your phone!"

Frankie Walker rang off leaving Tanner holding onto the phone. The bank manager put the phone down, slowly turned and then had to run along the corridor to the staff toilet and into the nearest cubicle, where he vomited violently.

37

When Jake Sutton saw the two young and very attractive women approaching him in the hotel lounge, he grimaced, thinking they were probably from one of the Spanish business magazines who had been tipped off by someone at the hotel and had come to try to get an interview with him.

"Good morning Mr Sutton. We'd like to have a word with you," said Holly.

'Good, confident opening line,' thought Greg, as he listened in on the open-mic comms.

"Look, I don't mean to be rude, but I don't do interviews off the cuff. You'll need to go through my corporate comms team and besides I'm here on holiday," said Sutton.

Sutton went to walk past them, when Terri put her hand on his arm. He thought she was just trying to gently persuade him to stop, until he felt her twist her hand across his wrist and he involuntarily buckled slightly, caught unawares.

"What the…"

"Jake, mate, just give us a minute," and Terri twisted his hand again. Although this time he was ready and resisted her.

"Who are you?" he demanded. *'Maybe they were from*

the Sanchez gang?'

"Mr Sutton," said Holly, retaining an air of formality. "My name's Holly Regus and I work for Premium Risk International and represent our client, Adamsons."

She saw Sutton blink, taken by surprise. She wasn't sure if a direct approach would work when it was first suggested, but she could see now that it had and she now had got the upper hand.

"Well I've no idea why you'd want to talk to me."

He tried to walk away again and this time Terri stepped directly in front of him.

"Now look Jake," she said. "We're asking nicely. I can see you look after yourself and you're in pretty good shape, but listen, going by what went on in Feltham, I don't reckon you're much of a fighter, so why don't we just sit down and you listen to what Holly here has to say?"

He thought, for just a moment, that he might ignore her and try to walk past her, but then he felt her hand again. This time on his chest and she gave him a firm shove backwards.

She was right of course. He wasn't a fighter and never had been. He didn't know who she was, but she certainly looked like she knew how to fight, just judging by the way she was standing - ready, poised and balanced.

"Alright, alright. What do you want?"

"Let's sit down Mr Sutton," suggested Holly.

*****

"You think I stole a picture from Adamsons in New York and then tried again just recently in Singapore?" Sutton said, trying his best sound to make it sound as though it was a ridiculous statement.

"We don't think Mr Sutton, or can I call you Jake?"

"Well, your friend here already is, so why not join her?" he said sarcastically.

"Okay, so yes Jake, you stole the first one and then took a fifteen million euro ransom to give it back. But you didn't stop there did you? You then tried to steal another one whilst you were in Singapore and now you've recently sent us this."

She put down a piece of paper with a copy of the email containing the riddle on it.

"Oh and by the way, we solved it, you're going to steal a picture from the Adamsons gallery in Sóller."

Sutton was shaken. It was bad enough they'd solved the riddle, but how had they known he was here?

"Listen, I don't know what you're talking about and whatever it is, you have no proof of any of this."

"Wrong answer Jake," said Terri, unable to resist joining in. "If you were completely innocent you wouldn't be saying Holly's got no proof."

"What I meant was…"

"Too late Jake," said Holly. "Look, we know it's you, but here's the deal. We won't involve the police if you just give the fifteen million back and drop any plans of stealing anything from Adamsons in Mallorca."

He meant to deny it again. Maybe they didn't have any substantive evidence against him that would stand up in court? But he delayed too long.

"I can see your mind turning over Jake. If you're thinking whether we'll stick to the deal, I can get something to you in writing within the hour, but that's it, a one hour window and after that we'll be coming for you, police and all."

Terri knew Holly was bluffing, as from the outset she'd made it clear that PRI would do their utmost to keep the police out of this because any resulting publicity would not be good news for their client, Adamson. But it was a damn good bluff, that was for sure. And it worked.

"Look, it was supposed to be a practical joke, but it

got out of hand." Sutton's voice had lost its combative edge.

"I'm not particularly interested in your reasons Jake. Just give back the money and you can go back to being the hotshot darling of the security industry."

Jake went quiet. He'd actually like to do nothing better than wind this all up and go back to just focussing on SIS, but he'd told Frankie that he had an idea to help him, although he hadn't actually told him what. He thought that if he stole the Joan Miró painting from the Adamsons gallery in Sóller, which was easily worth at least ten million euros, he could give it to Sanchez as payment for the safe return of Frankie's wife and kids.

'But how could he tell them that?'

'What's he waiting for?' thought Holly. *'He's admitted he did it.'*

Jake looked across at the two women again, hesitating, unsure as to what to say next.

"You look like you want to say something Jake?" suggested Terri, in a softer, gentler voice.

"Well that may be, but it's not as simple as giving the money back. There's a complication."

She heard Greg's voice in her earpiece.

"Ask him if this has something to do with Frankie Walker?"

"Jake, we know you've been seeing Frankie Walker," said Terri.

The look on Jake's face was enough to give him away.

"They've got his wife and kids and they want ten million from him to get them back safely."

"They being the Sanchez outfit?" said Terri.

Jake nodded.

*****

Terri spoke into her mic.

"Greg, Sam, did you get that?"

"Yes, yes," said Sam.

"Yes, got it loud and clear," said Greg.

Terri spoke to Jake again.

"What's happened?"

"Honestly, I don't really know. I met Frankie just by chance on the flight over here. I've no idea what sort of business he's mixed up in, but whatever it is, the people he's dealing with are even more dangerous than he is and that's saying something."

"Jake, just to confirm, you did come over here intending to steal another Adamsons painting?" asked Holly.

He looked at her. There didn't seem much point in denying it as things stood. He knew they wouldn't go to the police if they could possibly avoid it, so it wasn't as though he was losing anything by being straight with them.

"Yes, well at least I was going to scope it out first, but after you guys screwed up the Singapore job, I meant to get one over on Adamsons again."

"But why? Why are you doing this? Your business is successful, so what if Adamsons won't play ball and give you their business?"

He didn't answer immediately. Probably because he wasn't actually sure how he had got into this position. Maybe it was just the adrenalin rush? It wasn't the ransom money, at least not to start with, but what he'd told Frankie Walker was true. SIS was haemorrhaging money and at a rate he couldn't sustain.

"I don't know and anyway, I don't expect you to understand so I won't bother trying to explain as I'll just sound like some poor little rich boy trying to justify why he's been caught stealing sweets."

"But it's ten million euros worth of sweets Jake," said Holly.

"Like I said, it didn't start off being about the money.

I really was going to give all the money back and tell them, Adamsons I mean, that that's why they needed to work with me, to improve their security systems."

"But you didn't Jake. So why not?"

Terri had been watching Holly as she'd gone at Sutton. She was getting all the information she needed. She was pushing all the right buttons to get him to open up, whilst not letting him off the hook at any time.

"I had nothing, or at least, very little as a kid, although it wasn't for my parents' want of trying. I was good at athletics and the gym work, but then I screwed up. Just the once, but they threw me off the Olympics programme and I lost everything."

Sutton's voice had gone quiet as he was speaking, but then the edginess in it returned once more.

"I wasn't going to let that happen with SIS. I'd built that company up from square one, but the business took a dive when the R&D costs went through the roof and I needed to shore up the company. So I decided to use the ransom money. But not all of it."

He could hear himself trying to justify why he'd spent the fifteen million euros and it sounded like a bleating child caught doing something wrong. He tried to explain again.

"Look, it sounds lame I know, but without a cash injection SIS was in serious danger of going down the tubes, but I did also give some of it to a couple of key climate projects and the rest I reinvested in SIS."

"Whoopee for the climate projects Jake, that was pretty generous of you using Adamsons' money," said Terri.

Sutton kept his head looking down. It actually sounded worse hearing himself say it out aloud.

"So you don't have the money to give back?" asked Holly.

"No, well at least not at the moment. Look, can't we come to sort of arrangement? I can pay this back, I promise."

"Promise Jake, promise? That's a bit rich seeing as you've made two attempts to steal from Adamsons and are in the process of planning a third!"

Jake Sutton went quiet again. She was right. He knew he must sound like a guilty man pleading he was innocent. They were empty words that he wasn't sure he believed himself, let alone this woman who represented the very people he'd stolen from.

Greg saw Lori's name appear on his phone.

"Terri, Holly, can you hold it there. Grab a coffee or something. I need to take a call from Lori," said Greg.

"Copied that," said Terri. "Jake, let's take a break shall we and get a coffee."

38

"I hope this is business my love because I'm really busy at the moment," said Greg.

"Yes it is and you're not the only one who is busy!"

It was her no nonsense, professional voice, so he didn't hang about with his response.

"Okay, what's up?"

"Why is Terri at the Portixol with another young woman and Simon is outside prowling around?"

Her team had still clearly been watching the hotel in Portixol, thought Greg, presumably to see if Walker had been visiting Sutton again.

"Did you know Frankie Walker's family have been kidnapped by Sanchez?"

"What? And how the hell do you know that Greg? I told you to stay out of this!"

"That's two questions and a statement Lori and I'm guessing you didn't know. So how about you start with a *'thank you Greg'*?" he said cheerily.

"Answer my questions first and then maybe I might say thank you." She motioned to Nino to come into her office. "Greg, Nino's here now, so you're on speakphone."

"Buenas dias Nino."

"Greg, good to hear from you. What have you got for us?"

"First of all, we weren't interfering with your operation. We went to see Jake Sutton about the matter we're investigating. Something that is totally unrelated to the Sanchez family."

"Okay, go on," said Lori, "I'm listening."

'Listening, but not necessarily believing,' he thought.

"Now this is in confidence, okay?"

"Yes of course," she snapped, clearly irritated. "Just tell me what's going on."

"Jake Sutton, as well as being the head of one of the most successful security companies currently in the market, is also an art thief. He stole a picture in New York about twelve months or so ago and then ransomed it back to the art gallery."

He paused.

"For fifteen million euros."

"Wow," said Nino.

"That's a lot of ransom," agreed Lori. "So what's he doing here? The same thing?"

"That's what we think, because Adamsons have a gallery out at Sóller, and after almost catching him at it in Singapore, we decided to just front him out here."

"Front him out? What do you mean?" asked Lori.

"Sorry, we put a direct challenge into him. We told Sutton what we thought he was doing and he's just admitted we were right."

"So where does the kidnap come into it Greg?" asked Nino.

"Yes, how does Sutton know that Walker's family have been kidnapped?" said Lori.

"Walker told him. He thought Sutton, because of the success of his business, might just have ten million in cash lying around."

"That's a lot of cash, even for a millionaire to have

readily accessible. Did Walker know about him stealing the painting?"

"No, they haven't seen each other for years, not really since Feltham, the young offenders' prison."

"Why would Walker think Sutton would give him the money?" asked Nino.

"Walker looked after him whilst they were both inside. Stopped him being used as a punch bag, or worse if you get my drift?"

"Yes, of course. Go on amigo."

"Jake Sutton taught Walker to read and write and they became friends of a sort," explained Greg.

"That's a lot of friendship," said Lori.

"Yes, but Sutton reckons he wouldn't be where he is today if Walker hadn't looked after him in Feltham."

"But presumably you're going to persuade him not to steal the painting?" asked Lori slowly.

"Yes, that's the plan."

Silence.

Greg could almost see her mind working.

"What are you thinking Lori?"

Nino was also looking at his boss wondering where she might be going with this.

Greg broke the silence.

"Are you thinking this might be a possible tactical option?"

"Perhaps," she said slowly.

"It's risky," said Greg.

"But potentially the only way we'll get into the Sanchez villa over here," said Lori. "Do you think your lady friend from Adamsons would go for it?"

Greg smiled at her description of Dr Holly Regus, but this didn't seem the time to tease her back.

"No, I don't and I don't think her boss, or Adamsons for that matter, would be best pleased either."

"But you solved her case, their case Greg. Surely that

would give you some leverage?"

"Oh, so now you want me to get involved with this?"

"Well it would be helpful for you to be the go-between."

"I'm still not sure what's in it for me, or Adamsons, for that matter?"

"Isn't helping me sufficient for you my dear?"

Lori frowned at her Sergeant as he grinned at her.

"Of course I want to help, but this is right at the top of high-end risk Lori. Are you sure?"

"I've been working to get these people for two years Greg and every time we get anywhere near them we lose the witness, or something else happens to undermine the case. I know this needs thinking through, but if we can somehow get inside using the stolen artwork, we might just get something we can finally pin on them."

Hearing the tone in her voice he decided this wasn't the time for levity.

"Well let's get together and start planning this. I know Holly wants some sort of retribution on the Sanchez family for what Diego Sanchez did to one of her people."

"Señor Theakston," said Lori.

"Yes. He's doing okay, but he could easily have been killed, so I'll talk to her and we can probably convince Sutton that any threat of a charge, or him being exposed as an art thief, will disappear if he helps, which I think he may want to do anyway, given his friendship and history with Walker."

"Good, we have a plan. Can you tie up with Nino to sort out a meeting place and times?" She didn't wait for his reply before saying, "See you soon," and ringing off.

*****

"Terri, Holly? Sorry it took so long. You still there?"

The two women heard what Greg had said in their

earpieces.

"Yes, we're here," said Holly.

"Looks like things are moving fast. Lori, that's DI Garcia, Holly, the investigating officer on the Sanchez case. She wants to meet, urgently to discuss the Walker kidnap and Jake Sutton," said Greg.

"Okay," said Holly, "but I'm not sure how I can be part of this?"

"With what we have in mind Holly, you're very much part of it, as is our friend Mr Sutton."

"Tell us where you want to meet and I'll make sure I'm there and that Jake stays where he is, so we know where to find him."

At the mention of his name Jake Sutton looked up from his coffee.

"What's going on? What do you mean, *'you'll make sure Jake stays where he is?'* You can't keep me under some sort of house arrest!"

"Jake, I know you want to help your friend Walker with his family, yes?"

"Well yes, but..."

"No buts, just listen. Sit tight here until I call you and we'll come and see you again. If Walker contacts you in the meantime tell him you're trying to come up with the money and that you have a plan, but you can't tell him what it is. Say it's so he can't give the game away to the Sanchezes."

"I don't understand. You said..."

"I didn't ask you to understand. Just listen and do as I say and ring me if Walker contacts you," said Holly, pushing her business card across the table.

Terri saw Sutton was taken aback by the ferocity of what Holly had said and how she'd said it.

'Impressive,' she thought.

"I think the lady wants you to stay here until she calls you Jake, so best you just shut up and do as she says, okay?"

Sutton sat back in his chair, his shoulders slumped and simply nodded.

Terri called across one of the waiters.

"Otro café para el señor por favor."

"Nice Spanish," said Holly as they walked out, leaving Sutton sat at the table.

"I'm getting there," grinned Terri.

39

They needed to meet well away from the police headquarters in Palma city centre. Lori couldn't be certain that the Sanchez family didn't have some eyes and ears operating within the local police force, so Nino wasn't going to take any chances with where they'd meet.

It was Sam who had offered up the suggestion that Nino had quickly picked up on and it was just a couple of hours later that they were all sat in Contrabando in Llucmajor.

Sam had phoned Miquel earlier. He'd been happy to go with Sam's request that they use Contrabando for a meeting behind closed doors, as long as he could still open up as usual at 4.00pm.

"Welcome my friends," said Miquel. "Once I've served up some light lunch for you, we'll leave you in peace...."

"Muchas gracias amigo," said Sam.

"De nada my friend. We'll catch up later."

After Miquel had finished laying out some plates of Pa amb oli, a local selection of bread, cheese, meat and olives, he brought some water and a bottle of local white wine, before leaving them to their meeting.

Greg opened things up.

"Okay Lori, I think we've got all the key people here."

Other than Lori and himself, there was Terri, Sam, Nino and Anna, who'd travelled to Llucmajor on her own to continue to maintain a bit of distance from the rest of the team.

"I've outlined the basics to Dr Holly Regus here, who represents Premium Risk International and their client Adamson," said Greg.

"Dr Regus," Lori nodded and smiled towards her.

"Holly please, Inspectora."

"And please Holly, call me Lori."

"So you will help us Holly, with what we are trying to do with the Sanchez OCG?"

It was more of a statement requiring affirmation, than a question and Holly was slightly taken aback as Lori's voice went from a welcoming and friendly tone into a firm and business-like manner.

"Er well, it's not quite as simple as that Inspectora, I mean Lori."

"Why not?"

"Well, because you're asking me to risk a ten million euro painting."

"I know that, but the drugs industry on the Spanish mainland is worth fifty to a hundred times that."

Holly had regained her composure and was determined to stand up against Lori.

"Lori, I appreciate this piece of art is a very small part of the overall issue for you here. However, I will not give you permission to facilitate the theft one of my client's pictures without a lot more discussion, in order that I can approach my client with a clear proposal," she said firmly.

Terri was again impressed at how Holly had stood up to Lori Garcia. *'Good for you girl,'* she thought.

Greg had also realised that Holly wasn't going to simply roll over and was about to interject when Lori came back to Holly in a softer, more accommodating voice.

"Of course Holly, I'm sorry if I seemed to be rushing you into a decision. Let's get down to business shall we and I hope we can give you everything you need to speak positively to your client who should of course understand how much the Spanish Government would appreciate their cooperation."

Holly smiled back, understanding the implied threat if Adamsons chose not to support the police operation, but knowing she'd perhaps passed some unwritten test with Lori and that she could now do business with this woman.

Terri looked across at Greg and smiled. Lori had tried to bulldoze through the issue of Holly's agreement, but seeing Holly wouldn't give in easily, she'd stepped back taking a softer, more collaborative approach.

Now Greg did manage to get into the discussion.

"I do think that there is a good case here for everyone to benefit from working together on this issue."

He saw both Lori and Holly nod at his comment.

"If we don't somehow engage with Jake Sutton then there seems every likelihood that if he doesn't steal the Miró in Port de Sóller he could well go and steal another painting somewhere else in the world."

"And it could be another Adamsons gallery that he hits," said Sam.

It was a good point and it wasn't lost on Holly, who nodded back to Greg.

"Greg, the fact that Frankie Walker seems to be in a predicament with his family and yet has seemingly got away with the Attempted Murder of Jimmy is perhaps a factor we shouldn't lose sight of?" said Sam.

"Are you thinking he needs to agree to hand himself

in if we help get his family back? Would he do that?" asked Greg.

"I don't know, but I don't see why we shouldn't include Walker in the scope of this operation. Lori?"

"I've no objection Sam, but I'm sure you will understand if the Sanchez family remain my primary goal."

"Of course."

"How would you use the painting?" asked Holly.

"Good question Holly," said Greg. "Lori?"

"I can answer this," said Nino. "We have never been able to get any listening devices into the Sanchez camp, nor any informants. They seem to be able to quickly root them out and they end up either missing or dead."

"Go on," said Greg.

"They screen everyone for bugs who goes into anywhere where they are staying. So the painting gives us an opportunity to get a mic in there, secreted in the frame somewhere."

"How big are the bugs, the listening devices?" asked Holly.

Nino gave her a brief summary that it could just be a small length of wire, or something that might look like a nail head, or a button.

"That's definitely feasible," said Holly, "there's always generally room on the backs of these frames to hide something away that wouldn't be noticed by the casual observer."

"That's always assuming they keep the painting in the room where they're having their conversations," said Anna slowly.

Greg picked up on what she had said and more to the point, how she had said it.

"What are you thinking Anna?"

The whole table turned and looked at her.

"Now Lori, this is where it may be your turn to find

things could be a little tricky in terms of you getting the appropriate agreement from your bosses."

"Go on Anna," said Lori looking intently at her.

"Sam, you know the Walker family. Is Maggs's mother still alive?"

"Yes," he said slowly, wondering where his mother was going with this.

"How old is she?"

"Mid-sixties I think, something like that. Why?"

Anna ignored his question.

"Do they see much of each other?"

"No, I don't think they've spoken for a few years. Saoirse Murphy did not approve of Frankie one little bit."

"So she's got good sense of judgement then," laughed Anna.

"Yes, although last time I spoke to her, she wasn't exactly pro-police either."

"Where's she from?"

"London, well actually, she's from the West of Ireland I think."

"Okay, thanks. So the painting idea only gives you, I mean us, a half chance at best at listening to what the Sanchez gang are talking about, whereas if we had Maggs Walker's Irish mother in there…" Anna let her words trail off.

Greg immediately recognised the gentle Irish accent from County Donegal that Anna had adopted for her last few words.

"Mum, I'm really not sure that's a good..," started Sam.

"Anna," interrupted Lori. "I like it, but are you sure? Not that you couldn't do it. I know you can, but the risk? How do you get past Maggs Walker acknowledging you as her mother?"

"She's clearly smart as she seems to have running

the Walker operation whilst her husband's been inside for the past year. Plus we tee up Frankie and when I turn up at the Sanchez place banging on the door, he sets the storyline to the Sanchez family that he couldn't stop his mad Irish mother-in-law coming to the house."

Holly had sat back in her chair. This woman, Anna Martínez, continued to amaze her, volunteering to go into the proverbial lion's den.

Sam had to admit that it was actually a pretty good idea and since he'd found out about his mother's background in the security services, he'd learned not to underestimate her ability when it came to working undercover.

Lori was thinking through the implications of Anna's suggestion. It could work, but what about the background story?

"Can we cover the background story in London with her real mother?"

"Don't see why not," said Sam. "I'm sure she'll be happy to cooperate if she knows we're trying to save her daughter and grandkids."

"Do you think you'd get it past your boss?" asked Greg.

Lori thought for a moment. Using a civilian in an undercover police operation, even someone as experienced and capable as Anna Martínez, was likely to bring on the stress lines of her usually risk averse boss.

"That could be a problem. But to summarise for now, if we can't get Adamsons' agreement around Sutton stealing another of their paintings, we can still go with Anna's plan to get inside the Sanchez villa out here in Mallorca, yes?"

"Agreed," said Greg.

"I'll put it to my boss after we finish here," said Lori.

"Me too," said Holly firmly, although with a lot less confidence than it came across to the others at the meeting.

"Sam, can you just spell 'Ser-sha'? I'll need it for my report."

"Yes, of course Lori. It's a good old Irish name, but spelt nothing like it sounds, but it's very apt in the circumstances as it means liberty, or freedom," said Sam with a grin before he spelt out the name – S a o i r s e.

40

Maggs Walker called out again, more in hope than expectation.

"Will you please open this door? We're going nuts in this room!"

Whilst the room she and her two children had been taken to had an en-suite bathroom and toilet, the children were both getting restless and she needed to give them something to do to distract them from thinking about where their dad was.

This time she banged on the door.

"Look, this is a massive bloody estate and I'm hardly going to run away from you and leave my kids here, am I? So please just open the damn door and let us out."

Nothing. No noise and no response either from the guard she assumed was on the other side of the door. She gave up and slumped back on the bed were her children sat, looking scared, but trying not to cry.

"It's okay kids. The grown-ups are just playing a game and we just need to be patient. Daddy will come and get us soon and then we'll all play nicely together once again."

"When will he come Mummy?" said Olivia.

"Well that's the thing Livvy, Daddy's also playing the game and he's hiding somewhere as well, but don't worry, we'll get this sorted very soon, I promise."

"And then he'll come and make the Sanchezes wish they'd never met Frankie Walker," she said quietly herself.

Ten minutes later she heard the outside key in the lock turn and the door opened.

"Ah Maggs, I hear you've been asking to come out. Children, I'm so sorry you couldn't go out to play, but we had some problems with one of the dogs and we had to keep you all safe in here with your mama," said Alejandro Sanchez.

"I thought you said we were playing a game Mummy?" said Olivia.

"Hush now Livvy, let's just get out of this room shall we and go and play downstairs."

As the children ran skipping out of the room, Maggs turned to Sanchez.

"Alejandro, what the hell's going on? Have you heard from Frankie?"

"When Frankie comes up with the money, we can all settle down and work out the final details of the new deal."

"You expect us still to go through with the deal after you've kidnapped me and my kids?" she said incredulously.

"It's just business Maggs, just business, so just be patient and we can sort this out."

She went to say something, but he looked at her.

"Maggs, please, do not aggravate the situation."

She heard the tone in his voice and thought it better not to say anything else, but her mind was racing as she followed her children out and down the stairs to the main entrance hall.

But who the hell did he think he was? Don't aggravate the situation. I've been bloody kidnapped and being held to ransom!'

Then she collected herself.

"Alejandro, can we go outside to let the children play?" adding quietly, "I promise I won't play up, but in return can you try to make it look, at least for my kids' sake, that we aren't being held prisoner?"

He didn't reply, but he walked to the front door and opened it for them and motioned to one of his men to follow her outside into what was left of the afternoon sunshine.

*****

Frankie, good to hear from you. How are you doing pulling together our little deal?" asked Alejandro Sanchez cheerily.

"I don't call finding ten million any sort of little deal, but I'm doing it. Just make sure you don't harm a hair on my wife or kids, understand?" growled Walker.

"I really don't think you're in any sort of position to threaten me Frankie, so let's keep this civil shall we?"

Frankie ignored what he said as he continued.

"Look, I'm trying, but I don't have that sort of cash lying around, but I'm calling in favours and I'll get as much as I can by close of play today, okay?"

"As much as you can? Hmm, that may not be enough my friend. But let me be fair, I'll give you another forty eight hours to get all the money together."

Even that wasn't going to be enough time, thought Walker, but Sanchez was right, he wasn't in any sort of position to argue.

"Frankie? I said forty eight hours."

"I heard you, I heard you."

*****

Frankie Walker had been able to deal with most things in his life including, when sometimes required, resorting to a brutal level of violence when threats weren't enough. But he knew neither was a viable option in this case. There was no way he could get enough people across to Mallorca in time to do anything, let alone know what any sort of direct action against the Sanchezes might look like without having any weapons.

He didn't have enough money himself to cover the ransom and nor could he call on any loans from his so-called 'friends,' because as soon as they sensed a weakness in him they'd be planning a takeover.

He was hanging on to a slim hope that Jake would come up with something, but he still hadn't heard anything back from him since the previous night, when Jake had said he might have an idea that might help. He texted him.

Jake Sutton was still sat in the lounge with his coffee, a little shell shocked after his encounter with the two women who he'd just thought were after an interview with him. He saw Walker's text.

'Any progress?'

Jake knew he couldn't ignore the text, but how could he tell Frankie that he'd just been warned off in no uncertain terms from stealing anything from Adamsons? Then another text appeared.

'I'm coming down.'

Walker wasn't the sort of guy to say 'No' too, so Sutton picked up Holly's business card and phoned her.

"Jake, what's up?" said Holly.

"Frankie's asking what's going on and he's coming down to see me."

Holly muted her phone and thought for a moment. She had been on the phone to her boss trying to explain everything that had been going on and she hadn't been getting very far.

"Jake, we'll be down with you shortly. Keep Walker there."

"Okay, I'll try."

"Do better than try Jake. Tell him it's for his benefit."

She rang off and immediately called Greg.

"I'm struggling with my boss and I haven't even tried calling Christine Harrison at Adamsons yet."

"Can I help?" asked Greg.

"It'll have to wait Greg. Sutton has just called me and Frankie Walker is on his way down to Portixol to see him. I've told him we'll go down and meet them."

"Good, I'll pick you up with Terri. Ring him back and tell him we'll see him in his room, probably best we're not on open view, just in case Sanchez has anyone watching him."

"Okay, I'll do it now and we'll be waiting down in the car park."

It turned out to be a useful precaution because Alejandro Sanchez still had one of his men, Andres, on watch in a Seat, parked on the side road that ran around the outside perimeter of the Hotel Portixol.

Although where Andres was parked only gave the man sight of the entrance and reception area to the hotel and so whilst he'd seen Sutton walk from the staircase and into the hotel lounge, he hadn't then seen him meet up with Terri and Holly.

When Walker arrived at the hotel, to meet Sutton, Andres saw him and called Alejandro Sanchez who listened as Andres told him he'd seen the two men meet up, but that they'd gone up the stairs, rather than into the lounge area.

"You think they're still in the hotel Andres?"

"Yes Boss."

"Okay, good, they've probably gone to Sutton's room. Stay where you are and update me when Walker leaves."

Simon Barnes was drinking coffee at one of the tables outside the front of the hotel. From there he had a good view of the side road that ran along the side of the marina, as well as the road by the hotel and he'd been keeping an eye on the Sanchez man since Holly and Terri first went to meet Sutton.

Greg phoned him to tell him he was on his way back down to the hotel with Holly, Terri and Sam.

"Presumably Greg, we could do without this guy reporting back to Sanchez that you're back at the hotel? Because if he sees Terri and Holly again, he's likely to guess that they're back to see Sutton."

"Yes, that would be useful. What are you thinking?"

"The guy's double parked, so why not get Lori to get a patrol car down here and just move him on. It will give you guys enough time to get in and upstairs to Sutton's room and I'll shift your car."

"I'm on it. Give me a couple of minutes Simon. Then text me when the Policía come down and move him on."

"Yes, yes."

Simon appeared to be slowly finishing his already empty coffee as he slowly scanned the side road to check if the Sanchez lookout had moved. The Seat was still there, in the same position, double parked just across from the front of the hotel.

*****

"Yes, I can do that no problem," said Lori when she heard Greg's request. "Now, do you want me down there to meet Sutton and Walker with you?"

"I don't think so Lori, maybe not just yet. You definitely need to meet this guy Walker at some stage, but let's set the scene first and see what we've got. How does that sound?"

He didn't want her feeling he was blocking her out, but it was also more likely they could get the business done a lot easier without having to record anything formally as Lori would have to do as an SIO, a Senior Investigating Officer.

"No, I can see where you are coming from, but Greg, please try to ensure we can still take this forward as a police prosecution and not lose it because of …," she hesitated.

"Don't worry, I know what you're saying and we'll make sure we've not bulldozed our way through the entire Spanish Judicial legislative requirements."

"Hmm, *'don't worry'*?" she said. "Remember, I know how you and your team operate my love, so that might not be your best advice to me. Now, leave me to sort out a marked car for you and we'll get someone down to move the Sanchez lookout along. And Greg? Please come back to me with an update soon."

"That's great and yes, of course Lori, I'll ring you as soon as we know where we are."

*****

As soon as Simon saw Greg's text that the plan was being actioned, he moved his chair slightly back, so he could more easily start to move towards the front of the hotel.

Less than five minutes later Simon saw a local police marked patrol car appear on the other side of the marina and drive slowly along the road into Portixol, as though on a routine patrol. The police car then indicated right and turned into the side road leading to the Hotel Portixol.

Simon could see that the Sanchez man was so focused on the hotel that he hadn't noticed the police car, at least not until it was right behind him.

He texted Greg.

'Move forward and hold at the junction into the side road.'

'Copied,' Greg's text came back.

Simon, saw the officer get out of his car and walk purposely towards the Seat with a notebook in his hand. It looked as though the patrol officer wasn't just going to move the driver on for double parking, but he was going to issue a parking ticket, or maybe even do some sort of a stop-check, potentially gaining some further intelligence on the Sanchez gang.

He saw the Sanchez lookout gesticulating and starting to raise his voice at the police officer trying to intimidate him, but the officer was standing firm, with his hand on his sidearm.

Simon looked again, closer this time at the officer. It was Sergeant Fernando Pérez, one of Lori's GEO team! Dressed in a local police officer's uniform, rather than his GEO kit, obviously so as not to give the game away that the GEO were on the island watching the Sanchez family.

After a few minutes, when the lookout had seemed to quieten down after some sort of warning from Pérez, Simon saw the lookout get back in his car and start to drive away. He then saw Pérez get back in his police vehicle and follow the lookout's Seat up the side road and away from the hotel back towards the junction, presumably to make sure the lookout didn't double back to the hotel, nor stop in a position where he could see Greg's car stopping at the front of the hotel.

'Move up now.'

Greg saw Simon's next text and accelerated forward along the narrow side road, parking tight in against the hotel entrance.

41

"That went well," said Greg with a grin as he walked past Simon.

"Worked like clockwork," said Simon. "It was Pérez, he was brilliant. Good luck."

He waited until Greg and the others had walked into the hotel and gone straight to the stairs, before he got in the car and moved it to where the Sanchez lookout had been parked up.

A minute or so later, the others were standing outside Sutton's room. They stood back, two either side of the door, as Sam knocked twice. It was unlikely, but they didn't know for certain if Walker had a firearm of some sort, so there was no need to be careless, especially when they knew he was very likely to be on edge after his family's kidnap.

The door opened and Sutton stood back to let them in. Frankie Walker looked up from the chair he was sitting in, but shot out of it when he saw Sam.

"Martínez! Jake, what's going on? What's he doing here?"

"And a very good morning to you too Frankie," said Sam.

"Jake, you need to tell me and quickly, what the hell is going on?"

"Frankie, calm down and just sit back and listen.

This is to do with Maggs and your kids and how we may be able to help," said Sam.

"You, help me?" snapped Walker, unable to believe what he'd just heard from the copper whose mate he'd shot and nearly killed a year or so ago.

"I said, sit down," said Sam quietly, but this time with a firmer voice. "Every minute you waste now may make this harder to get your wife and kids back."

"How do you know about Maggs?" Walker looked accusingly at Jake, who held his hands up.

"I told them Frankie. I needed their agreement for the idea I've got to get you something to bargain with, with the Sanchezes."

Frankie was looking from Jake to Sam and back again, trying to get a hold on what was being said, but then noticed Greg, Terri and Holly.

"And who are you lot? Old Bill?"

"No," said Greg, "but as Sam said, we can help you, but it will be on our strict terms."

Walker eyed Greg suspiciously. He knew Martínez was a cop, or rather an ex-cop, but this guy was older and seemed very full of himself. He then looked at the two women. One was a tall blonde, good looking, in fact very good looking and a slightly smaller woman, who was a little bit younger, but also very attractive.

"So who are you then?" He glared at the two women, trying to stare them down.

Terri immediately went on the offensive.

"At the moment mate," she said, catching him off guard as she pushed him hard on his chest, into the chair behind him, "we're your best, no let me rephrase that, we're your only hope of getting your darling Maggs and kids back safely out of the hands of your business partners. So do as Sam says and shut up and listen."

He didn't know whether it was the Australian

accent that side-stepped him, or maybe it was just he wasn't expecting her to start pushing him a round, but Walker just sat there.

"Good," said Sam. "Now Frankie, this is Holly Regus, she works for an insurance company and it's pretty much down to her as to whether we can help you, so perhaps you'd like to stop snarling at her and let's see what we can do to help you."

"Okay, okay, I'm listening, but look, it's been doing my head in knowing they've got my girls. And they want ten million euros within the next forty eight hours!" He was gabbling. "And why would you help me? Especially you Martínez, no offence mate, but I sort of nearly killed your mate."

"Yes you did, we'll come to that Frankie. First of all, with Jake's help here, we can perhaps get the bargaining chip for you to negotiate with."

"But negotiate? With what? They want ten million euros."

"Yes," said Greg, "but they haven't stipulated cash have they?"

"Well no," said Walker. "What are you thinking?"

Greg looked across at Holly who nodded. She'd been taking everything in as things unfolded. Walker was intimidating and yet she saw he was unsettled because of his family's kidnap, so she went in with all the confidence she could muster.

"Frankie, I can call you Frankie can't I?" But she didn't wait for a response. "You need our help. Jake here, is willing to steal a ten million euro painting from an art gallery here on Mallorca that my client's operate."

"And you're going to let him?" asked Walker slowly.

Now it was Jake Sutton who was looking at Holly with a look of confusion on his face.

"I thought you warned me off earlier this morning?"

"That was then, this is now," said Holly firmly.

"I'm sorry if I'm missing something here," said Walker, "but I still don't get why you want to help me, unless...." He went quiet. "You want, or maybe the Spanish Old Bill want the Sanchez lot don't you?" He smiled, knowing he perhaps now had something of a bargaining chip of his own with whoever these people were.

"Got it in one Frankie my boy. But listen," Sam's voice suddenly went hard. "I saw that look in your eye. You need to forget it if you think you have anywhere to go with all of this except where we tell you to go and when we tell you to go. Do you understand? Any sign of shit from you Frankie and we withdraw all help."

"Look Sam, I can call you Sam can't I?" Now it was Frankie Walker's time to push back, to test this new relationship with the former police officer. "If you get my Maggs and our kids back then I swear on my mother's life that I won't do anything to upset anything you've got in mind to do with the Sanchez lot."

"Frankie, that's very good of you, but there's just one thing," said Sam.

"Yes," said Walker.

"Your mother's been dead for ten years, so I won't be counting on any of your promises, got it?"

Walker smiled back at him. "Look Martínez, truce, okay?" Then his face took on a much more serious look. "Get Maggs and my kids back and I'll hand the Sanchezes to you on a plate."

Sam was thinking that Walker could hardly do anything else, given the position he was in, but he needed to work with this guy. "Okay good, now I think we can properly get down to business."

"Can I come in here?" said Jake, "as I think you need me to do something and I want to know where that leaves me."

"Yes, why would you steal anything Jake? I mean you're minted aren't you?" asked Walker.

"Long story Frankie," said Jake.

"Yes, which we haven't got time to bother with just now. So Jake, now that you ask, we need you to play your part in this to get the Sanchez family to believe you're bringing them a genuine Miró."

"A what?" asked Walker.

"He's a Spanish painter Frankie, very well-known. He lived here on the island for many years," said Jake.

"And his paintings go for ten million?"

"Some more, some less," said Holly. "Jake, first things first. You said you wanted to help Frankie by stealing the picture?"

"Well yes, that was the only way I could see of helping him get anything worth the ransom they want."

"So let me get this straight," said Walker. "You'll let Jake nick a painting and I'll take it to Sanchez."

"Yes," said Sam.

"And which bit haven't you told me yet then?"

Sam smiled. Frankie Walker was nobody's idiot. He knew there must be something else as well as handing over a picture as part of the ransom.

"Okay, so this is when it gets a bit riskier."

Ten minutes after Sam had finished outlining the plan, Frankie Walker was pacing up and down Jake's hotel bedroom floor.

"This is nuts!"

"No, not nuts," said Greg. "We have a plan. It is admittedly, at the top end of risky, but we will have contingencies in place."

"What bloody contingency, as you call it, do you have if they discover I've set them up? Where will you and the 7th Cavalry be then amigo?"

Walker was boiling over. He'd felt relieved to see a possible way of getting his family back, even if it meant working with Martínez of all people, but talk about risky! This was madness.

"Let me get this straight in my head, just so I know I'm not going completely mad." Walker paused for a moment. "You want some woman, posing as Maggs's mum, to turn up unannounced at the Sanchez villa. Jake here then appears with a ten million euro painting he's been allowed by Holly's lot to steal. Then what?"

"Couple of things Frankie. Jake will still have to physically steal it. We can't risk anyone leaking the fact that it isn't a bona fide theft."

"Okay, I get that," said Walker, although Jake Sutton was now looking even more uncertain. "What's the other bit?"

"The 'then what' is something you're better not knowing the detail about."

Greg saw Walker look as though he was going to say something.

"Just in case you inadvertently give it away," said Greg.

Walker thought for a moment. That made sense. He was living on his wits at the moment as he was worried sick about his wife and kids. The only thing he wouldn't tell this lot was that if he got the chance to knock off one, or the whole bloody Sanchez family, he'd do it in a second to make them pay. But that was for him to know and for the others to find out if it came to that.

"Okay, I can go with that. What about the Spanish Old Bill? Where do they come into all this? Presumably they'll be there?"

"Yes, they'll come in at the end to pick up the pieces

so to speak," said Sam.

It wasn't lost on Sam that Walker might look for any opportunity for revenge if he got the chance. It wasn't ideal, since if it went wrong, his mother would be in there masquerading as part of the Walker family and so could be caught up in any subsequent retribution by Alberto Sanchez, or his two sons. But that was something he knew his mother would have already taken into account in her own planning.

Walker was thinking. He didn't like the idea of working with these people. He'd never trusted a copper in his life, but he had nothing else. This seemed the only thing to go for.

"Look, you need to know something. Her mum hates me."

"Why?" asked Sam.

"Because I took her little girl away. The Murphys were an ordinary family, hard-working and almost on the right side of honest."

"Almost?"

"Back in the day I think they might have had some ties with the IRA."

"Ah, and then their daughter fell in love with a London criminal?" said Sam.

"Yes, but look Martínez I don't expect you to understand, but Maggs loves me for me, not because of what I do," he paused, "and I, well, I just love her."

It was a sudden outburst of emotion from Walker that caught them all a bit by surprise. Sam was the first to react.

"Actually I do, and whilst I thought I'd never say it, you're a lucky man. So you need to use those feelings for Maggs and your kids Frankie, when you tell the Sanchezes that you can get them a Miró, rather than ten million in cash."

"Why don't you just give me the cash? Surely you

can get your hands on it?" asked Walker.

"We've been through that idea," said Greg. "It brings too many other people into the equation, where questions could be asked and we don't know the extent of the Sanchez network, so it's a no-go for that reason."

Walker realised they'd clearly thought through their plan.

"One other thing with my mother-in-law that you'll need to know when you approach her."

"Are you going to tell us they haven't spoken for a few years?" said Sam.

"How did you know? I wouldn't have thought the Met would have known that?"

"Obviously you're not the only one who has someone watching your mother-in-law," said Sam, "but look, it's good you told us Frankie, as it confirms what we thought and we think it will actually help, as your kids probably won't remember their grandmother," said Sam.

Walker looked around the room, his confidence just starting to rise a little that this wasn't such a crazy idea.

"Looks like job's a good'un then. What do you need me to do?"

42

Tommy Williams, the long serving, ex-para, member of the team was still in London. He'd been kept updated by Simon as to what was going on, but since solving Sutton's riddle his main focus had been back managing 3R International's day to day business in the UK.

It was late afternoon and he was still in the office when he saw the call coming in from Greg.

"Hi Greg, how's it going out there?"

"All good my friend, all good, although things are starting to move quickly, so I need your help on setting something up over there."

Tommy listened as Greg walked him through the plan.

"Okay, got it. I'll call Sharon in for support and we'll get someone on site this evening, ready to go first thing tomorrow morning."

"Great, speak later Tommy."

*****

Sharon Bridger was one of the most experienced of 3R's team leaders and once briefed she started calling her team to be ready to implement the plan Tommy had talked through with her.

"We're just waiting on an address Sharon and then

you can get the team to take a look."

"Okay Tommy, speak soon."

*****

Greg and Sam had gone to Anna's villa to sort out how best to go about getting Anna into the Sanchez villa on the island.

"Where have we got to?" she asked.

"Okay, so Tommy's ready to go. We just need the address for Maggs Walker's Mum," said Greg.

"Shouldn't be too long. I told Jimmy that he should run it past his DI. I don't want him getting in trouble over this. You know, data protection and all that stuff."

"Absolutely. Now Greg, what about Lori? Has she got her boss's agreement?" asked Anna. "I'd prefer to know that we've got the police tee'd up ready to come rushing in, should I need them on the hurry-up."

"Good point. I left it with her and then we had the meeting with Walker and Sutton, so I'd better check in and see."

Greg rang Lori and she answered quicker than he expected.

"If you're ringing to see if I've got the go ahead for this from my boss, then this isn't a good time. He couldn't make a decision if his life depended on it."

"What now then?"

"He's now in a meeting and apparently uncontactable. That just means he's hiding from me. He's done it before. He's such an infuriating man!"

Greg didn't need to say anything. He could tell she was furious and that this would put a block on her moving things forward.

"Problem?" mouthed Anna.

"Hang on a moment Lori, Anna and Sam are here. I'll put us all on speakerphone."

"Maybe I could help Lori? A phone call from London perhaps?" said Anna.

Lori knew Anna had re-engaged with the British Secret Intelligence Service, MI6.

"Well yes, that might well work Anna, but isn't this just a little outside their jurisdiction?"

"There's always some leeway with these things. This isn't just a little drugs operation you've got going here now is it? It's got to be in the region of a hundred, or even two hundred million pounds plus of street value drugs, therefore I'm sure I can suggest it hits an appropriate threat level to UK national security. That might well enable someone in London to put in a call to someone in Madrid, as well as to PRI and Adamsons to ask for some support."

Greg looked at Anna.

"You mean Martin?"

She nodded.

Martin Carruthers headed up a small team responsible for specialist operations in MI6. He was what was known in the service as a fixer and on his return to London, he'd told Anna that the reason they'd not given his role a title was primarily because it meant that his boss, Henry Greenfield, MI6's Deputy Director, could effectively give him any job that was in the too difficult box.

"Yes, I think he owes 3R more than a small favour or two," smiled Anna.

Greg grinned at her.

"Well I definitely think it's worth trying," said Lori. "My boss will not back down once he's made his mind up, but something from further up the chain of command, if you can get a call into them from London, might just give him the motivation to make the decision we need."

"Good, I'll get onto Martin straight away," said Anna.

"Do we know if Holly has secured the necessary agreement from her boss and Adamsons?" asked Lori.

Sam was shaking his head.

"We don't know at the moment. Holly spoke as though she did, when we were with Walker and Sutton, but to be honest I'll need to double check."

"Keep me posted please Greg, on what you intend to do," said Lori.

"I know you're busy Lori," said Anna, "but can you come here for dinner this evening? Be a good opportunity to fill you in on the detail."

"Bueno! See you later."

*****

When Sam rang Holly to see if her boss, Charles Hacker, had agreed, he soon found out that he hadn't.

"He won't even let me speak to Christine Harrison from Adamsons."

"What now then?" asked Sam. "You do need their authority?"

He asked the question slowly, knowing the potential implications for her if she went ahead without it.

"If we did this and something happened to the Miró…"

"I understand Holly." He paused. "I wonder.."

"Wonder what?" asked Holly.

"Sorry, I didn't realise I was talking out aloud. Look, Lori's having similar problems with her boss, so Anna is going to put a call into London."

"You're involving MI6?" asked Holly incredulously.

"Yes, but we need to keep that closely under wraps Holly and it's certainly not for Sutton or Walker to know. National security and all that stuff," said Sam, "but it may be useful if a call went into your boss at PRI, as well as the Chairman at Adamsons."

"Okay understood."

She thought for a moment.

"You know what Sam, this might just work," said Holly. "Keith Smalling, the Managing Partner is very old school, so a call to him and to the Adamsons' Chairman that it's a matter of national security and I think we might just get it through."

*****

It didn't take long for things to start happening once Anna put the call into 85, Albert Embankment, Vauxhall, the headquarters of the Secret Intelligence Service, otherwise known as MI6.

Martin Carruthers listened carefully to Anna as she outlined the plan and why she thought it was something that he should lend his weight to, although he didn't agree straight away and not until he'd fired some challenging questions into her.

"What's your primary reason for wanting this to go ahead Anna and please don't tell me it's national security?"

She knew he wasn't going to be bamboozled into anything. He was far too switched on to have any sort of wool pulled over him.

"Look Martin, this is nothing to do with our commercial contract with Adamsons, or rather their insurers Premium Risk International."

"Good, well that's a start, although I'd have been surprised if you'd have come to me with just that. So come on, what is it?"

"It's simply a situation where two plus two actually ends up with five for the good guys. If Lori can break this drugs route between Spain and the UK we'll keep millions of pounds worth of drugs off the street and you'll effectively put a London OCG boss, Frankie Walker out of business, at least for a while, plus we won't have the British private security industry thrown into turmoil at the demise of SIS."

"SIS, isn't that the young entrepreneur chap, Jason Sutton?"

"It's Jake and yes, that's him."

"So why should I worry about him?"

"It's what he can bring to you in terms of knowledge and skills that I think you'll be interested in. Far better that than have him languishing in a Spanish prison, if he goes ahead and steals a ten million euro picture, which we know he's going to do to help his gang boss friend get his wife and kids back."

She saw Martin's eyes twinkle. She'd noticed they always did that when he was seeing possibilities arising from chaos.

"You're going to recruit him?"

"Exactly. He needs to give something back for the hole I'm about to get him out of, that is if we all survive this and don't end up as fish food in the bottom of the Med," she grinned.

He smiled back at her.

"Who do I need to ring?" he said.

43

Holly saw the call was from her boss, Charles Hacker.

"Holly, I've been giving this thought and whilst it took some persuading, I think this is something we need to try."

She couldn't help but smile. Anna's call to London had clearly worked, but she couldn't risk upsetting Hacker by telling him she knew why he was calling her.

"Oh Charles, that's great. Have you spoken with Christine?"

"Yes, yes, of course and we've got her hundred percent backing too."

"That's great Charles, thanks so much for your help," she said, trying to not sound too sarcastic.

"Holly, just one thing," he said almost casually.

"Yes Charles."

"If you do lose the bloody Miró, don't bother coming back."

She knew he wasn't joking.

"Understood."

DI Lori Garcia also received a call that she could proceed with her operation. It was from her previously uncontactable boss. He'd been unceremoniously pulled out from his so-called important meeting to take a call from the head of the GEO and to round things up, DI Sandra Chisholm got a call from Commander Katy Dawson, Head of Special Ops in the Met.

"Sandra, anything going on that I should know about?"

Dawson was known as a no-nonsense, get things done type of senior officer who had flown up through the ranks.

"Er, no Boss, nothing special other than what was on the morning briefing."

"I've just taken a call from our friends at Vauxhall Cross. We've been asked to assist the Spanish Police and in particular their GEO, with something they're doing with a Spanish OCG and Frankie Walker."

"Really! What are Six getting involved for?"

"So you know about this?"

"Well yes, sort of Boss. We had a call for some info from an officer one of our intel guys knows over there, just for some background on Walker. It seems he's in Mallorca, but we're monitoring it Boss and helping where we can."

"Does that help extend to a certain former DCI, Sandra?"

She knew the Commander was talking about Sam Martínez, but she wasn't too sure how to answer without getting either Jimmy Mellor, herself or both of them into a whole load of trouble for unlawful disclosure of information.

Commander Dawson didn't leave her hanging too long, but definitely long enough to make sure the DI got the point.

"Let me take your pause as a yes, however, on this occasion Sandra, you'll no doubt be pleased to know that it is okay for us to assist an organisation who, whilst outside of the usual law enforcement agency family, are still on the side of the good guys."

"Yes Ma'am, understood."

"It seems that our former colleague's new associates have the support of some very well-connected people in Vauxhall. So let's help them as best we can."

Sandra Chisholm breathed a sigh as the Commander hung up. She had already given Jimmy Mellor the go ahead to give out the home address of Saoirse Murphy, Maggs Walker's mother to Sam Martínez, even though she hadn't sought any sort of official confirmation from further up her own chain of command.

She was glad Jimmy had asked her, as it showed his confidence in her and just as well he did because she certainly wouldn't have wanted to have taken that call from Dawson without knowing what was going on. She smiled when she thought about Jimmy telling her that it had been Sam's idea to ask for her permission.

"He was a good guy then, your Sam Martínez?" she'd said.

"Yes Boss, very much so."

She left her office and walked across the corridor to where the main intel team were based and sat down next to Jimmy Mellor.

"Trouble Boss?" asked Jimmy, knowing enough about the behaviours of senior officers that they didn't usually just sidle up and sit down next to you for a chat.

"Jimmy, did you know MI6 are showing an interest in what's going on in Mallorca?" asked Chisholm.

"No Boss, but to be honest, it doesn't surprise me. Sam's Mum has some very old friends from her life before she had him."

He didn't want to go into more detail and seeing his boss's smile he realised he didn't need to.

*****

Maggs Walker's mother lived on one of the estates in South London, near the Elephant and Castle, where it was difficult, but not impossible to do any sort of static surveillance.

"You know what it's like around there Sam," said Jimmy when he'd called him with the address. "I don't want to go teaching your 3R guys to suck eggs, but don't go sitting around in any cars. They'll stand out like a sore thumb, plus we've got no houses in that immediate area that I can call safe. You know, where you could chance a door knock to get an OP?"

It was an old technique, where the police would sometimes look at previous reports of victims of crime in an area. They'd then contact them either by phone, or sometimes even a cold call knock on the door, to ask for help where they couldn't easily get an OP, an observation point for a static surveillance operation.

"I think we'll be okay with a drive-by to check the area Jimmy, but have you got anything on Mrs Murphy and her immediate neighbours?"

"Nothing much to worry about with the Murphys. Neither Saoirse, nor the late hubby have had any police contact, except as victims of crime, for burglaries on a couple of occasions. Probably not relevant here Sam, but there's some E5, uncorroborated intel of a connection between Saoirse's mother to the IRA, maybe her brother or an uncle. Interestingly though, they've had no trouble since Maggs started going out with Frankie, funny that, eh?"

"Ah yes, their very own knight in shining armour who no doubt made it known that no one should be bothering his in-laws."

"Looks that way Sam, so you'd better be mindful about number four, the immediate neighbours. The voters register shows it should be a family called the Staples, but we think it's a guy called Colin Muldoon who is actually living there."

"What? Have they got someone at Housing sewn up on their books?" asked Sam.

"Probably nothing as complicated as that Sam. Frankie could have just told the others to get out, or if he was feeling generous he may have given them some money, or even have rehoused them if Maggs said she wanted her Mum kept an eye on."

"What do you know about Muldoon?"

"He's got form and we think he's one of Frankie's enforcers. Judging by his form he can handle himself, so he's probably been put there to make sure his mother-in-law's not bothered by any of the locals."

"Good point Jimmy, I'll let Tommy know. Anything else?"

"No, not from our end? But I've got the go-ahead now from the boss that if you need help, just let me know."

"Okay tell her thanks from me, it's appreciated."

"I'll pass it on."

*****

"Sam, we've done the drive-by of the house. Sharon did it. Fortunately there were a lot of parked cars either side of the road so her driving slowly past didn't look out of the ordinary."

"That was handy, especially in that neighbourhood."

"Yes, she said she saw there were lights on in number two, that's the Murphy place and she also managed to have a quick look at four as they went past. That's where the minder Muldoon is. He's got cameras on the outside of his place, so he's clearly keeping a good eye on the Murphy place."

"So you're set then Tommy?"

"Yep, I'll go in tomorrow morning. Sharon's team will be there as back-up, just in case Muldoon has anyone else in there with him."

"That's good to hear mate. Let's talk again in the morning to finalise the call with Frankie Walker."

After he'd rang off Sam turned to the others around Anna's dining room table. Greg, Anna and Lori looked across at him.

"Things all set for tomorrow?" asked Greg.

"Yes," said Sam. "We just need to tee up Frankie Walker to ring his mother-in-law when Tommy knocks on the door."

"You may need to get him to call his guard dog, Muldoon, too," said Anna.

"Yes, good thinking Mum, although I suspect Tommy can probably manage him anyway."

It was then like a rapid fire Q&A session as they each threw questions in during their planning session.

"Greg, do you want to use your kit to go in the house with Anna, or do you want to use ours?" asked Lori.

"No thanks, we're good for that Lori. We'll use the kit that Anna is already familiar with, so it'll be one less thing she has to be concerned about. I'll sort out the frequencies we're operating on and let Nino know so we can all listen in. Now what about the gallery in Sóller, Sam?"

"I told Holly that we shouldn't go warning anyone there, not even the gallery manager. Sutton needs to do his thing and get in and out without any risk of anyone letting it out of the bag that he's been allowed to take this picture."

"What will he do once he's got the picture?" asked Lori.

"I think we need him to take it to Walker and then Frankie will take the picture to the Sanchez place. It shouldn't take long as it's around halfway between Palma and Sóller. I don't see the need for Sutton to go to the Sanchez place. He'll just be one more thing to be thinking of and possibly getting in the way," said Anna.

"I agree," said Greg. "Sam?"

"Yes, definitely. There will be more than enough for

us and your team Lori to worry about with Walker's family and you being in there Mum."

"That sounds good to me," said Lori. "There's no point making this easy as it might arouse suspicion if any of the Sanchez lot are watching."

"Anything else from anybody?" asked Greg.

"I'd like to talk to Frankie Walker," said Lori.

"Me too," said Anna. "I need to get some information on his mother-in-law."

"And I need to make sure he's not going to do anything stupid. I don't care about him, but we have you Anna, plus two innocent kids in there too," said Lori.

Anna nodded. Despite her professional approach to all of this, it wasn't lost on her that this was risky. Actually not just risky, but downright dangerous. It was the uncertainty of the Walkers that was giving her most cause for concern.

'How would they react in the heat of the moment if things got tricky?'

"Okay, so we'll have to either meet him at Sutton's place again or just ring, or video call him, because we can't afford to be seen with him by any of Sanchez's lookouts," said Sam.

"I'd rather see him in person," said Lori, "and I don't mean by video call."

"Me too," said Anna. "I don't want it to be the first time we've seen each other when I see him in the Sanchez villa."

There were nods of agreement from around the table and given the time restrictions on them it was decided to act quickly and set up a meeting with Walker at his hotel in a couple of hours' time.

44

Holly rang Frankie Walker at 10.00pm.

"Yes, I know it's late, but I've got a couple of people who need to speak to you face to face before the morning."

"What, now?"

"Yes, give me your room number and listen out for another call."

He realised this wasn't a request and despite some deep held reservations of working with them, especially someone like Martínez, he knew they might be the only way of getting his wife and kids out safely.

"I'm in 232, second floor."

"We'll text before we enter your hotel."

"When I came back in they still had someone out front parked up in a dark blue or black SUV."

"Okay, thanks."

Holly rang off.

"He's in 232 on the second floor, but he says someone's watching his hotel."

"He's in the Sant Francesc isn't he? It's in a little plaza just up from the cathedral, La Seu," said Terri, looking at Simon.

"I'll go and do a recce and then call Anna and Lori in. Can you sort them out getting down there?"

"I'll ring Greg now," said Terri.

With that Simon went down to the cycle store in the underground car park. The streets in the city were small and parking was limited, so a car would stand out. On a bike it would only take him ten minutes to get into the city from Terri's apartment in Portixol. Then he could easily leave it somewhere before continuing on foot into the Plaza de Sant Francesc, where he'd get a good view of the hotel.

It was just after ten as he made his way along the main road into the city, before turning right and going through the Parc de la Mar and up past the Banys Arabs, the Arab Baths and through the back streets and alleyways towards Walker's hotel.

Even on a slightly chilly October evening there was still a fair number of people about, some coming out of restaurants and bars, but others looked like they were only just going in for a late dinner.

It took only ten minutes hard cycling until he reached Carrer del Pare Nadal, an alleyway south of the Plaza de Sant Francesc.

He left the bike leaned up against a wall before he took a quick look from the shadows out into the square. The Sanchez man was clearly making no effort to conceal the fact he was watching the hotel. The SUV was parked about thirty yards from the hotel entrance, just across from the impressive church, the Basílica de Sant Francesc.

He then went looking for the back entrance to the hotel where the deliveries would be made. He might have been a lot more wary if he'd been in the Sanchez's home city, as they might well have eyes and ears in many of the hotels and bars, however, this wasn't their home turf, so it was unlikely and anyway, time was now of the essence and so this was a calculated risk worth taking.

Years of service with the SAS had given him the skills and knowledge of blending into situations when required, but one of the key things he'd learned was that sometimes a bit of brazen confidence, that you should be in a particular place, often meant people didn't challenge you.

After a few checks of the side alleys, he found one of the service doors to the Sant Francesc. It was propped open, which wasn't unusual as it led out to the waste bins and usual staff habits often meant doors, even fire doors, got left open.

He walked through the door and into the kitchens. A couple of staff looked up as he passed through, but ignored him, thinking he was probably just another security guy checking out safe routes in and out of the hotel for their client.

He kept walking, taking a route that appeared to take him towards the staff corridors. Confident that this would give him access to the guest bedrooms, he retraced his route back through the kitchens, nodding to some of the staff knowing he'd see them again in just a few minutes and familiarity was a useful step towards acceptance.

Back outside in the side street he rang Greg.

"We're just down the road Simon, about a hundred yards away, I'll send them down."

Simon saw the two women approaching, chatting away as though just out for the night. He texted Walker to expect them shortly.

"Evening ladies," he said.

"Buenas noches Simon," said Lori.

"It's this way."

As before, few of the staff looked up, but those who did saw the same guy from a few minutes before, but this time he was with two women, presumably his clients, who smiled at them as they walked passed.

"This way please ladies," said Simon, adding to the theatre, as he led them out of the kitchen and in to the staff lift.

"Nice to see you again Simon," said Lori.

"You too Lori," smiled Simon.

The lift door opened and Walker's room was just a few yards along the corridor.

"Okay, we're here, I'll stay outside."

Anna nodded and knocked on the door. A man opened it immediately before stepping back to let Lori and Anna in.

"Come in," said Walker.

No pleasantries, not that Anna expected any.

"Frankie, apologies for the late visit, but we're going to see Saoirse first thing tomorrow morning," said Anna.

"Well you've got the accent spot on. You Irish?"

She smiled. She'd thought it best to get straight into character, so that when he next saw her he wouldn't be swayed by a different accent.

"There's Irish in my blood Frankie, that's for sure. Now we just need a few answers about your mother-in-law and the layout of the Sanchez place and then we just need to set out some rules of engagement."

"What do you mean *'rules of engagement'*?"

Anna heard the tone in his voice change. She'd need to be careful with him as he had the potential to blow at some stage of the operation.

"I want to make sure you don't go off on one until we've got your wife and kids safe," she said firmly.

He'd been taken in when he first saw her. The way she'd come into the room had given him the sense that she had a gentleness about her. He realised now that it was just an act and he'd fallen for it.

He nodded and this time it was Anna's turn to sense something in him. For all his arrogance and outgoing bravado as a London gang boss, he was genuinely worried about his family.

"Frankie," she said quietly, "we can do this, but you must do as I tell you, do you understand?"

"What are you, or were you? A cop?" he asked, but this time without the aggression in his voice.

"No, but I've done a lot of this sort of thing."

He gathered he wasn't going to get any more from her.

"Okay, what do I call you?"

"Let's stick with Saoirse, shall we, it will save you from calling me by my real name by mistake."

"Oh no Missus, it's always Mrs M, never by her first name."

Anna saw almost a grin from Walker.

"And you? You're the Spanish police?" he continued.

"Yes Señor. DI Garcia, GEO. You can call me Inspectora."

"GEO huh," he muttered. He knew they were one of the elite squads in Spain and he'd heard they didn't mess about when it came to how they tackled organised crime on the mainland.

Lori wasn't sure if she heard a bit of grudging respect from him, but she needed him to know that he needed to play ball with her, so she wasn't going to get on friendly terms with him.

"Let's get started Frankie," said Anna.

They spent the next hour or so going over the detail Anna wanted to know about Maggs, before Lori quizzed him on the layout of the Sanchez villa.

"So you think you can pull this off then?" Walker asked at the end.

"We wouldn't be doing this if we didn't Frankie," said Anna as she stood up. She'd got what she wanted from him, especially some key personal details in terms of the relationship Maggs had with her mother, like what they called each other, how she addressed her grandchildren and what they called her.

When Walker didn't have any recent photos of Saoirse, Anna made a mental note to make sure Tommy messaged her a photo as soon as he made contact the following morning.

"Frankie, we're done. So contact Alejandro Sanchez tomorrow and arrange a meet to talk about the money around eleven. If you do get to see Maggs, then you need to feed in the story we've given you about your plan to ask her mum to come for a reconciliation holiday. If she's primed for that and that it's come from you, then she should be able to read through the lines to understand what's going on."

Walker nodded.

"One final thing Frankie. Be ready in the morning to talk to Saoirse, and possibly your guy at number 4. Should be around ten o'clock our time, nine o'clock UK time."

"I got that, but I've been thinking," said Walker, "why would they take a picture and not cash?"

"This isn't any old painting Señor Walker. I don't suppose for one moment that the Sanchez family necessarily need another ten million euros in cash, but the opportunity to own a Miró? Even a stolen one? They won't be able to resist, I promise," said Lori.

45

Traffic was fairly light when Tommy and Sharon Bridger set off for Saoirse Murphy's house near the Elephant and Castle in South London.

"You set for this Tom?"

"Yes hun, I think we've got it all covered haven't we?"

They'd worked together for some time now and were a good team, so there was a lot of trust there.

"I'll be close by and we can call the boys and girls in if Muldoon turns out to have reinforcements in there with him."

"Thanks Sharon," grinned Tommy. "If all goes well, I'll be in and out in about fifteen minutes with Maggs's mum in tow."

Sharon went through one final radio check with the two other cars following them before she turned into the estate. She dropped him off as planned, about seventy five yards down the road from Murphy's house and far enough away to be out of camera range of Muldoon's CCTV at number 4.

"Lights on in number 2," said Tommy. "I'm approaching the door."

"Roger that," said Sharon and pushed SEND on her phone for the text to Anna that said Tommy was making his approach and Anna immediately sent a *'Stand by, call her in 5'* text to Walker.

Tommy knocked on the door firmly, but not aggressively.

"Hello, who is it?" a soft, gentle Irish voice called out.

"I'm a friend of Maggs."

She'd hardly spoken to her daughter for two years. She kept wanting to try to make up with her, but she was hurt. Maggs had said some horrible things to her, when all she had ever wanted was to try to help her daughter make the right choices. The problem was, in her mind at least, that her daughter hadn't made the right choice when she'd married that thug Walker. She felt her body twitch as she thought about him. She knew what he was, a violent criminal.

But Margaret was still her daughter, so she started worrying that something was wrong with her daughter, or her grandchildren. She opened the door and saw a stocky, well-built black man.

"Mrs Murphy? Maggs's mum?" he asked.

"Yes," she said carefully. "Who's asking?"

"My name's Tommy, Mrs Murphy. Have you got your phone close by? Frankie would like a quick chat?"

"What's happened? Is it my Margaret? Stop messing with me and just tell me!"

Her voice had hardened. She was in her late sixties, maybe early seventies, but she'd grown up on the mainland for most of her adult life and underneath a soft and gentle exterior, she was a tough South Londoner.

"I know this must be a bit of a shock for you Mrs Murphy, but we need your help. Frankie is ready to talk to you if you want, but I'll explain everything if you would please let me come in?"

He didn't look or sound like one of Walker's thugs,

but just as she was deciding whether to let him in or not, she saw her guard dog, or rather Colin Muldoon, coming towards her.

"Incoming Tommy," said Sharon as she saw Muldoon running across the road.

"Thanks Sharon," said Tommy quietly. "Is he alone?"

"Yes, yes."

"Who are you? What the hell do you think you're doing?" yelled Muldoon.

Tommy had already turned to see the man running towards him. He was big, about the same size as he was, but he was out of shape. He looked like he relied on his weight and the fact he was part of Walker's gang to intimidate people.

"Do you like this man Mrs Murphy?" Tommy asked, tilting his head to one side so she could hear him.

"Can't stand the man. It's like having your every move followed."

Muldoon had now reached Tommy only to realise the man before him was quite a bit bigger than he'd looked on the CCTV screen from the safety of his house across the road.

"Look, I'm here at your boss's request, so why don't you just ring him and he'll tell you to back off and get back in your kennel," said Tommy.

"He'd have told me if you were coming," said Muldoon, jabbing a finger towards Tommy's chest. "You need to shift your arse now before I do it for you."

Tommy would normally have had more of a dialogue with the man to resolve the issue, but he knew time was of the essence and so he feinted, as though to start walking away, before grabbing Muldoon's right arm with his right hand. He wrapped it sharply backwards, spinning Muldoon around towards him and exposing his belly, into which Tommy sunk a hard left jab.

He was expecting Muldoon to be able to react more quickly, but he didn't, maybe he was a lot more out of condition than Tommy had given him credit for. Tommy went at him again, pushing him hard up against the porch wall and punched him in the belly again, this time with a driving right and Muldoon crumpled to the floor.

"Not much of a guard dog are you now Muldoon," said Saoirse Murphy. "It's Tommy is it? Come in son, let's have a cup of tea."

Five minutes later they were sat at her kitchen table and after a few tears when Tommy had explained her daughter and grandchildren had been kidnapped, she took the call from her son-in-law.

"Frankie, I swear if my darling girl, or my grandchildren are harmed in any way I will make sure you are hunted down and dealt with. Do you understand me?"

Tommy listened and hearing the threat, he realised that Murphy's connections back home might be very real and not as far back in the past as the Met had perhaps thought.

"Mrs M," said Frankie. She'd never allowed him to call her anything else. "Please listen to me and believe me when I tell you I love your daughter and your grandchildren more than anything in the world. Just right now, I need you to help whoever is at your door. They aren't Old Bill, but they can help me get Margaret and the kids back."

Again, he called his wife by the name her mother always used.

She really didn't like him. She blamed him for taking her baby away, but Margaret had made her own choice and she knew she had to let her daughter live her own life, despite the complete misgivings both she and her husband had.

"Just get her back Frankie, get her back safely. You can deal with the people responsible for this later, do you understand me?"

"I do Mrs M, I do."

She rang off. Tommy saw more tears in her eyes, but also a steely look of determination.

"Now then, what do you need me to be doing?"

*****

Saoirse Murphy showered and changed and then packed quickly and efficiently. Tommy took some photos of her and sent them to Anna as she asked, to give her time out in Mallorca to find some similar looking clothes, as well as to work on Murphy's hairstyle and colour, to ensure she had the right overall look of the woman she'd be using as her cover.

"Tommy, I need to tell my neighbour where I'm going, well at least tell her I'm going to Mallorca. Known her for years, but if anyone comes to check, she'll know something's wrong if I haven't told her."

"Mrs Murphy, you're a star," said Tommy with a grin, realising that whilst it might be unlikely the Sanchez gang had someone to check up on Murphy's address, it was better to have it covered than not.

As they left the house, Saoirse Murphy rang her neighbour's doorbell whilst Tommy took her bags to the car Sharon had brought to the front of the house. Two minutes later she was sitting in the back.

"All done?"

"All done Tommy, she's so pleased I'm going for the reconciliation."

Tommy glanced back and seeing what he thought could be a tear at the corner of her eye, he smiled at her.

"Well you never know, this may be something that brings you two back together again."

Murphy wiped the tear away and forced a smile.

That would be nice, Tommy, that would be very

nice."

*****

Anna saw the picture of Saoirse Murphy and nodded to herself. The woman was smartly, but not expensively dressed. She obviously took care when choosing her clothes because they were good quality and would last. Her hair was a mix of brown colouring, presumably from trips to the hairdressers, and grey that was trying to take over as the dominant colour.

"Well I can absolutely understand that," Anna said out aloud to herself as she looked in her mirror.

She thought her hair would need a little bit of work and colour to get it somewhere close to resembling that of Murphy's photo, but the clothes would be much less of an issue. Since meeting back up with Martin Carruthers she'd gathered together an assortment of items in differing styles, some of which she knew would be suitable to help her take on Murphy's persona.

She checked her watch. It would be tight, but she had just enough time to get everything done and get a case packed and be ready to appear as Mrs Saoirse Murphy arriving on the afternoon BA flight from London City.

*****

"Frankie, how good to hear from you," said Alejandro Sanchez. "Can we expect the money anytime soon?"

"Can I come and talk to you and your father?"

"Frankie, you aren't going to let me down are you?"

"No, not at all."

"Good, I thought I might have to go and get your darling Maggs to help persuade you."

Walker felt the anger rising, but gripped his left hand tight, digging his nails into his own hand until he saw blood appearing.

"That won't be necessary Alejandro. I just have a

suggestion that I think would interest you and perhaps especially your father. Can I come up to the villa, for about eleven?"

"How intriguing Frankie, yes, by all means."

"I need to bring someone with me, Jake Sutton."

Sanchez thought for a moment. They'd seen enough of Sutton to realise he seemed to offer little threat in terms of violence.

"Well yes, of course then, we'd be delighted to meet Mr Sutton. I'll send a car."

Frankie rang off and called Jake Sutton.

"You want me to go in with you!" exclaimed Jake.

"Yes! What are you worried about?"

"Well possibly because they might also take me hostage and try to ransom me too!"

"Fair point," admitted Frankie.

Walker hadn't actually thought that might be a consequence of him taking Jake with him, but he needed him there to show them he was serious about what they were going to do.

"I'm not sure Frankie."

Walker lost what little patience he was hanging on to.

"Jake, stop bleating and be ready in ten. They're sending a car."

Walker rang off before Jake could say anything. Sutton just sat on the edge of his hotel bed wondering how he had ever got into this situation, then saw a call come in from Jeannie. He'd been dodging calls from his company's CEO for the past day and knew he couldn't keep avoiding her.

"Jeannie, how are you," he tried to sound bright and cheerful.

"It's not working Jake, what's up?"

"What's not working Jeannie, I'm fine."

"And I'm a flying dutchman, so just tell me what the

matter is," she said gently. "Are you in trouble?"

He didn't say anything. Mostly because he didn't know what to say. He didn't want to bring her into something that would leave her exposed reputationally.

"I take it that that's a yes. Don't tell me what it is if you don't want to, but is it something I can help with?"

"No," he said quietly.

"Are you likely to be arrested?"

"I don't think so, not now."

Her mind was racing at what she was hearing from him. She decided to take a positive tack.

"Well that's good."

"I suppose so," said Jake.

"But you're still in trouble?" she asked again.

"Yes, I need to do something to help a friend."

"Is it dangerous?"

"Not what I need to do, but the people he's involved with might make it dangerous."

"Hell's teeth Jake, can we stop talking in bloody riddles and just tell me."

"But I don't want to involve you Jeannie."

"Now you're pissing me off young man. Remember I worked in the City for a long time and there's nothing much I haven't seen in terms of dodgy dealing, drugs and extortion rackets, so come on, spit it out because if this ever gets out I'll be the one having to answer questions to the press."

He wanted to tell her, but he knew if he told her everything she'd probably not want any more to do with him.

"I'm sorry Jeannie, I need to do this on my own. I'll be back in three days I promise."

"Jake, …," she tried again.

"I'm sorry."

Her phone went dead as he rang off.

'What on earth has he got himself into?'

46

Sutton got into the car that was waiting for him outside his hotel.

"You alright mate?" said Walker.

"Not really Frankie, not at the prospect of going into some Spanish crime gang's villa where they're already holding your missus and kids hostage. No, not great at all!"

"Alright Jake, calm down for Christ's sake," said Frankie as quietly as he could. "Look, just follow my lead and fill in the bits if they start asking any questions about how you're going to nick this painting."

"Oh well that's easy then. I don't know why I was worrying," said Jake sarcastically.

*****

But it went a lot easier than even Frankie Walker could have anticipated. The Spanish cop had been right. Whilst he didn't know anything about this guy Miró, it was soon very apparent that the offer of the painting proved to be a real temptation to Alberto Sanchez.

"This is an interesting suggestion Señor Walker, but let me ask your friend, Señor Sutton, how do you propose to steal the Miró and more importantly how will you guarantee that it doesn't ever end up with the police coming through my doors looking for it?"

Frankie looked to Sutton hoping he had some sort of answer for the Sanchez patriarch.

Jake smiled as confidently as he could as he spoke, "Señor Sanchez, I hope you aren't asking me to divulge my craft secrets?"

But he saw Alberto Sanchez wasn't smiling back at him, so he quickly continued.

"Basically, I have the technology to freeze most alarm systems and make them think they are still operating. I then choose the most appropriate route into a building, take what I want and then once I've left and I'm a safe distance away I unfreeze the alarm system."

"That sounds very simple, so why hasn't anybody else thought of it?" asked Alejandro Sanchez.

"Simply because no one is as smart as me Señor. You need some very special technology to make this type of thing work and as I designed it, we're the only company that's got it."

"So you use this to demonstrate your company's products to new clients?"

"Yes."

"But you're willing to use this to steal a picture for your friend, Señor Walker here? That seems remarkably generous considering the risks?" asked Alberto Sanchez, his eyes narrowing.

"I owe him a lot Señor and he would dearly like his family returned to him and for you to get on with your original business deal. I seem to have somehow caused an issue for you, so I hope by doing this we can return to the original status quo."

Frankie looked at his friend. He was turning them towards the deal, slowly but surely.

Jake continued.

"But you asked Señor Sanchez," looking directly at Alberto, the patriarch, "you asked how I can guarantee the police won't find out you have it. Well I can only say that we won't tell them and no one will know I have taken it and even if by chance the police do find out it was me? Well I still won't tell them because I have a good idea as to what might happen if I did."

There was a faint smile beginning to appear on Alberto Sanchez's lips. His son, Alejandro, saw it too and knew his father was going to accept Walker's suggestion. Frankie was right of course. The family didn't need the money. This was all about a matter of principle for his father. It was Alejandro's deal and his father had been watching carefully as it progressed, but whilst he seemed to like the woman, Maggs Walker, his father had appeared to have taken a dislike to her husband, although Alejandro didn't know why.

Alejandro thought it may have been because Frankie was a little brash, or it might simply have been because his father wanted to impress on both him and Diego that he was still very much the head of the family business. Maybe he was using the excuse of Walker bringing a third person into play, even unwittingly, as a reason to show he was still in charge and that meant there would be serious consequences if Walker didn't come up with the money his father had demanded.

Whatever it was, Alejandro couldn't help but feel some embarrassment over losing face because of his father taking control of the deal. It didn't help that he could also feel Diego, his brother, smirking at him from across the other side of the room.

But if he could just get his father to agree to the Miró he could get the whole thing back on track.

"Papa, I think Jake here understands what would happen if anyone was to ever find out about the Miró. Don't you Jake?"

"Yes, Señor Sanchez, I do."

Jake was already beginning to understand that if he ever got out of this thing alive and even that he realised was currently going to be a very big ask, then he'd probably need to go into long term hiding. He shook his head to get rid of the idea, but Alberto Sanchez had seen him.

"What is it Señor Sutton?"

"Nothing," he stopped for a moment. "No, actually, I was thinking I might have screwed this up for Frankie if you don't want the painting. I mean, what's going to happen to Maggs and their kids? Señor, please, I can do this, just give me a chance."

Even Frankie Walker wasn't sure if it was a genuine impassioned plea, or a clever performance, but whatever it was, he saw Adeline Sanchez walk slowly across to her husband and say something quietly in to his ear.

There was another smile from Alberto as he said, "Well there is no need to be disappointed young man, Señora Sanchez here would like to have the Miró."

He turned to Walker, still with a smile, although it now seemed to be a lot less friendly, "So we have an agreement Señor Walker, but do not let us down."

*****

Frankie asked to see his wife and children but had been given a firm 'no' from Alejandro Sanchez. He could see them when he brought them the painting. He went to argue, but Jake gently nudged his arm and led him outside to the waiting car, a Seat SUV. They then sat in silence on the way back to Sutton's hotel.

From higher up the road and using long range binoculars, Juan 'Cecil' Moriarty the GEO surveillance motorcyclist, saw the Sanchez car turn out of the villa driveway and on to the main road. With a top speed of around 300kph, Moriarty knew he'd have no trouble in following them on his Suzuki GSX and he could always quickly make up lost ground if he needed to hang back, especially if it looked like the driver was surveillance savvy and kept stopping or doing 'U' turns.

The quarter of a mile away Moriarty had been from the villa driveway was soon swallowed up by the superbike before he settled into a safe holding position some way back from the car, ensuring the driver wouldn't spot anything unusual in his rear view mirrors.

"Charlie Four to control," called up Moriarty.

"Come in Four," said Nino, who was operating the comms channel.

"We've got movement. It's the same car that picked them up at the hotel. We're heading back towards Palma. I can't confirm for sure if they're both in the back of the car, because I'm holding off a bit because there's not much traffic about."

"Roger that."

As they turned on to the Ma20, Moriarty called up again.

"Control from Charlie Four, I'm ready to hand over."

DS Fernando Pérez was waiting at the next motorway bridge, looking back down the motorway. He knew Cecil would have moved up a little closer towards the Seat to help him spot the SUV as it approached.

"Alpha One to Control, we've got eyeball on Charlie Four and the subject vehicle. Joining the motorway now."

"I can see you Alpha One," said Moriarty. "I'll drop back, so just give me a call if you need me."

"Cheers Cecil," said Fernando Pérez who was sat in the front passenger seat of an unmarked BMW looking ahead. *'Good,'* he thought. There was enough lunchtime traffic to limit the likelihood that the

Sanchez driver would see he was being followed.

"Nino, we're with the Seat, with good cover."

"All copied Alpha One."

The team continued to follow the Sanchez car without incident, before leaving it when the Seat turned right towards Portixol, when they held back once more.

When it was safe Pérez told his driver to pull in and he jumped out of the BMW and started running along the road towards Portixol, looking across the marina towards Sutton's hotel.

"Alpha One control," said Pérez.

"Go ahead," said Nino.

"I'm now on foot with eyeball on the car. Looks like it's going to the Portixol hotel."

Nino heard Pérez breathing heavily.

"Yes, yes, confirmed," continued Pérez, "the Seat has stopped. Two men, repeat two men, are out of the rear of the vehicle. Vehicle moving off and our men are walking into the hotel."

"You a little out of breath Alpha One?" teased the comms operator.

*****

Only when they were safely back in Jake's hotel room did Frankie speak.

"You did it boy! You only went and bloody did it!"

It was the first time Jake had seen some real hope in his friend's eyes.

"Stage one done Frankie. We'd better report in."

Walker's phone then rang, with caller ID withheld.

"You're safely back then Señor Walker."

He recognised her voice. The Spanish cops obviously saw them arrive back.

"Yes Inspectora."

"So, how did your meeting go?"

"They went for it, just like you said. Jake did a great

job convincing them."

"Good. Did you see your family?"

"No, the bastard said I had to wait until we bring them the picture."

"Okay, remember, we need you to go and collect your mother-in-law when she arrives at the airport," said Lori.

"Yes, I've already booked an extra room where I'm staying and I'll be at the airport for when you said, half three this afternoon."

"Can you put your friend on please?"

He handed the phone to Sutton.

"Hello?"

"We haven't met yet Señor Sutton, I'm DI Garcia and well done for successfully negotiating for the Sanchezes to accept the painting. Now can I assume you're ready to go for the next stage?"

"Yes, it'll be done tonight," said Jake. "Do you need me to do anything before I take it to Frankie?"

"No, just go straight to his hotel and Greg Chambers will be there waiting with him."

"You're going to put something on the frame aren't you?" asked Jake, who saw the concern on Frankie's face. "Isn't that just increasing the risk of this whole thing going wrong?"

"Put me on speakerphone please Señor."

Sutton pushed the icon on the phone screen.

"Now look guys, you might be good at the particular things you do, but you need to trust us on this. Okay?"

Walker thought for a moment. This lot didn't seem to have got anything wrong so far, so it seemed fair to let them get on and do what they wanted.

"Presumably this is some sort of wire you're putting on it?" said Walker.

"Yes, Señor," said Lori.

"You know we've been searched every time we go

in?"

"Yes Señor, you told us that when we visited you at your hotel," she said patiently. She didn't want Walker getting jittery now. "But you also said they use search wands?"

"True, but won't they still pick the wire up?"

"For a start, we're anticipating that they won't put the search wand across the painting. They're much more likely to be focussed on people bringing in weapons or covert listening devices. But, if they do pass the wand over it and it bleeps, there's a very good chance they'll assume it's the tacks or picture hooks."

Jake looked at Frankie and nodded.

"Okay Inspectora, that makes sense. Right, I'll get ready to go and get my dear mother-in-law."

As Lori came off the phone Greg grinned at her.

"Sanchez went for it then?"

"Yes!" said Lori, with a little fist pump.

47

Anna was collected from her villa by DS Nino Castilla, who then drove her to the airport, taking her in through the police entrance, well away from the public.

Once inside the police offices, Nino paused and then took a quick look out of the door and saw some people at the top of the escalator. He quickly spoke into his radio and nodded at the response.

"Anna, sorry, I mean Señora Murphy, we've got the first of the passengers coming off the latest BA London City flight coming down the escalators now. Are you ready?"

"I am that."

Since he'd picked her up she'd only spoken in what he knew was an Irish accent. It was a soft and gentle tone and yet he could see she also spoke with her eyes. Lori had said Anna Martínez was good, but this was his first look close up and he realised just how immersed into her character she was.

He'd needed a double take when he'd gone to her villa to collect her. The transformation, with a change of hair colour and style and her clothes, was startling. The skirt and coat she was wearing were still smart, but she wore them differently to her normal clothes, or was it the way she walked? Whatever it was, she looked very natural in her role, but nevertheless he couldn't help but admire her bravery for walking into the Sanchez stronghold.

"Time to go. Good luck Señora."

"Don't worry Nino, I will see you soon and all will be well."

He watched as she walked towards the baggage reclaim area, pulling her cabin trolley behind her. Then as he closed the door he said a silent prayer, before turning back to the CCTV camera operator who was following Anna's progress towards the Arrivals door.

"Boss, Sierra Mike One is in Arrivals," said Nino through his radio.

"Gracias Nino," said Lori.

'And now we need to be patient and wait,' she thought.

*****

Frankie Walker had a similar feeling to DS Nino Castilla when he looked at the woman coming out of the Arrivals door.

'Is that her?'

She looked like his mother-in-law, but definitely nothing like the woman he'd met just the previous day.

Anna saw him and his uncertainty, so she quickly called out.

"So come and take this bag off me then Frankie."

She saw the recognition in his face.

"Mrs M, it's great to see you."

He went to give her a hug which she shrugged off.

"Great is it? You haven't seen me for two years, so why is it suddenly great? And where's Margaret and my grandchildren?"

Walker had to smile. She was good, very good. This is exactly the reaction he would have got from his mother-in-law. But he needed to keep things going just in case Sanchez had someone watching him.

"She's staying at a friend's villa for a couple of days."

"That's grand, you can take me there now then."

"It's not quite as simple as that Mrs M. I'll explain everything when we get to the hotel."

If it really had been his mother-in-law he would have had no idea how to tell her that her daughter was being hostage with her grandchildren, so this didn't need him to do any play acting.

"I don't like the sound of this Frankie. Not one little bit, but I'll wait a while for you to tell me what's really going on."

They walked to the taxi rank and Frankie looked around, trying to identify anyone who might be watching them.

"Stop looking about Frankie and just talk to me," said Anna quietly.

The last thing she needed was for him to make any Sanchez lookouts think anything was untoward.

"Sorry," he whispered before settling his composure. "We've been having a great time and Maggs, sorry Margaret, is so looking forward to seeing you again. She was really excited when I told her I'd asked you to come. It'll be good to get you two back together again."

"I can't say it wasn't a surprise when you asked. But I'm glad you did Frankie, it's been too long."

'Let's just hope my 'daughter and grandchildren' recognise me when they see me,' she thought.

*****

The Sanchez lookout watching and following Walker had called his boss, Alejandro when he'd seen his man leave the hotel and go to the airport.

Alejandro Sanchez's immediate reaction was to wonder if Walker was going to leave the island.

'But surely he wouldn't leave his family?'

When the lookout called in again to say Walker

was waiting at the Arrivals gate, Alejandro thought he might have called for reinforcements from London.

"Get the cars and four men," he shouted to his personal minder, "and quickly."

Two black Mercedes SUVs were soon en route towards the airport in a high speed convoy, with the drivers ignoring the speed limits. They slowed as they approached the city, because the local police would then be much more likely to be on the lookout for speeding offences and the last thing Sanchez wanted was to be pulled over, not with two cars full of men carrying guns.

Alejandro was tapping the front of the armrest of the passenger seat as he thought of how to handle this. He knew that if Walker had men coming through the Arrivals gate they wouldn't have any firearms on them, as they'd never have got them through security.

He was going to confront Walker, that was for sure, if only to ask him what the hell he was doing. But there were too many armed police in the airport for any sort of direct confrontation, however, he was also mindful that he didn't want to be exposed in any sort of situation, where Walker could potentially grab him and try to exchange him in return for his family.

The convoy had made rapid progress and as they drove into the airport complex Sanchez motioned to his driver to pull up by the coach parking area and then waved out of the car window to indicate to the car following to hold back by the car park entrance.

He got out of the Mercedes with his driver, telling him to leave his weapon in the car, before walking quickly towards the airport entrance.

He rang the lookout.

"Where is he now amigo?"

"Boss, he's at the Arrivals gate. He's just met a woman."

"Describe her, quickly."

"Old, well sixties, maybe seventy. They're starting to walk towards...."

"Got them, gracias," he rang off as he saw them approaching him.

"Frankie, what a lovely surprise," smiled Sanchez.

"Sanchez, what are you doing here?" growled Walker.

"We were just passing. So who do we have here?"

"My mother-in-law, Saoirse Murphy," said Walker quietly. "But please leave her out of this Alejandro."

"Ah, Alejandro is it now?" smirked Sanchez.

"Señora, welcome to Mallorca. Are you here on holiday?"

"I am, although what it's got to do with you I don't know," said Anna.

*****

The CCTV operator had seen the two Mercs as she scanned the bank of camera screens and pointed them out to the GEO man, Nino Castilla.

"Boss?" Nino called up on the radio.

"Go ahead," said Lori, who was sat at the desk in the office she'd previously used in the police headquarters in Palma. Greg Chambers was sitting opposite her.

"We might have a problem. Alejandro Sanchez is here. He's got a team with him. Two cars, Merc SUVs, with blacked out windows. We can see at least two with each vehicle, but there maybe more. At the moment it's just him, plus his minder, inside the airport, the other two are with their car up near the car park."

Armed major criminals in an airport was not something Lori wanted to hear. She certainly didn't want any sort of shoot-out with so many people about.

"Nino, alert the airport commander. Give him my regards and suggest he moves his team into a wide holding position near the two cars and boosts the people he'll have in and around Arrivals, but to make no approach unless absolutely necessary."

"We're on it Boss."

*****

"Frankie, you didn't mention your mother-in-law was coming? What a delightful surprise Señora Murphy, I'm sure Maggs will be pleased to see you, but I'm very surprised Frankie that you never mentioned this before?"

It was plainly obvious to both Anna and Walker that Sanchez was suspicious. However they'd worked on what Frankie could say and Anna crossed her fingers that he'd play his part as they'd planned.

"Alejandro, this was going to be a surprise for Maggs. She doesn't even know Mrs M is coming out, so please can we leave her out of this?"

Anna couldn't believe how well Walker had just dealt with Sanchez's challenge.

"Leave me out of what?" she said, seeing an opportunity to interject and steer things the way she wanted. "Is this the friend you said Margaret is staying with?"

"Si Señora, you must come and stay with us as well, at least for a few days, especially whilst Frankie is going to be busy completing some business we are doing together."

Anna looked at Sanchez and then to Frankie, as though for guidance, but hoping he would play his part as they'd discussed.

"But Alejandro, I think Mrs M might be more comfortable at my hotel until we settle things," Frankie said in a firmer voice.

"No, I insist. Señora, you shall come with us and you'll get to see your daughter and grandchildren. Is that okay with you?"

The way Sanchez looked at Walker suggested this

was a non-negotiable issue unless Frankie wanted things to suddenly become difficult for his family back at the Sanchez villa.

"Frankie, is that okay?" Anna's voice was faltering slightly.

Walker looked at Sanchez and then back to Anna, his 'mother-in-law and nodded slowly.

"Good, that's settled then. Now come, let's all go back to the villa. Frankie, we've got two cars. You ride in the second one and I'll sit and have a nice little chat with Señora Murphy."

*****

Lori flicked the transmit button on her radio.

"Nino, what's happening?"

"It's all looking good. There was some talking and now they're walking back to the cars. Doesn't seem to be any problems and the second Merc has joined the first one in the coach park."

"Good, keep the airport commander posted. Looks like they can stand their people down."

Nino acknowledged and then looked back at the CCTV screens.

"Okay, Walker has got in the back of the second Merc and Alejandro Sanchez is helping Sierra Mike One into the back of first SUV and he's now got in the back with her."

"Gracias Nino. Great work by you guys down there. Give my thanks to the CCTV operator and the airport commander please."

"Will do Boss."

She pushed her chair back from the desk and stood up.

"This is going well Greg. Let's hope it keeps going like this."

"Yes, she's in. We just need to hope Maggs Walker quickly buys into what is happening."

"I know, I've got the team on stand-by. Pérez has worked through a dynamic action plan in the event we need to go in quickly."

"I hope we don't, but it's bloody good that you're prepared for it," said Greg. "I'll leave you to it now Lori and get back to Sam and Terri to check we're good to go with Sutton this evening."

She smiled at him.

"We will get that dinner together, just the two of us, but not yet my love, eh?"

He grinned back.

"Not yet, but we can wait."

He hugged her and kissed her gently on both cheeks.

She quickly glanced out into the outside office. It was practically empty. She pulled him closer to her and kissed him again, this time on the lips.

"I need you to take care with these people Greg. They are ruthless and won't hesitate to kill you, Anna or anybody who they see as presenting a threat to them."

He was going to make light of what she said, but he saw how serious she was and he remembered it was an organised crime gang who had murdered her husband nearly twenty years ago.

"I'll be careful, I promise."

48

As the Mercedes sped away from Palma, heading north, Alejandro Sanchez was making small talk with Anna and she was playing along as he first asked her about her flight and then moved on to her grandchildren.

Anna was ready for his questions and started to set the background scene, giving him what was the real background story of Maggs and her mother and how they hadn't seen each other for a couple of years after a serious fallout.

"This is because of Frankie then?"

She turned and looked at Sanchez and stared hard at him.

"I'm not in the business of sharing my family issues with most of my closest friends Mr Sanchez, so I'm not about to start telling you."

"Señora, my sincere apologies. I did not mean to intrude." smiled Sanchez.

'*Not much,*' thought Anna, but she'd done what she'd wanted to do, creating the reason why she was there and importantly, why her grandchildren were unlikely to recognise her.

"But this is to be a reunion then? How wonderful if you can reconcile your differences."

"Well, we'll see about that!" she said quietly.

"But you will be pleased to see your grandchildren again Mrs Murphy?"

Anna made a point of sighing and smiling.

"Oh yes, I've missed them so much. They probably won't even remember their old Grandma." She looked away out of the window whispering, "They must be so big now."

"They are beautiful children Mrs Murphy and I'm sure they will be thrilled to see you again. Tell me, do you have any pictures of them at all?"

"Only from two years ago."

This was the test she thought. Taking her phone out of her handbag, she touched the photo icon and started flicking through the photos.

When Tommy had been taking Saoirse away from her house, he'd asked to borrow her phone. He'd then rang Anju on his phone. She was one of 3R's latest recruits out in India and in his words, a 'techno-geek.' She talked him through how to clone Saoirse's phone, uploading all the contents of to the Cloud. Anju then rang Anna and guided her through the final part of the process, downloading the content back into the clone, a second hand phone Sam had sourced for Anna in Palma.

Tommy had also scanned copies of some printed photos Saoirse had of her late husband and emailed these to Anna. She'd printed them out and then 'doctored' the images to give them an old look, by teasing the edges of the photos to create a frayed effect and adding some creases, before the final ageing touch of wiping them with cold tea and drying them with a hot hairdryer.

"That's amazing Mum," Sam said.

"I had a fair bit of practice when I was out in the field and needed something quickly," she grinned, "and the technique still works for at least a quick look."

She now showed Sanchez the phone and flicked through some of Saoirse's personal photos of her grandchildren and then some with her daughter.

"Where was this?"

"We all went to Brighton for the day, That's the pier in the background."

"Well they've certainly grown up since then Mrs Murphy. It won't be long now and we'll be there," Sanchez replied as he passed her back her phone.

She made a point of leaving her handbag open just enough, as she put the phone back, for him to see one of the paper photos of Saoirse's husband.

"I'm sorry, I didn't mean to look Señora Murphy, but is that your husband?"

"Yes, he's been a gone a while, but he'd have never have wanted me and Margaret to fall out, so that's why I'm here."

Anna sat in her seat watching him as he picked up his phone. She heard him say "Hola Papa." It seemed he clearly hadn't even thought to consider whether she spoke or understood Spanish, because he was soon telling his father that the Englishman had met his mother-in-law at the airport. He was even laughing as he said how easy it had been to take yet another hostage to ensure the Walkers played ball with them.

"No Papa, I had no idea he'd invited her out here."

Another pause as his father fired in another question.

"Yes, it's definitely her," Alejandro replied, "I got her to show me her phone on the pretext of seeing pictures of her grandkids and I even saw an old photo of her husband."

'Test passed,' thought Anna.

Now all she needed was for Maggs Walker to quickly pick up on the storyline.

*****

Less than fifteen minutes later Anna felt the car slowing and saw a gated entrance on the left hand side of the road. High wooden gates were swinging open as they turned into a tree lined driveway, although the driver barely slowed as the car went through the gap where the gates had been just a few moments before.

It was another quarter of a mile before the car pulled up outside the front doors of the villa.

"Welcome to my home Señora," said Sanchez. "Come, you must see your daughter and grandchildren and then you must meet my family."

"Gracias Señor," said Anna, with her best impression of someone who had little grasp of Spanish.

Anna was watching the windows on the first floor and she thought she saw a woman looking out, possibly Maggs Walker. As she walked towards the doors the second SUV arrived and stopped behind the first Mercedes.

Walker was quickly out and looked across at Anna.

"It's a lovely place isn't it Mrs M?"

"I suppose so," she replied stiffly.

"Can we see Maggs then Alejandro?"

Walker caught Anna looking at him, "Sorry, I mean Margaret?"

"But of course Frankie. Why on earth do you feel you need to ask?" said Sanchez.

'Don't bite Frankie!' thought Anna.

And he didn't, he simply smiled and followed Sanchez and Anna into the hallway where a man stepped forward and waved a search wand around her and Walker.

Anna looked suitably confused as though it was unexpected.

"It's alright Mrs M, they're just a bit cautious about security."

She nodded to him and then, hearing children's chatter, she looked up. Maggs Walker was walking down the stairs, with her children holding her hands and with Adeline Sanchez at her side.

Maggs Walker gasped and stopped when she saw Anna look up at her. She looked like her mother! Anna knew she needed to act fast and she was already on her way up the stairs, calling out as she did.

"Margaret, it's been so long, too long, but I'm so happy to see you," said Anna, hugging her close.

Before Maggs could say anything, Frankie cut in.

"I know it's a shock love, but I wanted to surprise you and bring your Mum out here. You know? So we could kiss and make up, at least that was the plan."

That Maggs Walker was clearly surprised didn't even come close to how she was feeling.

A voice inside her head was screaming, *'Who is this woman?'* She looked a little like her, but even though it was two years since she'd seen her, she knew it wasn't her bloody mum. *'Who the hell are you?'* she thought, her sense of confusion rising.

Maggs heard the woman's voice again. The voice and her accent, a gentle Donegal lilt? It sounded so much like her Mum.

"And you two, my lovely little girls! I don't suppose you even remember Grandma Murphy now do you?" Anna said, looking down at Maggs's children, Olivia and Charlotte.

Anna could see confusion in Maggs's face, but also now on the children's faces, especially Olivia's, who was possibly old enough to remember her real grandmother from two years before.

This was going to go badly wrong unless Maggs Walker reacted the way she needed to in the next five seconds. Anna looked straight into Maggs Walker's eyes and held her gaze for a moment, before she glanced across to Frankie Walker. As Frankie smiled back at his wife, she read his message loud and clear.

"Oh Mum, I've missed you so much," she said, hugging Anna. "I'm so sorry we fell out. Look girls! It's Grandma M, give her a big hug now."

Anna thought she saw tears in Maggs Walker's eyes. *'Nice touch,'* she thought, to finish off what had been a remarkable performance.

"Frankie, this is such a lovely surprise," Maggs paused, looking across to Alejandro with concern on her face as to what her mother had been brought into. "But couldn't my mother have stayed at our hotel until," she hesitated, "...until we're ready to go back there?"

Sanchez smiled, but there was no warmth in the smile.

"Oh no Maggs. I insisted your mother came and stayed here. We have plenty of room and my parents wouldn't have had it any other way, would you Mama?"

"Of course not Alejandro. Señora Murphy, I am Adelina Sanchez and you are most welcome in my house. My husband and sons are just completing some business with your daughter and her husband and we thought it would be nice if they stayed here."

Like her son, the smile on Adeline's face gave off no sense of emotion.

"Well it's a beautiful place you have here Señora Sanchez and thank you very much for asking me to stay, but I don't want to be a nuisance and can just as easily go to the hotel Frankie's booked for me," said Anna, who knew there was no point in playing this too easily, just in case one of the Sanchez family smelled a rat.

"It's no problem at all," said Adeline, "and I'm sure you'll be much more comfortable here and besides, you'll have more time with your daughter and grandchildren whilst the men sort out their business."

"Well if you insist Señora then that would be just lovely and please call me Saoirse."

"Alejandro, get Saoirse's bag taken upstairs and then we can have some dinner later, you must be hungry my dear and please, call me Adeline."

"How kind of you Adeline," smiled Anna, as she turned and hugged her *'daughter'* who smiled back.

"Mum, the girls are almost ready for their dinner. We usually let them have it in our room."

Maggs looked across at Adeline Sanchez who nodded.

"I will get it sent up."

"Gracias Señora Sanchez and afterwards Mum, you can help bath them and put them to bed."

"Oh, I'd love that Margaret," said Anna with tears in her eyes, all of which she hoped wasn't lost on Adeline Sanchez.

*****

Anna had no idea as to whether Maggs's bedroom was bugged or not, so she went straight into the bathroom and turned the taps on, calling out as she went, "I'll just freshen up Margaret."

Maggs Walker got the girls playing with one of the games they'd been given, although the eldest, Olivia was looking suspiciously at her 'grandmother.'

"Mummy will be back in a moment," before she went and joined Anna in the bathroom, gently pushing the door to behind her.

"Copper?" she whispered.

"No, but I am here to help. You just need to keep playing your part as you are and we'll be fine."

"My mum?"

"She's fine and she sends her love."

Tommy had told her that Saoirse was really worried when she knew what was going on and wanted her daughter to know she was thinking of her.

"She's praying for you," Anna added.

"Ah, that definitely sounds like my Mum, although I think she thinks I'm beyond redemption, getting involved with a guy like Frankie."

"Maggs, we need to be really careful with all of this, so please go with the flow and take my lead when you need to, okay?"

"Frankie knows all about this then, does he?"

"Yes, but we've a long way to go. You've heard that his friend Jake Sutton is going to steal a picture to fulfil the ransom money?"

"Yes, Alejandro told me what was happening, but I don't understand. Sutton is supposed to be sort some of hotshot tech guy isn't he? A multi-millionaire in his own right? Why's he stealing a bloody picture for Frankie, can't he just give him the sodding cash?"

"Woah, hang on, that's a lot of questions. I'll come back to you with answers, but for now, we should get back out to the girls before anyone suspects anything."

Anna turned off the taps and opened the door.

"Come on then now my darlings, what game are you playing here and can Grandma join in?"

"By the way," whispered Maggs. "What do I call you?"

Anna looked at her.

"Call me whatever you call your mum!"

"The *'to her face'* name, or the one I sometimes call her behind her back?" Maggs laughed.

Anna grinned back. Another stage successfully completed.

49

Jake Sutton had hired a car from an on-line website as he made his preparations for removing the Miró from the gallery in Sóller and it had just been dropped off at his hotel.

A silver Ford Fiesta, one of many on the island used as hire cars, that he knew would blend nicely into the background.

He'd tried to insist that Sam Martínez stayed well away from him when he went to check out the gallery in Sóller, but he'd lost that argument.

"This is more about your protection than me watching over you Jake. I know Frankie told the Sanchez lot that you needed free space on how you went about getting the picture, but you do know we can't trust these guys, don't you?"

Sutton had realised Martínez was making sense. Just because he'd heard the Old Man Sanchez promise Frankie that no one would be following him into Sóller didn't mean they'd be keeping to their promise.

"Okay, I guess so, but just give me room will you?"

"We will, if you stay in touch," said Sam, handing Jake a comms set.

"You want me to wear a wire?"

"No, this is just a mic and an ear plug, so we can keep

our distance, but we'll be able to talk to you if need be and you can talk to us too, if something goes wrong."

Sutton was relieved and just nodded.

"I don't need to know how you'll do this. But when you're going to do it, well that would be useful Jake."

"I'll go and look at it during this evening and then decide if it's going to be daytime or at night."

"Any early thoughts?" asked Sam.

"Not yet, but I'll let you know when I decide."

*****

Sutton left the hotel not long after Frankie had gone to the airport to collect his 'mother-in-law' and made his way to the ring road, the Ma20. The late afternoon sun was still quite warm, even for October. He checked his watch again. Four o'clock and the traffic wasn't too busy yet. Directions he'd got from his phone app suggested travel time was around half an hour and he was making good time as he turned off Junction 5A on to the Ma11.

He followed the road, passing through the impressive 3km Sóller tunnel, that seemed to literally drop down the side of the mountains, before coming out a just a short distance from Sóller.

Within a few minutes he'd parked in one of the car parks near the railway station and put on his anti-facial recognition glasses that he'd got in Singapore. No point in risking anything, he thought, as he walked down into the Plaça de Constitutió, where he had a choice of cafes and bars to choose from. He chose one and sat outside, taking in the location.

He'd read about the famous Sóller trams and seen the tram tracks along the streets and as he sat with a coffee and one of the local almond pastries, a tram came through the square, catching the light on its windows as it passed by him.

He looked around, trying to look like a casual tourist

taking in the sights, whilst actually looking for anyone who might be following him, whether it was from the Sanchezes or the police, or whoever else the other lot were.

He was thinking he'd managed to avoid anyone following him when he heard a slight crackle in his earpiece, the one Martínez had told him to wear.

"Good trip then Jake?"

He recognised the voice. It was Martínez.

"Just click your mic wire once."

Sutton slowly moved his hand to the buttons on his shirt, where the mic wire was located and clicked it once. Then holding it open he spoke, "So where are you then?"

"Well if you can't see me, I must be far enough away," said Sam cheerfully. "Nice glasses by the way, and don't worry there's no one else nearby."

Sutton breathed out. He'd promised himself that if he got through all of this he wouldn't do anything like it ever again. But first things first, he had to steal this picture for Frankie.

He left enough money to cover a tip and then slowly walked around the square looking for any town council CCTV cameras, as well as any other security equipment on any of the local shops close by to the gallery.

Seeing nothing to concern him he walked into Carrer de sa Lluna where he saw the Adamsons gallery. Housed in an impressive century old building it was, according to his guide book, one of a number of early 20th Century mansions built in the style of Catalan Modernisme and French Art-nouveau.

It was certainly a grand looking old building, but more to the point, it was only three stories high and there were plenty of hand and foot holds because of the style of the brickwork.

Whilst not quite a piece of cake, getting in and out

of the building really didn't look like it should pose a problem. This was especially the case given that he knew the Adamsons' alarm and security systems couldn't withstand his blocking equipment. They'd effectively be neutralised until he turned them back on again, by which time he would be long gone. He smiled, if it wasn't for Holly Regus, he could have got away with it again.

But this wasn't for him this time. He wasn't making another point to Adamsons. This time he was trying to help a friend. Someone he hadn't seen for nearly ten years, but who nevertheless was someone he owed a lot to, possibly his life.

"I'm done," he said into his mic.

"That was quick. Don't you need to go inside?"

Sam realised he'd just asked someone who so far had successfully stolen one ten million euro picture and had almost got away with another.

"Er, don't answer that. Stupid question."

"But I'm grateful for your interest," laughed Sutton as he walked back to the square.

"Look, there's no point hanging about. We can do this tonight. I'll head back to the hotel and come back later, but there is something you can do if you're going to be riding shotgun over me?"

"Yes?" said Sam.

"I'll need another car, but don't leave it too near my hotel."

"No problem, I'll get it sorted and text you when it's ready. And Jake?"

"Yes?"

"We're impressed."

Sutton wasn't sure what to make of that. Who was impressed?

*****

Diego Sanchez was being sidelined. At least that was

how it felt. His father was giving his brother, Alejandro, more of the business to look after, including this deal with these Walker people.

He'd actually been pleased when things had seemed to be going wrong when first Sutton and then the gallery security guy, Theakston, had appeared on the scene. But then there were the guys who did the exchange for him with Theakston. Who were they?

He didn't trust either of the Walkers and yet his father had agreed to Walker's crazy plan for Sutton to steal a Miró as the ransom deal to get his wife back. If he had his way he'd teach the Englishman a lesson he'd never forget and get rid of both the wife and his kids. Yes, they needed the distribution deal to get their product into the UK, but there were plenty of other drug dealers who'd want the business and he'd make sure he found a replacement for the Walkers.

But his father had told him to stay out of things because it was Alejandro's job. When he'd complained, his father had at least said he might review things if his brother made a mess of things.

'I might just need to help make that happen,' he thought.

50

The surveillance motorcyclist was well hidden behind a small crop of olive trees high above the Sanchez villa. He'd seen the two Mercs go in through the entrance gate and called it in via his radio an hour before.

'Cecil' Moriarty was set up for a long night. He'd be losing the last of evening light anytime soon, but he'd got his night vision binoculars ready for when darkness finally fell.

He'd been surveillance trained for some time now and knew the challenges of working alone, especially when watching from distance. After a while your mind could play tricks on you, almost setting the scene you were looking at on a permanent setting, so if you weren't careful you could easily miss something.

He had his own strategies for coping with this sort of thing. Regular movement, shifting his body slightly, as well as keeping hydrated and warm, which even in Mallorca could be an issue as the heat of the day was falling away as the October evening closed in.

"Charlie Four, you all okay?"

That was another strategy. Someone good on Comms who would help keep your mind ticking over by checking in with you.

"All good Nino, gracias amigo. No change here since the cars went in. Hang on though."

He saw someone come from the side of the villa and get in one of the cars. The headlights had come on.

"A guy has just come out and started up one of the Mercs. Oh, and now here comes another one. Looks like we've got someone going out for the night."

"Can you ID them Cecil?"

"Wait one."

He was caught between the light. It wasn't yet dark enough for the night light glasses, but the dusky evening light wasn't helping as he tried to focus in on the person who was now walking to the front passenger door of the Mercedes.

"Both definitely male," said Moriarty. "The driver came from the side, so I'm guessing he's just a driver. But the passenger came through the main doors, so I'm thinking there's a good chance it's going to be a Sanchez."

"Okay, received," said Nino. "Any idea which one?"

"No, apologies Nino, the light's really bad now and so I can't be sure. From here, the guy looked smaller than Alejandro, so if I was to take a guess, I'd say it was Diego, because this guy isn't as thickset as the father."

"I wonder where he's off to then? We'll try and pick them up on one of the CCTV cameras if they head back into Palma," said Nino.

Inside the villa, Diego's exit hadn't been noticed until his mother went to check on the numbers for dinner.

"Alejandro, is Frankie staying for dinner?"

Frankie looked across at Adeline, but she ignored him.

"No he's not mama, he's leaving shortly."

Sanchez hadn't even asked Walker if he wanted to stay to be with his wife and mother-in-law a little longer.

"We're done then?"

Sanchez nodded.

"Can I see my wife and kids for a moment?"

"Perhaps it's best you do, just in case."

Sanchez left his words hanging, the threat being obvious as to what might happen if he didn't deliver on the ransom.

"Oh and Frankie, you'd better not be playing games with us with your mother-in-law."

"Alejandro, why on earth would you think I'd be risking anything like that? On my mother's life, please just trust me. We'll get this bloody painting and then we can all get back to where we were."

"Trust you Frankie? That's an interesting one which you'll have to leave me to think about. But clearly I don't need to remind you whose lives are at stake if you are thinking of trying to screw me over."

All attempts by Sanchez to maintain his charm had gone out of the window. Instead his face looked hard and cold and left Walker in no doubt that his family would be in serious trouble if things went wrong.

"No, you don't need to remind me Sanchez," said Walker angrily. "But I promise you this, once this is over..."

But Sanchez stopped him with a wave of his hand.

"Once this is over Frankie, we can get on with the business in hand and you and my family will make an enormous amount of money. Remember this is business, it's not personal." His charm had returned as he continued, "Right, let's go and see your family for a few moments and then we'll get you back to your hotel."

Walker responded with a grunt, thinking it better to not continue talking, just in case he backed himself into a corner, but as he went upstairs Sanchez's last comment had him thinking,

'Business may be just business to you mate, but it's always bloody personal to me!'

*****

"Look who has come to say goodnight?" said Alejandro as he breezed into Maggs's room.

"Don't bother knocking will you!" said Maggs, glaring at him.

Frankie gritted his teeth and took hold of his wife in his arms.

"I'll get this sorted, okay?" he whispered.

"You damn well make sure you do."

Anna butted in, playing her part.

"Sort what out Margaret? Look is something going on here that you haven't told me Frankie Walker?"

"Mum, it's okay. Please let it go. I'll explain later, but not now," said Maggs, lowering her eyes to the children and then back to her mother.

"Yes, I'm sure she'll explain everything later Señora Murphy, but after we've had some dinner," said Alejandro. "Now Frankie, you need to go."

It was a statement more than a request.

"My kids, Sanchez."

Walker looked at him.

"Two minutes and then you go."

"Thank you."

He went into the children's bedroom that was off the main bedroom and his children screamed in delight when they saw him.

"Hush now kids. Time for you to sleep and I promise you this will be soon to be over and we can get back to having our holiday, okay?"

He bent down and kissed his youngest, Charlotte, who carried on playing with a doll, before turning to Olivia.

"Okay Daddy," she said as he kissed her. "But Dad,

who is that lady?" she whispered.

'*Shit! She knows.*'

"I know I've also said not to keep secrets haven't I? Well, this is just a little bit of fun we're playing with these people who you're staying with."

"Why?"

He smiled. It was usually Charlotte who was the one who was always asking the '*why?*' question, as by now Livvy had grown out of it a little.

"It's just a game and we need to make sure that they don't find out that this lady isn't Grannie Murphy okay?"

His daughter grinned at him.

"Do we get a prize?"

"Of course my darling. A giant ice cream, with all your favourite flavours."

"Does Mummy know?"

"Yes, she does sweetie. Does Charlotte know she isn't Grannie?"

"Oh no, she was way too young to remember."

"Okay, well that's good, so let's not tell her shall we and then the ice cream will be a surprise."

"Walker."

He heard Sanchez's voice.

"I've got to go now Livvy, so you be good for Mum and Grannie," he winked at her.

"Okay Daddy. Night, night."

He closed their bedroom door.

"That was longer than two minutes Señor. Please do not abuse my indulgence again."

'*Indulgence!*' Walker could barely contain himself, but Maggs got to him before he could react.

"I'm sorry Alejandro. Thank you for letting Frankie see us. Now go hun and I *will* see you soon."

He knew that if he got half a chance he would make this man suffer for what he was putting his wife through, but that would have to come later.

"Yes, I'll see you all soon," he forced a smile and then hugged his wife, whispering quietly in her ear.

'Livvy knows.'

He felt her squeeze his arm and then he looked at Anna, "I'm glad you were able to come Mrs M. I hope you can sort things out with Margaret."

"I have no idea what is going on here, but yes, thank you Frankie, I'm glad I came too," Anna took hold of his arm and squeezed it gently. She needed him to keep his head and to do as Maggs had said and go quietly.

Walker left their room and as he went down the stairs with Sanchez he saw Alberto Sanchez was standing at the bottom.

"Alejandro, where's Diego?"

"I've no idea Papa. I thought he was in the lounge with you."

"No, he took a call and then disappeared."

Alejandro went to the front door and looked out. One of the cars had gone.

"Problem Alejandro?" smirked Walker.

"No, not at all, snapped Sanchez, although he was now wondering where the hell his brother had gone. The last thing he wanted was him getting involved in what was going on and making another mess of things like he did with Theakston.

"Come Frankie, there's a car outside for you. The driver will take you back to your hotel. I'll give you until midnight tomorrow to get that painting to us otherwise you'll be picking your family, or what's left of them, out of the Mediterranean."

"I'll be back, but make sure that brother of yours doesn't get in my way, or otherwise he might just end up in the Med too!"

Alejandro smiled, "Brave words Frankie, but I wouldn't advise trying to tackle my brother. He can be,

what do you say? *'el loco!'*
'He's not the only one amigo,' thought Walker.

51

Sam Martínez waited until he saw Jake Sutton get back to his car and then watched as he drove out of the car park.

"Sam to Greg?"

"Yes go ahead."

"Sutton is back in his car and is on his way. He's going to do it tonight."

"Wow, that doesn't give us a lot of time."

"No, but if we get Simon involved we should have enough to cover this."

"What about Terri? You know if you try and leave her out she'll go nuts," said Greg.

"I know. I think she's fit enough physically, but what about mentally Greg? She went through a hell of a lot with Marsden."

"She did, but I think she'll be okay. I spoke to her earlier and she's being upfront and saying she might be a bit ring rusty so to speak, but that she'd rather get back in there, than be kept on the outside."

"Well she'd certainly be a help. So, I'll go with the four of us covering this. You're still happy that it's us, rather than Lori's team?"

"Yes, definitely. Until we know where we are with all of this, I think we can operate much more fluidly without the confines of whatever legislative requirements Lori might have to comply with."

"Sounds good to me. I'm just going to take a quick look at the Adamsons place and then I'll meet you back in the square in ten."

Sam was back in eight. He reckoned Sutton knew what he was doing and so he didn't need to be getting in his way. But whilst he had no intention of getting too close to the guy, as he went about stealing the painting, Sam still wanted a look at the lie of the land, just in case things went pear-shaped.

"I've had a thought."

"Go on," said Greg.

"We've also got Holly."

"You're not thinking of putting her out with us are you?"

"Not unless it's absolutely necessary, but she could be a massive help with the Comms."

"True, plus I have a feeling she's going to pretty much insist she's part of this whole thing, if only to keep a track of the Miró."

"Good point and from what we've seen of her recently, she's not exactly a shrinking violet," grinned Sam.

Once they were back up through the Sóller tunnel, heading to Palma, Greg called Lori with an update.

"Hmm, if Sutton is planning on doing it tonight then we may have a problem. One of our guys is watching the villa and saw a black Merc leaving a while ago and it looked like it had Diego Sanchez in it," said Lori.

They were on speakerphone.

"Is Frankie still at the villa Lori?" said Sam.

"No, he's gone, but he left after Diego. You need to be careful guys. We know from source intel that there's been a rift between the two brothers for some time and the parents are barely keeping a lid on it."

"Do we know how many were in the car with Diego?" asked Sam.

"Just him and the driver, but he's mad enough to take on anything just on his own. We could go and try and find him and bring him in for questioning about Theakston," suggested Lori.

"Pros and cons?" said Greg.

"It gets him out of the way," said Sam.

"But it lets them know we're watching them," said Lori. "That's the bit I don't like about it."

"I agree," said Sam. "And there's a good chance a big fee lawyer will make a pretty compelling case for disclosure of documents which if they don't get, they'll demand his immediate release."

"The other thing is that it's possibly a bigger distraction having him inside rather than on the outside, where he may open up opportunities," said Greg.

"What sort of opportunities?" said Lori slowly.

"Arrest opportunities, to gain entry to the villa."

"You mean if he goes after Walker or Sutton?"

"Yes," said Greg.

"That's potentially a dangerous strategy Greg," said Lori.

"Agreed, but then again Diego may just have gone out for a nice meal and a few beers."

"I think that's highly unlikely Greg Chambers and I think you know that. But…"

"But what?" said Greg.

"But I think you're right about the distraction. However, I don't want this loose cannon running about the place, so if you see him anywhere near you, you call me and I will get a team on him to get him picked up. Agreed?"

Greg knew she wasn't asking for any further

opinion. She'd made her mind up as the SIO and this was the decision she was going with.

"Agreed," Sam and Greg said in unison.

"Good, now ring me when you're back in Palma and have got your team in place. I'll keep you posted if we spot Diego coming in on the Ma20."

After she'd rung off, Sam looked at Greg.

"Do you think Diego is going to get involved?"

"Oh yes," said Greg emphatically, "and knowing how bloody dangerous he can be, we need to be ready for anything."

*****

Diego had had enough of the games his father and brother were playing with the guy from London. He'd didn't care what they did to the woman and her kids, just as long as they got on with it and then got back to business.

He knew Alejandro would be annoyed, no actually he'd be fuming at what he was planning to do, but he didn't care. He'd made up his mind. He'd take care of things, just like he did with Theakston.

"Where to Boss?" said his driver, Pepe.

"Sóller."

Diego sat back in his seat. He'd heard about Walker's plan to get his father a Miró from a gallery in Sóller, but he didn't trust him and for the woman's mother to suddenly turn up.

'Was that all just a bit too much of a coincidence?'

Even if it was, he wasn't going to wait for Walker to bring the picture to the villa. He'd wait, but only until Walker had it and then he'd take it off him, before getting rid of both Walker and Sutton.

"You have got some kit in the car haven't you Pepe?"

The Mercedes, like most of their cars, had some carefully concealed hiding places built in to them to ensure a basic roadside check of the car by the police would reveal nothing. All the Sanchez drivers were responsible for keeping the equipment ready for use in their cars and Pepe had checked everything was okay that morning.

"Si, Patrón."

"Bueno amigo, I think we're going to need them tonight."

"Are you expecting trouble Patrón?"

"No, I'm not expecting it Pepe, because I know there will be."

*****

"Holly, Sutton's doing the job tonight," said Greg.

She knew it would be soon, but assumed he'd check the place out tonight and do it tomorrow.

"Okay, are you, I mean, are we ready for this?"

"I'm glad you said 'we' Holly, because we're going to need your help. I'm hoping you'll be okay to do the Comms for us?"

She thought for a moment. Was he trying to keep her out of any trouble, by being away from any of the action? Then she had a reality check. These people were trained to operate in the field, whilst she was an insurance analyst who'd had one run-in, albeit successfully, with a London gang boss and a crooked entrepreneur who seemed to get his kicks from stealing paintings.

"Yes, I can do that."

She hoped she sounded confident as even doing the Comms for the 3R team was potentially a high stress operation given the type of things that had already gone on with Tony Theakston nearly being killed and the Walker family being kidnapped.

"That's great Holly. Is Terri there?"

"Yes."

She passed her phone to Terri.

"Hi, what's going on?"

"It's on for tonight. I've asked Holly to do Comms. I'm thinking she can stay where she is at your place? And can you sort out the equipment for her?"

"Yes to both of those Sam," said Terri. "What do you need me and Simon to do?"

Sam smiled. There hadn't ever been a moment when she wasn't going to be involved in this, he thought to himself.

"We've got two people and two locations to watch over. Sutton and Walker, plus the gallery in Sóller and the Sanchez villa."

"Any preference Sam?"

"Lori's got someone watching the villa. Greg was originally going to stay with Walker, but I'd prefer us to stay with Sutton, as Greg and I have got a sense of the Adamsons' place already."

"Makes sense," said Terri.

"So can you guys keep an eye on Walker?" asked Sam.

"Sounds good to me. We'll go and get set up near his hotel."

"You need to be aware that Diego, the younger brother who took out Tony Theakston, is out and about at the moment in a black Merc SUV. We don't know where he is, but Lori's team are keeping an eye out for him if he comes into the city on the Ma20."

"How much do we need to worry about him Sam?"

"A lot. His nickname is 'el loco'."

"Got you," said Terri. "Everything else all okay?"

"As far as we know, yes. We think Frankie is on his way back to his hotel now, so I'm expecting him to call me shortly and then I'll update you as soon as I can."

"We'll move out shortly after we've got Holly set up with the Comms and she's been through a radio check."

"Copied. Speak later Sis."

52

The promise of a sit down dinner with the Sanchez family hadn't come to anything. Under cover once again of running tap water in the bathroom, Maggs had told Anna that she'd been having all her meals brought up to her in the room, but at least they'd been treated okay and the kids had been allowed outside to play during the daytime.

"Do you actually have a plan then?" asked Maggs.

"We wait until Frankie brings the painting and then if they keep to their word, you should be released and as that's happening, we try to get them to say enough about their operations for the police to use as evidence."

Anna didn't want to give too much away, because as with Frankie, she wasn't too sure how much she could trust this woman who certainly wasn't an innocent sitting on the sidelines as her husband ran an organised crime gang. After all, she'd been the one who had been running the Walker business for the past year whilst her husband had been in prison.

"I'm not a grass."

"I know that Maggs, but listen and listen well. Without us helping make this happen, you and your dear kids were probably not going to make it out of here alive."

Anna had dropped the soft Irish accent and replaced it with a hard and cold English accent. It had the effect she was looking for. Maggs looked at her, confused and completely thrown by the change in not just her voice, but the tone and intimation.

"Okay, I hear you," said Maggs quietly.

"Good, so keep doing what you've been doing and follow my lead as and when something happens."

"But Livvy knows. That's what Frankie whispered to me."

Maggs couldn't tell from the woman's reaction in front of her whether this had had any impact on her. Anna made sure she gave away nothing. But it had thrown a spanner in the works, that was for sure. But she was thinking that if little Livvy had realised she wasn't her grandmother, then so far, she'd hadn't given the game away.

"Well she's doing very well then and playing along with us, probably because you are Maggs, so let's keep her thinking it's a game of some sort."

Even though she wasn't feeling it, Anna spoke confidently and calmly and Maggs seemed to react to how she was speaking, perhaps more than to what she was actually saying.

"Okay, come on, we'd better get back out into the main bedroom in case they are listening in and begin to suspect something."

Making a play that they'd been clearing up the bathroom after bathing the children, Anna spoke once again in the Donegal accent. "Well that's that all done." She went quiet for a moment and then said quietly, "I've so missed you and your darling girls."

As Maggs replied she was actually thinking that she really wished it was her mum in front of her. It had been a silly argument that had just got out of hand and things had been said that shouldn't have and then they couldn't easily be taken back or forgiven.

"I'm so sorry Mum. Whatever the rights and wrongs of what we argued about, I shouldn't have said those things and I know I can't take them back, but even though I can't, I hope you know how much I still love you."

Anna saw the tears in her eyes. It might have been because of the realisation that the situation she was in with her kids was very likely to come to an end, one way or another, sometime in the next twenty four hours, or, it might be because she really did regret what had happened between her and her mother.

"I know you do my darling," and Anna hugged her and whispered, "and she knows you do too."

Maggs shook as the tears ran down her face and Anna kept hold of her as the emotion, from not just the past few days, poured out of her.

*****

"I'm not going to say be careful, but please come back safely, both of you," said Josie, as she watched as her daughter and Simon got ready to go.

"We will Mum, I promise," grinned Terri, although she'd been careful that her mother hadn't see the two Glock hand pistols she'd taken out of her secret storage area.

"I'll make sure she's fine Josie," said Simon.

Terri looked across to Holly who was checking the signals on her phone and radio yet again.

"Holly, the equipment's good. You've checked it and double checked it. You've got this girl, okay?"

Holly had been getting ever more jittery about managing the Comms, but Terri's words seemed to calm her.

"Sorry, I just don't want to mess things up."

"You won't. I know you won't. Now as I said, only

come up on air if there's something we need to know, otherwise we'll be the ones doing the calling up as and when we've got something to tell you, or Greg and Sam."

"Understood. Less is better, yes?" said Holly.

"Definitely," said Simon with a grin. "We'll be back before you know it, so we'll see you both soon."

As they stepped out of the door and headed for the lift down to the car park Terri suddenly stopped.

"This is the first time we've ever actually worked together since we…"

"Became a bit more than colleagues," finished Simon.

"Yes."

Was that a shy grin he'd seen from her?

"And?" said Simon.

"We're okay doing this? Working together I mean. It won't affect how we do things?"

He could see she was concerned, if not worried.

"Look, I've learned my lesson. I won't be mollycoddling you if that's what you're thinking. I know you're a big girl and can handle yourself, but it doesn't mean I still won't be looking out for you, but I've been doing that since I joined your Dad's outfit."

She kissed him gently on the lips.

"I do love you." Then she ran off to the car, "Come on slow coach."

"I love you too," he said quietly, adding to himself, "and I'd never forgive myself if I let anything happen to you."

*****

Jake Sutton was ready. He'd got the text from Martínez that a car was in position. Dressed in loose, casual dark coloured clothing, he'd put on a new pair of Onitsuka Tigers, specialist Parkour training shoes that usually only lasted a month given the wear and tear put on them through the sort of vigorous regime that came with Parkour and Freerunning activities.

In his jacket he was carrying some of the most technically advanced anti-security equipment that his company, Sutton Innovation Security, had developed. Essentially it was a blocking device that he could set to cover a base area from the size of a three metre square to a hundred metre square office block. Rather than 'switching off' any alarm system, Sutton's device effectively tricked the system into thinking it was still working, when in fact it wasn't. It also removed any 'memory' of an alarm intrusion, meaning that when the device was turned off, the alarm it had been blocking didn't then automatically activate.

The counter to this was of course his own security systems, which he'd designed to withstand any such device.

'You've got to build the best blocking device in the industry to know how to beat it,' he'd told Jeannie Marshall, his CEO, when he started creating what was now their highest selling security system.

And this new system, together with his blocker device, was what he'd used to try to convince Adamsons that their outdated security system really did need updating. His intention had been to prove to them that he could provide them with a new improved system capable of keeping all of their galleries across the world safe.

'If only their Board hadn't rejected what was a bloody fair offer to update their entire global security system,' he thought. *'I wouldn't be in this position now if they'd have just accepted it.'*

But then again, he wouldn't have been in Mallorca and seen Frankie Walker and it was Frankie who'd helped him survive Feltham, so maybe this was all just fate?

With that thought in his head, he made his way back towards Portixol and into one of the side roads where he saw a dark grey Seat Leon. He felt under the front wing and found a set of keys resting on the tyre.

'Time to do this.'

53

Jake knew he didn't need to rush. He'd have plenty of time to get there and get the job done, so he made a point of keeping to the speed limit. Retracing the route he'd taken just a few hours before, he turned right at the Portixol junction, opposite a new modern looking building, and out onto the main road. He then stayed in the nearside lane before filtering on to the northbound city ring road, the Ma20.

This late in the evening meant there was less traffic about on the ring road making it easy for Lori's team, who were positioned up on one of the motorway bridges, to report no suspicious cars following the grey Seat as it passed under them.

They also didn't see the black Mercedes Diego Sanchez was in. They hadn't missed it, because Sanchez had gone straight to Sóller to wait for the Englishman, Jake Sutton.

"Boss, how long do you want to wait here? I'm just asking because we'll stick out a bit if we're here too long."

"Good point Pablo. Tell you what, you go and park up somewhere and I'll hang about here in the square."

"You sure Boss?"

The driver regretted what he'd said as soon as he'd

finished.

"Pablo," Sanchez's voice had gone quiet. Never a good sign as Pablo knew only too well when he'd seen his boss working on some poor unfortunate who'd incurred his displeasure. "Perhaps leave me to make the decisions, shall we?"

"Yes, Boss, sorry, I was just trying to ….."

"Well don't."

Sanchez cut him off and Pablo got the message loud and clear and counted himself fortunate, if not very lucky, that he'd not fallen foul of his boss's violent temper.

"Sorry Boss."

Diego ignored him. He was already thinking about Sutton. He knew that what he really wanted to do was screw up his brother's plan. That meant that rather than simply taking the picture off Sutton or Walker, he'd just stop Sutton getting it in the first place.

"Forget it Pablo," he said cheerfully.

Pablo smiled, but he knew Diego Sanchez well enough to know that his boss being cheerful was also not necessarily a good sign, but at least it looked like he was off the hook himself.

"Text me when you're parked up. I'll just be floating around here."

Sanchez got out of the car and pulled his coat around his neck. It was getting colder as the night air was drawing in. Some of the restaurants in the square had those outside heaters around the tables where there were still a few people having late dinners.

Making his way in to the Carrer de sa Lluna, he walked on past the Adamsons gallery before doubling back on himself, turning right and then right again and coming back into the Plaça de Constitutió. He heard his phone buzz and saw the text from Pablo.

'Pl.Mercat. 200m.'

The Market Place. Close enough thought Diego. He sat down at an empty table at a café nearest to the Carrer de sa Lluna and ordered a coffee when a waiter appeared. He wasn't thinking Sutton would drive into the square and park up and casually walk across to the gallery, but he had to be somewhere and at least here he had something of a partial view towards the gallery.

With his attention focussed towards the gallery, he missed the white SUV as it drove slowly into the square behind his line of sight.

Sudden moves, or not moving quickly enough, were common mistakes for anyone untrained in surveillance techniques. Greg was driving and made sure it looked like they were simply manoeuvring around the square, looking for a possible parking space. It was Sam who noticed the man sitting at a café in the corner of the square closest to the Carrer de sa Lluna.

He recognised the place next to the café. C'an Pau was the old gelateria his mum and dad used to take him to when they went to Sóller on the old train from Palma.

The man seemed to be looking in the direction of the Adamsons gallery and not at anything much else.

"I think we've just found Diego," Sam said calmly.

Greg kept driving, without making any sudden moves to look for Sanchez.

"That's interesting then. Is he here to check on Sutton? What do you think Sam?"

"I think we've got a problem. Should we tell Sutton?" said Sam.

"No, it could spook him and we need him to get that painting. Besides I don't think we'll be seeing a lot of Jake Sutton tonight, at least not here in Sóller," said Greg, looking up to the rooftops.

"I think you may be right. I'm wondering where Diego's driver is though. We don't want another re-run of what happened to Tony Theakston."

"He can't be far away as presumably Sanchez would want him pretty close. Let's go and see if we can find him," said Greg.

Greg started a wide trawl of the side streets looking for the Mercedes as Sam rang Holly.

"We've found Diego Sanchez, Holly. He's sat up in the main square in Sóller."

"Shall I tell Lori and Terri?"

"Yes, yes. Lori's probably got people out looking for him, so at least she'll know where he is now."

"What if she asks me what you're planning on doing?"

"Good question."

"That sounds as though you might be thinking of doing something?" said Holly.

"If she asks, tell her we won't do anything unless he makes a move on Sutton, plus we're not going to tell Jake as we don't want to distract him."

"Will she believe me Sam? I mean about not doing anything about Sanchez."

"Possibly not," laughed Sam. "But tell her we'll call her straight away if anything happens. Greg will ring her direct."

"Will that reassure her?" asked Holly.

"I doubt it," he laughed again.

"Are you sure you wouldn't prefer to ring her yourself Sam?" suggested Holly.

"Oh Lord no Holly. This is definitely a job for someone with your persuasive powers."

She knew he must be grinning and was about to say something.

"Sorry Holly, got to go," Sam said urgently as Greg pointed a finger at the road ahead. He rang off.

"Seen something?"

"There's a black SUV just down the road," said Greg.

"We've got some cover from that van. Why don't you jump out and go and check it out? And Sam, take this."

He handing him an emergency car window glass hammer.

Sam looked at him, amazed that he had this piece of equipment with him.

"Boy scout stuff," laughed Greg. "Always be prepared."

There was a tall sided van parked just ahead of them that Greg would need to pull around to get by. As he slowed to pull out to pass the van Sam quickly jumped out of the car and up onto the footpath, going to the right of the van, whilst Greg drove on.

Sam could see the Mercedes was parked facing them, on the opposite side of the road. As Greg eased slowly down the road towards it, Sam kept walking, keeping abreast of him, which gave him cover from the eye-line of the driver, whilst Greg tried to see who the driver was without being too obvious.

"Couldn't see him Sam. It's too dark," said Greg into his mic.

"Copied," said Sam, who then crossed the road and turned back towards the rear of the SUV.

He was exposed. The footpath was narrow and the car was the only one parked there. He could see a shape in the driver's wing mirror, but he was still just a bit too far away. He was getting closer when he suddenly heard the engine start up and the car pulled away.

"Change of plan Greg. He's just moved off."

"Be with you shortly."

54

Jake Sutton was already high up on the Sóller skyline. He'd parked the Seat away from the main square and had taken to the rooftops some way away from Adamsons gallery.

The streets in the town were quite narrow in places and many of the buildings had overhangs and this was where his skills in Parkour came into their own.

Accessing high walls and buildings, where your body is moving at speed, rather than at a slow climb, was what Parkour was all about and Jake was a master practitioner. It wasn't just a case of him being strong and athletic. He had practiced long and hard to achieve the level of balance and precision, not to mention the mental toughness, to become one of the elite Parkour specialists operating across Europe.

After he'd stopped competing in the Olympics programme he'd needed something to give him the adrenalin rush he had previously got from elite competition and he knew he'd found it in Parkour.

As he sat perched high up on the building next to the Adamsons gallery, he looked around. The gallery was only three stories high and getting on to it and then back up away should be a walk in the park, certainly compared to some of the climbs he'd undertaken in different cities across the world, sometimes with the owner's permission and sometimes not, he grinned to himself.

There was a fair amount of cloud cover in the sky and this was giving him a good level of darkness, not that he was particularly overlooked by anyone up there. He took a quick look about and then made up his mind on the best way to get down onto the Adamsons roof.

He'd need a rolling leap forward off the wall to clear the fence, which he could easily do within the fifteen foot drop down to the roof surface. He took off his backpack and unzipped it and took out a small black box, the alarm blocker he'd designed. Once he'd activated it he'd pretty much have free rein to take as much time as he wanted, not that he expected he'd need much more than five minutes.

The alarm blocker was just a box of electronics, but it was an exceptionally advanced box of electronics. It worked a little bit like when searching for a Wi-Fi signal. Once turned on, it would pick up alarm signals from the immediate surroundings and they would be listed on the screen. All he needed to do was to select the Adamsons alarm code, which he already knew from the security review he'd undertaken at their behest last year.

Jake turned the device on and moments later four codes appeared on the screen. Adamsons was the first one and he clicked on it. There was no password needed. The blocker just piggy-backed onto the selected system and once it locked in a green light would show. This meant the alarm was now blocked from activating and nothing would register that there was anything untoward. To all intents and purpose the system still thought it was operating properly.

Green light.

He took one final look at the jump he'd need to pull off and started some deep breathing exercises. Compared to some galleries he'd inspected there were some pretty good physical security barriers here, with electric shutters on the windows and alarmed wire fencing offering some protection to the roof. However, he knew the fencing wouldn't pose a problem to him.

He backed up a little from where he was standing on the high wall on the neighbouring building. Then, taking one long breath in, he paused before he pushed off, running hard as he breathed out as he jumped long into the space below, in a falling, tumbling Parkour somersault that took him well over the fence, before he landed in a semi-squat position, with his breathing controlled and regular. It wasn't the sort of move your usual burglar would make, thought Jake.

'*Still got it!*' he grinned.

Now he was on the gallery roof it was unlikely that there was anything else to worry about. There was a fire escape door which, according to fire regs, wouldn't be cross bolted on the inside. It wasn't. It just needed a firm bit of pressure with a jemmy and it popped open and he went inside.

He ignored the CCTV cameras as he knew Adamsons wouldn't be reporting this particular burglary, so it was habit, rather than necessity, which saw him still pull on his usual face and head covering.

He found the picture soon enough. All of Miró's art was on the gallery's first floor. Whilst it was dark inside there was some low light from the fire exit signs and he had a small Maglite torch to help remove the picture.

He saw some of the artist's early work and a few smaller, later half-finished sketches, but even with his untrained eye he could see why the particular picture he'd chosen was the most valuable by some way.

However, he'd not chosen it because of its artistic

content, but because of its size. It was relatively small – around 50cm x 30cm and size clearly didn't matter in the art world, he thought, with such a relatively small painting being worth nearly ten million quid.

There would be the usual Adamsons picture alarm on the back of the frame, plus a security chain. Both were intended to deter, rather than necessarily stop an opportunist thief grabbing the picture. However, they might just give the security staff time to apprehend the would-be thief.

When he'd researched security systems in the art world he'd been surprised to find that art thefts weren't always sophisticated and intricately planned burglaries or robberies. Many were simply opportunist thefts where the thief stepped over the customary rope, intended to keep the public from touching the painting, and pulled it off the wall.

He looked at the picture before him and ran his fingers along the frame. He'd already discounted cutting it out of the frame, as he'd discovered that was something the art world deplored, partially because of the significant impact on the value, but mostly because it destroyed part of the very essence and fabric of the picture which, despite the amazing skills of art restorers, was something that could never be replaced.

Actually removing the Miró turned out to be comparatively easy, with a mini-screwdriver dealing with the screws holding the brackets to the wall. He then removed the single screw that attached the security chain to the wall sensor, which wasn't going to activate whilst the alarm blocker was in operation.

He gently pulled the frame away from the wall and then carefully wrapped it in a protective covering and put it in his backpack.

He checked his watch. Three minutes from the time he'd entered the building. He made his way back up the stairs and out through the fire door and onto the roof. With the alarm still blocked, it was easy enough to just climb up the wire mesh fencing and then find a couple of footholds in the brickwork to clamber up the wall of the adjacent building.

From there he retraced his route back across the rooftops. It was an easy route across the roof tops, as there were a lot of same height roofs and he'd only had one reasonably small jump to make across a couple of buildings and the tiles, although old, were firm and stayed in place.

He took a wide berth around the Plaça de Constitutió on his way back before dropping down off a building close to where he'd parked the Seat. By this stage he knew he was on the limit of the Wi-Fi signal to the gallery alarm. However, there was no need to worry about de-activating the blocker because he knew the Adamsons' system didn't possess an active 'memory' as such. Therefore it would only recognise any new alarm breaches, so it wouldn't realise it had already been breached, even with the fire door being forced open.

*****

Greg barely stopped the Kia as he pulled up by the kerb where the Mercedes had been moments before and Sam jumped in just as his phone went.

"Jake?"

"It's done."

"That was quick."

"Well I don't exactly hang about."

"Point taken."

"Where are you now?" asked Sam.

"Back in the car about to set off."

Sutton paused.

"Why?"

His voice had changed. Sam recognised the difference in tone. Jake must have picked up on something in his last question.

"You're here aren't you? What's up?" Jake demanded.

"Yes we are," said Sam.

He stopped, then made up his mind.

"Diego Sanchez is here too. He's in a black Merc, a GLC."

"He's the loose cannon isn't he? Do I need to be worried?"

Sam decided there was no point trying to hide anything now.

"Yes and yes. He may want to try to stop you getting to the villa. He won't know you've got the picture so you head off now and we'll keep Sanchez off your back."

"Just make sure you do!"

*****

Sutton could feel his hands trembling. He knew what adrenalin was and how it affected your body, but this was different, very different from what had started as something more akin to a game, albeit an illegal game between him and Adamsons.

If Diego Sanchez did get to him, then there was every chance he'd end up dead.

'Calm yourself. Breathe, breathe!'

55

Terri and Simon were carefully checking the area around Walker's hotel, the Sant Francesc and so far they hadn't seen anyone looking or acting suspiciously.

"Let's get inside and see how Frankie is," said Terri.

Simon nodded and they made their way in through the main doors as there was no need for subterfuge now, with Terri texting Walker of their arrival.

As she knocked quietly on the door they both stood to one side. It was basic 'expect the worse' stuff to take such precautions, but if someone was inside holding Walker and decided to start shooting through the door, it would be too late to take evasive action.

The door opened quickly.

"Jake's just phoned me. He's got it! He's only gone and nicked it."

"Good to hear mate," said Terri. "But did he tell you we've got a bit of a problem?"

"Diego? Yes, he did and he's shit-scared bless him. I shouldn't have dragged him into this. He was no bloody good in Feltham at looking after himself, so God help him if Diego gets to him before we do."

Terri was surprised at Walker's apparent heartfelt concern.

"You care for him don't you?" said Terri.

"Look, I'm not one of the good guys alright? I know that and you know that. But this guy, well he did something for me that no teacher ever could. He helped me to read and write and because of that I'd go to the end of the bleeding world to protect him."

"Let's hope we don't need you doing that Frankie-boy, but what we do need to do is get that painting back to the Sanchez place, get your family out and then close down this operation."

"What's next then?"

"As soon as Jake's here, we fit the listening device to the frame, have a quick check in with the rest of the team and a bit of a final briefing and then we're off. Jake stays here and you take his car and get yourself back up to the Sanchez place and get your family back."

Walker got a sense there was something she wasn't saying, but he let things go. He was in spitting distance now of getting his family back and that was all that mattered. Dealing with the Sanchez lot? Well that would come later.

"I'll go down stairs and see Jake in to the hotel," said Simon.

"Take care," said Terri.

After Simon had gone, Walker looked at her.

"You two got something going?"

She was annoyed that she'd let her feelings show and tried to recover things.

"Nope, just colleagues. No such luck as he's a good bloke."

Walker smiled back at her, but didn't believe a word she'd just said.

*****

Diego Sanchez had phoned Pablo his driver to pick him up from the Plaça de Constitutío and that was when Pablo had taken off, just as Sam Martínez was about to walk past the Mercedes to see who was driving.

"Where to Boss?" asked Pablo.

"Back to Palma. Make it quick Pablo, it was a mistake coming here. Head for Walker's hotel, the Sant Francesc. I'll sort things out there."

Pablo wondered what *'sort things out'* meant, but he wasn't about to venture another opinion to his boss.

Diego felt the surge from the car's engine as Pablo accelerated hard out of Sóller and up towards the tunnel. He pushed the speed dial on his mobile and heard his brother pick up the call.

"Diego, where are you?" said Alejandro.

"Something doesn't feel right about this Alejo."

Alejandro knew his brother often felt undermined that he was the younger brother and that their father, Alberto, had always said that he, Alejandro, as the oldest son, would take on the mantle of leader of the family business when his father eventually retired.

"Look Diego this isn't the time to be getting precious about who's going to run the business when Papa retires."

'Easy for you to say,' thought Diego.

"I'm not getting precious my dear brother. I just don't want you to screw things up for what Papa has spent his life building."

"Look, come back to the villa and we can talk about it, but please, just don't go interfering with this job. Not for my sake Diego, but Papa's. We're really close to getting this distribution route into the UK sorted and screwing the Walkers over for another ten million euro bonus to go with it."

"I think you're the one who'll end up being screwed Alejo!"

"Not me brother. Now come on, just come back."

Diego had no intention of going back to the villa

until he was good and ready. He wanted to see what was going on with Sutton and Walker and if there was any chance to grab the painting, to take it in himself, then he would make sure he did just that.

"Yes, yes, Alejo, but all in good time. I'll be back soon though, I promise."

Now Alejandro was worried. Anytime his brother promised anything it pretty much meant that he would do the opposite. He didn't bother arguing any more with him, but rang off.

His father had heard him take the call as he'd walked into the lounge, but had held back trying to discreetly listen to what his sons were talking about.

"Was that Diego, Alejandro? Problem?"

"Yes it was Papa and no, no problem. He's on his way back in. He said he just popped out to see someone for a quick drink."

His father nodded and Alejandro wondered if he'd bought the story he'd given about his brother.

His father nodded to him, but of course he hadn't.

*****

Simon left Walker's hotel through the kitchen and walked back around and into the Plaza de Sant Francesc and stood in the shadows, watching the main entrance to the hotel.

"All clear at the moment Terri," said Simon.

"Copied. Shouldn't be long."

Simon was looking around the square. There were a couple of possible routes Sutton could choose to get to the Plaza and he had a good view of both of them.

It was less than a minute later when he radioed in again.

"Grey Seat Leon has just come into the square. The vehicle is stopping by the hotel. The driver is out. Yes, confirmed. It's Sutton. He's just parking up."

"Cheers Simon. Holly, can you call Greg as I think

he's maybe still out of radio range and let him know Sutton is back please?" asked Terri.

"Will do," said Holly, who put the call in immediately to update Greg.

"Okay, thanks Holly, we're not too far away, so we should be able to do comms via the radio very soon."

"Understood. Any sign of Diego?"

"No, which is a bit worrying. I think we'd have heard from Lori if any of her team had seen him. I don't like the idea of him running loose out there."

"Where are you now?" asked Holly.

"Ma20, the ring road. I'll try calling you on the radio," said Greg.

"Greg to Holly, are you receiving?"

"Yes, loud and clear."

"Good. Simon? We'll be with you soon."

"I hear you Greg. All quiet here. No, cancel that."

Greg heard concern in Simon's voice.

"A Mercedes GLC has just come into square. He's coming in at speed. It's got to be them Greg."

"Can you get to Sutton, Simon?"

"I'm on my way."

Simon's radio was still on transmit as Greg heard Simon shouting a warning.

"Sutton, get inside. Now!"

Then they all heard it.

It wasn't loud, but it was loud enough for those who recognised the sound to immediately know what it was.

A suppressed gunshot.

Sam accelerated hard, but they were still three minutes away.

"Simon!"

It was Terri, who was still upstairs with Walker in his hotel room.

No response.

"Dad, I'm going down."

She rarely, if ever called him *'Dad'* at work. He was going to tell her 'No,' because this looked like it might be a rescue mission and like the rest of the team she was unarmed. To be specific, none of them were carrying firearms, which was something Lori had insisted on as she couldn't countenance any of the 3R team carrying guns illegally around Palma.

"Be careful my girl," said Greg quietly.

"Less than two minutes," said Sam, as Greg looked at him, worry spreading across his face.

"Hello, hello, Martínez! He's been shot."

It was Jake on the comms Sam had fitted him with for Sóller.

"Jake, stay calm. We're on our way. Try to get inside the hotel."

"He's coming!"

Sam heard the panic in Jake's voice.

"Greg, we need a firearms team there and quickly," said Sam.

"Holly, tell Lori we need armed back-up and quickly. Shot fired in Plaza de Sant Francesc," said Greg.

"Yes, calling her now."

He was surprised at how calm Holly was. This wasn't her usual arena of work and yet she was holding up remarkably well.

"Well done Holly."

Terri got to the front lobby of the hotel.

"I've got Sutton, but Diego is outside with Simon. Simon's on the ground. Looks like he's injured."

"Jake, call the police and say shots fired at Hotel Sant Francesc," shouted Terri.

"I'm going out," she said into her radio.

"Terri don't!"

She ignored her father and was already running out of the lobby and into the square. She didn't have a plan as such, but knew she needed to create a distraction and hope Sam and her father got there soon.

"What are you doing! Get away from him!" she screamed as she saw Diego Sanchez standing over Simon with a pistol in his hand.

56

Diego Sanchez hadn't meant to shoot the man who was now lying on the floor in front of the Hotel Sant Francesc, but he'd got in his way as he'd gone to stop Sutton.

"That was a very stupid thing to do Señor."

The man was looking up at him.

"Now, who are you Señor? A friend of Señor Walker maybe?"

Simon could feel the blood seeping through his shirt. The bullet had gone in through his side, just under his ribs. He'd been shot a couple of times, but this felt different, and not in a good way.

Then he heard Terri's voice.

"Shit! No Terri!" he tried to shout, but his voice sounded weak. "Get back inside!"

For a second it looked like a stand-off, although it was much too one-sided with Diego the only one who was holding a gun.

"So, you have a friend? Now look, let's be reasonable. All I want is what your other friend Sutton has with him. Then we can all go our own ways and you can get some medical help for the señor here."

"Boss?" said Pablo who was standing slightly away by the Mercedes.

"What is it now? Not some more of your great advice is it Pablo?" said Diego not trying to hide his annoyance at his driver interrupting him once again.

"Boss, I can hear sirens."

Diego had missed them. He nodded at Pablo. A small and unexpected acknowledgement his driver thought.

"He shouldn't have got in my way. Now just give me the damn painting."

Terri was now with Simon and could see his blood on the pavement. She was about to shout to Sutton to get out there and give up the picture when Frankie Walker appeared at the hotel entrance.

Ignoring the gun in Sanchez's hand, Walker walked up to him stood directly in front of him, almost nose to nose.

"Diego, I don't know what the hell you think you're doing, but there's only one person taking that painting to your old man and that's me."

"Frankie, I was just trying to help…."

"Help? How are you helping when you shoot one of my people! Yes, these are my people. What? Did you think I was out here on my own? If you did then you've seriously underestimated me mate and if you've done that, you've made a very bad mistake. Now run along home to your daddy like a good little boy and tell him I'll be there soon."

Diego went to raise his gun and Walker pushed him back hard.

"I've come up against men a lot harder than you Diego and most of those didn't need a gun to front me out, so if you want to try something, then go ahead, but you'll only get one shot off before I break your neck. So go for it if you fancy your chances, or back off, because the Old Bill, the Policía, are almost here."

Walker continued to stand his ground.

"Boss?" said Pablo, urgently.

"We'll see you soon Frankie and I hope you bring your nice friend here along as I'd really like to get to meet her," smirked Sanchez as he got in the car and Pablo accelerated hard away, just as Sam and Greg drove in from the other side of the square.

*****

They saw the Mercedes leaving on the opposite side of the square as Sam brought the Kia to a halt with the tyres squealing for grip on the paving stones.

"Terri?" said Greg as he leapt out of the car.

"We need an ambulance Dad and quickly," she said quietly.

"Hello mate," said Greg gently, kneeling down beside Simon.

Simon forced a smile. He was finding it hard to speak, so he knew the best thing was to conserve energy and focus on breathing as gently as he could.

Sam was now out of the car and at Simon's side with Terri who was holding her hand over the wound. He could see she was having to apply a lot of pressure to try to limit the blood loss.

"He's losing a lot of blood and starting to lose consciousness Sam."

"Shall I take over?" he asked.

"I'm okay, but can you try to get some bandages."

Frankie Walker was already taking his shirt off and shouting at Jake.

"Quick mucker, get your shirt off."

Walker folded his shirt into a pad and handed his to Terri who took it, mouthing a *'thank you'* to him before she pressed it on to Simon's wound and then held it there.

"Here, here's mine too Terri," said Sutton, who'd also folded his into a makeshift bandage.

The square was suddenly filled with sirens and two unmarked cars, presumably the GEO arrived, followed by two marked local police cars. The four GEO officers took the lead shouting at orders in Spanish and English to get down on the floor.

Terri was already kneeling, but because she was applying pressure to the wound, she just held one hand up, whilst Greg, Sam, Walker and Sutton all lay face down on the floor with their arms out wide.

"Jake, put your hands palm up mate, so they can see you're not armed," called Walker.

Sam risked a glance at the officers and saw Fernando Pérez.

"Sam, is it just you 3R guys here?"

"Yes, it was Diego Sanchez. He's gone, but Simon needs to get to a hospital and quickly."

"Simon, stay with me. Come on big man," said Terri.

"Okay, everyone stay where you are until you've been searched. You too please Sam and Señor Chambers. Señora, please lift your hand carefully and reapply the other one. I just want to see you have nothing in your hand."

She looked at Pérez and went to say something, but Sam stopped her.

"He needs to check Terri. If it was you, you'd be doing the same."

She slowly lifted her right hand and replaced it with her left, whilst momentarily showing her right hand was clear.

"Gracias Señora."

He could see from her close fitting trousers and top she was wearing that she wasn't hiding any other sort of weapon.

"Please feel free to reapply your right hand Señora. An ambulance will be here in just a moment."

He signalled to one of his colleagues, who said something into his radio. Almost immediately there was a noise of another vehicle, the ambulance, entering the square.

The GEO officers were quick, but thorough, as they checked the rest of them before Pérez allowed them all to stand up.

"My apologies guys, but I'm sure you will appreciate this is standard procedure."

"Of course, of course Sergeant," said Greg. "But what do you need to do now and can we continue with what we need to do?"

"DI Garcia is on her way Señor and she suggests she meets you in Señor Walker's room whilst we sort things out here."

"I'm not being difficult here Officer," said Walker, "but I really need to be going."

"She won't keep you waiting long Señor Walker, in fact here she is now."

Another unmarked car drove into the square, albeit this time at a slightly slower speed than the first GEO cars and Lori and Nino got out.

"Pérez, are we good?" said Lori.

"Si Inspectora."

"Can you put a team on the ambulancia please?"

It was an order, rather than a request, for an armed escort to go with the ambulance. Pérez nodded.

She also hadn't missed the seriousness of the injury and that Simon had now fallen unconscious.

"Terri, I expect you will want to go with Simon. Si?" asked Lori, giving her a gentle squeeze on her shoulder.

"Please," said Terri and put her hand up to Lori's.

"Okay, let's let the paramedics get Simon comfortable and into the ambulance."

Sam could see Greg's face. It was tight and drawn, his concern was evident because he could now see the extent of the bleeding from Simon's injury.

"Greg," said Sam. "I've got this covered."

"If you're sure?"

Sam nodded.

"Come on then Terri, let's go and keep an eye on our Welsh dragon shall we?" Greg said, trying to be as positive as he could be.

"Thanks Dad."

Terri got up as the paramedics started to lift Simon on to a stretcher. Sam saw the almost indiscernible look they gave each other.

"Señora, would you like to come in the ambulance with us?"

Greg saw his daughter's right arm twitch and then start to shake and he took hold of her and held her tight.

"Go on," said Greg. "I know he'd like you to be there with him."

"But Dad?"

There were tears in her eyes.

"Is he going to make it?"

"You know how tough he is Terri. Now let's get him to hospital and remember, keep talking to him. Let him hear your voice. It'll keep his brain stimulated and help him fight the blood loss."

She reached out and hugged her father. They watched in silence as the paramedics finished loading Simon into the back of the ambulance, before one of them waved at Terri to get in.

"Keep us posted," said Sam.

"Of course. Good luck up at the villa guys," said Greg as he got into his car and then followed the ambulance out of the square, with an unmarked police car with two GEO officers just behind him.

Once Lori had seen the ambulance leave she turned back to the remaining group.

"Nino, can you take charge here please?"

Her gaze flashed around the crime scene.

"Si Inspectora."

"Right, I need you Sam, Señores Walker and Sutton upstairs and now."

The three men looked at her, nodded and followed her as she set off towards Walker's room.

57

Frankie Walker had immediately gone to one of the wardrobes in his room and found two new shirts for him and Sutton and he was pacing the floor as he was doing up his shirt buttons.

"Look Inspectora, I know you've got a job to do, especially now Diego has killed Simon…"

"He's not dead yet Walker," said Sam coldly.

Walker knew this wasn't perhaps the best time to mention the amount of blood he'd seen that the guy had lost.

"No, sorry. You're right, I just meant…"

This time it was Sam's turn to interrupt. He'd seen that Walker had stripped off his shirt and given it to Terri as a bandage, plus she'd told him that Walker had stepped in between her and Simon when Diego was threatening them. A surprising act of bravery and humanity from someone Sam had previously had precious little regard for.

"I know," said Sam. "It's my turn to be sorry Frankie. You did your bit to save Simon, so thanks, it's appreciated."

Walker was a little taken aback by the apology and he could only think to grunt an acknowledgement, although as he did, he couldn't help thinking, *Strange times when a copper apologises to you.'*

Lori brought them both back to order.

"If we can get on gentleman?" she demanded. "Señor Walker, was there any specific mention for you to be alone when you took the painting back?"

Walker thought for a moment.

"Not as such. They had said they wanted to send a car, but I told them I'd make my own way there."

"Good," said Lori. "Señor Sutton, I need you to go with Señor Walker here. It will give an added distraction and allow our contact in there to do what she needs to do."

"I'm not sure about that Inspectora...," Sutton started to say.

"Jake, I don't think you understood the Inspectora," said Walker. "She's not asking. You're coming in with me."

Sutton looked at Frankie and then back to Lori Garcia.

"But..."

"Señor Walker is right, I'm not asking. I don't think I need to remind you that you've previously stolen a ten million euro painting in the US and tried to do the same in Singapore?"

Sutton realised he had no choice in the matter.

"What do you need me to do?"

"You'll be an added distraction for the Sanchez family and with you and our contact in there, I need you to get them to open up about their whole drug import export business."

"And if Diego is there, our contact will also be working on getting him to admit to trying to kill Tony Theakston," said Sam.

"Okay, not much then," grumbled Sutton.

Lori Garcia ignored his comment, but asked, "But I also need to know, can you negate the external security system at the Sanchez villa?"

"Yes, shouldn't be a problem. It's far enough away from any other property, so whatever comes up on the blocker reader should be their system."

"Bueno," said Lori.

"What about the search wands inside the villa?" said Sam.

"No, it won't work on them. They're more than likely to be off the shelf products and not specifically connected to the villa system. That means they're just indicators, so they won't give off any signals for my kit to pick up."

"What are you thinking Inspectora?" asked Walker.

"I want to get the Sanchezes talking about their business and get it recorded. We don't think the search wands will pick up the transmitter we'll have on the painting, but I'd rather not risk it."

"I've only seen them scan people, so I'll take a guess and say they won't scan it anyway," said Walker.

"Bit of a leap of faith," said Sam.

Lori looked at Sam, who was fitting the audio wire transmitter to the frame. Not to the back as she'd expected, but to the front, on the gilded framework where he was blending it into the waves and curls of the woodwork and securing it with a fine gel.

By the time he'd finished fitting it she was finding it very difficult to see where he'd actually put it.

"I thought it would be on the back Sam?" Lori said.

"Sometimes the least obvious place is right in front of your eyes," said Sam, who pointed to it and she then saw the very slim wire that looked like it was part of the gold leaf around the ornate frame.

This was still the part of the operation she'd had most concern about. She needed to get the Sanchez family talking about their drugs business and getting it all down on tape.

She smiled to herself. It obviously wasn't tape these days, but the principle was the same, she needed the evidence to be rock solid, but she also needed to know when she could send Pérez in, so this transmitter really needed to work.

"Well if they do find it," said Walker, who'd been watching Sam fit the transmitter, "I'll just tell them you've bugged it! So you'd better be listening and be ready to send in the cavalry."

Walker was grinning, but Sam couldn't tell if he was joking, or if it was just bravado.

"I'm not sure I can go with your optimism Frankie, but it's also not some sort of bloody game either, especially not for your wife and kids and certainly not for my mother!"

"Don't you think I know that copper!" growled Walker, who was now standing nose to nose with Sam, his body flexing as the adrenalin rushed through him.

"Señores! Calm down, both of you. Señor Walker, you need to do your very best to ensure they don't go anywhere near the painting with their search wands, okay?"

"Yes okay, I get it. I'm not bloody stupid."

Jake tried to calm the situation.

"Look, I'll take it in and make a bit of a fuss and make sure I hand it to one of the Sanchezes before we have to go through any sort of search."

Lori thought for a moment.

"That should work. Now when we do come in, it will be quietly, unless we get you telling us it's urgent. So, Señor Walker, you need to make sure you've got your wife and kids in a safe place, okay?"

"Yes, understood, but what about your woman, my mother-in-law?"

"Don't worry about her," said Sam, "she's more than capable of looking after herself."

"I think we are good to go," said Lori. "Good luck gentlemen and we will see you shortly."

She looked across at Sam. They'd already decided it wasn't a good idea to tell Walker or Sutton that Anna already had a set of ear pods that would activate once the transmitter was in the villa and she was now even more certain that this had definitely been the right decision.

*****

Terri was holding Simon's hand as the ambulance, with blue lights flashing and sirens blaring, made its way to Mallorca's largest hospital, Son Espases. With a thousand beds and over twenty operating theatres it had the best facilities on the island, including a modern and well equipped trauma unit.

She could hear the paramedic talking to someone on the phone, but even though her Spanish was improving, she couldn't follow much of what was being said, but the paramedic was calm and going through a number of checks and routines.

"I'm giving him fluids and pain relief," the paramedic told her in English as he fitted a cannula in Simon's right arm. "The trauma team are getting ready and will be there to meet us. We'll be there soon."

"Gracias."

She looked down again at Simon as he lay still unconscious on the stretcher. "Come on mate. This isn't the time to go leaving me now you big lump. Not just as we've finally told one another what we actually feel."

The paramedic had continued what he was doing, but he'd heard enough of what the young woman had said to know that these two people meant a lot to each other. The man was very badly injured and although he'd controlled the bleeding for now, he was very worried about a significant risk of internal bleeding."

"José," he called out urgently to the driver. "Vamos amigo!"

Terri felt the surge of the vehicle push forward again. The knot inside her stomach was tightening as the fear took over. The paramedic saw the look on her face as concern started to turn to panic.

"Not long now Señora," he said, calmly and gently.

But then, all hell seemed to break loose inside the ambulance. Alarms started going off and lights started flashing on the diagnostic machine Simon was attached to by a series of tubes and cables.

Then she heard it. The flat lining sound. Whilst she'd seen enough hospital dramas on TV and film, she'd also seen the real thing in field hospitals while on active service in the army.

The paramedic stayed calm and started checking switches and buttons, before moving to Simon.

"Come on Señor, come on, stay with us, stay with us. You've too much to lose if you go now Simon."

The panic was getting worse for Terri. She could almost feel him going. She knew she was losing him and there didn't seem anything the paramedic could do.

She watched in vain as the paramedic tried to restart his heart with chest compressions and then an adrenalin injection.

The hospital was only just off the Ma20, to the north of the city, but it still took another three minutes to get there, but suddenly the vehicle was stopping and the back doors were flung open and there were men and women there in surgical gowns and masks and things were being shouted by a woman standing just towards the back, but not in panic, but in clear decisive tones, letting everyone know what they needed to do.

"Don't give up hope Señora," said the paramedic as he stood back to let the trauma crash team take Simon through to surgery.

Terri tried to say something, but there were no words coming out. Then she saw her father. He ran forward and held her as the tears flowed from her.

"He's stopped breathing Dad! He's not responding."

Greg didn't know what to say. He'd been in situations where colleagues were dying, or had died, but this was the man his daughter had finally fallen in love in. The man who had saved her from that monster Marsden just a few months before.

'This can't be happening, not now.'

"It's not over yet my love. He'll keep fighting and not just for himself. He's got you to think about remember."

His daughter just held him even tighter.

58

Lori Garcia watched as Jake Sutton and Frankie Walker drove away from the hotel with a ten million euro painting, by Mallorca's famous adopted son Joan Miró, wrapped up in a rucksack in the back.

For two years the operation had been beset with challenges where they'd make an arrest, or seize drugs, before hitting brick wall after brick wall, as witness after witness either disappeared, or mysteriously suffered a memory loss as the police prosecution case neared the court process.

Although it wasn't actually one of the Sanchez family who had murdered Lori's husband twenty years ago, it was somebody very much like them. Someone who thought they were above the law and couldn't be touched, but since re-joining the police as a detective she had made it her business to bring exactly these type of criminals to justice.

There was still much that could potentially go wrong during this stage of the operation, but she knew only too well that there was never an easy route to bringing major criminals down. You sometimes needed a bit of luck, and sometimes you needed to do something different and that might include taking a bit of a risk.

'*A bit of a risk?*' she thought. '*More like a hell of a risk!*'

Here she was working in collaboration with Greg's 3R team and not one, but two criminals, no actually make that three including Maggs Walker.

"Inspectora?"

It was Nino, who'd seen her staring into the distance after the Seat Leon.

"Everything okay?"

"Si, Nino, si," she said. "I was just thinking about this as a scenario in a policing exam where you're asked if one, you would do it, two, would you refer it to your line manager or three, you must be out of your mind to even think about doing it."

"I know which one I'd pick Lori," said Nino, who only called her by her first name when they were alone and talking privately.

"None of the above?" said Lori, with a laugh.

"Maybe, before I met you. But you've taught me more than any text book could do about detecting crime, so I'd be going for number three," he grinned. "Come on Boss. Let's go and get this done!"

*****

Walker wondered if he'd see any of Garcia's GEO team on the way. He didn't have much respect for the investigatory skills of coppers in the UK, let alone in Spain, but he had to admit, if they were there, then he'd not seen them.

"Looking for Old Bill Frankie?" said Jake.

"Yes, not sure if I'd be reassured or worried if I'd seen them."

"Probably best we haven't seen any, because if we had, then maybe the Sanchez lot would have too."

They reached the gate house to the Sanchez villa. Jake saw the CCTV cameras mounted on the walls each side of the main doors. Presumably they'd been picked up on the cameras because a side door had opened and a man was coming out to them. He didn't say anything, but merely looked inside at them, presumably checking there was just the two of them. He waved his arm towards one of the cameras and presumably someone inside the gatehouse flicked a switch and the main door started to swing open.

"You ready for this Jake?"

"Yes mate, let's go and get Maggs and your kids back."

*****

Walker had been right to think the GEO were there, because they were. Lori had her strike force held in readiness down by an abandoned finca about a kilometre from the Sanchez villa. Nino had posted spotters along the route from Palma to the villa and they had seen a black Mercedes GLC heading towards the villa, followed about fifteen minutes later, by a report that Frankie Walker's grey Seat was turning off the Ma20 heading that way as well.

Twenty minutes or so after the GLC was first sighted, Cecil Moriarty was reporting into Pérez that it was being let through the main gates to the villa and that he was pretty sure it was Diego Sanchez who had got out of the front passenger seat.

Pérez was well prepared, as was the whole GEO team. He was leading the Alpha team and his long-time colleague and friend Sergeant Jorge Cruz, Bravo One, would lead the Bravo team. They'd both already been up to where Cecil Moriarty had based himself, to get a good look at the land surrounding the Sanchez villa. It was almost three quarters of a kilometre from the road entrance up to the villa's front door, so with their night glasses they had a really good view of the approach to the villa and the surrounding land.

Pérez knew it would be a difficult entry, not least

because it was dark, although to be fair, the darkness also brought its own benefit. But there was a lot of ground to cover before they would get to the actual villa and a dynamic entry, at least according to the tactical theory books, primarily requires speed and surprise.

Pérez knew only too well that dynamic entry was best used when the suspects are not expecting to have to immediately repel an attack. Therefore, the other key issue concerning him, other than the distance, was the likely presence of alarms and cameras at the gatehouse. So it was like music to his ears when Lori told him that Sutton would block the alarm system immediately after they'd been allowed through the front entrance.

After that the alarm system would look like it was functioning normally, whilst not changing any images on the CCTV cameras or reacting to any alarm activations.

He went through the final briefing with Jorge, who said, "We'll still need to get up to the villa damn quick amigo, but if they don't know we're coming I reckon we can do this."

"Good, glad you agree Jorge."

Pérez's radio crackled.

"Alpha One from Charlie Four. Grey Seat has arrived at the gatehouse. One guard is out the side gate and to the vehicle. Front gates now opening. Seat is in through the doors."

Pérez flicked his radio transmit button.

"Gracias Cecil. To confirm the Seat is now inside the villa grounds?"

"Yes, yes, Sarge."

"Bueno," Pérez said, "and there's been no change to the number of guards you've seen?"

"Confirmed. No change, no change. We've still got

just the eight guards. Currently two on the gate and six up at the house. It still looks like they run a three on, three off system during the hours of darkness. I keep seeing two circling the villa and then there's always one who comes out of the villa if anyone turns up or goes out of the front door."

"Nothing changed with what you're seeing with their weaponry Cecil?"

"It's as before Sarge. They're all carrying side arms holstered inside their jackets and one of the gate guys takes out an automatic rifle when he does his walkabout inside the grounds."

"We're getting set to go Cecil. Keep us posted if anything changes."

"Will do, and Sarge? Those doors by the road entrance? They do look pretty hefty. Are you thinking force, or blagging our way in?"

Blagging wasn't just a police term, given to getting your own way by gentle persuasion or a bit of guile, but anyone working in the world of surveillance knew the term well, especially given the fact they might often need to quickly 'blag' their way into somewhere when they quickly needed to take cover from someone they were following.

"Not sure we'll do an outright blag Cecil, but I think the Trojan horse might work well enough and Jorge will come in from around the back if we need any help persuading them to let us in."

"I think it'll work a treat," radioed Cecil and grinned.

*****

"Is there any news Doctor?"

Terri had seen the woman who had been giving the instructions at the back of the ambulance walking towards them. Then she saw the look on the woman's face and felt her body go rigid.

"I'm so sorry Señora, Señor. We did everything we

could, however the bullet had done too much damage internally."

"Thank you."

That was all Greg heard his daughter say. He thanked the doctor as well and started to say something to Terri.

"Dad, it's okay. We've both been through this. I just need a bit of time. Can I just borrow the car keys for a moment? I think I left my coat in there."

"Yes, yes, of course."

He watched as she went out of the hospital entrance to where he'd parked the car. He'd be in some tough scrapes with Simon Barnes but never thought he'd lose him. There were people he needed to tell, like Tommy and James, but for now the operation had to come first.

59

Frankie drove slowly towards the Sanchez villa, the headlights of the Seat flickering against the olive trees that lined the driveway. As he did Jake waited for the main doors to close and then he flicked the switch on the alarm blocker that he had down by the side of his seat.

The villa was so far away from any other properties that only one line appeared on the options list. Jake clicked on it and then pushed the activate button and saw the green light appear.

"Guys, if you're hearing me," Jake said, "the alarm blocker is on."

Just over a kilometre away, at a deserted abandoned finca, Sam heard Jake and passed the message to Lori who was standing next to him.

She waved to Pérez who was going through last minute checks with his team.

"Fernando, they're in and the alarm is blocked."

"Si, Inspectora."

Pérez flicked transmit on his radio.

"Bravo One, Jorge, the alarm is off, get your guys ready, we're on."

"Copied Alpha One. We're held off just short of the fence. We'll be over in two minutes and in position close to the gatehouse in around five and ready for when you need us."

"Gracias amigo," said Pérez.

"Inspectora, Bravo team are going over the wall now."

She nodded and then she and Sam watched as Pérez started loading up the Alpha team into the 'Trojan horse', a large plain green box van with side and rear doors for easy entry and exit.

Sam was thinking back to his days as an operational firearms officer in the Met and going over Pérez's tactics in his head. How many people to breach and secure the outer wall? How many would they need overall? Pérez had eight, with him and the driver dressed in casual clothing over their protective vests and sat up front in the van. Sam saw the remaining six officers load up in the back. All of them were wearing Kevlar protective vests, with full ballistic armour plating, good enough to stop, or at least reduce the damage, from handguns and all but the most powerful automatic and specialist rifles.

Together with Bravo team, Pérez would have sixteen officers to secure the villa, which going on the intel on numbers Lori had been given by her Obs man, Cecil, seemed to be a good number to Sam to get the job done.

His phone buzzed.

"Greg, how's Simon?" asked Sam.

Sam was Greg's first call.

Greg paused just for a moment and Sam instinctively knew.

"He's gone hasn't he?" said Sam.

"Yes," said Greg quietly. "There was too much internal damage."

"Stupid question I know, but how's Terri?"

"We've literally just found out. She's just gone to the car to get her coat...."

As soon as he said it, Greg realised his mistake.

"Shit!"

"What's up?" said Sam.

"She asked me for my car keys. Told me she was going for her coat. But she didn't have one Sam! She didn't have a bloody coat! What the hell's she going to do?"

It didn't take Sam long to think about what she probably had in mind.

"She'll be going to her flat. Better warn Josie and Holly to try to stop her," said Sam.

"Stop her?"

Greg's mind was going into overload at what had happened and what his daughter was going to do. "Why am I even asking? I know my girl. She's going to go after Diego! She'll want blood for this Sam. His blood!"

Lori had seen the concern on Sam's face.

"What's up?" she whispered.

"Simon's dead and Greg thinks Terri is going after Diego."

Lori held her hand out for his phone.

"I'm putting Lori on whilst I ring Holly, okay Greg?"

"Greg, I'm so sorry about Simon. Now are you sure about Terri? She's really going after Diego?"

He thought for a moment. He didn't actually know what Terri was going to do, but knowing his daughter as he did, he had a pretty good idea of what she'd have in mind.

"I can't say a hundred percent Lori, but I think that's the most likely thing she's going to do."

"Greg, me more than most people can understand what she's feeling, but we can't let her do this. Do you hear me? We cannot let her throw her life away to avenge Simon's murder."

"I hear you, but I'm not sure how we'll stop her."

"Where is she now?"

"Heading for her flat I imagine, probably to pick up her kit. One of your guys is going to take me there now."

*****

The tears of sadness had gone. Replaced by a cold stare as Terri looked straight ahead as she headed towards Portixol.

She was already thinking ahead, planning her next move. She knew her father would be trying to stop her if he could, but she was beyond caring what happened to her. She'd lost the man she had fallen head over heels in love with and she was going to make damn sure that the man responsible for his death paid dearly with his own life.

She had ignored the flashes of the speed cameras activating along the Ma20 as she flew past the other traffic as though it was standing still.

She heard her phone ringing and saw 'DAD' appear on the screen. She switched it to silent. But when the calls kept coming, from both her father and Sam, she turned the phone over so she couldn't see the screen and then accelerated hard, knowing she had to get to her apartment as soon as she could, before her dad or Lori sent someone there to stop her.

She took the exit towards Portixol and then swung the Kia hard left into the underground car park entrance before driving towards her own parking bay before abandoning the car in the first empty space she saw.

She knew time was against her. Her father, or Sam, had probably already phoned her mother. So she was expecting a hard time from her mum, not that anything was going to stop her. She ran straight past the lift. No point getting caught in an enclosed space if someone was waiting for her on her floor. Instead she went up the first flight of stairs, then turned and ran down the corridor to the other end of the apartment block before then going up the stairs furthest away from her apartment.

Coming out of the stairwell door on her floor, she had a good line of sight of the corridor where her apartment was. There was no one there, at least not from where she could see and the entrance spaces into each apartment weren't that big that somebody could easily hide in.

She moved quickly along the corridor and put her key in the lock and turned it. The door opened partially, but only onto a lock chain. She could see her mother Josie standing behind the door, tears streaming down her face.

"Terri, I'm so sorry my love. You must be heartbroken, but you can't do this. You mustn't do this. He wouldn't want you to do it my darling, honestly."

Josie could see her daughter's face. It sent a shiver through her. She'd never seen her looking that this. Terri's eyes were boring in to her, pupils wide and cold.

"Open the door Mum."

A flat unemotional voice.

"I don't think that's a good idea Terri. Why don't you just wait until your father gets here?"

"Mum, I said, open the door."

Terri's voice raised a notch in volume.

Josie glanced behind at Holly, who was on the phone to Greg and whispered, "How far away is he?"

"Mum, I can hear you talking to Holly. Look, I know you're worried, but this is something I've got to do, so just open the damn door, or I'll smash it in."

She saw her mother back away from the door and without waiting for her to say anything else Terri took a step back onto her right foot and then using her left foot like a springboard she catapulted her right leg forwards, smashing her right foot into the door lock, behind which she knew the chain lock was secured by just a few short screws.

The door sprang open and Terri walked in.

"I did ask nicely Mum," she said, before nodding at Holly who was standing just behind her mother, still with a phone in her hand.

"Terri, Greg says he wants to talk to you," said Holly.

She had never, even as a slightly uncontrollable teenager, done anything to go against her biological father. But she knew if she spoke to him now she might well back away from what she wanted to do, which was avenge the murder of the man she loved.

Terri shook her head slowly and then saw Holly muttering something into the phone before she looked back hopefully towards her.

"He's asking if you'll just wait there and if need be, he'll come with you," said Holly.

"Good try Holly, but just let me get a few things and then I'll be on my way."

Holly couldn't believe the change in the woman before her. She knew Terri was tough and had apparently been in some pretty dangerous situations in her army service, but it was the look in her eyes that most disturbed her. It was as though she wasn't thinking of anything other than hunting Diego Sanchez down, whatever the consequences to herself.

Terri was already in her bedroom and had gone into the secret compartment Tommy had made for her, where she kept a cache of weapons and specialist equipment. She grabbed a kitbag and selected two Glock handguns, a box of fifty rounds, a combat knife, together with some camouflage clothing and netting, plus her night vision glasses and telescopic sights before picking up her old Australian sniper's rifle and another box of ammunition.

Holly was waiting for her outside the walk-in

compartment as she came out. She was in a fighting stance with a determined look on her face.

"Holly, I know you think you're trying to help, but please!" said Terri.

"I'm not letting you leave without at least trying to stop you Terri."

"I haven't got time for this Holly. You ever been in a fight?"

As Holly went to answer, Terri didn't give her a chance, lunging forward and grabbing Holly's right hand. She pulled it down sharply, forcing Holly to her knees and making her cry out in pain as Terri applied pressure to the back of her hand.

"Thought not," said Terri.

"Terri! Let go of her now!" yelled her mother.

"Mum, I'm sorry," said Terri, still holding on to Holly's right hand and keeping her on the floor. "I know you don't want me to do this and nor does Dad, but I'm going to get the bastard who murdered Simon and make him pay."

She didn't wait for her mother to answer, but as she went out of the door she called out, "Holly, I'm sorry, but your hand should be okay, it shouldn't be broken."

With that she was gone, leaving Holly on the floor rubbing her hand.

60

Greg had heard everything his daughter had said on Holly's phone that had gone flying when Terri had forced her to the floor.

"She's gone Greg, I couldn't stop her. I'm so sorry."

"Not your fault Holly and thank you for trying, but you could have got yourself hurt. Are you okay?"

"Yes, she barely touched me. She didn't want to hurt me Greg, but she wasn't going to let me stop her going that's for sure."

"Well at least I'm glad you're okay. Look, I'm two minutes away. Do you know if she's taken the Kia?"

Josie looked around and saw a set of Kia keys on the side.

"No, she left those here Greg. Look, don't bother coming here. Just go and find her. We're fine."

He heard Josie calling out in the background too.

"We're okay Greg. Just find her!"

"Holly, let me talk to Josie."

He knew Terri would be smarter than to take the Kia, but she didn't have a car of her own. She went everywhere by taxi, or hired a car on the odd occasions she needed one.

"Josie, do you know if she has the keys to any of her neighbours' cars?"

Josie thought for a moment.

"I think she might have. She said she was going out the other day to check on someone's car, but I don't know who they are. She said something about them not being here all year round and so she keeps the battery ticking over for them with the odd run. You're going to ask me what type of car aren't you?"

"Well it would be handy if you knew."

"Well I've spectacularly failed then Greg. I've no bloody idea."

"Not to worry. Look, it's just an idea and it's a long shot at that, but it might be worth you and Holly going and banging on a few doors and see if the neighbours know which car it is, that and go and take a look down in the car park and see if there's any cars that aren't there around Terri's parking space."

"We're on it," said Josie. "And Greg?"

"Yes?"

"Go and find our baby and bring her back home safe!"

*****

Terri was in a Range Rover Evoque. The English owners were usually there over the winter months, so Terri would keep the car charged up by taking it out for a drive over the summer. She took out one of the Glocks and put it in her waist band and then dumped her kitbag in the back. As she drove out of the car park she went left, to go out of Portixol the back way rather than risk meeting her father coming in from the marina side.

She was committed now, she knew that. She was going to find Diego Sanchez and kill him.

*****

"Sam, I can't let Terri get anywhere near Diego Sanchez," said Lori quietly.

"I know, but what are you actually saying Lori?"

"I mean that if she kills him in cold blood I'll have no option but to arrest her."

Sam looked at her, but decided against saying anything. He knew she was right and go back a few months when he'd been in the Met, then he'd have been of the very same view. It wasn't that he necessarily agreed with what Terri was going to do, which was to basically follow the old saying of 'take an eye for an eye', but he was now also operating outside of the boundaries he'd followed when he'd been in the police.

"I can see your mind turning over Sam Martínez. Don't get me wrong, Sanchez is a bad one, we both know that. But we have to respect the law even if the OCGs don't, otherwise what have we got?"

He knew she was right, but what was deemed right and wrong had always been something of a grey area for him and it hadn't got any easier for him since he'd left the Met.

"Maybe you're right Lori, but as of a few months ago this woman became my sister and that just makes it that much harder to rationalise all of this."

"For you and me both Sam. Look, here's what we'll do if you're up for it?"

"Go on," said Sam.

"I can pull Moriarty off the Obs post and get him to go and find her. He's a trained marksman and will know the sort of area where she's most likely to head for. But I need to cover his post and see what the hell is going on in the villa. I know you're listening in to the wire, but can you cover the Obs too?"

"Lori, you're a star! And of course I'll do it."

She took her radio out of her waistband.

"Sierra One to Charlie Four."

"Si Inspectora," came Cecil's cheerful voice.

"Expect a visitor in the next few minutes. One of the 3R team is going to take over from you. Start getting ready to deploy on foot. He'll brief you on what I need you to do. Understood?"

"Si Inspectora," said Cecil, who was now wondering what task he was being given when through his night binoculars he could see the Bravo team had already gone over the fence into the grounds of the Sanchez villa and far to his left, by the finca, Pérez had just loaded up his team into a van.

"Sam," said Lori handing him her car keys. "I hope for all our sakes, but especially Terri's, that she doesn't get into a position where she can take a shot at Sanchez."

He could see the look on her face. How would she deal with the dilemma, if it came to it, of protecting a criminal like Diego Sanchez? Would she authorise a shot at Terri to stop her killing Sanchez?

He tried to put himself in Lori's shoes. She was emotionally connected with what was happening, yet it was far too late for Lori to back out and hand responsibility to Pérez or Nino who, albeit were clearly not in love with Greg, were almost as much connected with the whole situation. No, he thought, she had to go with this and manage as best she could. Finding Terri before she could do anything was the best, or maybe the only option she had.

*****

Within minutes Sam was with Moriarty after he'd guided him into his location.

"Señor Martínez, a pleasure to meet you."

Sam saw the long range rifle set up in position and grimaced, thinking about Terri.

"It's Sam please Cecil. We've got a problem."

Sam outlined what had happened and what Lori wanted him to do. Cecil listened, asking questions and clarifying if Sam knew the type of weaponry Terri might be carrying.

He then nodded and put a hand on Sam's shoulder. "Amigo, leave it to me. If she's out there I'll find her."

Sam watched him go.

"I just hope you find her before it's too late amigo."

*****

Although she hadn't seen the villa itself, Terri knew the road reasonably well because it was the main road out of Palma to Sóller, plus she'd seen enough from the terrain maps Sam had been using in the planning process to know what the lay of the land was like.

She remembered Lori saying how she had one of her team in an Obs position, looking down on the villa from across the main road. Apparently they had a really good line of sight of the little gatehouse by the road and right up the driveway, to the villa itself and the surrounding gardens.

Knowing her father and possibly Sam might be out looking for her she stayed on the back roads and approached the villa from the East, keeping to the other side of the hill, where she expected Lori's Obs man to be positioned. As she got within half a kilometre of the main road, she found a spot and parked the Evoque.

Terri knew she needed to tread carefully, because the GEO were no mugs, not by a long stretch. Although it was still dark, it wouldn't be that long before the early dawn started to appear.

That said, she knew Anna would be trying to wrap this up as soon as Walker and Sutton got the painting into the villa. She'd be pushing the Sanchez family to talk about their drugs deal with Walker, to get it all recorded via the wire they'd put on the Miró. Anna wouldn't want to be hanging around any longer than she needed to in there, so Terri knew she didn't have much time to get in position, before the expected assault by the GEO on the Sanchez villa.

She changed into full camouflage gear, adding masking paint to her face and hands. Slipping the sniper rifle bag over her shoulder she set off, heading up the hill, but staying wide of the area she expected the GEO guy to be in. She could confidently take a shot from up to a mile, so a kilometre or so was no problem to her, therefore she intended to be well above him.

She thought back to the last time she had used the rifle other than for practice. It had been in India, with the Kaur woman. Simon had been with her, helping with the wind and distance data. She felt a shiver down her back. He was gone just when they were…, she stopped herself thinking about him, refocused and then pushed on even harder to the top of the escarpment.

It didn't take long to get to the top and she peered carefully over and saw the gatehouse below and the villa in the distance.

She was fit, but not maybe as fit as she'd been before she'd been shot and although she'd trained damn hard, she was feeling the effects of the quick climb she'd put in to get up to the top of the hill, so she lay there for a while, getting her breathing back under control.

As she took in her surroundings she saw there were lights on in the villa and with a scan of the area with her night glasses, she spotted movement of what must be Lori's team at an old finca.

She wondered who'd be looking for her. Would it be her dad? Probably, she smiled to herself and he was good, bloody good. But who else? Sam? Maybe? Whoever it was, she was a long way up and she should see them before they saw her and anyway if things went well, then they would know full well it was her who had shot Sanchez, but she certainly wasn't intending to get caught.

She'd thought about where Lori's man Obs man would be. He was primarily, she guessed, in an observation capacity, to monitor movements and guide the assault team in, rather than as a sniper. That would suggest they would be lower down the hill, because line of fire and any wind factor was less of an issue than having the best overall view of the area. She guessed they were maybe halfway up, so she started moving slowly down the hillside until she spotted a hollow behind a piece of rock. There wasn't much cover, but she gathered some olive branches on her way down that would give her enough cover, together with the camouflage netting, to make it almost impossible to see her from below, or above once she was settled in.

It took her less than a few minutes to get prepped and in position and looking down her night sight at the villa. As she lay there she started her breathing drills. Box breathing they called it in sniper training. There were a number of different connotations, but she liked the four in and four out ratio. Breathing slowly, she let her body adapt to her environment until she was relaxed, but with her senses on full alert.

Now all she had to do was wait for the bastard to come out of the front door and she'd be ready.

*****

Juan 'Cecil' Moriarty had packed up his rifle into its carry bag and left Sam setting himself up in the small clump of bushes, concealed from sight below. Cecil went immediately to his left and then started heading further up the hill, before stopping behind an old untended olive tree that gave him plenty of cover.

He leaned back against the tree, facing away from the villa and then took out his map and mini-lite. Then shrouding the torch light as much as he could, so that any light would project away from the villa and not towards it, he scanned the map.

There was no point in just walking around the hill trying to find this woman. Martínez had said she was good, a trained army sniper who would know all about identifying 'shoot' locations, even in the most difficult terrain. However, it wasn't quite a needle in a haystack search. He knew, because of where he'd positioned himself, that there were not that many areas up on the hill where she was likely to go.

DI Garcia had previously given him authority to use lethal force if a situation arose involving the immediate protection of the Walker woman and her children, so he'd already done his calculations on line of fire, trajectory and managing the wind factor which was how he'd arrived at the location he'd left Sam in.

He was an experienced police marksman, but she was a professional soldier and a trained sniper. Like her, he was trained to shoot at targets, but as a sniper, she would be doing it from a concealed location and at a far longer range than he was competent to shoot from. However, he'd had some long range shooting training from concealed positions and in many ways it was quite closely linked with his Covert Rural Observation Post training, or CROPs, as it was known for short.

He started sketching a new line of sight from the villa, but this time on a higher line to where he'd been positioned. After looking at a few of the options he'd drawn, he decided that if it was him, then where he would go would be somewhere along a line about forty to fifty metres above where Sam Martínez now was.

That meant he'd have to go even higher than that. Staying well away from where he had been, he started the climb. It wouldn't have been that arduous in light climbing gear and in daylight, but he was kitted out in full Kevlar protective ballistic gear, and he was carrying a rifle gun case. It was only because he had night vision glasses on that he could see anything as it was still pretty dark.

He'd told Sam he wouldn't be calling up unless he had to, but he felt he had enough cover at the moment to risk a short transmission.

"Charlie Four to Sierra One."

"Si, si Charlie Four," said Lori.

"Boss, I'm heading seventy metres up the hill and then I'm going to go across, heading north. I reckon she's going to be about fifty metres above my previous location. Copied?"

"Gracias Charlie Four."

"Also copied," said Sam.

He didn't know if he wanted Moriarty to find Terri or not, because he didn't know how she'd react, or indeed what Moriarty's orders might be if he needed to stop her taking a shot. He tried calling her again, but her phone was still going straight to ansaphone. She must have turned it off, so that she couldn't be tracked and had probably even taken the battery out, to make sure it was properly untraceable.

'Bloody hell Terri,' he swore to himself. *'Please don't do this!'*

61

Walker brought the Seat to a halt outside the front doors of the villa. Alejandro was there, together with his father.

He and Jake got out of the car and Jake opened the back door and pulled out his rucksack that had the painting in it. He was breathing heavily trying to control his nerves. This was nothing like anything he had ever done before.

"Jake, for Christ's sake, relax will you! You're getting me all bloody jittery too," snapped Walker.

"I'm trying, I'm trying," said Jake, who was subconsciously combing his hair back with his fingers. "Shit!" he whispered.

"What is it now?" said Walker, as they got closer to the doors where Alejandro was standing to greet them.

"I've still got my bloody ear piece in. The one Martínez gave me."

"Do not touch your ear," Walker said calmly, "but when I move, which I'm going to any second now, make sure you get rid of it."

Jake didn't have time to respond. Walker had seen Diego standing back in the entrance hall, a smirk across his face. One of the Sanchez guards was about to step forward to pass the security wand over Walker, when

Frankie burst past him and ran straight at Diego.

"You bastard!" Walker shouted. "You killed one of my best people!"

Whilst Jake was taken aback by Walker's sudden onrush, he was switched on enough to quickly ditch the earpiece and flick it across the driveway into some bedding plants.

"Frankie, Frankie, hold up! What's this you're saying?" said Alejandro.

"Your piece of shit brother here killed one of my best guys back at the hotel. Now we've got the cops swarming all over the place."

Alberto Sanchez, the Old Man, stepped forward.

"Diego? Is this true?"

The smirk was still on Diego's face.

Back up on the hill Terri was trying to work out what was going on. She'd seen Walker run forward into the villa, but didn't know why and she couldn't see any sign of Diego.

"Papa, I was just trying to help," said Diego. "I thought I'd bring you the picture myself to save Frankie here a trip."

"That's total bollocks and you know it," shouted Walker.

"Frankie," said Alberto. "If Diego says he was trying to help, then he was trying to help."

Walker had chanced a quick look to see if Jake had got rid of the earpiece and was relieved to see his friend give a quick nod.

"You can think all you want Señor Sanchez, but he was not helping, and he has killed one of my people. Now here's your bloody picture, now please get my wife and kids and I will be out of here."

Adeline Sanchez had heard the shouting and had come down the stairs.

"Come, come, now Frankie, let us not leave on a

bad note. Now we can celebrate the start of what is going to be a very profitable relationship for both of us," she said. "Alejandro, go and get Señora Walker and her mother. Perhaps let's leave the children to sleep Frankie, just until everything is settled."

Her eldest son smiled at her, "Si Mama."

*****

Up on the hillside Sam was hearing what was being said down at the villa.

"Greg from Sam?" He called up on the 3R radio.

"Go ahead Sam, I've just got to the finca. I picked it up too. Looks like the transmitter on the frame is working."

"Yes, so they're in, but why did Walker go for Diego?"

"No idea," said Greg, "but he must have been inside the house as we didn't get any reaction from Terri, who I'm guessing must be somewhere up on the hillside by now."

"Greg, Lori has sent her Obs guy to find her." Sam paused. "He's armed Greg, but I don't know what Lori's told him to do."

"Okay," said Greg quietly. "I'm with her now, so I'll ask her."

Lori was looking at him.

"Ask me what?"

"Sam says you've got someone out looking for my daughter."

She heard the tone in his voice. She knew he'd of course be worried, but what did he think? She'd sent someone up there to shoot Terri?

"Before you start and say something that you, and then I, might regret Greg, I've got Cecil looking for her okay. She must not, I repeat, must not be allowed to shoot Diego, or anyone else for that matter in cold blood, do you hear me?"

He could see the passion coming out in her. She was mad at him, but he still didn't know what she intended to do if Terri got in the way.

"But..," he started to say.

"No 'buts' Greg. I don't have a master plan, but Terri won't be shooting anyone. If anybody does any shooting up on that hill it will be my guy, not your daughter!"

She turned and walked away from him. She knew he must be worried sick, but she also had a job to do and she'd need to cool down before she said anything else to him.

*****

Frankie was relieved to see his wife coming down the stairs with a smile on her face and he nodded at his 'mother-in-law' who was a step behind her.

"Are we sorted?" said Maggs.

"Yes we are, all bar a bit of admin apparently."

Walker looked across at Señor Sanchez.

"Señora Walker, Frankie and his friend here have done a splendid job in providing us with such a nice gift."

Maggs looked at Alberto and his wife and wondered where they got off pretending everyone was playing happy families, when the reality was that they'd kidnapped her and her kids and held them to ransom.

But she bit her lip. She knew the woman next to her needed the Sanchezes to come and talk about the drugs distribution stuff, otherwise she had pretty much assured her that Frankie's team would be the number one target for the Met, the National Crime Agency and not to mention MI5, for the next decade and more.

"Well I'm glad you like it. Now when can we expect to get this business plan up and running? I assume you have still got your supply guaranteed?"

She was careful not to feed them too much, that's

what her 'mother' had said to her.

"Yes of course, it's coming in with the cannabis on container ships from Bolivia, via Ghana," said Alejandro.

"And you're sure you can guarantee both products? Maggs pushed back.

"Yes of course Maggs. Look you must trust us. We have a very good arrangement with our suppliers for both the cannabis and the cocaine. The prices are very competitive and we shall make a lot a money."

"I don't like what I'm hearing here Margaret," said Anna, trying to show her concern for the business her daughter was in.

"Señora Murphy, we are merely importers and distributors of products that society has seen fit to use," Alejandro said. "For example, did you know the UK is, along with Spain and Germany the highest users of cocaine outside of the United States?"

"I didn't and I wish I still didn't," said Anna indignantly. "But why are you are doing this? You seem to have more than enough money already judging by this place?"

It was Adeline who answered this time.

"Perhaps you're right Saoirse, maybe we have. However, we come from a very poor family and I never want any of my family to experience what I went through."

"So you'll import and sell these drugs that addict and kill people just to make more money?" mocked Anna.

"I don't like your tone Señora Murphy," said Old Man Sanchez. "We will not only keep doing this, but we are expanding. We will blow the market wide open by undercutting those Albanian gangs who have tried to muscle in on our business in our own country."

Anna could see she had got Old Man Sanchez on the

run now. He was angry with the Albanians for taking a major slice of the drug importation business in the UK and he was going to make sure he got a share of it.

"So how do you propose to do that in the UK when you're sitting over here in sunny Spain?" Anna asked. She had appreciated how Maggs had started things, but she needed to get this done and quickly before any of them smelt a rat.

"We were too soft with the Albanians when they started bringing the coke into the UK. We thought they'd only take a small share and keep the margins small, but they got greedy and now they're undermining our business. But we have your daughter here to thank for helping us get back our rightful position as the number one supplier into your country. With her help and should I say also with Frankie's help, now he is out of one of your Majesty's prisons, we will see our first ship dock at Felixstowe in a week's time."

"Can't wait Señor," said Frankie. "What's it called again?"

Anna winced. He was trying to help, but she knew it was one question too many.

Alberto Sanchez had realised it as well and he turned away slightly, before turning back to face them again, this time with a gun in his hand.

"It's the MS Cotopaxi, after a volcano in Ecuador, but Frankie, I think you know that all too well don't you?"

62

Greg had heard Anna drawing out Old Man Sanchez and getting him to outline their drugs business and he'd found Lori and given her an earpiece to follow what was being said.

She'd given him a thumbs up as she heard Sanchez talking about the Albanians and then she smiled at him when he gently laid a hand on her arm and mouthed *'Sorry'* to her.

"It's okay my love," she said gently. We're all under a lot of pressure and I know how worried you are about Terri and I am too, believe me."

But the moment was interrupted when they heard Frankie Walker ask about the ship.

They both groaned and Lori immediately radioed to Pérez to move in.

"Roger that Inspectora. Bravo One, did you copy? Be ready to get an entry into the gatehouse, but hold off until you hear my call."

"Copied Alpha One," said Jorge Cruz, Bravo One.

Pérez checked his team were ready to deploy and signalled to the driver to head out. He checked his clothing, to make sure it was covering his protective vest and then did a quick visual check of his driver too.

They quickly covered the kilometre up towards the

villa and as they approached the gatehouse he heard Sam Martínez call up.

"Alpha One, I have you in sight. Both guards are currently in the gatehouse."

"Gracias Sam," said Pérez as the van turned into the villa driveway and stopped by the main doors.

"One guard coming out to you."

"Seen him," said Pérez. "Bravo One, move in now please."

"Si, si," replied Bravo One and he motioned to two of his men. They stepped out from their cover and ran forward to the gatehouse and quietly opened the door. The guard inside didn't see them until he felt the muzzle of an automatic rifle in the back of his head and heard a GEO officer quietly telling him to put his hands slowly on top of his head.

"One in custody," said Bravo One.

"Gracias," smiled Pérez, as the other guard approached the van. Pérez then slowly nodded to the two men in the back who were poised by the side door, which they had already taken off the lock, so it was ready to be flung open.

The guard had a grim face and didn't say anything, but just indicated to the driver that he wanted him to wind his window down.

"Sorry amigo," said the driver in a friendly voice. "I know it's late, but we're here with some deliveries."

"What sort of deliveries? We're not expecting..."

He didn't get his last word out. Suddenly the side door of the van flew open and one of the GEO officers launched himself at the guard taking him to the ground, whilst the second officer was quickly followed him and stood over the guard with a pistol aimed at the man's head.

"Sierra One from Alpha One, we now have two in custody."

The two guards were left in the gatehouse, handcuffed with their hands to the rear and both ankles plasti-cuffed, with a GEO officer for company.

Bravo One had already deployed the rest of his team, moving up towards the villa, keeping to the shadows, whilst the Alpha team followed in the van with the lights off.

"Sam, can you tell what's going on in the villa?" said Pérez.

"Frankie's having a hard time. I think they're roughing him up a bit, so perhaps you might want to get a bit of shift on?"

"We're not exactly dawdling amigo."

"Copied that Alpha One, apologies."

For a minute Sam had thought himself back as an OFC, an operational firearms commander, directing his tactical teams into place, but he wasn't there for that this time. It was Lori's show and in any event he knew Pérez was a first class operational cop who would be doing the right thing, without some former Met Chief Inspector interfering.

*****

Greg felt his phone buzzing. He'd put it onto silent when he was listening to what was being said in the villa. It was Josie.

"Have you found her?"

He could hear the worry in her voice. There was almost a rattle in there, as the concern must have been flooding through her body causing her vocal muscles to tighten.

"No, not yet, but we think she's up on the hill close by to us and we've got someone up there trying to find her."

"But find her and do what Greg? What are they going to do if they find her?" Josie was trying to hold on to herself, but it was hard and just being told someone was looking for her daughter just wasn't enough. "And why aren't you out there Greg? You were a bloody spy weren't you?"

Now the anger was coming through. He knew it would. She needed someone to blame, so it might as well be him, so he let her rant.

"If I thought I was the best person to be out there then that's where I'd be Josie, but we've got someone better, far better and he thinks he knows roughly whereabouts Terri is and as soon as he spots her we have a plan to get her to back off."

He didn't have a specific plan and nor did he think Lori had one, but it was probably for the best that he didn't tell Josie that, but he seemed to have reassured her, at least for the moment.

"Okay, now Holly wants to talk to you."

"Greg?"

"Holly, I'm sorry I haven't kept you posted, it's been a bit..."

"Yes, so I gather and Greg, I'm so sorry again about Simon."

"Thanks Holly, now you probably need to report in to your guys too, so you can tell them that the GEO are currently moving in on the Sanchez villa, so we should have a resolution sometime soon."

Holly thanked him and sat back and thought it had only been a few days before when she was dealing with art thefts from a desk bound analytical perspective, rather than being out in the field, where a man had lost his life.

She shivered and then saw Josie, who was trying to keep a grip on herself, but not too successfully, Holly thought she'd be better keeping her busy.

"Josie, I need some help if you can manage it?"

Josie looked at her and smiled. She knew what Holly was doing and she definitely needed something to do to keep herself from worrying about her little girl.

"What can do I to help?"

*****

As he ended the call Greg looked across and back up to the hill where he knew his daughter must be.

'Don't do anything stupid my girl,' he thought, then knowing he needed to let Anna know help was on its way, he called up on the radio frequency of the earpiece she had.

"Greg to Anna. Help will be with you very soon."

63

Alberto Sanchez had been a criminal for long enough in his lifetime to get a feeling for when someone was doing something they shouldn't. He cursed himself that he'd let the older woman lull him into some sort of false sense of security, enough for him to start blabbing about his business.

"Very clever, very clever Saoirse, or is that actually your real name?"

Anna just looked at him blankly. She'd heard Greg's transmission, so she had to try to play things out for as long as she could and hope Lori's team made it to them soon, before one of them was killed.

"Don't play dumb with me Señora," and he caught Anna unawares as he hit her, a vicious slap with the back of his hand that stunned her and she felt a trickle of blood from her lip.

Frankie Walker went to grab Old Man Sanchez, but Alejandro hit him on the back of the head with a pistol.

"Now, now Frankie, just sit still and then we can get to the bottom of this."

Walker had fallen to his knees and was groggy, but conscious. His wife, Maggs went to him, but he waved her away. He didn't want them seeing he was down and out of it. He tried to clear his head as he first got up on one and then the other leg, trying hard to keep his balance.

"I don't know what you're thinking of here Señor," said Anna, trying to keep the pretence up, "but now you've got your pretty picture can't you just let my family go?"

"Ah, but you see Señora, I have been in this business long enough to know when I think something isn't right. Now all we have to do is find a way to see if I am correct. Of course, if I am wrong, then I will wholeheartedly apologise and indeed, I will make you a gift of this fine painting."

"You are wrong, with whatever it is you're thinking and in any case, I don't want your damn picture."

"Perhaps we should wake your children Margarita? They may be able to help one of you come forward with the truth?" said Adeline.

"So you're not just the mother sitting in the back, looking after the family are you, you old cow?" hissed Maggs.

"Do not speak to my mother like that again you bitch," said Alejandro, as he lashed out at her and sent Maggs sprawling across the floor.

"If you think I'm going to let you get away with any of this Sanchez, you've another think coming," said Walker.

"Oh, but you see Frankie, we will get away with it. If you don't want to do business with us, then I'm sure we'll find one of your competitors in London who will no doubt be pleased to step into your shoes. Besides, I'm not so sure we want to do business with you anymore, do we Papa?"

His father looked back at his son and then said, "No, I don't believe we do my boy."

With that Alejandro smiled as he raised his pistol and shot Walker through the chest.

Maggs was stunned, but Anna was quick to react and let Greg and whoever else was listening to the transmission know what had happened.

"Alejandro Sanchez just shot Frankie Walker."

Sam was first to acknowledge.

"Roger that, shot fired."

Lori immediately radioed through to Pérez.

"Alpha One, be advised, shot fired. Frankie Walker is down. ETA please?"

"Going in now," replied Alpha One.

Alejandro Sanchez had stopped smiling.

"Señora? What did you just say and to who?" as he raised the pistol towards Anna.

*****

Both Pérez and Jorge Cruz had heard the shot. The two guards, who were walking around the villa, one at the front and one to the back, both heard it too and instinctively turned and looked into the villa.

They were distracted just enough to miss a GEO officer come up behind each of them and push a handgun deep into their neck and then pull them backwards to the side of the villa, where they were handcuffed and plasti-cuffed.

Pérez signalled to one of his Alpha team, who had found the electric fuse box in an outhouse at the side of the villa, to go on his countdown.

"Three, two, one, go!"

The lights went out in the villa and Anna instinctively dived for the floor, pulling Maggs Walker with her and then she rolled, and kept rolling to the side of the room, knowing she had to take cover in case anyone of the Sanchezes starting firing indiscriminately, but also knowing what was coming next.

At least two shots were fired, followed by a scream and then Old Man Sanchez started shouting for everyone to stop firing.

"Are you hit?" whispered Anna.

"No," said Maggs.

"Put your hands over your ears and shield your eyes! Do it now."

Anna knew it wouldn't stop the full effects, but then she heard the glass smash and then waited for the stun grenades. Bravo team took the French windows, smashing the glass and throwing in the grenades, whilst Pérez took his team in through the front door, hurling a two more stun grenades down the long corridor just as three of the guards were coming out of a back room.

Anna knew how loud the flash-bangs from the stun grenades were in open spaces – they were louder than a jet engine, but add that to a confined space like the villa and the noise can literally knock people over and cause temporary deafness and even blindness, but certainly complete disorientation.

The flash-bangs did their jobs and by the time the three guards were getting to their feet the Alpha team were on them and they were knocked back down to the ground and held firm with automatic rifles aimed at them.

Bravo team had gone in fast, literally bursting through the set of wooden French windows. Wearing night glasses, they'd easily identified the two Sanchez men and the mother, Adeline.

They shouted at them to get to the floor. Alberto and Adeline went down onto their knees and then lay down, but one of their two sons stood there defiantly.

"I said get down on the floor. Do it now!" said Bravo One.

"Or what?" said Alejandro. "You're not going to shoot me, I'm unarmed."

"Alejandro, no!" cried his mother.

"Listen to your mother my boy and get down on the floor. We can sort this. All of it," said his father.

Bravo One held steady, his gun pointed at Alejandro Sanchez's chest.

"Bring your right arm up slowly to the side and drop your weapon. Do it now."

"Weapon, I don't …."

Alejandro went to pull his hand up to shoot when Bravo One fired. It was point blank and Sanchez wasn't wearing a vest of any sort, so the bullet smashed into his body and straight into his chest, creating chaos amongst his vital organs and he was dead by the time he hit the floor.

"Alejandro!! screamed his mother.

"Goggles off and lights back on, now please," said Pérez and the electric was flicked back on once more lighting up the villa.

Bravo One walked across to where Anna and Maggs were still curled up tight against the wall.

"Señora, good to see you again," he said smiling at Anna.

"And you Bravo One. Perfect timing too."

"Sierra One," radioed Pérez. "We have control of the villa, but we've lost Diego. He must have got out when the lights went out. We'll start with the villa and then widen it to the gardens."

"Shit" said Lori. "Diego has got away."

"Not good," said Greg. "If she sees him…"

"I know," said Lori. "Let's hope we get to him before she does."

*****

"Señora Walker! Por favor!" shouted one of the GEO officers who had found the children crying in the bedroom upstairs.

"The kids! God, what will I tell them?" yelled Maggs.

"Yes, come with me," said Bravo One, taking her arm

and guiding her through the bodies. Maggs stopped for a moment and quickly knelt by her husband.

"Oh, my love."

Wiping the tears from her face, she got up and followed Cruz up the stairs.

64

Terri had seen the action taking place at the villa. The flashes from the stun grenades were clear to see even if she hadn't been wearing night vision glasses.

She had also seen someone down below her, presumably Lori's Obs man. Once it looked like the GEO team had secured the villa the guy in the Obs post had sat up, which is when she saw him. Then as he turned around, looking up the hill, she saw it was Sam. He was scanning the hill, but he clearly couldn't see her.

She refocused her telescopic sight back on the villa. There was still activity going on. The police were completing a full search of the place. Not unusual, but they seemed to be taking their time. Did that mean not everyone was accounted for? She'd heard at least four shots. One before the GEO went in, then two more when the lights in the villa had gone off and then another one after the lights came back on.

'*What the hell's going on down there?*'

Who hadn't they found? It was unlikely the police would be all that bothered to find one of the guards missing, so presumably it must be one the Sanchezes. Could it be Diego?

She watched as a car moved from the gatehouse up

the driveway and stopped at the front doors to the villa.

Two people got out. As soon as they did she recognised them. It was Lori and her father. She watched as they both looked up the hill in her direction, but obviously they wouldn't be able to see her from where they were.

She knew she must be worrying them and for the first time she wondered if she was doing the right thing. But then she felt the anger and then sadness come over her, as she thought about Simon and how Sanchez had shot him in cold blood.

Her father was on his phone. He was probably trying to ring her again, but she still had it turned off, with the battery out. She wasn't ready to talk, not yet. He looked up at the hill once more and then turned and followed Lori into the building leaving Terri to scan the rest of the grounds of the villa.

"Where are you Diego?"

*****

When the lights had gone out Diego had instinctively known it was some sort of attack. He didn't know, but whether it was some of Walker's men, the police, or even a rival OCG, it didn't matter. He needed to get out of there and quickly!

He stood pressed back to the side of the French doors and only just got his hands up to his ears as first of the flash-bangs were thrown in. Seconds later the noise exploded in the room and he felt his ears ringing and he struggled to keep his balance.

He counted the men coming in through the doors, one, two, three, four, five. They were shouting as they came in and then a sixth guy stopped and stood in the doorway. He, or maybe it was a woman, he didn't care, must be the last one. They had to be police he thought, with that sort of controlled entry. He probably only had moments to make his move, before the lights were likely to come back on. He heard more shouting and then heard his brother say something, but he couldn't catch what he'd said as his ears were still ringing.

He needed to go now. He swivelled from where he was and ran out through the doors, straight through the guy who was standing there. Bravo Six didn't see him coming as, still wearing his night glasses, he only had limited peripheral vision.

Sanchez pushed the man out the way and kept running, out the back and into the gardens and headed for the rear yard. He heard a shot, but it seemed to be within the villa and not out towards him. He knew there were three more cars in the back yard and that they should all have the keys in them. At least that was the general rule, as some of the idiots who worked for them had been prone to lose too many sets of keys in the past.

He checked the first one, a Land Rover discovery. No bloody key. He swore, but kept looking and the next one, a Skoda SUV, had the key in it.

He got in and switched the lights off automatic and onto manual so as not to alert the police. The engine started up, but sounded like a rocket firing up in the night air. He gently pulled away from the villa and out onto a dirt road that he knew led towards a rear gate that would take him out on to one of the back roads.

As soon as he felt it was safe to do so, he flicked the headlights on. Terri saw the lights come on before she saw the vehicle. She knew it must be one of the Sanchezes escaping and she wasn't about to let that happen.

It was a moving target and it was still dark, but she was confident she could take out a tyre, even on a moving vehicle. There was little or no wind to be concerned about, so she took aim at the rear nearside tyre, taking into account the direction of travel of the vehicle. In effect she was aiming in front of the vehicle, with the expectation that it would 'catch up' as the bullet arrived in the space where the rear wheel was going to be by that time.

Even if she missed the tyre itself, she knew there was a good chance the bullet would take a sizeable chunk out of the alloy wheel, which was likely to cause it to collapse. Either way, there was a good chance the SUV would go into a swerve and with any luck it might even flip over.

She fired.

Diego was pushing the car as fast as he could even though the lights weren't great on the Skoda and there was no other light from around. At the last minute he saw a bend on the dirt track and went to turn the steering wheel, but suddenly heard a loud bang at the rear of the car, then he felt it start to buck and sway to the right.

Sanchez hadn't heard anything with the noise of the car on the track surface, but he guessed he must have burst tyre or something. He stopped the SUV and got out. The tyre wasn't just flat, it was shredded. His mind was trying to take in why that might have happened when he heard a faint noise and then the rear window shattered.

Someone was shooting at him!

He dived for cover behind the front of the Skoda. He was trying to get his head around who was firing at him. Surely it wasn't the police?

'They don't shoot at people who are trying to get away,' he thought. 'So who is it?'

He had a handgun, but there seemed little point in firing it as whoever was shooting at him must be high up on the hill. He thought about making a run for it, or even crawling away under cover of what darkness was still there, but it was starting to get lighter, so he'd need to go quickly if he went at all. But how far would he get before he'd be exposed to the shooter? That, he decided, wasn't something he wanted to find out.

*****

She knew she had him pinned down.

'But now what?' she thought.

It was a sort of a stalemate, because if he stayed behind the car she couldn't get to him and she wasn't in any sort of position to move from where she was without giving him a chance to escape.

She fired off another round at the Skoda, just to keep Sanchez occupied and heard the noise as more glass in the SUV shattered. Then as she was lining up her sights, this time looking for him, she sensed something. It wasn't anything she heard, but it was like a flicker that she caught out of her right eye. She glanced down from her telescopic sight to her right hand, her trigger hand.

There was a red dot on the top of her thumb. She tried not to react, but forty metres or so above her, Cecil Moriarty saw her flinch.

'Got you,' he said to himself.

"Señora," he called out calmly. "My boss wants to talk to you."

She guessed it was one of Lori's men. She'd missed him and he must be good, very good to have spotted her. But then again, even with the rifle fitted with a sound suppressor, the noise of the shot wasn't ever completely silenced, so perhaps he had heard that as well.

"We gather you have your phone switched off Señora Anderson, please switch it on."

She didn't know if he had orders to shoot her or not. Would Lori do that? She decided she didn't know, because if she was in Lori's shoes then she wasn't sure what she'd do in these circumstances.

Whoever was calling her must have radioed Lori, because she came out of the front door of the villa, together with her dad, both of them looking up in her direction again. Lori had her phone to her ear.

'She must be ringing me,' thought Terri.

The guy aiming the red dot at her hand must have read her thoughts because he called out again.

"Don't worry Señora, I will make sure Diego does not get away and if the boss says you can shoot him, I'll back off, okay?"

'Fat chance of that,' thought Terri, but she called back to him, "Okay, I'm putting my phone back on."

As soon as the battery slipped into the phone it started ringing.

"Terri?"

"Yes, Lori."

"Terri, I'm so sorry about Simon. We all are, but look, I know how you're feeling. Remember I've been through this too, when they murdered my Felipe in front of my kids."

"He killed him in cold blood Lori," said Terri quietly.

"I know, I know my darling girl. You're hurting so much, just like I did, when your whole body aches for the man you've lost. I tell you, I wanted to do exactly what you're thinking about doing now and worse. I wanted to round them all up and string them up by their balls and watch them bleed to death."

Terri took a deep breath and wiped away the tear that had formed in her left eye. That was exactly how she felt. She wanted Diego to suffer, to feel the tightness in his stomach of pain and loss and then watch him slowly die in front of her. That's what Simon would have done for her. That's what he did when he killed Marsden.

Greg motioned to Lori for the phone and she passed it over.

"Teresa, it's Dad."

Terri half-smiled. He only ever called by her full name when he was being serious.

"Your Mum wants me to bring you back home. So can we do that my girl? Please? We can leave Lori to deal with Diego and the rest of these lowlifes."

"But I want him to suffer Dad, for what he did to Simon."

Greg took a deep breath.

"I know, but we've done what we set out to do. We need to go back now and have a drink to Simon. That's the Regiment way isn't it?"

"Yes," she whispered, barely able to get the words out. "A drink to him would be good Dad."

"Can I come too Sis?" asked Sam, who'd quietly made his way up towards her and was now standing right in front of her.

"I'd like that," she said, forcing a smile towards her half-brother.

The quiet was interrupted by Cecil Moriarty calling up.

"I've got movement at the Skoda Boss. Do I have authority?"

It took DI Lori Garcia less than a second to make her mind up. She wasn't in the business of executing criminals, no matter what their crime.

"Negative Charlie Four. Negative."

65

The tidy up had begun at the villa. Pérez had sent the Bravo team to find Diego Sanchez, but he'd got away after deciding he wasn't going to wait around for the police to come and get him.

After a thorough area search of the grounds produced nothing, Bravo One extended the search parameters. Then after waking up the residents at a number of the nearby villas, they eventually found one where a car had been stolen sometime overnight.

Sam brought Terri down the hill and Greg ran and hugged her.

"I'm so sorry Terri, Simon was a really good man and I know he loved you dearly.

"I know he did Dad, I know."

"Terri?" said Lori.

"Yes."

"Please believe when I say I will hunt this man down myself, like I did for Felipe's killer and I'll make sure he's brought to justice."

"I do," said Terri.

And she knew Lori would move heaven and earth to find Diego Sanchez and get him before a court of law.

*****

Jake was looking down at Frankie Walker, still

unable to digest what had played out. Two men had been shot and killed right in front of him.

Anna saw him and saw the slight shudder go through his body.

"Jake, we got Maggs and the children back safe. Remember that and it's because you were able to get the painting. You did very well, so don't blame yourself for what happened to Frankie."

"I sort of don't. Which is what I can't get my head around."

"He lived in a world you left a long time ago Jake, except of course for your recent excursions, although those were like light years away from the drugs business Frankie and Maggs became embroiled in."

"Is she going to be okay? And the kids?" asked Jake.

"Children can be very resilient and I somehow don't think Maggs will stay in this line of work for long, but who knows," said Anna.

"I'm sorry, I don't even know your real name," Jake said suddenly.

"It's Anna," she said in her usual voice.

"You're not Irish then?"

"No," she smiled.

"So am I off the hook? I mean with the stuff I was doing with Adamsons?"

"Are you going to put a stop to all that nonsense then?"

"Well yes, now you know it's me, I can't exactly carry on can I?"

"No, but to answer your question, are you off the hook? Well, not quite."

He looked at her, confusion on his face.

"But you said if I helped you?"

"I know and as far as the police are concerned then you are, as you say 'off the hook.' But there's someone you need to meet. His name's Martin Carruthers and I'll contact you when you're back in London."

"Who is he?"

"All in good time Jake, all in good time."

*****

Three weeks later Sam Martínez was reflecting that funerals were usually a celebration of someone's life, but inevitably there's always a sadness, whether it's a life cut short as in Simon's case, or just the feeling that the person, however long they may have lived, will be missed.

They had been to Wales for the funeral and there had been a presence there from Simon's old regiment, the SAS. Terri, together with Greg and Tommy, who'd known Simon as long as Greg, had been to spend time with Simon's mother, Aderyn Barnes. She was trying to come to terms with having now lost both her sons. Jim had been murdered by Tom Marsden, who Simon had subsequently shot and killed when he tried to kill Terri, and then Simon himself, murdered by Diego Sanchez who was still out there running loose, despite Lori's best efforts to track him down.

Now the 3R International team were back at Contrabando. Miquel, who owned the tapas bar and was Sam's best friend from their school days, had laid on a quiet lunch for them all to come together for a bit of much needed R&R. Sam had asked him for help because he knew if Miquel invited Terri then she might just go, because other than a couple of lunches with Lily up in Puerto Pollensa at her friend Aina's Restaurante Bar Coral, Terri seemed to be finding reasons not to leave her apartment.

As for himself, well since that night at the Sanchez villa, Sam had been busy, in fact really busy. He'd been tidying up the loose ends of the Adamsons contract with Holly Regus, together with Christine Harrison and Charles Hacker, as well as spending time with Tony

Theakston who was recovering well. But on top of that he was still managing the day to day business of 3R because Terri, for obvious reasons, still hadn't felt up to it.

But as he looked around the table he wasn't the only one who'd had a lot on their plate.

Lori had been managing the prosecution case against the Sanchez family, with Old Man Sanchez, Alberto, together with his wife Adeline both having been arrested and subsequently charged with drug trafficking offences and kidnap. Maggs Walker's support for the kidnap charge had been part of a plea bargain agreed between the prosecutors and Maggs's defence team which his mother, Anna, had been instrumental in negotiating between Maggs and the Spanish Judicial Authorities to ensure her freedom, in exchange for her cooperation in providing evidence against the Sanchez OCG.

Although Maggs had apparently contemplated taking over Frankie's business, as she had done when he'd been in prison, his death had hit her harder than she had at first thought and she'd become very worried about how her children were dealing with losing their father.

Their behaviour was worrying her more and more and it created an opportunity for Anna to intervene and help manage the reconciliation between Maggs and her mother, Saoirse, after she returned to the UK.

Deciding to get out of the world she'd been in since meeting and falling in love with Frankie wasn't an easy choice, but Maggs knew it was the best choice for her children's future safety. Even with a number of other 'investors' in the Walkers' drug importation business, Maggs was able to deal with the compensation they required and she wasn't going to go hungry. Far from it in fact, as she still had a significant amount of money to support her and her family, whilst the subsequent disruption caused, with the Walker OCG effectively disbanding, was also very well received when it was reported by DI Sandra Chisholm to Commander Katy Dawson in the Met.

With Anna's support and encouragement, Maggs was able to set herself up in a legitimate business as a business coach, using, as she described it, her expertise in running an international import and export organisation.

Greg had agreed, as part of the plea bargain to get Walker's support for the Sanchez prosecution case in Spain, that he could help her get her business off the ground with a few introductions back in London. Although whenever he was asked about her previous background, in terms of product base experience, it seemed easiest to just say she'd been in pharmaceuticals.

For Sam, the final part of the jigsaw was him dealing with the sense of unfairness that Frankie Walker had literally got away with attempted murder of his friend Jimmy. But in some ways, although not all, he'd found this was tempered with a side he hadn't seen in Walker before, especially how he'd stood up against first Diego and then Alejandro before paying the ultimate price for doing so.

What was for sure was that the nightmares he'd been having started to drop off in frequency. This surprised him, as much as the psychiatrist he'd started seeing who thought the nightmares relating to his PTSD might well continue for some time to come.

How long would it continue like that? He didn't know, but although he couldn't bring himself to celebrate Frankie Walker's death, he was happy to accept that those who live by the sword, as Frankie did, would often die by the sword.

They were all still worried about Terri though, although they were seeing some improvements, especially with the help of Lily Green. Lily was like a ray of sunshine and positivity, despite all she had been through at the hands of Tom Marsden and Terri was showing some signs of wanting to get her life back on track.

"Sam, I've been thinking," said Terri, from across the table.

"What about?"

"Getting back on the bike, you know, getting back to work?"

Sam nodded.

"I reckon I've probably wallowed enough about losing him," she went a little quiet, "but he'd be bollocking me if he thought I wasn't going to get on with things."

Sam smiled and saw Greg was listening, but trying not to show he was.

"I think you're right, but only if you want to. The place hasn't quite fallen apart, but…,"

"It's creaking?" grinned Terri.

"Groaning might be a better word," laughed Sam. "So whenever you're ready, I'll happily step aside."

"How about Monday?"

"Perfect! It'll give me time to try and sort some of the mess before you take over again."

"You sure?" asked Greg, reaching out and gently taking hold of his daughter's hand.

"Yes Dad, it's time."

THE END

BOOK FOUR

The 3R team will return in Book Four.

Keep up to date with what's happening on the 3R International Series Facebook Group

Find me on a Facebook search:
The 3R International Series
and join up now!

You can also follow me on Instagram
the_mallorcan_bookseller

ACKNOWLEDGEMENT

My huge thanks once again to my growing army of helpers across the globe, be they my Beta (proof) readers, location hunters, early reviewers, or language advisors.

Particular thanks go to Dr Siv Rebekka Runhovde, a specialist in international art and antiquities crime, for all her support and advice.

Special thanks also to Dave Parker, one of my Beta readers, for his huge support in keeping me up to speed on all things tactical in the world of firearms, together with my four other trusted Beta readers: Chris Back, Caroline Green, Shonagh MacMaster and Tony Monks for their sterling efforts in striving to make sure I haven't made too many glaring grammatical or spelling errors.

I also want to thank the continued support of my favourite restaurant and bar owners, Miquel and Aina, who go along with my crazy requests to get them somehow involved in the storyline.

A few final words of thanks to you - the people who have taken my writing to heart and support me by buying my books and posting all of the supportive comments I see across a multitude of social media sites - thank you, I'm truly humbled.

Finally, more thanks must go to my cousin, Brian Tarr, for his massive support in producing the images and backgrounds for these first three books. The reaction from people has been amazing and I'm so pleased to be able to have Brian as part of this design process yet again.

THE SÓLLER SOLUTION LOCATION TOUR

I included this page in the two previous books, The Mallorcan Bookseller and The Pollensa Connection, after the tremendous interest I had from readers about the locations I used, so I'm doing it again for this one.

We're back at some of our now well known regular (and favourite) restaurants on the island, together with some new ones, especially in Palma.

Both Miquel at Contrabando in Llucmajor and Aina at Coral Bar Restaurant in Puerto de Pollensa will be pleased to see you - Aina even has some hardback copies of my books incase your Kindle breaks down whilst you're on holiday!

Mallorca
Contrabando Tapas Restaurant, Llucmajor
Quina Brasa Restaurant, Llucmajor
(Contact: Miquel)

Coral Bar Restaurant, Puerto de Pollensa
(Contact: Aina and all her family)

The Sóller tram runs between Sóller and Port de Sóller

Plaza de la Constitución, Sóller
Carrer de sa Lluna, Sóller
C'an Pau Gelateria, Sóller

Hotel Portixol, Portixol, Palma de Mallorca

Hotel San Francesc, Plaza de San Francesc, Palma de Mallorca

London
Elephant and Castle, South London
Threadneedle Street, City of London
HMP Belmarsh

Singapore
The Shangri-La Hotel, Orchard Road, Singapore

MS Cotopaxi
This was actually a real freighter built in the 1950s and was the ship I chose to follow as part of a school project when I was in primary school. I got the pleasure to visit it with my father when it docked in Liverpool. Sadly it was scrapped a few years later.

REVIEWS AND TYPOS

Book reviews are the life blood of all authors and so finding out what you thought about my book is really important to me.

Whether you have been given this as a gift, or purchased it new or from a charity shop, or perhaps you've borrowed it from your local library, please can I ask you to take a moment to submit a review on Amazon or goodreads.com

Finally, the book gets checked and treble checked by a host of people, but sometimes errors still slip through! Please email me with any typo errors you see and we'll quickly get them changed.

Please join The 3R International Series Facebook Group to find out more about me, my books and when the Book 4 may be coming out!

Thanks again for reading my book.
Pete Davies
Email: petedavies01@hotmail.co.uk

BOOKS IN THIS SERIES

The 3R International Series

An exciting action crime series set primarily on the beautiful island of Mallorca, featuring the 3R International team, where Greg, Anna, Sam and Terri find themselves drawn into complex crime adventures where danger is never very far away.

The Mallorcan Bookseller

"Is Anna in?"
It took just three words to change his life.

Sam Martínez, a London detective, is put on sick leave suffering with PTSD resulting from a firearms incident that went wrong and his best friend was shot.

Going home to Mallorca, where he grew up, he helps out in the family bookshop. But before long, he finds himself caught up with helping a family friend who has fallen prey to an IT scam.

When another scam victim is murdered, Sam finds he has to learn to play by a new set of rules and a different type of justice when he goes up against a ruthless boss of an Armenian organised crime gang.

The Pollensa Connection

The 3R team are back in action in the second of the series!

Lily Green is scared stiff. Kidnapped after she leaves her work in Pollensa, Mallorca, she doesn't know why this has happened and even when drugged and interrogated, she still has no idea what they want from her.

When her grandparents ask for their help, Anna and Sam Martínez start to look into Lily's disappearance. Together with the rest of the team, they soon realise there's a lot more at stake when they find themselves pitched against Sir Charles Groom, the CEO of a corporate giant and Oleg Makarovich, a ruthless Russian billionaire, in a 'deniable' operation sanctioned by MI6.

What does Lily know and how is it linked to a shopping centre collapse in London and a multi-million pound money laundering operation? The more the team discover about The Pollensa Connection, the wider the net extends, leading to far greater danger for everyone concerned.

ABOUT THE AUTHOR

Pete Davies

Retiring after a thirty year career in the British Police Service, Pete had held a wide variety of operational and training roles, including being a firearms commander.

In 2012 he started a new career as an executive coach, working with clients within the public, private and voluntary sectors before committing to writing full time in 2020.

Enjoying the beautiful island of Mallorca for many family holidays over the years led him to base his books on the island.

Pete lives with his wife and their Labrador in Berkshire, England.

Printed in Great Britain
by Amazon